ON TO
AFRICA

To Dom;
The Best "Capo" on earth.

ON TO AFRICA

WALTER F. CURRAN

ISBN: 0999364901
ISBN 13: 9780999364901
Library of Congress Control Number: 2017918016
WFC Associates LLC, Ocean View, DE

CONTENTS

PRAISE FOR ON TO AFRICA

"This is a fine book. It's as if Richard Halliburton, Graham Greene and Agatha Christie staged a cruise across the Atlantic and decided to make things happen before writing about it. Marvelous."
Rick Ollerman
Editor, Down & Out; The Magazine

"An intimate, detailed, account of a young man's life aboard a merchant marine vessel."
Bernard Schaffer
Author: The Thief of all Light

ACKNOWLEDGMENTS

On to Africa is my second novel, continuing the saga of William Connolly, merchant mariner, as he explores new countries, engages interesting people, and delves into his psyche and soul, discovering himself.

The writer within me continues to soar, aided and abetted by the members of the Rehoboth Beach Writer's Guild, a wonderful group of writers led by Maribeth Fischer, and especially the Gray Head Group, masters of supportive critique.

Unbounded thanks to my wife, Marie, who tolerates my hermit sessions in my office while writing, occasionally checking to see if I'm still breathing.

On to Africa is a work of fiction, but many of the elements of the book, including how a commercial ship operates, are taken from my experiences sailing as a deck officer. Whenever the name MorMac or *Pride* is used, believe only the good attributes. Anything bad is a figment of my overactive imagination.

Cover and interior photos by Michael McGowan

It's all in your point of view. If you've never been outside your neighborhood, then the other side of town may as well be a different planet. Overcoming this stagnation, this alien outlook, and altering your point of view is the path to understanding in our world.

POINT OF VIEW

Often have I traveled, through lands both far and near
Each in turn an alien, fraught with angst and fear
Yet also each in turn have changed, as have my views of old
Once familiarity stamps its mark indelibly on mind and soul

As each has been revisited, in body or in mind
A mellowing occurs, dimming features, less defined
Once imminent images, meld and fade, ne'er the same again
Yet somehow larger than before, more symbolic now than then

So be not quick to look and judge, or worse, not even see
The fullness of each sign and sight, as they were meant to be
For perchance, it might well be, true destiny of you and yours
By narrowed vision brushed aside, ne'er to regain rightful course

Chapter 1

HOMECOMING

My finding Sparky, the radio operator, dead in the alley with his tongue skewered to his chest was an exclamation point to a chapter of life's book that I didn't want to reread. But here I am, walking up the gangway, stubbornness winning over common sense.

Monday, October 3, 1966: I've been home a week after signing off the ship in New York, and I'll rejoin her here in Boston…Bean Town…hometown and now port of call for the *MorMacPride*, my new home away from home. I did a lot of thinking in a short time about whether I wanted to return to the *Pride*, given the circumstances in which I left.

After finding Sparky dead in the alley in Brooklyn, I made it to Third Avenue and, given the time of night, was lucky to get a cab to stop for me and take me to the port authority Greyhound depot, where I got the last bus out for Boston. Getting off at South Station, a massive edifice at the edge of downtown Boston and South Boston at 7:15 a.m., I waited in the taxi line along with the daily commuters and listened to the grumbling of the rat-race crowd, glad I wasn't part of it. Thirteenth in line, a guy tried to jump ahead of me, saying he was late. Southie manners took over, and I told him to fuck off, shoving him back as I climbed in and gave the driver the address of my ma's apartment on Marine Road in Southie. This was the third place that Ma and my sister Betty had lived since Dad had died in my first year of college, and the living room couch was my official residence.

In my first year at MMA, Dad died just before the training cruise started in January of 1963. When I returned from that training cruise, I went home to the Viking Street house and found the door locked, something we never did. Figuring Ma was taking a nap, I knocked hard at the door, and a big guy I had never seen before answered.

"Who are you?"

"Who the hell are you?" he asked, semi-belligerent.

"William Connolly. I live here!"

With a glimmer of a smile on his face, he said, "Ahh, you're the son who went to sea. Your mother thought she wouldn't get your letters and asked me to forward any that came here. I gave her three. That was all that showed up."

"Damn!" I said. Then, I immediately said, "Sorry, it's not your fault, but I wrote twelve letters, one a week."

"Sorry, kid. They moved a month ago; somewhere up on Fourth Street, between L and M streets. Can't remember the exact address. Hold on a minute; the missus knows." Turning, he called out, "Sonya, where did the Connollys move to?"

A disembodied voice replied, "847 Fourth Street."

"Thanks," I said, reaching to shake his hand.

Enveloping mine in his, he said, "Things change, kid. It'll work out." And he closed the door.

That was a shocker, but the same thing happened at the end of my second-year training cruise. The apartment was next door to one of my classmate's girlfriends, and when I was walking up the steps to go into Ma's apartment, Doris came out of her place and said,

"Hi, William. What are you doing here?"

"What do you mean?"

"Your mom and sister moved two weeks ago down to a place on Marine Road."

"Jesus, not again."

On both those occasions, Ma mailed me a letter telling me where they were going, but that just showed the inefficiency of the military-mail service.

This apartment was on the first floor of a typical three-decker, with two small bedrooms. It also had a kitchen, bathroom, and living room, which we always called the "front room," and it looked out onto Carson Beach, with a view of the Columbia Point projects across the bay. As I walked up the stairs, the front door opened, and Ma stood there with that wonderful smile to greet me. She had been up early as usual, keeping watch on the neighborhood from her wingback chair by the window in the front room, smoking Old Gold cigarettes. Giving her a hug, always gentle since she had gotten frailer over the last two years, I kissed her on the top of her head.

"Do you want something to eat?" It was a perpetual question whenever I walked through her door.

I said, "Sure," knowing that to say otherwise would disappoint her. At that stage of life, the last thing I wanted to do was disappoint Ma.

I dropped my bag at the faux fireplace in the front room, used the bathroom, then settled at the kitchen table and absorbed the aroma of Ma's cooking.

"How many eggs, hon?" she asked.

"Three Ma, and toast."

She eyed me with that, "Would I ever serve you breakfast without toast?" look, and I grinned.

"Coffee or milk?"

"Both. I'll get it, Ma." I grabbed a glass from the cupboard, noticing that the glasses matched, a rarity growing up. Opening the fridge—a GE that came with the apartment, years newer than the old GE on Viking Street—I poured a glass of milk, drank half of it, and refilled it before sitting down.

"Is Betty working?" I asked as Ma put the plate of bacon, eggs, and toast in front of me, patting the back of my head as she turned away, another habit she had developed in later years. Were I younger, I might have resisted it, but now, there was something reassuring in her touch, as if she convinced herself of my reality when she touched me. Being the youngest of six kids and the first to graduate from college, I was Ma's pet. Whatever trouble I got into paled in comparison to my older brothers, so I got off the hook…a lot. Mature enough now to understand, I made sure Ma knew I understood and respected her appreciation of me, without getting egotistical about it. Since Dad died, I had elevated Ma to near sainthood.

"Yeah." Ma never articulated the word "yes" but was articulate in so many other ways. "She'll be home a little after four." Setting a cup of coffee down, she retrieved her cup and sat opposite me. "What are your plans?"

"I don't know. Maybe I'll go down to the yacht club and see if any of the guys are around."

The South Boston Yacht Club was one of four yacht clubs in a row on the boulevard at City Point. Boston Yacht Club was where the hoity-toits belonged, the Boston Brahmin aspirers and wannabes. South Boston Yacht Club was a blue-collar club popular with the sailboat crowd. There were a lot of good, competitive racers; Two-Tens (thirty-foot, double-ended, flat-bottomed racing machines) and One-Tens (smaller-brother versions of the Two-Tens) were the largest part of the fleet. A handful of Lightnings, Stars and Hustlers, ungainly catboats, made up the rest of the fleet. Columbia Yacht Club was also blue collar but oriented toward motorboats. The fourth club, the Puritan Canoe Club, comprised canoes and rowboats—shells rather than dory types—and was the least active of the four clubs.

I was never a member of the South Boston Yacht Club (couldn't afford it), but I would often hang out there with friends since racing sailboats was a big part of our lives during high school. It was by crewing for some of the rich guys that I got my first glimpses of how the elite lived. There was old money: third-generation folks born with silver spoons in their mouths. They were the friendlier, more down-to-earth types. They didn't remind you of your "place" as a poor city boy. Then, there were the nouveau riche: new to money, late to manners, and devoid of respect for others. They were obvious and tended toward the glitzy motor yachts rather than sailboats, so I avoided them as much as they avoided the likes of me.

Finished eating, I put my dishes in the sink, kissed Ma on the top of her head again, and went out.

I didn't own a car. The junker '55 Chevy that wouldn't shift into second gear that I had in college died, and I scrapped it. The '49 Ford Fairlane convertible preceding it that my uncle bought for me for one hundred dollars had bad shock absorbers, and the ride back and forth to school on Route 3 was enough to make you seasick. No need for a car when you aren't here to drive it.

Turning left off the stairs, I walked the eight blocks along Carson Beach, past the L Street bathhouses and M Street beach until coming to boathouse row. I could smell the pungent reek of low tide, and it smelled good. Folks who weren't raised at the edge of the ocean think it stinks. For me, it's nostalgia, a homecoming of sorts.

Ringing the bell on the gate, a steward named Jimmy, an older guy in his sixties, a veteran of WWII and the Korean War, came and let me in, asking me how the seafarer life was going.

"Pretty good, Jimmy. Traveled to South America and the Great Lakes over the last three months, and it was interesting."

"Glad to hear it. So many of you young guys are going to Vietnam, and that's no picnic. I'm glad at least some of you didn't get dragged over there." Jimmy used to tell us tales of his war days when he got a little drunk, and we were in awe of him and skeptical of his tales, but when Vietnam heated up and stories of what it was like there came back, the skepticism faded, and admiration replaced it.

"Anybody around, Jimmy?"

"Not a soul, other than a few guys up in their lockers, still drying out from the weekend." On the upper floor of the club were sail lockers. Many of the adjoining lockers got combined and renovated into a recreation room, complete with sink and refrigerator and a cot to sleep it off. One guy wanted to put in a stove, but the club governors refused, saying it was a fire hazard. The entire club was wooden and a tinderbox.

Going to the phone on the wall, I dropped in a dime and called Muriel. We had maintained an on-again, off-again relationship for the last two years. The last time I saw her before leaving on the trip to South America, I had spent the day at the beach with her, and it had ended with us making love—a first, at least for me. There was no answer, so I said the hell with it, said good-bye to Jimmy, and walked back to Ma's. I went to sleep on the couch.

Betty woke me up around five thirty and asked me if I wanted supper. I wasn't hungry, but before I could reply, she said, "Ma's already cooked it." So I got up, went to the bathroom to take a leak, and sat with them for supper: meat-loaf, boiled red potatoes, and green beans.

"How's the job going, Betty?"

"It's okay. Business is dropping off, but they treat me pretty well, and I'm hoping the company will last long enough for me to retire."

"That's a long way off. Are they that shaky? Maybe you should look for another job."

"Nah. I'll be okay. Ma is getting Dad's social-security money now, and we're getting by."

"I gave Ma my money for you to deposit in my savings account and gave her some, too."

Throughout the conversation, Ma was sitting at the table in her green housecoat, cigarette in hand, four feet away from us and pretending she wasn't there, wary of being an eavesdropper.

"Yeah, Ma told me, and I'll do that tomorrow. Maybe you should start a checking account, too, so you can pay bills."

"Pay bills? I don't have any bills, other than the life-insurance policy I got just before graduation. Nah, I'll wait."

"Suit yourself, but you'll have to open one sometime."

"I've been thinking about applying for one of those credit-card things. There's one called Diners Club that says you can use it all over the world. That would be convenient when I'm overseas."

"I don't trust those things."

"Well, it's just a thought."

After supper, I called Muriel again.

"Hello?"

"Hi, Muriel. It's William. How are you?" Silence.

"Muriel? Are you there?"

"Wait a minute." I heard a shuffling and a clicking sound and knew she was stretching the phone cord around the corner into their kitchenette.

"Okay, I'm here."

"You sound funny. Is everything okay? I missed you a lot on the trip." Again, silence.

"Muriel, what's wrong?"

I heard her inhale, and then she said, "William, I got a new boyfriend, and we're gonna get married, and I can't see you anymore. I'm sorry, but that's the way it is." And she hung up.

Wham! Right between the eyes. I never saw it coming, although I should have. She had broken up with me before, but I figured that after our last tryst in the sand at the beach, things would be more serious. Wrongo! Now, with nothing to keep me here, I wanted to get back on the ship and just go.

Chapter 2

BACK ON BOARD

H oosac Pier, in Charlestown, sat opposite the berth of the USS *Constitution*, Old Ironsides. In five years, I would be sitting in that office, looking at Old Ironsides as the general superintendent of a stevedoring company, but that was still a lifetime away. Built to handle general cargo, Hoosac was an active pier in a port on the cusp of change, as containerization was just coming into vogue. SeaLand was leading the parade in containerization, and there was talk that they would set up a container crane at the Castle Island marine terminal. That would be interesting since the terminal is directly under the approach to Logan airport, and those planes come in low. I know, because it's what I listened to every day growing up: the roar of the planes passing overhead as they landed.

As a teenager, I worked both at Hoosac Pier and Castle Island on weekends as a scalawag, the longshoreman term for a nonunion, part-time worker. It was a scam in that I worked on a real longshoreman's ID-card number. Many of the longshoremen had full-time jobs, and longshoring was a sideshow. The longshoreman got paid and was credited with the hours worked for his union benefits, and he gave me half the net money earned. At age fourteen, it was a great deal for me, but as Bob Dylan says, "The times, they are a-changin."

I didn't know if Boston will keep pace with ports like New York and Philadelphia. It seemed to be slipping, and as the ships got bigger and containerization got a foothold, the steamship lines may be reluctant to come to a port that had such a checkered history of contentiousness. We would see.

Standing at the top of the gangway, I felt a similar rush to when I first boarded the *Pride* at the dry dock in Brooklyn, New York, three months earlier. The *MorMacPride* was a general cargo ship built for Moore McCormack Lines to use primarily in the Great Lakes trade. Known as a 1624, it was a Class C-3 ship built specifically for the trade routes known to MorMac as Routes 1, 16, and 24. It was 483 feet, three inches in length overall (LOA), with a sixty-eight-foot beam, weighing 9,252 gross tons. It was launched on February 1, 1960, at the Sun Ship Building & Dry Dock Company in Chester, Pennsylvania. With five cargo hatches using conventional booms/derricks, as well as a heavy lift boom that could be swung between hatches 2 and 3, it was a workhorse. They also built in accommodations for up to twelve passengers and a postage-stamp-size swimming pool behind the bridge. Twin steam turbines, linked to one propeller shaft, generated 12,100 horsepower, so it could do 21 knots in calm weather. Standing there again, looking at the smokestack insignia—a green background with a white circle and a large red *M* in the middle—I felt like I belonged, especially after enduring the gamut of larceny and murder from the first trip.

More than a little nervous, I stepped off the gangway platform onto the deck, said "Hi" to the ordinary seaman on watch, and went into the house. The ship smelled the same, an overlay of old fish oil and new paint on the outside and a mixture of food, body odor, stale cigarette smoke, and acrid engine room—itself a combination of bunker fuel, steam, and diesel fumes. I was back.

I climbed the inside ladderway to the mate's deck, lugging my full duffel bag. I had packed everything when I signed off, not really sure whether I was coming back. I left the bag just inside the door to my room and went to check in with the chief mate, Dennis Hughes. Dennis was a solid six feet tall; his love handles had grown continuously larger than when I had first met him on the last trip. They still gave his belt a problem in the continuous tug-of-war to keep his shirt tucked in. Although he had told me that he looked forward to sailing with me when I left the ship in New York, I was leery and pretty skittish as to how I would be treated when I returned. To my knowledge, I was the only one who knew that Sparky, the radio operator, had been murdered, and I wasn't about to reveal that fact, lest I get more implicated.

Knocking on the chief mate's door, which was slightly ajar, I called, "Dennis?" I was somewhat timid but hopeful that the use of his first name rather than title of "mate" was a friendly opening.

"Who is it?" came from inside.

"William Connolly, Dennis."

"William!" It was loud but likeable. "Come in."

Pushing the door open, I stepped in as he came from his bedroom into his office, wearing nothing but a towel, which desperately clung to his love handles, and a big smile. I was grateful for the smile. Keeping his left hand on the towel to ensure that there was no slippage (something else I was grateful for), he reached out with his right, still damp from what I hoped was his shower, and shook hands. I let out an inaudible sigh of relief in appreciation of the friendly greeting. Backing into the edge of his desk, he rested his ample butt on it and said, "I'm glad you came back, William. Bill and I were talking last night, speculating as to whether you would." The "Bill" he referred to was the chief engineer, Bill Bradley. Bill's leanness was a counterpoint to the chief mate's bulk. Bill was built for endurance; he had a marathoner's body.

I was still tentative. "I'm glad to be back, Dennis. The week away gave me time to think, and this is where I want to be."

Fixing me with a not-unkind stare, he said, "One of these days, William, you and I will have a long, quiet talk about what happened last trip, but not now. Put your gear in your room; it's the same one, and I'll see you in the officers' salon. We've got a few surprises this trip." Then, obviously recalling the "surprises" of last trip, he added, "These are good surprises."

Turning, I said, "See you in a while." And I left.

I unpacked my duffel, hanging up my uniform shirts in the limited hanger space, and crammed the rest into the drawers built in under the bunk. My cabin was akin to a monk's cell, but after living for three years on the training ship *Bay State*, stacked three high on a pipe rack (a pipe frame with a piece of canvas laced to it for a bed), I felt that it was a palace. The bed was built into the bulkhead thirty inches off the deck, with two long drawers underneath. Attached to the bed on the inside was a twelve-inch rail that could be raised and locked in place in heavy weather, a shorter version of a baby's crib rail. I went to the head at the end of the companionway and took a leak, washed up, and went to meet the mate in the salon.

Stepping into the open doorway, I almost bumped into the captain on his way out. Captain Coltrain was the master of the *MorMacPride*, and to a third mate, he was God. Jerking myself back to avoid contact, I said, "Excuse me. Good morning, Captain." It came out all at once.

"Good morning, Mr. Connolly," he said, fixing me with that piercing stare of his, a hint of a smile—or was it a smirk?—on his face. "Glad you returned. The odds were even-steven on whether you would or not." With that, he walked out the door.

Stepping back in, I saw Bill Bradley, the chief engineer, sitting in his usual spot at the middle table. The officer's salon was at the forward part of the "house," that part of the ship where the crew quarters are on the centerline, about twenty feet forward to aft, which ran two-thirds of the width of the ship. The forward bulkhead had large, rectangular portholes that let in a lot of daylight. At night, there were six fluorescent overhead lights. It consisted of four square tables for the officers and two round tables for the passengers. If there were no passengers, the captain always sat alone at one of the round tables. On the port side was a pull-down screen for watching movies, and in the aft corner, up high, was a TV set. Under the TV set were some bookshelves with issues of *National Geographic*, a few issues of *Life* magazine, and some nondescript books whose titles I had never heard of. On the starboard side of the salon was the scullery, a pantry if it were in a house instead of a ship. The scullery was where the food was brought up by dumbwaiter and where the dishes were rinsed and cleaned. There was a door that led into it and an opening in the bulkhead through which things could be passed. On the aft bulkhead, next to the scullery door, was a sideboard. The food for the night watch was usually laid out there. All the tables had four-inch edge boards that could be raised and latched in place during rough weather to keep the dishes and utensils from flying off the table. In especially rough weather, the messman or pantryman would dampen the tablecloths to give them better friction for the plates, glasses, and cups.

Sitting next to Bill Bradley was the first assistant engineer, Mark Quigley. Mark, six feet two inches tall and 220 pounds, was the proverbial gentle giant. He never raised his voice and was always polite and deferential, but when he did speak, the others listened. His oddity was a pair of hands that looked almost deformed, they were so small and frail for a man of his size. His mop of chestnut hair was a frozen caricature of stormy seas.

I asked the chief if Roy Oliver, the second assistant engineer, was still with them, and he said that Roy would be joining them when they got back to New York. On the previous trip, Roy, a lanky six-footer weighing in at 180 pounds, with thinning brown hair and excessive attitude, had come close to getting himself and the chief mate killed late at night, conducting an illicit explosives deal with an unsavory "friend." When I left the ship in New York, the chief mate had almost convinced the chief engineer to fire Roy.

Getting a cup of coffee from the sideboard, I sat down just as the chief mate came in. He half-heartedly waved to everyone else and came and sat on the opposite side of the table from me. "Joey!" he called, and the pantryman peeked through the scullery window. Joey had been the pantryman on the last trip, and, while a little odd to look at because of his bald, tattooed skull, he was good at his job.

"Yeah, Mate?"

"Two eggs, sunny side up, ham, and toast. Got any orange juice?"

"Yeah. Large or small glass?"

"Large, thanks."

"Hey, Mr. Connolly. Good to see ya. Ya want anything to eat?"

"Just some toast, thanks, Joey."

"Right away," he said, ducking back into the scullery.

The chief mate said, "You're still on the twelve-to-four William. Tony should be rejoining us this afternoon. We've had temporary mates covering for you." The twelve-to-four to which he referred was the span of the watch hours. Typically, the second mate and two third mates, one sometimes called a junior third, would stand the sea watches; they would be four hours on watch and eight hours off. The second mate always had the four-to-eight in the morning and evening because he was the navigation officer. Early morning and late evening was when one could take star sightings. I was assigned the twelve-to-four hours, and the other third mate, Tony Adams, who had joined the ship when I did at the beginning of the previous voyage, was assigned the eight-to-twelve hours. The chief mate was in charge of cargo operations and deck-department maintenance, so he was on duty during the day from eight to five.

The engine department had similar rankings and watch-standing duties. The chief engineer was in overall charge of the engine department and reported directly to the captain. The chief engineer had a first-assistant engineer who worked eight to five daily, one second-assistant engineer on the four-to-eight watches, and two third-assistant engineers who stood the twelve-to-four and eight-to-twelve watches. The captain was in total command of the ship.

Dennis continued, "The longshore gangs will start at 1300 hours today. We weren't sure we would get here in time for an 0700 hours start, and the company didn't want to pay the standby time if we were late."

One of the problems the Port of Boston has was the inflexibility of its labor rules. Cargo ships weren't buses or trains and couldn't run on an exact schedule. They were subject to delays due to weather while steaming and also delays in prior ports due to slow cargo operations or breakdowns. Therefore, for them to order a day ahead of time for labor, they had to be sure of their arrival times. It was made more difficult because the labor contract insisted that orders for a Monday start—whether at 0700, 1300, or 1900 hours—had to be made by no later than 1700 hours on the previous Friday. Longshore labor was a large part of the cost of doing business, so the company always had to strike a balance between the cost of the labor to stand by and the cost of the delay to the ship if it didn't order labor. The companies always griped about the unreasonableness of the longshoremen, and the longshoremen always griped about the companies' unwillingness to guarantee wages for times the longshoremen made themselves available for work but didn't have any. Both sides complained, but both sides also overlooked the fact that, together, they had negotiated the labor contract. The union didn't have anything that management didn't give them, so no one had a legitimate complaint about anything. The angst often expressed by management and labor was mutually inflicted.

Chapter 3

BOSTON/TROIS-RIVIÈRES

The ship docked stern in to the shore, starboard side to the pier. The actual origin of the words "port" (left) and "starboard" (right) was thought to be because the right side of old merchant-sailing vessels had steering boards that hung over the right sides (before they created rudders), and loading or entry ports were on the left sides. Over time, steering board evolved into "starboard" due to sailors' laziness and lack of enunciation.

On deck at 1300 hours, I watched the longshoremen climb the gangway. Half of them wore long overcoats, despite the day being a warm 74 degrees and sunny. Those coats had a history, not just in Boston but on many waterfronts. Most of them had multiple large pockets sewn into the inside and were used by the longshoremen to hide whatever they stole from the cargo. I have never known an American longshoreman to steal anything from crew members, but the cargo was fair game, especially if it was cigarettes or liquor.

I recognized half a dozen guys I know from Southie and greeted them as they pass. One of them, Jimmy "Hands" O'Brien, was a notorious thief, and I made a mental note to warn the chief mate. If Jimmy was working in the locker unloading the canned beef, some of it would definitely take a walk.

There were twenty men to a gang, and we had two gangs of longshore-men working that day. The only cargo to discharge was cases of canned beef stowed in the no. 3 upper-tween-deck portside locker. General cargo ships the size of the *Pride* consisted of five hatches, each containing a lower hold, a lower-tween deck, and an upper-tween deck. On the *Pride*, we had deep tanks in the no. 3 hatch, one each on the port and starboard sides. They could be used for both dry and liquid cargoes and could be heated to lower the viscos-ity of heavy liquids like tallow to make them flow. In addition, we had two lockers, one each on the port and starboard sides in the upper-tween deck of the no. 3 hatch. These could be refrigerated to zero degrees to carry perishable cargoes. We also used them when nonrefrigerated to carry high-value cargo because we could lock the doors. Each locker had a forward and an aft door, and the doors were just wide enough to place a pallet. To accommodate the flow of the cold air required to refrigerate, the floors were latticed, making it difficult to use hand trucks, so the longshoremen had to walk the cargo to and from the interior. It was hard work.

As one gang went into the locker, including Hands O'Brien, the other went on deck to the no. 2 hatch and began laying dunnage in preparation for the loading of two bulldozers and one locomotive. Dunnage was a term for loose boards placed on the steel deck to protect the deck and to prevent steel-on-steel situations to minimize slipping of the cargo. The dunnage can be anything from 1" x 6" pine boards of various lengths up to 4" x 4" hardwood, depending on the cargo loaded.

The mate had assigned me to keep watch on the canned beef, and he oversaw the loading of the bulldozers and locomotive. For ease of loading, the mate had decided that the bulldozers would be on the port side and the locomotive on the starboard side. We could use our heavy-lift cargo boom for the dozers but needed a shore crane to handle the 126-ton locomotive. Laying 1" x 6" boards on the port side for the bulldozers, we used the heavy-lift boom positioned between the no. 2 and no. 3 hatches. The dozers were Caterpillar D8 models, weighing forty-four tons each. Using chains, the gang placed each one on the dunnage, making sure that no part of the steel treads touched the deck.

Most people seeing a ship alongside the pier think it's so big that it can't move. Unlike a French crane that hoists something onto a building under construction, when a ship's cargo boom hoists a piece of freight, the weight of the cargo makes the ship list or heel (tilt) toward whatever side the cargo is on. The difference between a list/heel and a roll is that a list is caused by the actions of the ship (lifting cargo or pumping liquids from one tank to another), and a roll is caused by the actions of the surrounding seas. The heavier the weight of the cargo, the more the severity of the list. The forty-four-ton dozer created a five-degree list to starboard when initially lifted. As the dozer got lifted, the cargo boom swung inboard, bringing it closer to the ship. Once it cleared the gunwale and hatch coaming, it swung across the width of the ship onto the offshore side. During this swing, the ship reduced the starboard list as the load got to the centerline of the ship and then started to list to port until it reached the spot where it was placed on deck. All during the loading, the whining of the cargo winches and the creaking of the lifting wires under strain were the symphony a deck officer listens to, hoping there were no sour notes that could spell trouble.

Dropping the hoisting gear, we stowed the heavy-lift boom in its vertical position between the hatches to keep it out of the way. A three-hundred-ton-capacity mobile crane came alongside on the pier, adjacent to the hatch. All mobile cranes had outrigger pads that are extended and placed on the ground to stabilize the crane and spread out the weight during the lifting process. Because the pier structure consisted of pilings with a deck built on top, the weight of the crane must be spread over a larger area than if it were on a solid-concrete surface. The crane crew accomplished this by laying steel plates, each ten feet square, under each of the outrigger pads.

Once the mobile crane was set up, the longshoremen hooked up four sets of fifty-ton wires and shackles and attached them to the locomotive. Built by the General Electric corporation, the locomotive was a model U28B with a B-B setup, meaning it had two identical trucks (that part comprising the wheels and axles) with each truck having two powered axles for a total of 2800 horsepower. It was big.

On deck, the longshoremen had built cradles of 4x4s to nest into the area where the trucks would normally be. The locomotive had arrived on a track alongside the ship, but when lifted, the trucks had to be detached. The truck crane lifted the locomotive one foot, and the longshoremen checked to ensure that the trucks were separated from the body of the locomotive, with no wires or hoses still attached. Verified to be clear of snags, the mobile crane slowly lifted the locomotive body and placed it on the blocks of 4x4s. As the weight settled onto the blocks, the ship listed to starboard again. Placed equally from the centerline of the ship, the 126 tons of the locomotive more than offset the combined eighty-eight tons of the bulldozers.

Since the mobile crane was already in place and we had to pay for a minimum of eight hours' rental, we used it to load the two locomotive trucks, placing them forward of the body of the locomotive. The longshoremen created rails out of 4x4 chocks and landed the trucks on the wooden rails. It took four hours to load the three heavy lifts and two trucks.

After the lifts were in place, a gang of carpenters, referred to as "wood butchers," secured them, using wooden bracing between the lifts and hatch coamings and gunwale framing. They then added additional steel wire, lashing them down to the permanent deck fittings.

At some point prior to sailing, the chief mate always checks the stability and trim of the ship to ensure that it was seaworthy. If there is a list on the ship or the trim (the measurement of difference between depth in the water forward and aft) is excessive, he will have the engine department pump fuel or water from one tank to another to offset the cargo effect and keep the ship upright and properly trimmed.

Another major factor in the seaworthiness of a ship is reserve buoyancy. All ships are designed to be buoyant and will displace enough water to equal the weight of the ship. Commercial ships have a Plimsoll line, which shows how far the ship can safely sink into the water, depending on the type of water (salt, fresh, or brackish). The Plimsoll line is always at the forward/aft centerline of the ship. If you overload the ship and put the Plimsoll line underwater, you are endangering the ship.

The longshoremen finished by 1700 hours and left the ship. The carpenters took until 1900 hours to finish. As Hands O'Brien walked down the gangway, I noticed he was moving slow, holding tight to the railings with both hands. I had tipped off the mate, and he had informed the stevedore company's security department; I knew they were waiting inside the cargo door of the shed. As Hands stepped off the lower platform of the gangway, he tripped and landed facedown on the apron of the pier. I expected him to get up and move on; instead, he lay spread-eagled and facedown, and his legs and arms were flapping. He looked like a butterfly pinned to paper. I started down the gangway just as the security guards came out from the doorway, and we reached him at the same time. I grabbed one arm to help him up and was astonished by the effort it took to get him to his feet. Hands is a skinny guy, maybe 130 pounds, but the mystery was solved when the security guard unbuttoned his coat. There were sixty-six cans of corned beef filling those inside pockets. He really had been pinned like a butterfly. Hands was the only one not laughing when they hauled him away.

We sailed for Trois-Rivières that evening at 2200 hours. Standing on the flying bridge between 2100 and 2130 hours, I looked up river toward the downtown section and thought about Muriel. When the mate called for mooring stations on the walkie-talkie, it startled me out of my reverie, and I headed aft to the fantail.

After being released from mooring stations, I stood on the flying bridge and watched the Boston skyline recede and Logan airport drift past to port. We passed the Boston Light perched on Little Brewster Island, the first lighthouse built in the United States in 1716 and the only lighthouse in the country still staffed by the US Coast Guard. The last lighthouse before reaching open seas is The Graves Light. Located on the outermost of the islands in Boston Harbor, it stands 113 feet tall and can be seen for fifteen nautical miles. I had passed both the Boston Light and The Graves Light many times when racing sailboats and was a little nostalgic, somewhat enhanced by it being the Fourth of July, watching them fade away. I no longer played on boats. Now, I made my living on them.

Sailing time to Trois-Rivières was three days and twelve hours, and we arrived at 1000 hours on Friday, October 7. Unlike the last trip to Montreal—when our radar and gyrocompass broke down and the captain was forced to sail by dead reckoning without navigational aid sightings, including having to take soundings as we rounded the tip of the Gaspe Peninsula—everything functioned perfectly. I smelled land about twenty miles out: the faint aroma of pine trees and coastal kelp with a tinge of periwinkle from the rocks at low tide.

We picked up the Saint Lawrence River pilot at Father Point and proceeded to Trois-Rivières without incident. Started as a private enterprise by Canadian business owners who needed to move their products, Trois-Rivières was created as a port in 1824. Matthew Bell owned the Forges du Saint-Maurice and built a dock and warehouse, followed by John Molson of Montreal, a ship owner who built three additional docks in 1825, which enabled his Montreal-Quebec steamship connection to dock there. The first public dock was built in 1858 to service the ferries that had been in business since 1845. Eventually, a harbor commission took over to coordinate the separate facilities and modernize them. The harbor commission dissolved in 1936 and was replaced by the National Harbour Board. Far enough up the Saint Lawrence River to be relatively unaffected by sea tide, the port is still subject to the river's water levels, depending on the season. Charts have its average depth at 10.7 meters, but typically in the summer, the available depth is 11.5 meters. This can be critical for the larger bulk carriers that arrive at the port.

Trois-Rivières was a limited stay since we were only loading rolls of paper and construction lumber consisting of two-by-fours in eight-, ten-, twelve-, and sixteen-foot lengths. We worked that day and the next day until 1800 hours and sailed for New York.

Chapter 4

NEW YORK

Sailed from Trois-Rivières at 2000 hours. Clear weather. Sixty-one degrees, low humidity, cloudless sky. Wind from the north at 6 mph. A light chop, less than a foot high. Bound for New York.

Three and a half days of sailing on calm, summertime seas had us at the Twenty-Third Street docks in Brooklyn at 1000 hours on Thursday, October 13. This was home port for the Moore McCormack Line and was a very busy pier.

Three weeks ago, the last time I was here, US customs agents had raided the ship, looking for contraband guns and drugs, and I had discovered the stabbed body of the ship's radio operator with his tongue skewered to his chest in an alley just off Twenty-Third Street. At 1300 hours, I stood looking over the rail at the longshoremen coming aboard.

Given the memories of my recent visit here and the fact I suspected that my Mafia benefactor, Frankie, had a hand in Sparky's demise, I was a little tentative. There was only three gangs; the normal is at least four, sometime five, gangs. The ship's schedule had put it in a time lag between the usual shipments; thus, there was less cargo to load.

The chief mate planned on loading cigarettes into the no. 3 hatch's upper-tween-deck portside locker, the same one from which we discharged the canned corned beef in Boston. Talking to the ship boss of the longshoremen, I reminded him I was on duty at that hatch. On the prior trip, thanks to my benefactor, Frankie, putting the word out, nothing was stolen from the hatch. I had hopes for a similar outcome today. We were also loading bags of milk powder, AID cargo, into the deep tanks at the no. 3 hatch. The loading of the cigarettes went well, with another miracle outturn showing no losses. Thank you, Frankie!

The cigarettes finished loading by 1600 hours, and the gang switched to the deep tanks. Using the ship's gear, the longshoremen lifted two pallets of bagged milk powder at a time using a tray. It's called that because it looks like a big steel tray, four and a half feet wide and eight feet long, hoisted at the corners by four wire straps. Every pallet carried thirty bags, five to a tier and six tiers high. Each bag weighed fifty-five pounds, for a total weight of 1,650 pounds. There was two pallets, so there was a little over a ton and a half per lift.

Longshoremen use hooks to handle cargo—different hooks depending on the cargo. Big hooks for crates and cases, and smaller palm hooks for bags (coffee and cocoa beans come in burlap bags). They were forbidden from using hooks on paper bags due to possible tearing; they handled them by the corners ("ears" to the longshoremen). The longshoremen weren't happy because it was harder to handle them. The powdered-milk bags were two-ply, with the outer ply being semiwaterproof. Before loading, they placed cardboard on the deck to act as a buffer between the steel deck and the paper bags.

The winch operator would place a tray in the center of the hatch, and a forklift operator would bring one pallet to one corner and the second pallet to another corner for the longshoremen to stack. While they were stacking bags, the winch operator took the tray out for another load, and they repeated this operation, only altering the tank corners to even out the loading.

Since they were in the deep tanks that had small hatch openings (hydraulic steel covers that lifted at right angles to allow access) and they used a fork lift, we placed blowers in the tanks to circulate the air and push out the carbon monoxide. At 1800 hours, they knocked off for the day.

Sitting in the officers' salon, the oniony smell of tonight's meat loaf pervasive, obscuring the hot diesel oil smell that the engineers' coveralls give off, the chief mate told me and Tony Adams what his "surprise" was: "Passengers!"

"Passengers?" we echoed together.

"What are you, deaf?" he said.

"No," I replied. "Just a little shocked. I mean, I know the ship is designed to carry up to a dozen passengers, but I didn't think they actually carried them. Kind of thought all the passengers traveled on the company's two cruise ships, the *Argentina* and the *Brazil*."

"You're not too far wrong," he said. "The *Argentina* and *Brazil* are popular and carry most of the passenger traffic, but other freighters have carried a few. This is the first time anyone other than the captain's wife has sailed as a passenger on the *Pride*. She ran a short coast-wise stretch with us two years ago."

"How many passengers?" Tony asked.

"Four for sure. A couple from Minnesota and a mother and daughter going back to South Africa. There may be one other guy, and the captain said he is waiting to hear from his wife. She may go, too."

"How old is the daughter?" Tony asked.

Pinning him with a glare, the mate said, "It makes no difference. Passengers are off-limits. Let me warn you right now: the captain doesn't like having passengers on board because he has to entertain them, and he has a low tolerance for anyone who upsets the passengers." Neither Tony nor I said anything, so the mate said, "Understand?"

"Sure, mate."

"Uh-huh."

"Good. They'll be coming aboard tomorrow sometime midmorning. Expect a lecture from the captain about manners and etiquette. Pay attention. He means it."

True to the mate's prediction, the next morning at 0715 hours, while we were eating breakfast and all the deck and engineering officers were present, the captain stood up and clinked his fork against his coffee cup twice. When he had everyone's attention, he launched into his lecture.

"Gentlemen. Today, for the first time since being put into service, the *MorMacPride* will board passengers for our trip to Africa." He paused. "Regardless of my opinion about the best use of cargo ships," he continued, a slight, supercilious smile on his face, "the company has booked them. Therefore, we shall treat them as the guests they are." Another pause while his eyes circled the room, looking for any dissenter, prey for the hawk. "You will, each and every one of you, treat them with respect at all times. The purser will tell you their names, and whenever you see them, which should be at a minimum except for meal hours, you will address them as Mr. or Mrs. So-and-So. You will *not* use their first names or get familiar with them in any manner. You will do your best to be invisible to them. The less contact made, the lower the chances of them getting upset about anything you may say or do or anything they may perceive you said or did." Another long pause. "Questions?"

There was a murmuring of "No, Captain" by the assemblage, followed by "Good!" by him. He sat down, and the normal buzz of conversation ensued as we finished our breakfast.

The mate told me and Tony that we had an additional gang starting this morning and that they would load used POVs (personally owned vehicles) into the lower-tween deck and upper-tween deck of the no. 4 hatch.

At 0800 hours, the longshoremen resumed loading bags of milk powder in the no. 3 hatch's deep tanks. The work went without incident until 0945 hours, when the winchman (who I later found out was a trainee) didn't lift the tray high enough coming in over the railing and caught the edge of the tray on the rail, stopping it dead in its tracks and causing most of the bags of milk powder to shoot inward and splatter all over the weather deck. Notwithstanding the double ply of the bags when they hit the steel deck and fittings, they exploded.

The ship boss, Ritchie, happened to be standing right there when it happened, and he let out a string of "Motherfucker's!" that would have done any bosun proud. A cloud of white powder that rose from the deck enveloped him, so the curses emanating from Casper the Ghost made it hilarious.

The winchman landed the tray back out on the pier, and they removed the damaged bags and replaced them with two good pallets of bags. Work resumed but with a different winchman. Ritchie told the guy who had caused the problem that he had to clean up the mess on deck. That would be the job of cleaners, a different union local than the longshoremen, but what Ritchie says goes, so the bosun spread out a cleaning tarpaulin, one with ropes attached at the corners, and the offending winchman shoveled and swept until he had it all cleaned up.

Back in the no. 4 hatch, the longshoremen were loading POVs into the lower-tween deck. They used an auto tray, a device that looked like a lift in an auto-repair shop. It consisted of two steel tracks suspended by four wires, one at each corner. The crane operator landed the tray flat on the pier, and the longshoremen would push a car (or pickup truck) onto the tracks. There were small, eighteen-inch long, ramps hinged to the ends of the tracks. When they lifted the tray, the wires would put tension on the spring attached to each individual ramp, and they would act as roll stops. As long as the longshoremen remembered to set the emergency brake, it was fine, but I had seen more than one auto roll through the stops, so I wasn't eager to stand near them when they came over the gunwale.

Many of the POVs were crammed with belongings being shipped to the POV owners. The company didn't care, so long as the goods were in the trunk or interior of the car. They allowed nothing in the back beds of pickup trucks. That was more of a "don't let it fall out when lifting" issue since we never signed for liability for anything other than the vehicles themselves.

All the while, I was keeping an eye on the gangway because I was curious about the passengers. At 1130 hours, the mate called me on the radio and told me to have the bosun bring a couple of seamen to the foot of the gangway to handle the passengers' baggage. I did and then stood at the top of the gangway, trying to look disinterested and important at the same time. I failed at both.

If the *Pride* were a passenger ship, the company would have to hire a separate gang of longshoremen to handle the baggage, but since passengers were only a sideline on our ship, they let the crew handle the bags.

A small tractor had pulled two connected dollies loaded with bags from the head of the pier to the foot of the gangway. Since the longshoremen were about to knock off for lunch, I called the mate and suggested we wait until they stop and then let the crew use the ship's booms to land the bags on the main deck. I made a few friends in the crew that day when the mate agreed. Many of those bags were heavy, and slogging them up a gangway was hard work.

After the bags landed on the main deck, the purser came out and told the crew what cabins to deliver them to. The mate told me to stand by in the passageway outside the cabins and make sure that everything got delivered to the correct room and intact.

The Simpsons, the couple from Minnesota, had a hodgepodge of mix-and-match luggage that was all mix and no match—nine bags in total, with one being an old-fashioned steamer trunk. It took two guys to handle that. The O'Briens, mother and daughter, had all Samsonite bags, matched, in pearl gray. In addition, there were two large, well-used duffel bags and two hard-sided, locked gun cases bearing the name of Pieter DeKuyper, our now confirmed fifth passenger.

The purser had assigned the O'Briens to the forward starboard cabin (no. 2, since all even numbers are starboard and all odd numbers port) and the Simpsons to the forward port cabin (no. 1). Mr. DeKuyper had the smaller no. 4 cabin, just aft of the O'Briens'. Once the bags were in the cabins and the doors closed, I reported to the mate, and he told me that the captain's wife would show up in about an hour. The other passengers were all at the head of the pier, being entertained by someone from the cruise department, and they would board when the captain's wife arrived.

"Will her luggage go to the captain's cabin?" I asked.

"No. Put her stuff in cabin no. 5." Without my asking, he offered, "She wants to be apart from the other passengers."

"Why wouldn't she stay with the captain?"

He *harumph*ed and said, "Not my business or yours. She stayed in that same cabin (no. 5) when we did the short coast-wise trip with just her as a passenger, and it seemed to work good for both her and the captain." His look made it clear that I shouldn't ask any more questions, but being pigheaded, I persisted.

"Okay, but why that cabin when she could have her pick of them?"

There was another *harumph* and then a pause; he then said, "I don't know, but I suspect because it's next to the aft door leading out to the ladderway. She liked to wander around the upper decks at night, smoking and drinking wine. She's a little strange. A good fit for the captain but a lot younger than him."

I nodded, content to not probe further.

"By the way," he said, "if she ever comes onto the bridge when you're on watch, tell her politely that she has to return to the pool deck. Tell her you don't want to get in trouble breaking the captain's rules. She'll be sympathetic. At least she was with the third mate on her last trip."

"Okay, mate."

I never got the chance to eat lunch, what with the baggage handling and listening to the mate, but I grabbed a piece of pound cake and a glass of milk before going back on deck at 1300 hours. The ship boss, Ritchie, was the first person to top the gangway. He had changed clothes and no longer looked like Casper, but he still didn't look happy.

I said, "Hi, Ritchie. You don't look so dusty now."

He snorted and said, "Yeah, everyone got a good laugh this morning. I wanted to strangle that little shit, but I was the one that let him get up there and practice on the winches, so I gotta grin and bear it. Besides, he's my nephew. He practically shit his pants, he was so worried about what I'd tell his mother." He grinned. "I'll use this as leverage for a while." He then walked off, forward.

They were still stowing bagged milk powder into the deep tanks at the number three hold, but they went a little faster now with the regular winchman on duty. It's interesting to watch the byplay between the winch operators, who pride themselves on moving the hook as fast as possible to show off their dexterity, and the holdmen, who have to lift, walk, and place the bags into their stowed position. They also have to interlock the bags in alternating rows, so they make a tighter stow. When the winch operator gets a little too fast for them, they counter him or her by having the forklift driver stop the machine right on the spot where the load has to land, so the winch operator has to hold the load in the air for a short while. It was a little tit-for-tat-game that never ended.

At 1415 hours, the mate called me on the radio and told me the passengers were coming down the pier now. He instructed me to greet them at the bottom of the gangway and assist them up the gangway if they needed help, while he would greet them at the top. He also told me we would sign articles around 1600 hours. I wasn't sure if I would shake hands with anyone, and my hands were dirty. I didn't always put on my work gloves, so I ran into the crew mess head and washed them, and then I trotted down the gangway.

Chapter 5

─────────◌◌◌─────────

PASSENGERS

I expected a van or car to pull up and disgorge the passengers, so I was a little surprised when a man wearing a suit and a MorMac tie walked out of the shadow of the shed doorway, leading the passengers single file—ducklings following the drake.

First came Bernard Simpson. He was in his mid-fifties and was heavy, with an enormous beer belly and a cue-ball bald head. With a rolling gait, he followed close in the wake of the MorMac staffer. Next was his wife Clara Simpson, also in her mid-fifties. She was somewhat heavyset, with large breasts—I mean the "Damn, that must be uncomfortable" kind of large. It was hard not to stare at them. Stalking her was Pieter DeKuyper, the great white hunter, carrying yet another gun case. The other guns shipped as luggage, so this one must be special for him to carry it. He was tall, about six foot, three inches and rangy, with a blond crewcut. His eyes missed nothing, always moving.

There was a small gap, and then Mrs. Grace O'Brien appeared. In her late forties, she stood at five feet six inches, a trim figure with fiery-red hair just tinged with gray. Self-assured, but not in a haughty way, she was a good-looking woman, and she knew it. Behind her came her daughter, Megan O'Brien, a younger clone of her mother—the same fiery-red hair, hazel-green eyes, athletic body, and perfect proportions. I fell in love!

Picking my chin up off the ground, I tried to stop drooling as the captain's wife, Eunice Coltrain, stepped into view. She was in her mid-forties and was five foot, eight inches tall, with a slim waist, long legs, and ample breasts; she, too, was a good-looking woman. The difference between her and Mrs. O'Brien was that O'Brien walked, and Coltrain strutted.

It was difficult for me to get my tongue working, but I somehow managed, greeting each one as he or she approached the gangway. If a hand was offered, I shook it. If not, I didn't offer mine. Mr. Simpson did. His wife and Mrs. O'Brien didn't. Megan (I was now five minutes in love, so I couldn't refer to her as "Miss O'Brien") extended her hand, and I turned to jelly when I heard her angelic voice with a South African accent say, "Hi. So very nice to meet you." I eloquently grunted.

As I greeted them, I helped them onto the bottom of the gangway. I damn near tripped when it came to Megan's turn because instead of watching where I turned, I was gazing into her eyes. She survived the incident and continued up the gangway. Tearing my eyes away from the obvious target, her derriere, I greeted Mrs. Coltrain. She had a sultry voice; she shook my hand, giggled like a young girl, and said, sotto voce, "Careful, young man. You're way too obvious." Then, she giggled again. I was too embarrassed to reply but helped her onto the gangway platform and followed her up the gangway, staying a few steps behind, certain she threw a few extra twitches into her ass as she walked. I just wasn't sure if it was for me or the entire world.

The mate greeted them at the top of the gangway, and the purser led them into the house and to their cabins.

Giving them about a half hour to get organized, the purser then asked them to come to the officers' salon for orientation and instructions on fire and boat drills. When they assembled, the captain introduced himself to them, gave his wife a buss on the cheek, and explained to the others with a supercilious smile, "I'm allowed. Eunice is my wife." Being in the presence of his wife didn't thaw his arrogance. He then introduced the chief mate, chief engineer, and purser.

"Ladies and gentlemen, Moore McCormack Line is proud to have you as passengers, and I am pleased that you chose my ship, the *MorMacPride*, to sail on. Have any of you ever ridden on a freighter before—or, for that matter, any passenger ship before?"

"I have," his wife said.

A shadow of annoyance flickered over his face before he replied, "Of course, dear. I meant, any of the others."

"Oh."

He continued, "While we don't have professional entertainment on board, we do have comfortable quarters, good food, and something the passenger liners don't: time in port. On a liner, you may be in port two days at most. Many times, we spend anywhere from four to ten days in port. That gives you more than ample time to see the sights. Mr. Hughes will run through the required boat and fire drill instructions. Does anyone have any questions?" Turning to the chief mate, he said, "Mr. Hughes, you have the floor."

"Thank you, Captain. Welcome aboard, folks. You've already seen your cabins. If anyone has any issues with them, please see the chief steward." He turned and nodded in Fran's direction. "He will take care of it. This," he said, waving his hand toward the round tables, "is the officers' salon, where you will have all your meals. You are free to use this room at any time. In port and up to about fifty miles out, we can receive most television-station signals. Every passenger room has an antenna connection for those who have broadband radios. If you need to send a message at sea, the radio operator will accommodate you. Keep in mind that in the middle of the ocean, the reception is subject to weather and other phenomena, so there may be delays."

Megan O'Brien asked, "Is it all right to play music in here?"

"Of course. I would ask that you keep it low after 10:00 at night. Both your fellow passengers and crew need to sleep."

"Thank you."

"Next topic: fire and boat drills. There are life preservers in each room on the shelf in the closets. We will let you know beforehand when we are having a drill. The first one will be tomorrow afternoon at 1500 hours." Seeing the questioning look on the Simpsons' faces, he added, "That's 3:00 p.m.; we use military time on board. When the alarm sounds, an announcement will follow, telling you to report to your fire or boat stations. Your fire station is here in the officers' salon. If necessary, you will receive further instructions after you are assembled here. Your boat station is at the loading platform on the boat deck. If you are in a port-side cabin, you go to the port lifeboat. If in a starboard cabin, go to the starboard lifeboat." He paused. "Is anyone not familiar with port and starboard? No? Good." Another pause. "Folks, it's unlikely that we will have a fire or need to abandon ship, *but* if we ever do, we need to react fast. When the alarm sounds, it's important that you go to your station as quick as possible. You don't have to run, but please don't dawdle. Also, wear your life jackets to *both* fire and boat drills; don't just carry it." There were nods of assent from all.

"Finally, this is a working freighter. When we are in port, you may not go out on the working areas near the hatches. It can be very dangerous. If you want to see what's going on, the best place to view it is from the flying bridge, which you can reach via exterior ladderways. You can see all the activity in the hatches, and you won't get in the crew's way…but, more important, in harm's way. The bridge and the engine room are off-limits at all times. If you want to tour either of them, see me, and I will arrange it, but please don't just wander into those spaces. Thank you." Turning to the chief steward, he said, "Fran, you're on."

"Thank you, Dennis." Beaming with pleasure, he said, "I'm Francis McGonigle, the chief steward. Please call me Fran. I'm here to serve you and make your journey as pleasant as possible." With a smirk, he continued, "And I'm your first line of defense against these bullies." He pointed at the captain, chief mate, and chief engineer. The Simpsons guffawed; the others smiled.

"Meal hours are posted on the chart in your cabin."

"Are they rigid?" asked Mr. DeKuyper.

"Semirigid. Most of the crew stands watches, so it's necessary to have fixed schedules; however, if you have an issue, please let me know, and I am sure we will be able to accommodate you."

DeKuyper nodded.

"While we are on that topic, if anyone wishes to have us prepare a box lunch for you when you go ashore, please let us know as soon as possible ahead of time."

"What kind of box lunch?" This came from Mr. Simpson.

"Sandwiches and a small snack or dessert."

Patting his huge belly, Simpson replied, "This body ain't made for snacks," and he then snickered.

"I am sure we can accommodate you."

"Glad to hear that."

The captain intervened. "Fran, please tell our guests about shoreside services and sailing times."

Nodding, Fran said, "What the captain is referring to, the posting of sailing times, is how we notify everyone when the ship is scheduled to depart port. There is a sailing board—a chalkboard, that is—on the bulkhead at the top of the gangway. The date and time of sailing is posted on that board at least twelve but no more than twenty-four hours prior to the scheduled time of sailing. Each crew member must make him- or herself aware of this by reading the board before going ashore. This rule will also apply to you. To avoid possible confusion, there are no separate notices given to anyone. For a crew member to miss the ship is a serious problem. For a passenger to miss the ship can also be a problem, depending on the country and whether you have your passport with you. Please, always carry your passport whenever you leave the ship."

Pausing but getting no questions, he continued, "Shoreside services, tours, dinner reservations, and so forth are not provided by the company. If you wish to make these arrangements, we will give you the name, address, and telephone number of the local ship's agent at each port, and the agent will usually make these arrangements for you. Some of them charge a small fee, so please inquire before you use them."

"Why not?" Simpson again.

"I beg your pardon?"

"Why won't the company provide those services?"

"Company policy."

"They do it for passengers on the cruise liners."

"Yes sir, they do, but their port calls and time in port is more fixed and focuses on nothing but passengers. As Mr. Hughes said, this is a working freighter, a different experience."

Sweating heavily, as if speaking were an exertion, Simpson said, "Make sure I get that list of agents right away. I thought we'd get better treatment than this." Shaking off his wife's hand and glaring at her, he continued, "You understand?"

"Of course, sir. I'll get the list to you immediately."

From behind Simpson came a clear but barely audible "Arsehole." Twisting, Simpson glared at Mr. DeKuyper, the obvious source.

The mate interjected, "Mr. DeKuyper. I've locked your other two guns in the locker of the ship's store. I'll also have to lock up the one you carried aboard with you."

DeKuyper's face was like stone and his eyes piercing. This was a formidable man. Simpson started to say something and thought better of it. He was obnoxious but not stupid. Staring at Simpson, DeKuyper replied to the mate, "Of course, Mr. Hughes. We wouldn't want to have a dangerous weapon loose on board, now, would we?"

"Thank you, Mr. DeKuyper."

An awkward pause ensued until Fran said, "Speaking of the ship's store, we carry cigarettes, cigars, pipe tobacco, beer, hard liquor, sodas, and miscellaneous toiletries. They are sold for ten percent above cost, but the store is open only when the ship is at sea. Due to possible conflict with local regulations, we keep it closed in port. You may purchase your own supplies and keep them in your rooms. The captain has a safe in his room if anyone wants to store valuables." Fran looked at the passengers and then nodded to the chief mate.

The mate said, "Thank you folks for your attention. If anyone wants to see the bridge or engine room, now would be a good time." Getting no response other than a murmured "Maybe later" from Mrs. Simpson, he said, "Okay, thanks again."

As they filed from the salon, with DeKuyper never taking his eye off Simpson and following him out the door, the captain turned to the mate and said, "DeKuyper is right. He is an arsehole."

At 1600 hours, I walked into the salon, and the signing of articles was underway, the same as on the last trip. The captain, chief steward in his purser role, and a coast guard lieutenant (junior grade) named Worrisom (pronounced "worrysome") witnessed the signing on of the crew.

This time, the crew totaled forty-one souls. The deck department comprised the officers—captain, chief mate, second mate, two third mates (one of whom was called a junior third)—and unlicensed deck hands. They were one bosun, one maintenance man, six able-bodied seamen (AB), and three ordinary seamen (OS).

The engine department comprised the officers—chief engineer, first-assistant engineer, second-assistant engineer, two third-assistant engineers (like the third mate, one is often referred to as junior third)—and the unlicensed hands. They were three oilers, three fireman water tenders (FWT), and one wiper. The oilers and firemen stood regular watches, like an AB and OS. The wiper was a day worker, like the bosun and deck-maintenance man. There were no cadets in training aboard this trip.

In addition, there was the radio officer (Sparky) and the stewards department. Under the chief steward were the chief cook; baker; third cook; salon messman; salon pantryman; officers' bedroom steward (BR); steward utility (gofer for the chief steward); the crew messman, who served the unlicensed crew; and the galley utility, who did most of the menial jobs, like peeling potatoes. Since the ship carried passengers, the additional passenger utility and BR were also here.

Each crew member stepped up to the table and handed over his Z-card to the LTJG, who examined it and handed it to the purser. A Z-card is a merchant mariner's standard ID card, issued by the US Coast Guard. The purser asked the man if he wanted any allotments sent. If he did, the purser handed him some forms. After each man signed the articles, he filled out the allotment forms, signed them, and returned them to the purser, who gave him a copy. It was all routine, and since I had done it once, I wasn't so impressed, but I was still very much aware that I was signing a contract with the steamship company. I and everyone else who signed ceded control of a good part of our lives to the captain.

The captain was again regally surveying his realm, one arm draped over the backrest, legs crossed and smoking a cigarette, a Dunhill. He used a cigarette holder, which lent him a Hollywood air.

When the crew finished at the captain's table, they went over to where the mate and first engineer sat, checking the men's union cards. The mate and the first engineer oversaw the maintenance and overtime of their respective departments, and they each kept a separate log for that purpose.

I said, "Good afternoon," to the captain and got in line behind the BR to sign up.

The purser looked up and said, "Welcome back, Mr. Connolly. We'll try not to make this too 'worrysome.'" And he smirked at the LTJG. This wasn't the first time the LTJG. had heard this, but he dutifully smiled and said hello.

This time, after my signing, the captain didn't shake my hand but said, "Welcome back aboard, Mr. Connolly."

"Thank you, Captain. I'm glad to be back."

I went off to the corner to fill out the allotment forms. Last trip, I had named my ma as the recipient, but this time, I changed it to my sister Betty since she had set up my savings account and it was easier for her to get to the bank than Ma. I signed them and returned them to the purser. Leery of the purser when we first met (he was obviously queer with a limp handshake), I overcame my reluctance when I saw him in action. On the last voyage, he had performed first aid when my AB, Pickerell, lost both his legs when a mooring line snapped. Fran stood tall, did his job, and saved Pickerell's life. You can't expect more of a crew member. I was learning to overcome my biases.

Back on deck after signing articles, I watched the longshoremen close the deep tanks and proceed to load a dozen medium-size cases into the after end of the no. 3 upper-tween deck. They were all for Ascension Island, the only cargo scheduled to be discharged there. The wood butchers secured them, blocking and chocking them, and then tying them into the bulkhead with wires and turnbuckles.

At 2000, hours we dropped the last line and sailed for Ascension Island on our way to Cape Town.

Chapter 6

FIRST DAY AT SEA

S̲ailed from New York at 2000 hours on Friday, 10/15/66. Partly cloudy.
Temperature 62 degrees. Wind from the southwest at 7 mph. Sailing time
from New York to Ascension Island, a speck of land in the middle of the Atlantic
Ocean halfway between South America and Africa, would be about twelve days.

Prudence mandated that everything loose get stowed in lockers or tied down,
so as the ship passed the Statue of Liberty, the crew finished stowing the
mooring lines.

After releasing the crew members—Sturm AB; Jaeger AB (he had replaced Pickerell, the AB who had lost both legs when a mooring line snapped
while undocking on the prior trip); and Brian Goode, OS—I walked up the
after ladder to the officers' deck, intending to go to the flying bridge, a habit I
had acquired when leaving port. Halfway up, I heard voices and realized that
some of the passengers were up there. Heeding the captain's advice of being
invisible, I went to my cabin instead, feeling a little put-upon at not being able
to occupy my heretofore private space. This might take getting used to. Lying
down on my bunk, I dozed off.

"Mate, it's time for your watch." The OS from the eight-to-twelve watch woke
me. Leaning in the door, he asked, "You awake?"

"Yeah, I'm up, thanks."

I splashed my face with cold water, walked to the head, and peed (remembering to close the door since we carried passengers), and then went to the salon to see what they set out to eat for the midwatch. Not surprisingly, the food included pound cake, the baker's specialty, and a tray of cold cuts. I made a Dagwood; he was one of my favorite Sunday-comics characters, famous for his sandwich creations of ham, cheese, salami, and bologna, slathered with mustard. I took two cartons of milk and sat down to eat. As I was halfway through the first bite, the captain's wife walked in and said hello.

It took a few chews before I could mumble, "Hello."

She walked up, stood in front of me, leaned over (exposing ample cleavage), looked at my sandwich, and said, "Sure you can handle something like this?" The double entendre was blatant, but before I could reply, she smiled, turned, and walked out. I was stunned and nervous; the last thing I wanted was the captain's wife coming on to me. The implications of that were frightening.

I scooped up my sandwich and milk and headed for the bridge. When I walked in, I set the food on the chart table and asked Tony, the other third mate, "How's it going?"

"Okay," he said and reeled off the course and speed, ship traffic, and the usual "Call the captain if anything looks close." But then, he whispered, "On the bridge wing," and I followed him out the door.

"What's the matter?" I asked.

"There's gonna be problems."

"Problems? What kind of problems?"

"Captain's-wife problems."

"Oh, shit, what did she do?"

"She came up here right after the captain went below and stood out on the starboard-bridge wing. So, doing what the mate said, I walked out and politely asked her to please return to the pool deck or flying bridge, adding that I didn't want to get in trouble disobeying the captain's standing orders."

"And…what happened?" I asked.

"She patted my cheek and said, 'I wouldn't want someone as cute as you getting in trouble for my being where I shouldn't be. I have better plans for you.' She stared at me for a few seconds and then went back to the pool deck and sat in one of the chaise lounges. When I closed the connecting door, I heard her laugh."

"Jesus, Tony, I had my own run-in with her in the salon, and she flashed her tits at me. This is not good. If the captain finds out, there will be hell to pay, and something tells me he won't see our point of view on this."

"What the hell can we do? It's his ship, his wife, but our asses on the line."

"I don't know. I just don't know."

Tony went below to his cabin, and I did a radar check, followed by a 360-degree visual check of the surrounding ocean. There was a ship, seven miles in front and just to starboard, separating faster since they were heading south down the coast and we were heading out to sea. The helmsman was my AB, Sturm, and the ship was on autopilot. He had asked permission to smoke, and I had agreed, giving him a light.

In his German accent, he started, "Mr. Connolly, I know it's none of my business, but the AB on Mr. Adams's vatch told me that the captain's vife came on the bridge." He eyed me to see if I would stop him, but I let him go on. "You know, I vas here when she rode the coast a while ago. At first, she came on the bridge but then spent a lot of time on the pool deck. The third mate on that trip, he found a lot of excuses to inspect the pool deck. The captain fired him before we finished the trip."

"Thanks, Sturm, I appreciate the heads-up. Both Tony and I will do our best to stay out of her gun sights."

Chuckling, he said, "Gun sights, ya. Ven she points those twin thirty-eights at you, you feel like a target."

I laughed, but it wasn't funny.

The rest of the watch was uneventful. The sea was flat calm, and the ship's movement wasn't noticeable unless I looked over the side at the bow wave. A sliver of crescent moon peeked through the clouds and ignited the sparkles of water surfing down the crest of the bow wave. There was engine vibration, but I knew that after a few days, even that would tune out.

When the second mate Charles (Chuck) Stewart relieved me, I stopped at the head to pee. When I came out, I stated at the door to cabin no. 5. Standing there, I felt a vague sensation of apprehension or déjà vu. I turned and scurried to my cabin, locking the door behind me, not wanting any surprises. Lying on my bunk, the irony of the situation struck me. I had a young man's dream of an older, good-looking woman coming on to me, and I was terrified.

My routine at sea on the previous trip had evolved to where I rarely ate breakfast. There's not much chance for aerobic exercise, and I tended to gain weight if idle. It was easier to skip the meal than to eat light. However, I wanted to take advantage of every opportunity to see Megan O'Brien, so I set my alarm and entered the officers' salon at 0715. The bacon-and-eggs aroma was in a head-to-head battle with the perfumes the women were wearing. My nose wasn't sophisticated enough to decipher what types of perfume, but there was more than one.

Megan and her mother sat at the round table closest to where I sat. I viewed her mother from the rear but had a perfect profile view of Megan. She stunned me. Did I mention I was in love with her?

The captain and his wife also sat at the table. When I entered the salon, and said good morning in the general direction of the captain, they all replied, "Good morning." Megan smiled at me, and Mrs. Coltrain smirked. The former gave me thrills, and the latter, chills.

The Simpsons ate alone at the other round table. When I sat down, the mate nodded toward the Simpsons and whispered, "They've been here since six thirty. Joey, the steward, told them we didn't serve until 0700, and Mr. This-Body-Ain't-Built-For-Snacks went into a snit. He's already on his second helping, and she's kept up with him."

Just then, Mr. DeKuyper entered, looked around, noted where the Simpsons sat, went to the captain's table, and inquired, "May I join you?"

"Of course," Eunice Coltrain replied before anyone else could speak and patted the table in front of the seat next to her. He sat down.

Joey, the steward, came over and asked what he wanted to eat. Each day, the chief steward would print a list of the day's meals. Without passengers, it resembled a list of ingredients rather than a menu. With passengers aboard, it was a menu.

"I'll have a muffin with jam and a cup of tea, please."

Eunice said, "That's not much for a man of your size. You'll waste away if you don't eat."

"Thank you for your concern," he said, an edge of sarcasm showing. "It's unlikely that I'll 'waste away,' but in fact, I feel a bit queasy so I'm going light on food."

At the mention of "queasy," the captain said, "The sea is calm now, but it will get rougher. Do you have Dramamine?"

"What's that?"

"A pill for seasickness. Have you ever been on a ship before?"

"I've never been on anything bigger than a riverboat."

"The steward has Dramamine in his medicine kit if you need it."

"Thank you. I'll see how it goes."

I had ordered coffee, toast, and milk. Until they ran out of fresh milk, usually ten days out, I would drink it. I had sworn off powdered milk after the first training cruise at MMA. Glancing at Megan, I saw her peeking at me, and a grin arose automatically. She grinned back. That's when I noticed the captain staring at me. I slammed my eyes onto the table and focused on my toast.

The mate nudged me with his knee and whispered, "Roll your tongue up; you're tripping over it." He chuckled.

By then, Bernie Simpson was on his third helping. Clara, his wife, had stopped after two rounds.

"Captain," Bernie said, between bites of runny eggs. Some of it had run all the way down to his shirt, a minimarathon. "This morning when Clara and I came in for breakfast, the steward"… He glanced at Joey. "He refused to serve us. That's not what I'd call good service."

Fran, the chief steward sitting at the square table next to me, started to reply, but the captain cut him off by raising a finger. Half turning in his chair, he said, "What time did you arrive for breakfast, Mr. Simpson?"

"I was here at 6:30, my usual breakfast time."

"Ah." He paused. "I believe at our orientation yesterday, both the chief mate and chief steward explained the working hours of the ship. Part of that explanation was the meal hours for crew and passengers. Breakfast is served from 0700 to 0900 hours."

"I don't remember hearing the meal times, but regardless, Clara and I eat breakfast at 6:30."

"I also believe," the captain continued, "it was mentioned that if you wished to make any special arrangements for anything, you would make a request to Mr. McGonigle, the chief steward, and he would make a reasonable effort to accommodate you." Turning fully in his chair and facing Simpson, he added, "Isn't that so?"

"I didn't think asking for breakfast was a special arrangement."

Before the captain could reply, Mr. DeKuyper interjected, "Is it asking for breakfast or thinking that requires a special arrangement for you?"

Clara Simpson said, "Well, I never!" to which DeKuyper responded, "Ahh, if that was an answer to my question, then the mystery is resolved. Looking at your husband, it's clear that breakfast is a regular occurrence." Standing, he continued, "Excuse me, but my queasiness has just intensified." He left the salon.

Bernie Simpson waited until the door had closed behind DeKuyper and then jumped in with, "Captain, I won't stand for this rude and belligerent behavior toward my wife and me."

"Mr. Simpson, are you saying I am rude and belligerent?"

"Oh, no, Captain. I'm talking about DaCoopa."

"It's DeKuyper, Mr. Simpson, not DaCoopa. I would hope that all the passengers would be civil and polite with one another. I know that my crew will." With that, the captain turned back facing his table and called, "Joey, may I have more coffee, please?"

"Yessir, Captain, right away."

Watching the Simpsons during this encounter, I bit my lip to keep from laughing. Stealing a peek at Megan, I could see she had her napkin to her face more than necessary, trying to hide her smile.

"Captain?" Simpson again, this time more restrained.

"Yes, Mr. Simpson?"

"Would it be possible to make arrangements for early breakfast?"

Keeping his back to Simpson, hiding a smirk that everyone at his table could see, he replied, "I'm sure that Mr. McGonigle will be able to work something out for you." Hearing no reply, the captain continued in a somewhat sharper tone, "Is that suitable, Mr. Simpson?"

"Yes, Captain, thank you."

"You're welcome."

Chapter 7

SOCIAL STRAINS

Bernie Simpson had managed to at least irritate, if not piss off, everyone he had come in contact with. Since I was in no position to rebuke his rudeness like the captain did, I decided to steer clear of him and his wife, Clara, as much as possible.

When the Simpsons left the salon, the captain's wife, Eunice, lit a cigarette and announced, "Must be terrible being married to such a rude person." Looking at the captain and patting his arm, she continued, "I'm so glad I have the perfect husband." Her smoldering voice was a perfect imitation of Marlene Dietrich in her prime.

The captain stared ahead, and the O'Briens, mother and daughter, made sympathetic, simpering noises. The rest of the salon was silent.

"Excuse me." The captain addressed the O'Briens as he rose. "There's things to attend to." He walked out, never even glancing at his wife.

The chief mate broke the silence by asking Joey for more coffee. As Joey brought the pot to the table, the O'Briens stood, nodded at Eunice Coltrain, said thank you to Joey, and left. Megan turned as she went by and smiled. I beamed back at her.

"The young lady seems to like you, William," the mate said, speaking low since the captain's wife was within earshot. "Touchy. Keep that in mind."

Standing, the mate patted my shoulder and left. Noticing Eunice staring, I got up and left before she could get a conversation started.

With over three hours remaining before my watch, I went up to the flying bridge and stood at the rail, staring forward at the ocean. Just as I pulled out a cigarette and opened my lighter, I felt a touch on my shoulder and jumped. Megan stood there. "Oh, I'm sorry. I didn't mean to startle you," she said.

"That's okay, Miss O'Brien. We didn't carry passengers the last trip, and no one else comes up here."

"Am I not supposed to be here?" She was innocent and coy.

"Oh, no." I was eager to please. "Go anywhere you want."

Her contagious smile lit up again, and I had to smile back.

"What a nice smile, Mr. Connolly."

"Call me William. You have a beautiful smile. Your face transforms when you smile."

She blushed; she was not red but had a pinkish tinge. It was mesmerizing.

"Thank you. I'm Megan, but my friends call me Meg."

Survival instincts kicked in. "Love your name, but the captain insists that we address all passengers by Mr., Mrs., or Miss."

Another coy smile. Looking around and waving her hands, she said, "But the captain isn't here. When he's here, we can be formal, but when he isn't, please call me Meg?"

I was defenseless. Whatever this girl wanted is what she would get. I agreed.

"Okay, it's a deal." Holding up my cigarette, I asked, "Do you mind if I smoke?"

"No. In fact, I'll join you if you have an extra one."

Handing her the one in my hand, I lit it, staring at her face the entire time. When she looked up, we were twelve inches apart. This close, she smelled fresh, with no perfume. The salon odor must have been the other women. She looked in my eyes, turned her head to the side to blow out the smoke, never losing eye contact, and said, "I find you fascinating."

"That's nice," was all I could say. "I mean…"

Touching my hand, she said, "I know what you mean."

Her touch was electric. Feeling overwhelmed, like a mumbling, fumbling idiot, but needing to get control, I took the plunge and told the truth. "Look,

I'm having a hard time getting words out, so I'll just say it. You're amazing! I've never met a more beautiful girl, and I can't believe the effect you have on me." Staring at her, I continued. "I hope I didn't upset you, but there's no getting around it."

She lowered the cigarette, took a breath, and said, "Wow! That's the nicest thing anyone has ever said to me." Reaching out with the noncigarette hand, she touched one cheek, leaned in, and kissed me on the other cheek. I damn near fainted.

Turning and leaning against the rail, she took a drag on the cigarette, exhaled, and said, "So where do you live?"

Spreading my hands, I said, "Here."

"No, I mean where do you live when you aren't on board the ship?"

"Oh, at my ma's in South Boston." A strange look from her made me apologetically add, "I'm never there. I don't even have a bed. I sleep on the couch. Besides, it's a convenient mailing address."

"A one-bedroom apartment, like the room I had in college, just enough room for her and your father?"

"No. My dad died in my first year at school. It's two bedrooms. My sister, Betty, lives with her. They look out for each other."

Megan processed this and then continued, "I went to Boston University, but I've never been to South Boston."

"Just another neighborhood. No big deal, other than a lot of Irish live there. What was your major at BU?"

"French. I love the language, the language of romance." She batted her eyes in an obvious gesture and laughed. Theatrical and funny.

"I take it you are fluent in French."

"*Certainement, monsieur, et tu?*"

"No. I'm barely fluent in English. Two years of French in high school and Spanish in college. I can read both languages pretty well but can't carry a conversation."

"*Je peux peut-être vous apprendre un pende de choses pendant le voyage.*" She smiled as she spoke.

Not sure what she said, I queried, "Teach me something?"

Staring straight in my eyes, she said, *"J'aimerais vous apprendre des choses."* She then blushed.

"Translate that, please."

"I said, 'I'd love to teach you things.'" And then, I blushed.

The cigarette was down to a stub, so I bent down and extinguished it on the scupper. She was about to flick hers overboard when I stopped her. "Never toss a lit cigarette anywhere on a ship. The wind can take it, and the last thing we want is a fire at sea." Reaching, I took it from her and put it out in the scupper but kept both dead butts since the wind was blowing astern; they would have landed on the pool deck or fantail if I tossed them. Old habits die hard.

I looked around, nervous, worried that someone would see us up here, and though reluctant, I said, "Got to go. I'm on watch in a couple of hours and have a few things to do."

"Okay. I'm staying awhile. I like it up here."

"See ya."

"Uh-huh."

As William walked away, Megan wondered, "Is this the one? He's good-looking and independent; he seems intelligent and easy to talk to. And, judging from his 'You're amazing! I've never met a more beautiful girl, and I can't believe the effect you have on me' speech, he knows a good thing when he sees it." She was mentally laughing. "Definitely in the running. I wonder what Mum will think?"

Starting down the aft ladder leading to the pool deck, I saw the captain's wife sitting on a lounge chair, holding a drink and smoking. She wore a flesh-colored bikini under a sheer coverall. We were out in the Gulf Stream and the temperature had warmed to sixty-nine degrees but still cool for that attire. I had to pass within ten feet of her and couldn't ignore her, so I said, "Hello, Mrs. Coltrain."

"Hello, Mr. Connolly. Enjoying the fresh air?"

"Yes, ma'am," I said, not wishing to prolong the encounter and trying not to stare.

"Oh, Mr. Connolly. Since you're here, would you be so kind as to get me a blanket? It's getting a little chilly."

"I'll have the steward bring one up right away, ma'am," I said and walked to the ladder.

"Can't you bring it to me?"

"Yes, ma'am, I could, but it's the steward's job, and I wouldn't want him to complain to his union that I was doing his job." All the time, I continued to walk away.

Pausing only to dump the cigarette butts in the trash bucket, imagining the scene if we had flipped them and they blew onto the captain's wife, I went straight to the chief steward and told him what she wanted. He smirked and said, with conspiracy written all over him, "Quick thinking, William. I'll bring the blanket myself. I doubt if she's interested in me."

"Thanks, Fran," I said, smiling.

The chief steward had just returned to his office, intent on setting up the menus for the rest of the week, a more difficult task now that the passengers' appetites and palates had to be considered. A rap on the doorframe made him look up. "Good morning, Mr. DeKuyper. What can I do for you?"

"I need something to settle my stomach."

"Still nauseous?"

"Yes, and getting worse. No vomiting, but I'm not too far from it. I've had nothing out of the ordinary to eat, so I must be getting seasick."

Turning back to his desk, the chief steward got a key from the top right-hand drawer and then stood and walked to a four-drawer file cabinet against the bulkhead. Unlocking it, he opened the second drawer from the top, removed a small packet, and then relocked the file. "Here, Mr. DeKuyper. This is Dramamine. Take one now, but just have a sip of water. Until your stomach settles down, go easy on liquids. Also, munch on saltines. They'll absorb stomach acid. I'll drop off some for you."

"Thank you, Mr. McGonigle; that's very good of you."

After DeKuyper left, Fran went to the galley, got a sleeve of saltines from the box, and delivered them to DeKuyper's cabin. When the door opened, DeKuyper, shirtless, looked worse than just ten minutes earlier—pasty and sweaty.

"Did you take the Dramamine yet?"

"Yes, and I could barely hold it down."

"You should lie down. It can take up to an hour for the Dramamine to act."

When DeKuyper sat on his bunk, McGonigle told him, "Lay on your left side. That reduces the effect of bile rising in your system."

"Thanks," he said, and he lay down, facing the bulkhead. The enormous scars on DeKuyper's back and right shoulder shocked McGonigle. When he pulled on the pillow, adjusting it, McGonigle saw the butt of a pistol underneath it. Glancing around the cabin, he also saw an enormous knife in a sheath and a machete lying on the table.

"If you need anything else, please let me know."

"Thanks again," came a muffled voice from the pillow.

Closing the door behind him, he turned to the aft stairway and then changed routes and went to the captain's office. Knocking on the door, which was open, he called, "Captain?"

"Yes, Fran," was the stentorian reply. "Come in." The captain emerged from his stateroom.

"Captain, I gave Mr. DeKuyper Dramamine and brought saltines to his cabin. I hope the Dramamine acts quick because he looked pretty bad."

With a hint of impatience, the captain said, "And you are telling me this because?"

"I am always concerned about the welfare of everyone on board." Fran was somewhat defensive. "But I thought you should know he has a large knife and a machete on his table."

"Fran, half the crew carry big knives, and the chief engineer has a machete mounted on his bulkhead. Why shouldn't Mr. DeKuyper have one?"

"Well, it seemed sinister because he also has a pistol under his pillow."

No longer impatient, the captain replied, "Thank you, Fran. All the guns were supposed to be locked up. I'll have the chief mate talk to him."

"Yes, sir." He turned and then hesitated. "Captain, one more thing. He has terrible scars on his back and shoulder."

"Well," the captain replied, "he spends a lot of time in the jungle. After all, he's a Great White Hunter."

McGonigle shuddered and left.

Chapter 8

EMERGENCY DRILLS

I slipped into the salon at 1130 hours to get a cup of coffee. The smell of beef stew hung tantalizingly in the air, but, still flying high from my encounter with Meg, I wasn't hungry. Greg Russell, the third engineer, was there, wearing his usual oil-stained jumpsuit. The Simpsons were there, he in shorts resembling pantaloons and a United Nations T-shirt; she sporting a bright-pink muumuu and a garish, kelly-green belt. The belt didn't clash with the muumuu; it had declared outright war with it. Joey, the steward, was in the scullery.

"Morning, Greg." Looking at the Simpsons, I would have greeted them, but they were staring at the menu, so I ignored them. Getting my coffee, I sat opposite Greg.

Leaning forward, he flicked his eyes toward the Simpsons and whispered, "What a pair."

"You noticed?" I whispered back.

"It's hard not to notice. I'm putting on weight just watching them eat."

"Me too." He smirked.

"The pretty redhead has taken a liking to you."

"Is it that obvious?"

"Yeah. You two making goo-goo eyes at each other has the chief mate nervous and the rest of us jealous. She's gorgeous."

"Yes, she is. Why is the mate nervous?"

"Doesn't want to see you do something stupid and get the captain pissed off. When the captain gets pissed, everyone feels his wrath."

Not sure whether I should say anything about the captain's wife's behavior, I opted to tell Greg. "The captain will get pissed even more if he finds out how his wife is coming on to me and Tony."

Greg had lifted his cup but set it down without drinking, an incredulous look on his face. "Serious?"

"Dead serious, and Tony and I are scared because we can't win if she keeps it up. If she gets pissed because we won't play her game, she tells the captain some story, and we're screwed. If Tony gives in and gets caught, he's screwed."

"Tony? What if you get caught?"

"I won't get caught because I ain't gonna screw around with her. She scares the crap out of me. Besides, if I'm gonna get in trouble, I want Meg to be the reason."

"Meg? First-name basis. What happened to 'Miss O'Brien'? Captain's orders."

"Believe me, when the captain is around, it will be 'Miss O'Brien.'"

Looking contemplative, Greg muttered, "This will be a long trip. Might have to spend a lot of time in the engine room or my cabin to avoid getting hit with all the loose flak that will fly around."

"Keep this captain's-wife thing to yourself, okay?"

"Sure."

I got up just as the chief engineer and the first engineer came in. "Morning, Bill, Mark," I said as I passed them. Both nodded and sat down with Greg. Getting a refill for my coffee, I went to the bridge to relieve Tony.

Greg started to speak. "Chief, I think there's something you should know."

On the bridge, I relieved Tony, and my AB, Sturm, relieved Tony's helmsman. Like Tony had done previously, I whispered to him, "Bridge wing," and walked out to the starboard wing.

"Just to let you know, I told Greg Russell about the captain's wife coming on to us."

"Oh shit! Why did you do that?"

"Because I think the more people know it before anything happens, the better off we are if we have to defend ourselves. Besides, you know there aren't any secrets on a ship."

Tony leaned on the forward rail with both hands as if stretching and then pulled back and looked at his hands, which were covered in a light soot. He said, in a less-than-assured tone, "I guess you're right."

"Where'd the soot come from?" I asked. "The wind is blowing aft."

"Yeah, but it was abeam when they blew the tubes. I don't know why they did it this morning. They usually do it at night." ("Blowing tubes" is a process done on ships with steam boilers. Once a day, the engine room blows steam across the outside of the boiler tubes, cleaning the soot off them that accumulated during the previous day and venting it through the smokestack. It's done at night because it creates a black cloud.)

Clapping his hands to shake off the soot, Tony went below.

Stepping into the bridge, I asked Sturm to get a few rags from the bosun. The ship was on autopilot, so I didn't need him to steer. When he returned in five minutes, I took the rags, went out to the bridge wing, and wiped the soot from the rails.

"Hey, mate," Sturm said, "I'll do that."

"Nah, that's okay. When I was on the school ship, we did a lot of 'soogy-ing.' It's good for the soul," I said, chuckling.

"Soogying? What's that?"

"Just what I'm doing. It's an old navy term. The difference between mopping decks and scrubbing bulkheads is only in the size of the mop and the angle you apply it."

Sturm grunted, shook his head, and went back to the helm.

In the officer's salon, everyone except the watch standers sat there as the usual buzz of nothingness filled the air. At the captain's table, the captain; his wife, Eunice; and the O'Briens chatted. No sign of Mr. Dekuyper. The Simpsons reigned supreme at their table, keeping Joey busy bringing refills of everything.

The captain, clinking on the edge of his cup with a spoon, broke the buzz. Addressing the entire room, he said, "Just a reminder we'll be having a boat and fire drill, in that order, this afternoon at 1500 hours, 3:00 p.m. for our passengers. Attendance is mandatory, so when you hear the alarms sound, please go to your stations. If you have any doubt about where your station is, please check with Mr. McGonigle. Thank you."

At 1450, the mate came on the bridge and told me about the drills. The mate would relieve me on the bridge. My fire station was on the fantail, and my lifeboat was the starboard boat. The captain arrived on the bridge and ordered the chief mate to sound the alarm. I went to the loading area of the lifeboat deck and counted heads.

Unless we were doing our annual test and in port, all we did was muster the crew and note the times. If doing our annual drill, we would loosen and remove the bindings, uncover the tarp from the boat, man the boat, and lower it into the water. This sounds simple enough, but try doing it at sea with twenty-foot waves. It takes dexterity, and you better be paying attention, or everyone gets dumped in the ocean. This is serious stuff.

When I did the final head count, the only ones missing were the engine room staff on watch. Unless it was a real emergency, they always stayed at their watch stations. Everyone showed up with life jackets on. Megan and her mother were the first ones there. I smiled at them. Megan smiled back. After glancing at Megan and then me, her mother smiled. I felt relieved when her mother smiled.

Mr. DeKuyper looked a little green in the gills, but he was there, and he didn't puke. I reported to the bridge that everyone was accounted for and waited for the all clear to come from the bridge. It took about five minutes more than I expected, and I wondered if they were having trouble on the port side.

On the port-side boat station, the second mate, Chuck Stewart, was in charge, and Tony Adams assisted him. The crew arrived, along with the captain's wife, who wore her life jacket, but it was unfastened. The Simpsons hadn't arrived, so Chuck told Tony to go check on them. As he opened the WT door to their cabin area, they sauntered out, carrying their life jackets in their hands. Chuck went up to them and said, "It's required that everyone wears their life jackets during an emergency drill. Please put them on."

"It's only a drill. The captain said so. What's the big deal?"

"Sir, the purpose of an emergency drill is to ensure that everyone gets into the habit of doing the right thing. That way, if it's a real emergency, it will be automatic for you, and you won't have to think about it when under stress."

"Well, I still think it's a pain. I know the difference between a real emergency and a drill, and I'll put it on if it's real. I can handle stress."

"Sir, I cannot report to the captain that the crew and passengers are ready unless everyone is on station and wearing their life jackets. Until you put on your life jackets, everyone has to stay at their stations."

"What a stupid rule."

"Sir, you are holding up everyone by not donning your life jacket."

Now seeing that everyone was staring at them, he turned to Clara and said, "Put it on," while shrugging into his jacket. She meekly donned hers, looking embarrassed, leading the others to think he had told her not to before coming out on deck.

"Thank you, sir," Chuck said. When they had donned their jackets, he reported to the bridge that all was ready.

Off in the corner, during the debate between Chuck and Simpson, Eunice had grabbed Tony's arm and breathed, "I'm having trouble fastening this jacket. Would you help?"

He didn't dare refuse, so he reached for the straps, pulled them tight, and tied them.

As he secured the last one, she said, "Thank you. I think it's tight because my breasts are so large. What do you think?"

He yanked his hands away and backed off, going toward the second mate. She smiled.

The captain ordered the chief mate to secure from the boat drill, and he radioed the mates on deck and called down to the engine room on the 1MC, the internal phone and loudspeaker system. As soon as the mate hung up the 1MC, the captain ordered the signal for the fire drill.

When the fire-drill alarm sounded, the mates instructed the passengers to report to the officers' salon but keep their life jackets on. Everyone else then went to his or her respective fire stations. My station was the fantail. AB Jaeger was still at the helm, so it was me, AB Sturm, and OS Goode. The other deck officers and crew members were scattered throughout the ship. The engine room staff manned various areas of the engine room.

At each station, we rolled out a fire hose and broke out the fire ax, trained the hose overboard, called in its readiness, and waited for the captain to order water pressure to the hose stations. On the inside stations, they led a hose out through a door and trained it overboard. All the fire systems on board were salt water. Fresh water was too precious to waste. When they turned on the water, the first fifteen seconds of flow showed rust from the piping in the system. We sprayed the hoses for a minute until the captain called to shut them down. An unexpected treat was a beautiful rainbow created by the sun, filtering through the mist of the hose spray.

Looking forward, I saw the O'Briens and Simpsons on the starboard-bridge wing. They had a bird's-eye view of everything. I don't know if they requested to come up on the bridge or if the captain was playing politics, but they got to see the rainbow.

Once we received the all clear, we disconnected and drained the hoses and then reconnected them and stowed them away. The bosun's job, after every drill, was to inspect all the lifeboats and fire stations and ensure that everything was secured and stowed. None of the crew, including the officers, wanted to piss off the bosun, so everyone double-checked before leaving his or her station.

When I returned to the bridge, the passengers had left. I relieved the chief mate, who acknowledged me with a wave of his hand. He was walking out to the port-bridge wing and joined the captain, listening to the second mate.

"I was polite, Captain," he said, explaining Simpson's behavior, "but it wasn't easy. That guy is determined to be obstinate. It seemed he wanted a confrontation."

"You handled it well."

"Aye, aye, Captain. Anything else?"

"That's all." The second mate left.

Turning to the chief mate, the captain said, "Dennis, that man is beginning to irritate me."

"He seems to be good at irritating people—too damn good."

"Yes. I'm sure the crew will behave, but I'm not sure how the other passengers will react, especially our great white hunter, Mr. DeKuyper. He's not the sort of fellow you want to mess with. That reminds me; Fran McGonigle was in DeKuyper's cabin, bringing him something, and saw a pistol sticking out from under his pillow, along with a large knife and a machete in the room. Fran also said he had severe scars on his back. Must be a tough guy."

"I'll go see him and get the pistol and lock it up with the other guns. I wouldn't want him to shoot Simpson."

"Well, if the scars are any proof, he'd probably use the knife or machete instead."

Knocking on the cabin door, Dennis called out, "Mr. DeKuyper?"

"Yes."

"This is the chief mate. I'd like to talk to you, please."

"Just a minute."

The door opened, and DeKuyper stood there in his skivvies. "Come in," he said, and he turned and walked to his bunk. "What's the topic?"

"We can't allow anyone to carry a gun when on board, and you forgot to give me one of your pistols when you turned over the other guns."

Staring at Dennis, DeKuyper replied, "I didn't forget. I don't think of my pistol as one of my 'guns.' However, if that is an issue, I will give it to you." And he reached under his pillow and withdrew a Colt M1911 .45 with remarkable engraving on it. "This was a gift, and it's very special, so please take care of it." He ejected the magazine, racked the round out of the pistol, and inserted the round into the magazine. Then, he handed the mate the pistol, butt first. "Do you want the magazine also?"

"No, that's okay. You keep it. Given your occupation and experience, I'm sure you know how to store it safely."

De Kuyper smiled. "Yes, I do."

"You're looking better. Is the Dramamine working?"

"Yes, it is. Getting seasick was a surprise. I've been on riverboats that bounced around quite a bit and never felt sick."

"The difference is that on a small boat, you're still connected to the water around you and can deal with the motion. On a ship, it's your whole world that's moving, and you can't relate to that unless you are standing on deck, looking at the ocean or horizon. If you start to feel queasy again, I suggest you do just that: stand on deck, and focus on the horizon. It helps."

"Thanks—Dennis, is it?"

"Yes, sir."

"I appreciate the concern and your diplomatic way of asking me to surrender my arms." A small smile flitted across his face.

"Glad to be of service," said Dennis, returning the smile. "Do you mind if I ask you a personal question?"

"How personal?"

"Your scars. They're severe. Was it a hunting accident?"

"No, it was hunting stupidity, arrogance on my part. My client had shot a lion, but it ran into the brush. I knew he wounded it and it's his job to finish off the lion, but he was afraid, so I had to do it. I kill animals, but I don't like to see the beasts suffer.

"My gun bearer, Joseph, a Swahili and excellent hunter in his own right, followed me into the brush, and I told him to circle around instead. The right thing to do is have him cover my rear, but as I said, it was my stupidity. The lion jumped me from behind, and by the time Joseph got there, I had managed to kill it with my Kisu." He pointed at the knife on the table. "I had my panga also," he said, pointing at the machete, "slung over my back, and that's what saved my life. The lion bit the panga and released, giving me a chance to use my Kisu. The lion damn near finished me off. I don't know who was the more surprised, me when he jumped me or him, when he bit the panga. It sliced the right side of his jaw wide open."

"How long were you laid up?"

"A good six months. It's still tender on cold, rainy days. A good reminder of the cost of stupidity and arrogance."

"That's some story."

"Yes, and I'm sure as I get older, the more garrulous the story will grow, and I will become less stupid and the lion more ferocious." He reached out his hand. "Anything else I can do for you?"

"No, thanks." Shaking his hand, the mate turned and left.

Chapter 9

Chapter 9

MIDOCEAN

It had been a week since we sailed from New York, and the weather had held up. Other than a few squalls, it had been perfect. The seas hadn't been higher than seven feet, although we had encountered a long, slow-rolling swell from the southeast. We were at 10.10.7 degrees north latitude and 36.38.0 degrees west longitude, 1,446 miles due east of Trinidad and Tobago. We were 150 miles north and 1,320 miles west of Freetown, Sierra Leone. There had been no sightings of other ships for two days, and we were alone in the world, in the middle of the Atlantic Ocean, except for our intermittent companions, the dolphins.

They were majestic shadow dancers, surfing the front of the ship's bow wave. Dark gray, luminescent shapes in a green, foam-flecked world, they flitted in and out of sight, diving under the bulbous bow and reappearing on the opposite side. Besides surfing the bow wave, dolphins can "surf" the invisible-pressure wave that the bulbous bow generates as it pushes through, rather than cleaving the water.

The crew had settled into their at-sea routine, the only difference being the passengers at mealtimes. Socially, the atmosphere had relaxed a little, with no confrontations between the Simpsons and Mr. DeKuyper. To DeKuyper's credit, on the third morning, when he had recovered enough from his seasickness to eat breakfast, he approached the Simpsons' table, causing Bernie

Simpson to lean back in his chair, wary. DeKuyper cleared his throat and announced, "I would like to apologize for my boorish behavior the other day. I have to attribute it to seasickness, since it's not my custom to insult strangers."

Bernie, with a crafty look on his face, started to say something, when the captain intoned, "Yes, Mr. DeKuyper, seasickness can throw you off stride. We're so glad you are feeling better." It was clear the captain wanted to leave a way out for DeKuyper because his "boorish behavior" had comprised uttering "Arsehole" twice before the ship ever left the pier.

Before Bernie could interject, DeKuyper turned and sat in his usual spot at the captain's table. By then, there was no way for Bernie to follow up without looking foolish.

Now, whenever DeKuyper was in their presence, Bernie Simpson looked the other way, avoiding eye contact. Clara seemed friendly with DeKuyper, to the obvious chagrin of Bernie.

I showed up for breakfast regularly now, so I would see and talk to Megan. Sitting at my usual spot, which abutted Greg Russell at the engineers' table, I came in late enough that Tony, sitting opposite me at the same table, would leave to go on watch, making Greg my regular conversation partner.

Still concerned about gaining weight, I ate little and had started "running ladders" for exercise. Starting at the main-deck level aft, I would run up all the exterior ladders to the flying bridge, reverse course, and run down them, doing at least ten sets. It was safer than running on the main deck because there were always handholds to grab. The weather, hot and humid, dictated my wearing thin running shorts, a T-shirt, and sneakers. The second day I was running the ladders, Megan came up to the flying bridge and stood at the top of the last ladder, within two feet of me when I cleared the top.

"You're sweating," she said, touching my brow and trailing her fingers down my cheek and along my arm. Sweat poured from me and emanated an odor not unlike a locker room, salty maybe but still locker room, without the socks. Meg had a fine bead of sweat on her brow. While both liquid, hers was a golden-champagne color; mine looked like urine.

"You should take your shirt off," she said in a sultry tone. "You'd be cooler." I hadn't worn a shirt since. Meg had been on the flying bridge every day when I exercised. I couldn't ask for a better incentive, finding reasons to flex and not make it too apparent. Like a puppy trying to please its master, I loved every minute.

After exercising, I'd stay on the flying bridge and take a Ben Franklin air bath, cooling off before going below and showering. Megan always stayed, too, and we'd talk. She'd talk, and I'd listen—about college, her experiences in America and South Africa, the building friction between the traditional Dutch (Boers) and the British South Africans, centered on apartheid. Meg's mother came up on the third day, looking for her. Meg told her what we discussed, and she joined in, holding an even stronger opposition to apartheid, but for reasons that surprised me. Thinking she would preach about the unfairness of racial and social disparity, she was more pragmatic.

Turning to face forward and leaning against the rail, she started. "You had slavery in your country, and there's been slavery in Africa forever. Most of your slaves started as slaves here in Africa. Slavery is a property-owning system. The slaves are property, to do with what you will. Everyone knew if he or she was a slave or owner; there was no ambiguity. Sometimes it made economic sense to use slaves as labor, but that proved false over time as people learned that incentive was more productive than threats.

"That's not what apartheid is. Apartheid is political and economic discrimination, disguised as racial segregation: separate but not equal. The Boers are foremost about doing business and making money. They believe they must control who can conduct business with whom. That they, and all whites, are a minority in their own country is the irony. This irony isn't lost on us non-Boer whites because we know the day of reckoning is inevitable. The Boers hide behind racial discrimination to keep control. Delusional? Maybe. Perhaps it allows them to hide from their conscience...who knows?"

Pausing, she collected her thoughts. "All persons of color in South Africa are discriminated against. The levels of discrimination vary. Long before apartheid, there was tribal discrimination, and the Boers rely on and use that continuing tribal discrimination to aid and abet their continuing discrimination. Divide and conquer."

Turning, she leaned back against the rail, looking straight into my eyes. She glanced down and just seemed to notice that I was wearing only shorts, which clung tightly in the heat. An assessing look came into her eyes, making me a little uneasy. She glanced at Meg and then continued. "I love my country, but I see hard times ahead. The world is changing, and unless the Boers figure out a way to allow people of color to integrate into our society, I fear that South Africa will become a pariah in the eyes of the Western world. We are already a focal point in the United Nations, as other countries in Africa, supported by Russia, try to gain dominance. There are already signs of it. That's why I wanted Megan to go to college in America, so she could see firsthand a nation trying to deal with racial issues rather than create them. It's difficult, but it is necessary."

Abruptly, she straightened up. "That's enough. You seem like a very nice young man. I trust Megan's instincts, and the fact she likes you says a lot."

Megan and I both turned crimson, and her mother continued, "Please continue to be a gentleman. You can get a lot further in this world with honey than you can with vinegar." Smiling, she walked away.

"Well," Meg said, "that was embarrassing."

"Yeah, a little, but I hope it's true."

Leaning in and clasping me behind the neck, she kissed me. It was short, chaste, and wonderful. "Yes, it's true. See you later." And she pranced away.

Did I mention it before? I was in love.

I walked over to the starboard rail, looked down, and saw Tony standing at the pelorus, leaning on it, staring up at me. The pelorus is a device used in navigation for measuring the bearing of an object relative to the direction in which a ship is traveling. There is one on each bridge wing.

"You seem to be a hit with both mom and daughter," he said. "Didn't hear all of it, but it seems like Mother O'Brien just cleared your path to Megan."

Sheepish but proud, I admitted, "Yeah, it seems so. At least, I hope so." Waving at him, I went below to clean up and get ready for watch.

In their cabin, Meg addressed her mother. "Mum, I know you meant well because you always do, but you embarrassed me and yourself."

"Sorry, dear, but when I saw him in his almost altogether, wearing only underpants—"

"Those are exercise shorts," Megan interrupted.

"Underpants! Looking at him I saw your father at that age and thought of how wonderful he was, so I blurted it out."

There was silence for a few seconds as they looked at each other. Stepping in, Meg hugged her mum and whispered, "I'm glad you did."

"Me, too," she said, hugging her tight.

At lunch, I nodded at Megan when I came into the salon, and she nodded back. She sat with Eunice Coltrain, engaged in conversation, although Eunice did most of the talking. The Simpsons were well into their meal, the usual trough sounds emitting from him. Bernie was a loud eater. He had also gotten into the habit of wearing a bib, an extra napkin he tucked under his chin. This ensured the sanctity of whatever multicolored jersey he wore. Clara was more refined in her eating habits, just as voracious but seemed to be easing up on her quantity of food consumed..

Mr. DeKuyper came in, said, "Good day," and sat down. Joey, the steward, approached and asked for his order. "Hullo, Joey, how are you today?"

"Just fine, Mr. DeKuyper. What can I get for you?"

"Let me have two muffins with grape jam and a teapot of hot water, please, boiling hot." When Joey looked at him, he explained, "I brought my own tea. Lapsang souchong, broken leaf, for morning and Darjeeling for afternoon."

When Joey left, Eunice asked him, "Why two teas? What is the difference?"

"Lapsang souchong is unique. They smoke it over a pine-wood fire, giving it a distinct flavor. Teas whose leaves are broken allow the water to extract more of the flavor in a shorter time. It is also higher in caffeine and is thus better for the morning. Darjeeling is lighter and more astringent, better suited for late afternoon."

"So you're a man who likes to sample exotic things?" she asked, playing the coquette.

"Exotic, yes. Forbidden, no. Some things are too dangerous to sample."

"How do you know what's dangerous?"

"Some things, Mrs. Coltrain, are obvious."

She responded by batting her eyes and smiling.

During this exchange, Meg sat staring at her plate, embarrassed and silent. When Eunice didn't continue her interplay, Meg asked DeKuyper, "Will you be getting off in Cape Town?"

Welcoming the interruption, he smiled and said, "Not now. That was my original thought. I have a brother in Cape Town and intended to ring him up and drop in for a visit, but we won't get there in time."

"How so?"

"He goes to England, Spain, and France on business every year at the same time. I miscalculated how long it would take for us to cross the ocean, so I will miss him by two days."

"So where will you get off the ship?"

"Durban."

"Do you live there?"

"Well, I have a small flat there, but most of the time, I am out in the bush, earning my keep."

"You have an exciting life. My father talked about going on a hunt from the time I was three. He would sometimes talk of the great adventures he expected to have. I loved listening to him." She was breathless in her explanation of the memory. "When I was a teenager, he got the chance. When he returned, he marveled at the time he had and regaled me with stories. I was fifteen but felt as if I was five. He told me stories regularly." Looking down at the table, she added, "Until he died, that is."

There was an awkward pause, and then he said, "I'm sorry to see your father died so young. I am glad he got to experience the hunt. It is unique."

"Thanks," she murmured. "Excuse me, please." She left the salon.

Jumping in at once, Eunice started, "At fifteen, I heard a lot of stories from older men, but I knew better than to believe them."

Holding her gaze, DeKuyper replied, "Your cynicism is exemplary. I somehow feel that, while young Miss O'Brien was captivated by her father's tales, your 'older men' were more captivated by yours."

Eunice smiled. "You seem to misunderstand me. Perhaps when you get to know me better, that will change."

"Unlikely, madam." He exposed an icy smile. "Excuse me." He rose, thanked Joey for his lunch, and left.

At dinner the evening prior, the captain had informed the passengers that we would cross the equator in the wee hours of the morning on Tuesday, October 25, and regaled them with a story of when he crossed the equator for the first time as a cadet on a Victory ship, just after WWII ended, getting very detailed in his description of kissing King Neptune's belly, drawing a few *ughs* from the ladies. He did a credible job, and the passengers enjoyed it. At the urging of the captain, supported by Eunice's breathy, "Oh, yes, do tell us", Mr. Dekuyper told a few stories of hunts he had conducted, including the one when he had been attacked by the lion and killed it with his knife. They reacted by exclaiming "Oh my God!" and "My goodness!"

Everyone had left the salon except Greg and me; we were each finishing a coffee when Meg walked back in.

"Hello, William…Greg."

We both stood up.

"Hello, Miss O'Brien," Greg replied.

"Hi, Meg," I said.

"Do you have a minute, William?"

"Yes, he does," Greg said. "I'm just leaving."

"After listening to the captain's story tonight, I thought it would be nice to be awake when we cross the equator," she said with a dramatic flair. "What time will we cross?"

"Around 0600 hours."

"I know you'll be awake all night on watch, but would you keep me company then? My mum would like to join us since this is her first ocean crossing."

"How did she get to the United States?"

"Same way I did. She flew from Johannesburg to Amsterdam and then to New York. So, is it all right?"

"Sure. Why don't we meet in the salon at 0530 hours? There's always coffee in the galley for the midwatch, so if you and your mother want some, help yourself."

"Thanks." She half turned and then turned back, leaned in, and kissed me on the cheek, holding my chin for a long two seconds. She stepped back, said "Ta-ta," and left.

When I got relieved by the second mate at 0400 hours, I told him that there would be people on the flying bridge when we crossed the equator. I had calculated the crossing time to be 0552 hours at 22.13.8 degrees west longitude.

We had crossed three time zones since leaving New York, and each time we did, the second mate would reset the shipboard clocks by moving them ahead one hour at midnight. The chronometers we used for navigation always remained set on Greenwich Mean Time (GMT).

Knowing I wouldn't be able to sleep, I went to the pool deck, sat on a lounge chair on the starboard side, lit up a cigarette, and leaned back, somewhat protected from the wind. I jumped when I heard, "It's nice up here this time of night." It was Eunice Coltrain. She reclined in a lounge chair on the far side of the pool.

Standing, I said, "I'm sorry for disturbing you. I didn't realize anyone was here."

"That's all right. Relax—though I'm not used to being ignored in such close quarters."

I didn't know how to respond, so I said nothing.

Sensing my discomfort, she continued, "I'm just toying with you. I do that on occasion with good-looking young men."

Again, there was silence from me.

Standing and walking around the pool, she asked, "May I have a cigarette? I was about to go get mine."

"Yes, ma'am."

"Please. Eunice...Mrs. Coltrain...anything but ma'am. That sounds so... old."

"I'm sorry, Mrs. Coltrain." My good manners kicked in. "You don't look old," I said, at once regretting the opening I had given her.

She didn't take advantage but asked, "Cigarette?" I gave her one and lit it. "Thank you, William."

"You're welcome."

I turned to leave, and she said, "Please, don't leave. I feel guilty chasing you away."

"No, ma'am—I mean, Mrs. Coltrain. This is the passenger area, and I shouldn't have sat down. I apologize for disturbing you."

She was silent for a few seconds and then said, "You are a rarity, William: a good-looking young man with impeccable manners who knows how to brush off an older woman without offending her. Young Megan seems to have landed herself quite a prize. I envy her." She turned and walked off.

I finished my cigarette and then went to my cabin.

At 0525, I walked into the salon and poured a cup of coffee, still pondering how to react to Eunice or whether I should react at all. When Meg and her mother arrived a few minutes later, I offered them coffee. Meg declined, but her mother accepted, black with one sugar.

I led them up to the flying bridge, and we stood in the firm breeze caused by the ship's headway, looking at the sea and the fading stars. The second mate had already taken his star sights. The horizon had been clear enough for that at 0515, with thin wisps of cirrus clouds dimming but not obscuring the stars. Everything was different in the early morning. A sense of expectancy heightened as the sun's fingernails clawed gingerly at the horizon, trying to peek at the waiting world. Even the tang of salt air was different in the coolness.

"Earlier, when I was on watch, I calculated that we would be on the equator at 0552 hours."

We stood at the rail, facing forward, Mrs. O'Brien between Meg and me. Knowing the morning dew would still be on the rails, I wiped them off with a rag I had brought with me.

Mrs. O'Brien said, "What made you go into this line, William?"

"I grew up on the water in Southie. Can't remember a time when I didn't want to go to sea. My father was in the merchant marine during the war. An engineer, but he didn't want me to go to sea. I never convinced him it was okay. No one is shooting at or torpedoing ships nowadays."

"And are you glad you ignored your father's advice?" She was somewhat chiding.

"I didn't ignore his advice. I paid close attention when my father talked because it wasn't that often. If he had lived to see me graduate, I think he would have agreed with me. Just wasn't meant to be."

"I'm sorry, William. That was rude of me."

"No, that's okay."

Meg glanced at her mother and then stepped around her and hugged me, seemingly in reaction to her mother's comment. Surprised, delighted, and a little nervous, I said to her mother, "Would you like to be rude again?" and she laughed.

"No, once is enough, I believe."

"Other than what the captain related in his story, are there any traditional things to do when crossing the equator?" Mrs. O'Brien asked.

"Not really. What he said only applies on your first crossing. There are variations of the story, but they are all disgusting and involve humiliation."

"What time is it?" This came from Meg.

"Two minutes to go. Hang onto the rail. Don't want you to fall when the ship bumps the line."

There was a leery look from Meg, followed by, "That's bull!"

"Yes, it is, but I had you thinking about it for a few seconds."

"Take a deep breath," I told them. "You're about to enter the southern ocean, and nothing is the same." I counted down from ten to zero, jumping when I reached zero, startling both of them.

"Why did you do that?"

"I jumped over the line. Didn't want to trip on it." We all laughed.

"Well, William, thank you for guiding us across the equator. It's always interesting to do something for the first time."

"Yes, ma'am," I said with a smile. "Hope you enjoyed the trip."

"I'm going back to bed for an hour. See you at breakfast." And she left Meg and me alone.

Meg took both my hands, looked up, and said, "I have an idea for a crossing tradition."

"What's that?" I felt my excitement rising.

"This," she said, and she kissed me. It was chaste at first like the previous ones, and then she slid her arms around my back and pressed in, infusing a little more ardor. Instinct prevailed. I became aroused, with no place to go and nowhere to hide it.

Pushing back, she said, "You like that tradition. I could tell."

Embarrassed, I said, "I did, and you could, but it's your fault."

She gave me a coy little grin. "I know. It'll always be my fault. At least, I hope so." She giggled and flounced off the deck, leaving me and my arousal to our ultimate fate.

Chapter 10

ASCENSION ISLAND

After Meg had left me on the flying bridge with an unanticipated erection, I did a few squats to kill it before heading below to my cabin. My embarrassment faded quickly once I realized that Meg took such a delight in getting me aroused, and then my imagination went into overdrive, which restarted the cycle. It was hard to tear my thoughts away from Meg, but I got things under control before going to breakfast at 0700 hours.

Meg, her mother, and I arrived at the same time, and I held the door for them. Meg was innocuous, but her mother smirked at me as she walked by, making me wonder what they had talked about in their room before coming to breakfast. The Simpsons were already there. Like clockwork, they arrived each day at 0630, and the chief steward had told Joey to feed them on arrival, so they were content. The aromas of bacon, eggs, and coffee seemed stronger, maybe due to my heightened awareness of all things sensual.

Greg was still there, as was Tony, since I had arrived earlier than usual. Tony muttered, "Did your great equator crossing show go well this morning?"

Smiling, I said, "It went great!"

"And what will you do for an encore?"

Shrugging, I answered, "I don't know, but whatever it is, I'm looking forward to it."

Tony laughed. "Getting a little cocky, are we?" He stood and headed for the door, calling back over his shoulder, "See you at noon."

Ten minutes later, the second mate came in and sat down opposite me. In a low voice, he said, "You had company this morning at your crossing ceremony, William."

"Yeah, Meg and her mom enjoyed it."

"Not them. The captain's wife. She was on the pool deck the entire time and seemed to be tuned in to you."

"I saw her when I came down from the flying bridge, but she left after I gave her a cigarette."

"She didn't leave. She scrunched up in a deck chair all the way forward next to the door. I heard the chair scrape and peeked in."

"Did she say anything?"

"No, I didn't talk to her. I listened, and if I could hear you, she could. She left right after you went below."

I don't know why this made me nervous, but it did. Other than the cigarette earlier, Eunice hadn't bothered me since she asked me to get her a blanket a few days ago. Tony had told me she had showed up on his watch a few times and tried to engage in conversation, so I figured she was aiming at him now.

When I relieved Tony at noon, he nodded toward the bridge wing, so I followed him out.

"What's up?" I asked.

"She's getting insistent."

"Who?"

"Who do you think? Eunice."

Something about the way he said "Eunice" rather than "Mrs. Coltrain" or "the captain's wife" told me things had changed.

"So, it's 'Eunice' now?"

"I told you, she's getting insistent. That's one thing she insists on."

"How often is she coming up here?"

"Every watch. In the morning she stops in, says hello, and then goes to the pool deck and reads. At night, she does the same thing, but when I'm on the bridge wing, she'll come over and talk."

"That's chancy, isn't it? The captain likes to drop in unannounced."

"I know, but ever since she started coming up at night, the captain doesn't come by. He's called up a couple of times but not walked in. It's like he knows she's here and deliberately stays away."

"So why are you telling me? You seem to have it under control."

"Yeah, that's what I thought. Up until last night, we talked about school, my family, her family—you know, normal stuff."

"And?"

"Last night around 1100, she said she was going below but wanted to tell me something first."

"What?"

"I was standing on one foot with the other braced behind me against the bulkhead, so my knee jutted out. She came right up, grabbed my hands, pressed her crotch against my extended knee, held my hands on her tits, and said, 'These are yours. Just tell me when and where.' Then, she reached down and grabbed my crotch and said, 'But this is mine. It's an even trade.' She wasn't wearing a bra, and her nipples poked my palms. She let go of my hands, stepped back, lifted her loose skirt to show she wasn't wearing panties either, and then laughed and went below."

"Whoa!" was all I could manage to say.

"Yeah," Tony said, looking miserable, scared, happy, and horny, all at the same time.

We arrived at the entrance to Clarence Bay on the northwest corner of Ascension Island on Wednesday, October 26, 1966, at 1900 hours local time. Although the island is geographically located in the middle of the fourth time-zone meridian, it is on Saint Helena time, which is GMT, one hour earlier. The strong trade winds blowing over the island brought the scent of musky vegetation and aged, rotting kelp, preceding our arrival by six hours.

Ascension Island is in the middle of nowhere in the South Atlantic Ocean, lying one thousand miles from the coast of Africa and 1,400 miles from the horn of South America—Brazil's northeastern shoulder. A volcanic island, Ascension resembles an amoeba shape, with a rounded point at the eastern end of the island. A relatively new geologic formation, its last volcanic eruption occurred near the sixteenth century. The soil consists of clinker. It's so barren people that from Saint Helena say, "We know we live on a rock, but the poor people of Ascension live on a cinder."

Named *Ilha da Ascensao* by its discoverer, Portuguese explorer Alfonso de Albuquerque, he named it because he discovered it on Ascension Day, May 21, 1503. Other than sea birds and large green turtles that lay eggs on its beaches, the island had little of value, and he didn't even claim the land for the Portuguese crown. Sporadically used, the island's first organized settlement was a British garrison in 1815, set up as a precaution when they imprisoned Napoleon I on Saint Helena some seven hundred miles to the southeast.

Ascension Island is such a barren spot with so little in basic sustenance (everything—from sheep, goats, guinea fowl, eucalyptus, bamboo and banana trees, and Norfolk pine—was imported), and such care was required of its inhabitants, that Charles Darwin compared it to a huge ship kept in first-rate order. The imported trees were so numerous they created a mini–rain forest on the top of Green Mountain in the center of the island.

Eastern Telegraph Company laid the first underwater cable in 1899, connecting Ascension to South Africa. In 1922, Ascension became a dependency of Saint Helena, managed by the senior officer of the Eastern Telegraph Company until 1964, when the British appointed an administrator, reporting to the governor of Saint Helena.

The United States built an airbase during World War II called "Wideawake," after a local colony of raucous birds, but ceased using it after the end of the war. Returning in 1956, the United States expanded the runway to handle larger aircraft. The US space agency NASA was building a tracking station, and the twelve crates we had on board were all related to that project.

British Customs officials boarded the ship at 0800 hours the next morning. The weather was bright, sunny, and warm; the aroma from the shore vegetation was overpowering the kelp smell. Customs cleared us within thirty minutes. The Simpsons wanted to go ashore, and the customs officers were gracious enough to offer them a ride in but warned them that they would have to make their own way back to the ship.

At the behest of the chief steward, Sparky, the radio operator, raised the local steamship agent and made arrangements for the Simpsons to get a tour of the town and also a ride back to the ship via a local launch service.

As the Simpsons waited in the salon, the captain warned them that the sailing time was 1800 hours that evening, with or without them on board. They left the salon and proceeded to the gangway. As he was leaving, the customs official said to the captain, "There's nothing much to see, you know. I think they'll be disappointed."

Smiling, the captain said, "Point them to a good restaurant; they won't care about anything else."

The customs official sniggered and said, "There are no good restaurants." He shook hands with the captain and left.

The port facility at Georgetown, the capital of Ascension, was too small for our ship to dock, so we stayed at anchor and unloaded the crates using our ship's booms onto a flat-decked barge delivered alongside by a small tugboat. Two of our ABs hooked up the crates on board, and the bosun ran the winches. Four men wearing blue jumpsuits with what looked like air-force patches on the arms stood on the barge. The operation ran smoothly, and by noon, all twelve crates were aboard the barge. The usual wind from the southeast had picked up, so the captain of the tugboat asked for the loan of some tarps to cover the crates. He didn't want the salt spray to get on the cases. The bosun gave him three of our older tarps and some quarter-inch sisal twine to tie it down. By the time the barge had the cases covered, our crew had covered the hatch and stowed and secured the ship's booms.

At noon, I relieved Tony on the bridge. We had anchored at the 20-fathoms line, the captain preferring to stay at that depth to minimize the swell from the south (the shallower the water, the more pronounced the swell) and avoid all the junk on the seabed in shallow waters. Known as a "foul" anchorage due to the abandoned mooring blocks, old ship anchors, and random lengths of chain strewn over the bottom, any boat or ship anchoring there, no matter what its size, had to be cautious.

Using the pelorus, I checked the bearing on the cupola of what looked like a Greek temple, which I believe was a courthouse or government building, and also the bearing on the water tower. The ship held fast with no drift. Behind the town was a large, rust-colored hill of clinker, which looked as if a giant dump truck had deposited it there.

Just as I lit up a Marlboro, using my windproof Zippo lighter, I heard voices back in the pool-deck area. Meg; her mom, Grace, and Eunice were setting up deck chairs to sun themselves. Meg was fiddling with her radio, trying to raise a station for music. When the atmospherics were good, she could pick up music from Brazil and even got a few channels from the States.

Clearing my throat, I said, "I'll close the doors to the bridge."

All three looked up and said, almost in unison, "You don't have to," and they all laughed like teenagers.

"Okay." I went back to the bridge wing to finish my cigarette. Surreptitiously peeking over my shoulder, I had a good view of Grace and Eunice but not Meg. Both Grace and Eunice wore bikinis, and they displayed their attributes in a stunning fashion. Watching them apply suntan lotion was a lesson in erotic art. Stubbing out the cigarette, I went into the bridge to reduce the stress on my libido. I heard a splash and then Meg saying, "It's chilly but feels good." After ten minutes, the splashing stopped. A knock on the frame of the open bridge door turned me, and there was Meg, barefoot, wrapped in a towel.

"Hi," I said, walking over to her.

"The water's nice, but it's cool."

"The same as the ocean. We fill it with salt water."

"I don't want to step inside; I'm dripping wet...come outside." She stepped back, but as I stepped over the sill, she stepped forward again, opened the towel with both arms, and hugged me, saying, "I need warming up."

She, too, was wearing a bikini, skimpier than the ones of the older ladies, so the effects of the hug were twofold, neither of which were helpful. The front of my shirt and pants got wet, and I got an immediate erection. I noticed both, but she, already being wet, only noticed the one.

"I seem to have the nicest effect on you," she said, grinding her hip. "We're going to have to do something about it. Maybe later tonight?"

As much as I loved it, I told her, "I am on duty, and it would be very embarrassing, at the least, if the captain or mate came looking for me and found me in this state."

Giving me one more grind, she backed away, folded the towel around her, and said, "I wouldn't want you to get in trouble on my account." She blew me a kiss as she walked back to the pool area.

Taking a deep breath, I walked back into the bridge, leaned against the forward handrail, and did a couple of squats to relieve the pressure, wondering if the ship's store carried condoms.

The Simpsons made it back in time for supper, riding in a fourteen-foot dinghy with a nine-and-a-half horsepower Evinrude outboard pushing it. They were low in the water, occasional splashes getting their shoes wet. The combined weight of the Simpsons added to the low-freeboard problem. The chief mate and I were standing at the top of the gangway when they approached, and he told me to go down and give them a hand. A low, three-foot swell was running, but the wind had added choppy waves, the crests of which lapped the bottom of the gangway platform, so the timing of stepping off the launch had to be exact. The launch couldn't tie up because it would be smashed against the foot of the gangway.

I told the boatman, a Colonel Sanders look-alike in a gray jumpsuit, to bring the bow and nudge it against the hull, right ahead of the gangway, and the passengers would have to jump from the tiny bow to the platform. I explained to the boatman and the Simpsons that they would only have time for one person to jump, and then the boatman would have to reverse and try it again; otherwise, the wave would push him into the platform.

Clara Simpson stood up, holding onto a light line attached to the bow, giving her some stability. Behind her, with one hand on her hip and one hand on her ass, her husband looked like he was backing up a scrum. When the boat nestled in, Clara jumped, agile for someone her size, and I grabbed her arm and pulled her, letting her go right up the gangway.

Bernie decided at the last second that he wasn't going to wait, and he started forward just as the boatman reversed the engine and pulled away. Two steps, later Bernie had taken a nosedive off the bow, made a wild grab for the rope at the bottom of the stanchion, twisted onto his back, and fell under the gangway platform. Seeing that the wave would bang his head on the platform, I instinctively reached down, grabbed his collar, and jumped off the platform, pulling him away. Even so, he scraped his face against the roller on the bottom, and blood flowed from his nose. He was panicking, so I grabbed him from behind with one arm in a loose choke-hold so he couldn't grab me, and swam toward the boat.

The boatman, who had no doubt witnessed dozens of such scenes, ran to the bow and threw the bow line to me. When I grabbed it, he pulled me to the side, and Bernie grabbed the gunnel of the boat.

"Do you think you can drag yourself aboard?" I asked him.

"I don't know," he said, wheezing.

"Okay. I'm going to climb in the boat first, and then the two of us will get you aboard. Don't let go of the gunnel."

"Yeah, okay."

I pulled myself over the gunnel and stepped forward. Telling the boatman to grab Bernie's right arm, I grabbed under his left, and at the count of three, we heaved. Bernie pulled, and we landed our big fish, all three of us flopping into the bilge. As soon as Bernie landed, the boatman went back to the stern and steered the boat back to the gangway. We had drifted fifty feet aft.

"Wait a minute," I said. "Give Mr. Simpson a chance to catch his breath." Bernie nodded in agreement.

After a couple minutes, Bernie croaked, "I'm okay," so I nodded to the boatman, and he approached the gangway again. Bernie assumed the position in the bow, holding onto the bowline while I crouched behind him, ready to push if necessary. This time, with the chief mate on the gangway, Bernie made it without incident. I waited until they both had gotten to the top of the gangway before I jumped off the boat. This was the second time today that my uniform had gotten wet. I liked the first time better. Saying thanks to the boatman, I watched as he shook his head and laughed, backing away from the ship, and then I climbed the gangway.

At the top, Bernie and Clara were there, along with the chief mate, bosun, and an AB. Going up to Bernie, I asked, "Are you all right?" and to my amazement, he started yelling.

"No, I'm not all right! I could have drowned! Why don't you have a better way to get onboard?"

Stunned, I didn't know how to reply, and before I could say something stupid, the chief mate jumped in, loudly.

"Mr. Simpson!" he roared. "That man," he said, pointing at me, "just saved your life, and the only reason you got in trouble to begin with is because you were too pigheaded to follow instructions."

Total silence. After what seemed a long time, Bernie turned and went into the house. With an embarrassed glance, Clara said, "Thank you" and followed him.

"What a fuckin' asshole," the mate muttered. Looking at me, he said, "Go get cleaned up." He patted my shoulder.

Thirty minutes later, dry and wearing a clean uniform, I entered the salon. The chief mate and the captain were conspicuous by their absence, but all the other officers and passengers were there, Bernie and Clara reigning over their six-foot, round gastronomical empire. I smiled at Meg, who smiled back with a slight questioning look.

Tony sat opposite me and whispered, "We heard."

I couldn't help myself, I barked out a laugh loud enough so that everyone looked at me. Mumbling "Sorry," to the assemblage, I continued in a subdued tone to Tony. "It was scary. I thought Bernie would get his skull crushed, but I'm thinking now it's way too hard for anything to hurt it." Switching subjects, I asked, "Are we still weighing anchor at 1800 hours?"

"Far as I know we are. I already relieved the second mate for his meal, so he's back up on the bridge." The words were barely out of his mouth when we heard the clanking of the anchor windlass as it strained to haul in the anchor. Five minutes later, we felt the pulse of the propeller as it bit into the water. We were heading for Cape Town.

Chapter 11

TRAUMA AND TRYST

*S**ailed from Ascension Island at 1800 hours on Thursday, 10/27/66. Low, heavy clouds. Temperature 73 degrees. Southeast winds at 10 to 15 mph. Seas running at eight to ten feet. Destination: Cape Town, South Africa.*

We'd changed time zones once again, and we were now on Cape Town, South Africa, local time. Ever since leaving Ascension Island, we had fought the southeast trade winds and were getting into the western shoulder of the Benguela current. The closer we got to Cape Town, the more we would feel its effect.

The Benguela current flows northwest, starting from Cape Point at the extreme southwest tip of Africa and traveling as far north as the country of Angola. Driven by the southeast trade winds, it is an amalgamation of cold water, rich in nutrients upwelling from deep in the Atlantic near the African coast, joined further offshore by warmer waters depleted of nutrients drifting from South America through the South Atlantic. The western edge where the two join isn't well-defined, made even more unpredictable by many seasonal variations caused by eddies. On the eastern edge, there is a significant and well-defined thermal front between the cold upwelling water and the eastward flowing Atlantic current. The Atlantic current splits when it meets Africa, with part of it curving north to join the Benguela and part of it continuing due east into the Indian Ocean.

From a navigator's point of view, the water temperature tells you which side of the thermal you are on. The further south we got, the lower the air temperature dropped—not excessive, but chilly enough for a sweater or jacket at night.

It was 0230 on a crystal night, starlight straining to reach down and touch the mast top, bright enough to be the masthead light. On the starboard-bridge wing, debating whether to smoke and pollute the pristine air, I heard a clunking noise from the pool deck. I walked back, peered through the open door, and saw Clara Simpson sitting on the end of a lounge chair, hunched over. She was a large woman, and the chair teetered.

"This is strange," I thought. "She rarely comes up here." Thinking I should ignore her and tiptoe back, as I turned, she slipped off the edge of the chair and sprawled on the deck, uttering a low "Fuck!" Then, she started to cry.

Walking toward her, I asked, "Mrs. Simpson, are you okay?"

She looked at me and then hung her head and sobbed.

Now in full alarm mode, not knowing what to do, I couldn't let her sit there, so I reached for her arm and said, "Please, let me help you up. Did you hurt yourself?"

Raising one arm as if to stop me, she snuffled, "No, I'm okay. This is so embarrassing."

Pulling her up, not an inconsiderable effort, I stood there, not saying anything, waiting for her to compose herself. The sobbing had stopped, but she still wept and sniffled. I handed her my handkerchief, and she sighed. "Thanks."

"Can I get you some water?"

Touching my arm, she asked, "Would you? Thanks."

I went into the bridge, poured cold water into a Dixie cup from the thermos I keep there, went back, and handed it to her.

She was calmer. She drank the water, blew once into the handkerchief, took a deep breath, looked down at the deck, and started. "I'm sorry, and I'm embarrassed—a grown woman, acting so foolish."

"Don't be embarrassed. Everyone has a bad day now and then."

"Bad day? More like the culmination of a bad decade." Lifting her head, she stared at me and continued. "I agreed to go on this trip because I thought it would be romantic, give me and Bernie a chance to relight the old spark, relive our youth." She paused. "He is a real shit, you know, but he wasn't always that way." She signed a heavy sigh and then said, "It didn't work. He's changed, and he can't go back. Neither can I, it seems. We'll have to put up with each other, at least until we get back to the States." Reaching out, she held my hand and said, "Thank you. I'll try not to repeat this." Then, she reached up with both hands, drew my head down, kissed me on the forehead, handed me my handkerchief, and walked aft and down to the passenger deck.

Stunned, I wanted to wake Meg and tell her what happened. A woman's perspective would be helpful. The last few conversations we'd had centered on family, and she had told me how devastated her mother was when her dad died. My dad died in my first year of college, but that's a whole different world. I couldn't imagine how it would be to have someone I love treat me like dirt. Sure, Muriel, my on-again, off-again girlfriend had done it to me, but I knew it wasn't the same. That's not years of investing your life, only to have it blow up on you. Shivering, I shook my head and went back into the bridge.

When the second mate, Chuck, relieved me at 0345 hours, I skipped my usual cup of coffee and went straight to bed, feeling sad for Clara Simpson and wondering how people got to that stage in marriage. I had a lot to learn.

When I went to breakfast later that morning, Bernie was sitting in his usual position, surrounded by food but no Clara. That is the first time she had missed a meal. Given the circumstances of last night, I wanted to ask Bernie where she was but thought better of it, sensing that there was no easy way through that quagmire.

Grace and Meg arrived, smiled, and said hello to everyone. Grace stood at the edge of Bernie's table and asked, "Where's Clara this morning?"

Without looking up from his food, he mumbled, "Not feeling well." He resumed eating.

"Maybe I'll stop in to see her after breakfast."

"No!" He sputtered, spitting out part of his eggs and toast, so he had to wipe his chin with his napkin. Looking around at the stares of the others, he realized how harsh it sounded and added, "She wants to rest for a while." He then lowered his head to the trough again.

Still standing, Grace said, "Oh," and then sat down. Joey's "Good morning, folks, what'll you have this morning?" broke the uneasy silence.

I was at it again, running the outside ladders late that morning. The air was cool and brisk, and the sun was brilliant as it danced off the wave tops. Meg showed up and ran with me, a practice she had started when we left Ascension Island. The bright part of Meg's running outfit was a pair of Keds, comprising dots of red, blue, pink, white, and purple on a dark-blue background, a paint-splatter effect. She never wore socks, which seemed weird; since my feet are so sensitive, I would have had blisters in five minutes without socks. The Keds were bright, but the most noticeable parts were the bikini bottom and T-shirt torn off so that it hung just above her belly button. The first day she joined me to run, I followed her up the ladder and tripped at least four times, I was so distracted. At the top deck, I cried out, "Whoa!"

Turning, she looked at me, curiosity filling her face.

"Follow me."

"Why?"

"Look at you. I'll kill myself, staring at your ass going up the ladder," I said, and she burst out laughing.

Doing a little moue, she half turned, cocked her hip, and said, "You like my ass?"

"Just follow me," I said, and I turned and ran down the ladderway. She followed, and she had followed me since, but at the start of every session, she asked, "Sure you don't want me to lead?" and wiggled her hips.

She usually stopped after five cycles, but today she went to seven before quitting and waiting on the flying bridge. After I finished my twenty cycles, I joined her in the crisp salt breeze to cool off.

Standing beside her at the rail, I rubbed her shoulders, saying, "You did seven today; that's good."

"I'm getting there." Arching her back, she said, "Scratch my back, under the shirt. I'm itchy." When I reached under the shirt, she directed me high to her left shoulder, and I discovered she wasn't wearing a bra. Why I hadn't noticed when we ran was a mystery. Instant arousal. It's a wonder she didn't hear a *sproing!* as my erection leaped to attention. Turning to face me, she leaned in, pressed her hips in, and said, "I know it's not the time or place, but I like to return favors." Sliding her left hand in, she rubbed my crotch with her hand.

"Not fair." Instinct forced my hands to slip below her waistline, gripping her cheeks.

Removing her hand, she pressed her hip in harder. "You're right; it isn't fair. When we get to Cape Town, we'll have a lot more privacy. I'll be good until then." Stepping back, she looked down at the bulge in my shorts. "You know I love you, don't you?"

"I hoped so, but it's nice to hear you say it, since I've told you a lot."

Standing on her toes, she kissed me lightly, leaned back, and kissed me again, running her tongue across my lip, and stepped back. "This is going to be great." She shivered, spun, ran to the ladder, turned, and blew me a kiss. She disappeared down the ladder. Standing there, hoping the cool breeze would be as effective as a cold shower, I discovered that it wasn't, so I squatted a few times (maybe more than a few) to alleviate the pressure in my shorts.

Skipping lunch, I settled for a piece of the good but monotonous pound cake and a cup of coffee and took them with me to the bridge. I relieved Tony and spent the afternoon reliving my flying-bridge experience. The watch was uneventful; the only excitement was in my mind.

At supper, I noticed that Clara Simpson was still absent, but after the weird commentary by Bernie at breakfast, no one seemed inclined to ask about Clara. Halfway through the meal, Grace O'Brien got up and left the salon. Looking over at Meg, she gave me an "I don't know" shrug. Just as I was getting up to leave, Grace returned, glared toward Bernie, went to the chief steward, and whispered something to him. Fran nodded, rose, and followed Grace out of the salon. Right behind, I saw them go to the Simpsons' cabin, knock, and then enter it. Presuming that he was checking on Clara for health reasons, I went to my room.

An hour later, I answered a knock on my door. It was Meg.

"We need to talk."

"Okay, but not here." I wasn't about to risk the captain's wrath.

I followed her aft and then up to the pool deck. At first, she seemed a little upset, but when she turned and faced me, I could see she was angry, really pissed off. Now, I was thinking, "What did I do?" I knew I hadn't done anything wrong, but it was a man's gut reaction to a pissed-off woman.

"That sonofabitch beat her up."

"Who? Who beat who up?"

"Simpson! He beat up Clara." I recalled Clara's crying jag on the pool deck the previous evening.

"Wait a minute. She was crying a lot, but I didn't see any bruises or anything."

"What are you talking about?"

"Clara," I said, and I explained the episode on the pool deck.

Meg then explained what her mom had seen when she brought the chief steward to Clara's cabin. "Both her eyes were bruised, and she had a bloody nose."

Absorbing this, I told Meg, "Go back to your cabin. I have to talk to the chief mate." Escorting her to her cabin, I continued to the chief mate's room, knocked on the open door, and walked in. The mate sat at his desk, reading. Closing the door, I said, "Something you gotta know." I told him everything I had seen and heard.

"That son of a bitch," he said, enunciating every syllable. "William, I'll take care of this. Don't talk about it to anyone else, and don't—" He pointed his finger in my face for emphasis. "Don't say anything to Simpson."

"Okay, Dennis, but if I ever see him doing anything to her, I'll rip his head off."

"Just cool it. I'll make sure it doesn't happen again."

Thirty minutes later, after talking to the chief steward, who told him Clara had no broken bones and just bruises, Dennis finished relating the story to the captain.

The captain said, "I can understand how a woman can get under a man's skin, but there's no excuse for this." It was a statement that would later prove to be paradoxical in its prescience. "Dennis, I want you to talk to Simpson and let him know there will be no reoccurrences of this type of behavior. You might let him know how easy it is to have an accident on a ship at sea. And Dennis, talk to him without any witnesses. He has no friends aboard, but you never know what tales people will tell after the fact."

"I'll talk to him, and believe me, he'll understand."

"In the meantime, have the chief steward serve Mrs. Simpson her meals in her cabin until she feels well enough to come out."

"Aye, aye, Captain."

Captain Coltrain sat at his desk, gazing out the porthole, re-running the entire Bernie-and-Clara-Simpson incident in his mind. It had been easy enough to instruct Dennis, the chief mate, to threaten Bernie to desist from violence or else. Bernie was a coward, and Dennis could be intimidating. The captain counted on that intimidation to quell the problem. He was contemplating whether he would ever get pushed to that limit by Eunice with her audacity when she sailed through the door, not knocking, sat on the edge of his desk, and said, "I'm going ashore in Cape Town when we dock, and I want an escort. Please see that *young* Tony gets off duty, so he can accompany me."

Standing up, he walked past her and closed the door of his cabin and then returned to his chair. "Eunice, ours is a loose marriage, convenient for the both of us, but I see no reason you should drag one of my officers into your affairs. You've kept a reasonable perspective in the past about who you had your trysts with. Picking on Tony isn't reasonable. He is young, as you so clearly pointed out, but he is also naive and doesn't understand you will toss him away afterward like a tissue in the wind." Pausing, he lit a cigarette and then continued. "I'm surprised you didn't try for our great white hunter, Mr. DeKuyper."

Tossing her hair, "I did try. He'd rather play with lions and guns."

"Smart man. Both are infinitely less dangerous."

Standing and turning, she said, "I'll be discreet. We won't leave the ship together, and we won't return together."

"Does Tony know of your plans yet?"

"I'll tell him tonight when I visit him on watch," she said, and she walked out.

"I wonder how Bernie Simpson would have reacted if Clara had that conversation with him," the captain mused, making a mental note to inform the chief mate of Tony's day off when they docked in Cape Town.

Shortly after 2200 hours that night, Eunice stood next to Tony on the starboard bridge wing. Tony faced aft, and she stood in front of him, having unzipped his pants, and held his engorged penis.

"I've made arrangements for you to get off duty and spend the day with me in Cape Town when we dock."

"Arrangements? With who?"

"Why, my husband, the captain. Who else?" Tony grew pale and instantly lost his erection, but she held onto him. "Don't worry; the captain and I have an understanding. You and I won't be seen leaving or returning together, so no eyebrows will be raised."

Despite the shock of the news, her gentle manipulation was having its desired effect on Tony, and he was soon standing at attention again.

"Give me your handkerchief," she said, and just seconds later, he ejaculated.

Tossing his handkerchief overboard, she said, "Always get rid of the evidence," and she smiled. "See you tomorrow at ten o'clock in the lobby of the Ritz at Sea Point. You'll have to last longer tomorrow."

Chapter 12

CAPE TOWN

Cape Town, Kaapstad in Afrikaans, is located at latitude 33.55 south and longitude 18.25 east. Table Bay fronts Table Mountain. The city lies in a large amphitheater-shaped area, adjacent to Table Bay and bordered by Signal Hill, Lion's Head. and Devil's Peak. Table Mountain is dominant, with its flat top at a height of 3,300 feet. Many times, a flat cloud layer referred to as the "tablecloth" forms on the mountaintop. It is a majestic sight, viewed from either the top of Table Mountain or from the bay, looking up at the mountain.

November is the beginning of summer here. The temperature averages 69°F during the day and 58°F at night, and the area is subject to cold fronts coming in from the Atlantic Ocean, bringing heavy rain and strong northwest winds.

Used by many trading ships as early as the late sixteenth century as a victualing port, it was the Dutch East India Company (Verenigde Oost-Indische Compagnie—VOC), under the leadership of Jan van Riebeeck, that established the first permanent European settlement in 1652. VOC imported many plants from other parts of the world, including cereals, grapes, apples, ground nuts, potatoes, and citrus, changing the natural environment in a permanent manner. This enhanced the overall viability of the area.

Approaching from the west, the nearing dawn painted the uppermost fringe of Table Mountain with a rich red-orange glow, a picturesque welcome to Africa. We picked up the pilot at 0515 hours a half mile outside of Green

Point Lighthouse and proceeded into Table Bay. The prevailing winds and most heavy seas came from the southeast, so Green Point protects the harbor. When, on occasion, a storm from the north or northwest hits, the harbor can get a little wild and choppy. Today, the weather was in our favor, and within an hour, we docked.

The ship's agent and South African customs officers boarded the ship as soon as we landed on the gangway and went directly to the captain's office. Following them was the representative of the stevedore company. He went to greet the chief mate to coordinate the discharging. By 0700 hours, the ship cleared by customs, the salon was busy as Joey the pantryman tried to keep up with break-fast orders. Both customs representatives and the ship's agent had accepted the captain's invitation to breakfast, and the chief mate told Joey to take care of them and the passengers first. The deck officers would wait, filling up on coffee.

The chief mate decided to not break sea watches since we would be in Cape Town only a day and a half. We wouldn't do any loading until the trip back and had only the cigarettes and POVs (privately owned vehicles) to discharge. He also told me to cover for Tony in the morning watch and left before I could ask him any questions.

The longshoremen came aboard at 0745 hours, two gangs comprising fifteen men each. With no unions here to say otherwise, the chief mate had me open the hatches. I also opened the no. 4 hatch covers to the upper-tween deck, where the POVs were stowed to be discharged in Cape Town.

The stevedore boss was a ruddy-faced, wide-bodied Afrikaner who looked to be in his late thirties; his name was Piet DeHaart, an affable guy. I talked to him as he stood watch over the working hatches with me, never leaving the scene while the men worked. All the longshoremen were native Africans, Bantu tribesmen from the interior, working on one-year contracts at the port.

"Is it hard to get people to take on a one-year contract?" I asked Piet.

"Not at all. There's competition by these boys," he said, pointing into the hatch. "In one year, they can earn enough to buy a wife or two and some cattle and retire."

ON TO AFRICA

"Buy a wife or two?" I asked, incredulous.

Looking oddly at me, he said, "They're native boys. They aren't like you and me. Cattle are valuable and a status symbol."

"The cattle I can see, but buy a wife?"

"Well, they don't really 'buy' a wife, but they pay a dowry to the father of the bride-to-be. It wasn't too long ago that white men did the same thing here. The only difference is white men learned that one woman was trouble enough; don't buy two of them." He snorted a laugh, sounding like a donkey bray. I simply gawked at him.

Going on, he said, "Mate, it's a good life for them. These are good boys. They live in the barrack, free of charge, get fed twice a day, and get paid one rand a day, whether there is work or not. If they stick it out for the whole year, they get a twenty-rand bonus. It's not work for a krimpie, but it's better than the mines."

"Krimpie? What's a krimpie?"

Chuckling, he said, "An old man. This is young man's work."

"One rand a day," I said, calculating. "The rand is worth US$1.40. That's not a lot of money."

"Not to you or me, living here in Kaapstad, but to a Bantu living in the bush, it's a small fortune." He now sounded defensive.

"Hey, Piet, I'm not criticizing, I'm just trying to understand."

Just then, one a man in the tween deck called out. "Laanie Piet."

"*Ya?*"

"No *motorsleutels.*"

Turning to me, he said, "He says there's no keys in the autos."

"Shit, I forgot. I'll get them."

As I called the bosun on the walkie-talkie, the same guy called up again and repeated, "No motorsleutels."

"*Hou jou bek*, Joseph!" Piet shouted, loudly but with a smile on his face. "Don't get your *broekies* in a knot." Turning to me, he said, "He's okay. He's a little *dof* and a bit of a *babbelbekkie.*" Seeing the question on my face, he said, "He's slow to understand—dof—and he talks a lot: babbelbekkie."

"Ah! What else did you say to him, something about 'brookies'?"

91

"I told him to shut his face and don't get his pants in a knot."

Nodding my head, I said, "Thanks for the language lesson."

The bosun showed up with the car keys. They were all tagged with the VINs, and numbers were soap chalked on the windshields; they corresponded to the last four numbers of the VINs.

They didn't use auto trays here. Instead, they used a pair of heavy woven nets hung from spreader bars to keep the nets from pinching the fenders of the cars. The men laid the nets on the hatch cover, one net for the front wheels and one for the rear wheels, and then pushed the car onto the nets. They hooked the nets to short, wire legs attached to the spreader bar and hoisted them, cradling the wheels. When on the dock, they reversed the process. They pushed them about twenty yards down the pier, where a mechanic connected the battery and started the car, and someone drove it to the storage area. The longshoremen were very careful to not let the wire legs snap against the cars and dent them. At noon, the longshoremen broke for lunch. Per the chief mate's advice, I invited Piet to have lunch on board.

In the salon was the chief mate, Dennis; Bill, the chief engineer; and Greg, the third engineer. Notably absent was Tony. I introduced Piet to Bill and Greg, having met Dennis when he came aboard in the morning. Joey took our orders for lunch, and we talked until he served us. When Joey cleaned up the lunch plates, I asked Dennis, "Where's Tony?"

"He asked for the day off. Said he had something to do. Why, you need to go somewhere?" Dennis sounded a little defensive.

"No, Dennis, just curious."

"Yeah, well, you know what curiosity did to the cat."

Taken aback by his response, I said nothing.

Greg asked Piet where he and I could go to get a good dinner in Cape Town, and Piet's answer stunned the both of us.

"Nowhere."

"What?" I said.

"Nowhere," he repeated. "Greg's a black man. Apartheid doesn't allow whites and blacks to mix socially. Greg can only go to the black townships to a restaurant or pub, and he would stand out there as an American. It's dangerous to be a stranger in a black or colored township. You," he said, turning and facing me, "can go to any public restaurant or pub, but not in the black or colored townships. It's dangerous for you there, but it's also not fair to the blacks or coloreds, because they can get in big trouble with the police if they get caught serving you."

"Is that everywhere in South Africa?" Greg asked.

"Yes, the laws are the same everywhere, but the enforcement's stricter here in Kaapstad. I'm sorry, but it's better I tell you than you get in trouble through your ignorance of our laws."

"Yes, Piet," Dennis broke in, "and we appreciate the warning. C'mon guys, it's time to go back to work." Dennis, Piet, and I went out on deck.

At 0945, Tony's taxi dropped him at the entrance to the Ritz. Not knowing what to expect, he wore a jacket and tie. Looking guilty, he strode into the lobby and spotted Eunice at the concierge desk, in conversation with the concierge. Walking over, he waited until she had finished and then said, "Good morning."

"Good morning, Tony. Aren't you looking dapper?" Taking him by the hand, she led him to the elevator. "I've made arrangements for dinner tonight at a very good restaurant." Leaning in close, she said, "A gentleman always buys a lady dinner when he gets to make love to her." Nothing else transpired until they reached the room, which faced out to the ocean. "There is a wonderful view from the balcony. We may even have time to look," she said, as she shut the door behind them.

Tony stood stock-still, not knowing how to proceed. Eunice took a step back, eyed him from head to toe, and said, "Get undressed." She then reached back to the clip at the top of her dress and shrugged once, and the dress fell away, revealing everything. Stepping in, she unbuckled Tony's pants while he wrestled with his tie and shirt. When he was naked, Eunice kissed him slowly and tantalizingly, her tongue darting and exploring, her body pressed hard against him. Pushing Tony back, she said, "I hope you're a good student, because I'm a great teacher. You should learn a lot today." And the lessons began.

Tony's first thought at seeing her naked was: "She has freckles on her chest." Then, the blood left his brain for other regions, inhibiting rational thought.

Tony reported back aboard at noon on Wednesday. The chief mate saw him coming up the gangway, smirked as he topped the platform at the rail, and said, "Everything go well?"

When Tony started to answer, the mate held up his hand, saying, "Never mind. I don't want to know. I suggest you take a shower and put your clothes in the laundry. I'm pretty sure the perfume isn't what you normally wear."

Tony just nodded and headed for his room to shower.

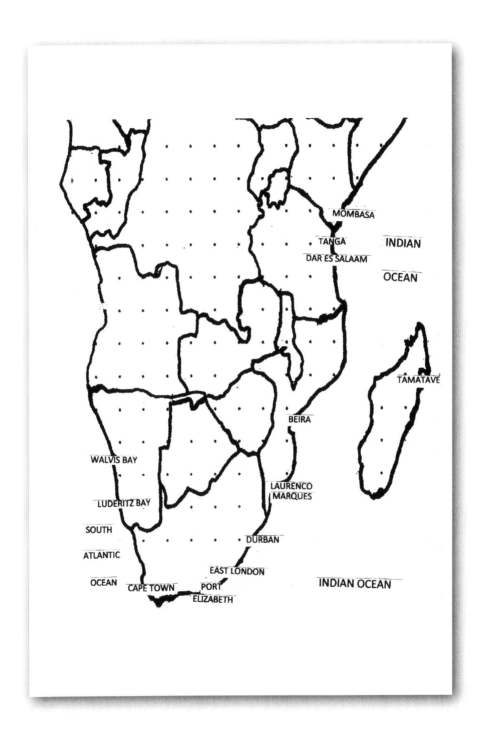

MOMBASA

TANGA
DAR ES SALAAM

INDIAN

OCEAN

TAMATAVE

BEIRA

WALVIS BAY

LAURENCO
MARQUES

LUDERITZ BAY

SOUTH

ATLANTIC

OCEAN

DURBAN

EAST LONDON

CAPE TOWN   PORT
          ELIZABETH

INDIAN OCEAN

Chapter 13

PORT ELIZABETH

Sailed from Cape Town at 1700 hours on Thursday, 11/3/66. Clear weather. Temperature 67 degrees with a light SE wind. We dropped the pilot when Green Point light was abeam to port. Once the pilot boat cleared away, the captain ordered full ahead and told the engine room to set revolutions for 19 knots. Destination: Port Elizabeth, South Africa.

We headed due west, passing through the southern edge of the former explosives-dumping grounds. Eight miles out from Green Point, we turned and headed due south, steaming twenty-nine miles until we reached a point due west of Cape Point Light. This was the Cape of Good Hope. Originally named Cape of Storms (Cabo das Tormentas) by Portuguese explorer Bartolomeu Dias in 1488, John II renamed it Cape of Good Hope (Cabo da Boa Esperanca) because of the optimism inspired by the opening of a sea route to India and the East.

Altering our course to 120 degrees, we cleared the cape by six miles and ran the coast, staying offshore ten miles until coming to 35.15 south latitude, 20.00 east longitude, twenty-four miles due South of Cape Aghulhas, the southernmost point of Africa. The seas were less than five feet, just enough to create a soft, rhythmic shushing sound as the bow cleaved through them. I loved that sound, soothing and peaceful. Changing heading to 90 degrees, we ran for forty-five miles, ensuring we stayed south and clear of the Alphard Banks before turning and heading on course 75 degrees. We followed this for 247 miles, bringing us south of the Cape Recife light. Since clearing Cape Agulhas, we had been in the Indian Ocean.

Unlike the approach to Cape Town, which was wide open, access to Port Elizabeth was protected by a long breakwater, built north to south to shelter the port from storm surges and gales. The approach channel is a thousand feet wide at its narrowest point, and a crosswind can play havoc with a ship when transiting.

From the Cape Recife light, we followed a course of 338 degrees, and the captain dropped speed to half ahead. As we neared the entrance sea buoy, we reduced speed to slow ahead and picked up the local pilot, an elderly man who displayed amazing agility coming up the Jacob's ladder from the pilot boat. The captain greeted him, remarking,

"Captain DeVoors, I thought you would retire by now."

"Hullo, Captain Coltrain," bellowed DeVoors, grabbing the captain's hand and shaking it vigorously. "It's been a few years since you were here. Good to see you. Why would I retire? I get to meet the finest people out here. Besides, my wife won't let me retire; she can only take so much of my companionship," he roared.

"The ship is yours, Captain," Coltrain replied, telling the second mate to track the course but follow the pilot's orders. Then, he stepped back and leaned against the chart table. He picked up the phone and called the chief steward, instructing him to tell the passengers we were approaching the port.

Starting at Ascension Island, the passengers, except for the captain's wife, Eunice, were in the habit of watching from the flying bridge when we were docking. When the chief steward first notified her as we approached Ascension Island, Eunice asked, "Fran, are there any good-looking young men to see?" When Fran stared at her without answering, she patted him on the cheek. "Call me when there are," she said, and she closed the cabin door in his face.

Checking the engine-order telegraph and the propeller-revolutions indicator, the pilot said to the helmsman, "Steady as you go. At the sea buoy, we'll come hard left to 238 degrees." A few minutes later, he ordered, "Hard left." The pilots in most ports spoke English, and most ship's officers understood basic English, so the more familiar "left and right" were used rather than "port and starboard" when giving helm orders. As the ship came around, the pilot said, "Ease your helm; steady on 238 degrees." This was followed by, "See the range lights direct ahead, the rear one flashing—keep those lined up."

"Aye, aye," the helmsman replied.

Another ten minutes passed, and then he said, "Hard left; bring her to 167 degrees."

"Hard left to 167 degrees," the helmsman repeated, and brought it around. "Steady on 167, Mr. Pilot."

"Okay. Mate, drop her down to dead slow ahead."

"Dead slow ahead it is," replied the second mate, and he rang the engine-order telegraph to dead slow.

"Come right to 200 degrees." The helmsman repeated it.

"Captain, we've got two tugs standing by. Have them tie on the port side, one at the bow and one at the stern. We're docking at berth no. 10, the outer berth."

The captain called on the walkie-talkie to the chief mate on the bow and to me on the stern and passed on the instructions.

With two tugs assisting, the pilot nestled the ship into the berth without incident, and by 2100 hours, we had all lines secured and were finished with engines. The pilot refused an offer of a drink with the captain but advised him that customs would be aboard at 0600 hours, and he departed. No one could go ashore until after clearing customs and immigration, so everyone went to his or her cabin. Since we were only here for one day, the chief mate kept sea watches.

I couldn't sleep and had three hours before my watch, so, grabbing a cup of coffee from the salon, I went up to the flying bridge and looked around the harbor. The air was cool and humid, with not a cloud in the sky. Being on the ocean mandates humidity, but this was a land-based, tropical humidity, infused with smells of jungle vegetation; petroleum carried across from the oil pier; and a pungent mix of pepper, clove, and leeks. Port Elizabeth isn't a spice port, so I presumed some of the odors emanated from the ships in front of us and across the pier from us.

The ship docked bow in, starboard side to the pier. Off to our left was an ore pier and further left and behind that, an oil-tanker pier. An empty huge, bulk carrier docked at the ore pier sat high in the water. The bow was missing. Getting binoculars from the bridge, I confirmed that at least one hundred feet of its bow was gone, sheared off clean. Puzzling over this, I was pleasantly interrupted by a kiss on the cheek and a "What's so interesting?" from Meg.

"Look for yourself," I said, handing her the binoculars.

"The front is square. Is that a big barge?"

"No, it's a ship, but it's missing the bow."

"How strange."

"Yeah. I'll ask the steamship agent about it in the morning." Changing the subject, I asked, "How come you and your mom didn't go ashore in Cape Town?"

"Mum doesn't like it there. When she and Dad first met, they lived there for a year. She says Cape Town exemplifies the worst of South Africa and prefers to stay in Durban."

"How about here in Port Elizabeth? This is a small port."

"We are going ashore here. Mum has a girlfriend who lives here she hasn't seen since before Dad died. Miss Lily, that's what I called her growing up, is picking us up at nine o'clock tomorrow morning." All during this conversation, Meg leaned on me, her left arm entwined in my right. Reaching up with her right hand, she turned my chin and kissed me; it was soft, not sensuous but tender. It still caused the usual reaction and tightness in my pants. "How long is the ship going to be in Durban?" she asked.

"Depends on whether they do any loading. There's not much to discharge. I'd guess a minimum of three days."

"Come to our house, and stay overnight. Mum already said it's all right. You can meet my soon-to-be stepfather. He's a nice man, and he makes Mum happy."

"Making your Mum happy seems to be a high priority for you."

"Yes, it is. Oh, we have our occasional tiff, but she never stifles me." Batting her eyelashes, she said, "I'm a big girl, in case you hadn't noticed."

"I've noticed everything about you and love everything I've noticed."

"Aren't you the charmer?" She kissed me again, longer this time and with more urgency. "I have my own apartment at home: the original overseer's house back when they farmed. Now, it's what they refer to as a 'gentlemen's farm,' more gardening than farming. Mum lets some of the black folks that used to work on the farm grow things for themselves. She even lets them use one of the old hothouses as a social center when they are working in the gardens. Mum's way of rebelling against apartheid."

"Can she get in trouble doing that?"

"No. She charges them a fee for the use of the gardens, so the government looks at it as if Mum were renting farmland."

"What does she charge?"

"She takes some of the vegetables they raise as the fee."

She smiled as she said this, so I asked, "What's funny about that?"

"Mum charges them one vegetable per year, a carrot or head of lettuce, and she makes a ceremony of receiving her annual rent. Most of the folks using the garden grew up with Mum, or their parents did. In some ways, it was like the workers on a plantation in the South in the United States, the difference being that the black folks aren't slaves. They're hired workers."

"I got a lesson about apartheid from the stevedore boss, Piet, in Cape Town. Greg and I wanted to go ashore and play tourist, but Piet shut that down when he explained about the segregation rules."

"Greg, the black engineer?"

"Yes."

"Piet was right. It's strict, even more so in Cape Town; that's why Mum doesn't like it there. Enough about that. Will you stay with me when we get to Durban?"

"There's nothing I'd rather do than spend a night with you. Let me talk to the chief mate and see what I can work out." I kissed her one more time, delicately, exquisitely, before she went back to her cabin.

The midwatch passed, uneventful, and when the second mate, Chuck, relieved me at 0400, hours I went to my cabin and fell asleep within minutes. I woke up at 0900, and after rinsing my face, brushing my teeth, and hitting the head for my morning constitutional, I grabbed a cup of coffee at the officers' salon and went looking for the chief mate. He was in his office, looking over the proposed loading plan.

"Morning, Dennis. Got a minute?"

Scratching his ample belly and his ear, he said, "Sure, what's up?"

"When we get to Durban, I've been invited to visit Meg and her mom at their home and spend the night there. Okay if I get Tony or Chuck to cover for me?"

"Sure. If they're willing to do it, it's fine with me."

"Thanks, Dennis. How come no one woke me up when customs came aboard ship? I thought they always wanted to see every member of the crew with their passport."

"Most of the time they do, but not always. Since we came direct from Cape Town, they looked at the crew list and asked the captain if it was accurate. When he said yes, they said okay, took their bottle of scotch and carton of cigarettes, and left. If this had been our first port of entry, they would have been more meticulous."

"Okay, what's happening today?"

"We've got two gangs. One will discharge the roll paper from the no. 2 hatch, and the other will discharge POVs from the no. 4 hatch. When you're out there, keep an eye on the roll-paper operation. They have to lift it over the locomotive on deck, and I want to make sure they don't run the cargo falls too tight, lifting the load up high. You gotta watch the fleet angle on the cargo falls. I already talked to the stevedore supervisor, Jodie, and warned him about it."

"Okay, anything else?"

"Yeah, your girlfriend and her mother went ashore earlier this morning. They had to walk to the end of the pier. Port security wouldn't let whoever picked them up come down to the ship."

"Yeah, Meg told me last night. By the way, did you see the bulk carrier across the harbor? She's missing about one hundred feet of her bow."

"The captain saw it coming in and asked the customs guys about it this morning. Customs said it was sailing empty, repositioning for a charter hire, and hit a storm south of the cape. A rogue wave buried the bow, and when the ship came up, the bow didn't. Snapped off clean, just the way you see it. There had to be a structural defect for it to break off so clean. Amazing the rest of the ship remained watertight. The captain put out a distress call and had the presence of mind to reverse the ship and keep it backed into the wind until the storm abated, and they got a tugboat out there to tow them in."

"That's really strange."

"Weirdest damn thing I ever heard of."

At 1145 in the officers' salon, I sat at the table with the chief mate, Dennis, and second mate, Chuck, picking at a lump of mislabeled mystery meat identified on the menu as beef tenderloin. It was neither beef nor tender, and if it was loin, it didn't come from anything that mooed. Crocodile, maybe? The chief cook had further disguised it by smothering it in onions, the odor of which filled the ship. When the steward, Joey, served it, his muttered comment was, "Don't blame me."

Tony came in and said to Dennis, "The gang working the POVs finished at 1130. The other gang knocked off for lunch." He sat down.

Looking at me playing with the food, he said, "What's that crap?"

"I have no idea, and you're insulting 'crap' by comparing it to this slop."

Calling to Joey, I said, "Let me have a peanut-butter-and-jelly sandwich and another glass of milk." We had picked up fresh dairy at Cape Town and would have fresh milk, at least until we left Durban. After that, it was iffy.

"Me too, Joey," Tony called.

When Joey delivered our PB&Js to us, he leaned over between us and whispered, "Mr. Simpson is on his third serving of the beef tenderloin. I don't think the man has any taste buds." We broke up laughing. Simpson didn't even look up.

At 1250, I asked Dennis if anything had changed regarding the cargo operation.

"No, just keep an eye on the roll paper. They banged a lot of the rolls up this morning, tipping and rolling them into slings. The supervisor said they'd have Jensen slings to use this afternoon, so that should help." A Jensen sling is best described as a cradle of rope that slips down over the top of the roll, and when lifted, it snugs up on the roll, spreading the strain around the entire girth.

Walking out on deck, I went to the top of the gangway just as the long-shoremen were clambering aboard. A tall, skinny guy introduced himself. "Good afternoon, Mr. Mate, I'm Jodie."

Shaking hands, I said, "Hello, Jodie. I'm William. I've got the watch this afternoon. The chief mate said you're switching and using Jensen slings on the roll paper."

"They're hooking them up on the dock now." Jodie and I walked forward and peered over the rail. I could see that the men were unfamiliar with the gear but said nothing. After wrestling with it for fifteen minutes, they got it hanging properly, and the winch operator swung the rig aboard.

Moving inboard, I looked down into the hatch and again saw that the men didn't know how to use the gear. Turning to Jodie, I said, "Have they ever used Jensen slings before?"

"It's been a while."

"Tell you what. Let's you and I go down there and show them how to hook up the rolls."

"Sure, mate."

We went down the manhole to the lower-tween deck and Jodie called out to the men, "The mate will show you how to rig the gear." It was a sure sign that Jodie didn't know how to use it, either. I called two men over and instructed them on how to spread the rope cradle as they lowered it and how to ensure that the cradle was low enough on the roll to grab it when the sling tightened up. They learned fast. Within two lifts, they had it down pat, so I climbed back up on deck, followed by Jodie.

Things went smoothly for a couple of hours. I had just returned to the deck after getting coffee when I noticed that the winch operator was lifting the load too high over the locomotive on deck. The fleet angle was obtuse, dangerously so. I yelled to the winchman to stop, using my arms crossed over my head in an *X*, and he stopped. I went closer to him and yelled up, "You're taking the load too high! You're putting too much strain on the gear!"

"Okay, boss," he replied, and he lowered the load.

I wandered over to the ship's rail and looked up toward the head of the pier. Meg and her mother, Grace, were walking down the pier apron, close to the water side, talking, oblivious to the cargo activity. I walked forward toward the no. 1 hatch and called over the railing to them, "Don't walk near the ship! Go over to the building, and walk along the wall. Wait until the load has landed on the dock before you walk past the cargo area."

Barely had I gotten the words out when I heard men yelling on the dock. I whipped around and saw the load of rolls swing way out over the dock. At the peak of its swing, with centrifugal force at its highest, one of the support wires holding the rig snapped, causing one end of the rolls to drop and slewing the entire rig. A split second later, the other wire broke, and the entire rig crashed onto the pier, splattering rolls of paper, missing the longshoremen by inches. The winchman, good to his word, had not let the load go too high but, instead, went too low and scraped the top of the locomotive with the load. That left slack in the offshore cargo fall, so when the load cleared the locomotive, it acted like a pendulum and swung ashore too fast.

Looking forward on the dock, I realized that Meg and Grace had escaped being under the load by just seconds. If I hadn't called to them, they would have been right in its path.

Getting on the walkie-talkie, I told Dennis what happened. He soon appeared on deck. During all this time, Jodie, the longshoremen's supervisor, was nowhere to be seen. Dennis went to the phone at the gangway, a temporary one for the convenience of calling the ship's agent, and talked for a minute. When he returned, he said, "Check the ship's gear. See if they damaged anything. No work until the supervisor shows up."

"Where's Jodie?" I asked. "I haven't seen him since the start of the shift this afternoon."

"Good question. Where is that fucker? We'll find out when the agent gets here."

I spent the next thirty minutes inspecting our gear and watching the long-shoremen clean up the mess on the pier. The agent, a young man usually referred to as a "runner," showed up at the same time and in the same car as Jodie. That's when Dennis exploded at both of them, starting with the agent. "You're supposed to have someone at the pier at all times the ship is in. Where the hell were you?" Before he could answer, Dennis turned on Jodie. "And you! Someone should be here whenever the ship is working. Where the hell were you?"

"It's my fault, mate," Jodie replied. Indicating the agent, he said, "I asked Simon to run me into town to pick up something I needed."

"What the hell was so important that it couldn't wait a couple of hours?"

Turning beet red, Jodie stammered out, "An engagement ring."

That ended the conversation. The mate shook his head and walked back into the house. I looked at Jodie, shrugged my shoulders, smiled, and said, "Hope she's worth it. Let's get everybody back to work."

Chapter 14

EAST LONDON

Sailed from Port Elizabeth at 2000 hours on Saturday, 11/5/66. Sixty-six degrees. Light winds from the east-southeast. Overcast skies. We cleared the narrow channel inside the breakwater and turned onto 58 degrees toward the flashing red-and-white sea buoy. Leaving the sea buoy to port, the captain ordered a course of 85 degrees and ordered the engines to full ahead. Destination: East London, South Africa.

When the captain said to secure from mooring stations, the crew had already stowed the mooring lines, so I released the crew members from our stern station and went to my cabin. Meg was waiting outside my door.

"I was going to wait inside for you, but it's locked." She pouted.

"Old habits die hard. Never can tell when some shifty young girl will try to get in and steal your heart. Besides, can't take a chance on ruining my virtuous reputation by letting a pretty woman be seen in my cabin."

Her smile broke through, banishing the pout. Sticking her tongue out at me, she said, "You can't wait for me to ruin your reputation, and you know it."

"Ah, so true." I pulled her close and kissed her, tempted to bring her into the cabin. Fear of the captain's reaction if we were caught made me opt instead to go up to the flying bridge with her. After a few minutes of pressing bodies and kissing, I had gotten into the habit of reaching around and fondling her cheeks, kneading them, a turn-on for both of us. I leaned away and said, "How was your visit with your mum in Port Elizabeth?"

Slowly licking her lips, a habit she had when we took a break from kissing and another erotic turn-on for me, she said, "It was fun. Miss Lily met us at the gate to the pier, and we spent the day at her home. Mum and Miss Lily did most of the talking while I listened. I felt like a little girl again, sitting on my swing in the garden while Mum and Miss Lily chatted on the *stoep*."

"Stoep? What's a stoep?"

"That's a veranda. It was a pleasant day, and Mum seemed so relaxed. I think she's been a little nervous as the wedding day gets closer."

"Is she having second thoughts about the guy?"

"No. I don't think so, but marriage is still a big step, and Mum is a practical lady who analyzes things."

"And how about you?" I leaned in close and brushed her lips with mine. "Do you analyze things?"

"Mmmhmm."

"Mmmhmm, what language is that?"

"Body language. It affects my vocabulary when you press your body against me." For the next hour, we practiced our vocabulary.

We were interrupted by the ordinary seaman on Tony's watch; he was standing at the top of the ladder on the rear of the flying bridge. "Uh, excuse me, mate, but Mr. Adams said to come and get you."

"Okay, thanks," I said, and he went below. Kissing Meg one more time, I said, "Gotta go. Have to relieve Tony."

"All right."

We had traveled forty-five miles, keeping well to the north of the shoals of Riy Bank. When we reached a point fifteen miles offshore, we adjusted course to 53 degrees, paralleling the shore, and ran for ninety-five miles until turning due north and working our way in until two miles from shore, where we picked up the pilot.

After boarding and greeting the captain, the pilot, Willem Voorhees, ordered slow ahead and instructed the helmsman to steer 249 degrees, further instructing him to line up the range lights with the occulting red light above and behind the flashing red. As we approached the turning basin, the captain asked, "Mr. Voorhees, what's the channel depth?"

"Plenty of water captain, just over ten and one-half meters. They finished dredging the channel late last year."

Turning to the second mate, the pilot ordered, "Dead slow ahead, 15 degrees right rudder." The second mate and helmsman echoed the orders. As we cleared the turning basin, we were now in the Buffalo River, which fed into the harbor. Other than a marking on the chart, there was no discernible difference; the water was still a dingy brown and gave off a fishy odor.

"Captain, we'll have one tug on the port side, and we're going into wharf no. 3." The captain nodded.

It took another forty-five minutes before being berthed at wharf no. 3, starboard side to the pier. This was necessary since we had to discharge the locomotive here in East London, and we had stowed it on the starboard side. There was a double railroad track running the length of the berth. It was 0600 on Sunday when we notified the engine room we were finished with engines. We wouldn't start discharging until Monday morning.

East London is South Africa's only river port, sandwiched between the Buffalo River and the Nahoon River. The town was founded in 1836 by Lieutenant John Bailey of the British Royal Navy, one of the original settlers in 1820. East London had its own frontier wars in the mid-nineteenth century between the local Xhosa tribesmen and the British settlers. Following this, circa 1876, as the port developed, an influx of permanent settlers, many of whom were German bachelors, imparted their heritage with small towns bearing German names, Gehring, Salzwedel, and Peinke, in the vicinity of East London. Originally called Port Rex, East London became a city in 1914. There is an unusual double-decker bridge over the Buffalo River, unique because it is the only one of its type in South Africa.

In 1961, the government declared areas on both sides of the city as Bantu homelands. The west is Ciskei, and the east is Transkei. Being almost surrounded by native lands was cause for unsettling times because of the imposition of apartheid. As part of their unofficial appeasement program, the apartheid government created wage and tax incentives to attract industries to the independent black states, including Ciskei, and created an unwitting exodus from East London. Labor union activity grew and hurt productivity. The port was beginning to slide down an economic hill when we called there.

At 0800, the salon was full since there was no work planned, and no one rushed to do anything. The usual aroma of eggs, bacon, fried onions, and coffee surrounded the conversations. Meg and her mother, Grace, and Clara Simpson were all talking at once, deciding what they wanted to do in East London. Bernie Simpson reigned supreme at his table, working on his seconds or thirds. The man's appetite was amazing.

Mr. DeKuyper stood near the door, talking to the chief mate about a possible motor safari when we reached Mombasa. DeKuyper only hunted in South Africa but had friends and acquaintances all over Africa, and Dennis tried to take advantage of his connections.

Greg, the third engineer, and I talked, sipping coffee, when Roy Oliver, the second engineer, sat opposite me. I hadn't avoided Roy but hadn't gone out of my way to talk to him, either.

"Hi, y'all," he said.

We both said hi.

"You boys going ashore?"

"Probably not," Greg replied.

"Why not? It's a nice little town."

"In case you hadn't noticed, the folks here don't socialize much with black folks. They even got a name for it: apartheid."

"There's parts of town you can go. There's black and colored areas." This drew a look of incredulity from Greg.

"You have got to be kidding. Tell me this is another of your lousy efforts at a joke." His voice raised a notch.

Roy put up his hands defensively. "Naw, Greg, I'm not joking, just thought you might want to see the town."

Greg rose and Roy leaned away as if he expected Greg to swing at him. Just then, Dennis stepped in, put his hand on Greg's shoulder, and said, "It's getting a little loud, Greg. If Roy is bothering you, take it away from the passengers."

There was silence for a few seconds, and then Greg relaxed. "No, it's okay, Dennis. Roy's not worth it." He walked out.

Stepping over to Roy, still seated at the table, Dennis leaned in, loomed over him, and said, "You've burned just about every bridge you've got. Keep your big mouth shut. You understand?"

"Hey, Dennis" was as far as he got when Dennis hissed "Shut!" He then turned and went back to Mr. DeKuyper.

Looking at me, Roy said, "Well?"

"I got nothing to say to you." I left the salon and went to Greg's cabin and knocked on the door. "It's me, Greg."

Greg opened the door and motioned me in. "I came close there to smacking that asshole."

"I know. If it wasn't for the passengers being there, I wish you had."

Rubbing his forehead, he said, "Remember last trip when you and I talked about Roy and how I put up with his shit?"

"Yeah, you said it was a test of your character, to not react."

"Well, I think the son of a bitch has stressed my character. I really wanted to hit him."

"He might have stressed it, but you didn't hit him, so he didn't break it."

Grudgingly, a smile appeared. Reaching out and tapping my arm, he said, "Thanks, William. Thanks for coming to talk and for reminding me to stay strong."

"No problem, Greg." I left and went to my cabin.

Mr. DeKuyper took Grace and Meg ashore later in the morning. Meg told me they planned to visit a previous business partner of DeKuyper and wanted me to go with her, but this was DeKuyper's event. They were South African, and I felt I was butting in, so I declined the offer.

I still ran the ladders to get my exercise, so at three o'clock that afternoon, I was hard at it for thirty minutes. When I finished, I stood on the bridge wing, cooling off, looking down over the deserted pier, when I heard the captain and his wife, Eunice, arguing. He must have left his porthole open because I heard them, loud and clear.

"Dammit, Eunice, you said you would be discreet, but the whole ship knows you're screwing Tony, and it's embarrassing."

"Embarrassing? Any more embarrassing than when I came home and found our next-door neighbor riding you like a bucking bronco? Our agreement was that home is off-limits. Any games had to be played elsewhere. You were the first one to break the rule, not me. Tit for tat, Marcus."

"This. Isn't. Home," he said, stressing every word. "This is a place of business, and for me to be effective, I have to maintain control. To do that, I have to have the respect of the crew."

"Respect? Why? You're the captain." Derision dripped from every word. "You're God on this ship. You have complete autonomy and authority. No one will say anything to you. They're all too scared of you."

"Goddammit, Eunice!" He was louder now. "You will do nothing else on board this ship with Tony or any other man, you understand?"

There was a pause, and then she said, "All right, Marcus. I won't rock your boat. You can still be the tin god here, but when we get back to New York, we are through. I expect you to have everything out of my apartment within two days after we return. If not," she said, showing a smarmy smile, "I'll donate everything of yours to charity. And remember, it's my money that keeps you in the style you've become accustomed to. You squandered all yours. You can go back to your sleazy, low-life friends." Then, I heard the captain's door slam.

I waited five minutes to ensure I wouldn't bump into her and then went below and took a shower, all the while thinking, "She didn't just pull the pin; she tossed the grenade."

After breakfast the next morning, the only ones left in the salon were Meg, Grace, and me. I stood at their table and asked, "How was your visit yesterday with Mr. DeKuyper's friend?"

"Very nice, thank you," Grace answered. "His friend George is quite the entrepreneur. He has started over a dozen small businesses, from arranging safaris to manufacturing and selling furniture. A very interesting man. What came as a surprise is that George is financed by my fiancé, Mark's, bank in Durban, and Mark knows George quite well. We came back last evening, but Pieter stayed on. He'll return on Monday."

"That is a coincidence. Did you or your fiancé know Mr. DeKuyper before this trip?"

"No, but now that we've made the connection with George, I'm sure Pieter will get to know Mark. I invited him to come visit us when we get to Durban."

Meg broke in. "What did you do yesterday?"

"Just hung around, exercised, missed you."

Putting her hand on Meg's arm, Grace said, "He always seems to say the right things. Will he always do the right things?" She gave me a questioning look as she rose and walked out.

"Was that a reprimand?" I asked Meg.

"No, Mum adores you. She likes to act mysterious at times. What will you do the rest of the day?"

"Other than exercise, I have no plans."

"Oh, good." She kissed me with just a hint of her tongue. "Let's go sweat together."

On Monday at 0800, we were back on sea watches. Tony had the watch, but Dennis, the chief mate, ran the show as we discharged the locomotive. The stevedore had arranged for two truck cranes to lift the locomotive in tandem. Reversing the loading sequence, they discharged the locomotive wheel trucks from the deck at the no. 2 hatch and landed them on the rail tracks alongside. Once on the pier, a mechanic checked all the hydraulic hoses and connections and greased the wheels and bearing surfaces. With the wheel trucks in place, both truck cranes positioned themselves, one at each end of the locomotive, and two signalmen on deck communicated to the crane operators via walkie-talkie. Ever so slowly, they lifted the locomotive. The trick was to balance the load and keep equal weight on each crane. To do that, they both had to lift and swing and lower at exactly the same time. Everything moved in slow motion. As they lowered the locomotive onto the wheel trucks, they pried the trucks with crowbars to get them in the exact positions to receive the bearing pins on the locomotive. That was a little nerve-racking because a couple of longshoremen kept leaning under the load to move the trucks, a very dangerous place to be if anything went wrong. Half an hour later, we were done.

Sailing from East London took a little longer than docking. Where we docked, the river was narrow—450 feet at its widest. Since the ship was 483 feet long, we had to back out of the channel all the way to the turning basin, about six hundred yards, before we could spin the ship. We had two tugs to assist us and needed them since there was a fifteen-knot wind blowing from the south, trying to push us onto the northern shore. Once we headed out the channel, one tug dropped off, and the other accompanied us as far as the end of the east-pier breakwater. After clearing the breakwater, we dropped the pilot, the same Mr. Voorhees, and headed out to sea.

Chapter 15

DURBAN

Sailed from East London at 1400 hours on Tuesday 11/8/66. Partly cloudy. Temperature 71 degrees. Wind from the southwest at 20 mph and increasing. Seas at twelve feet and growing. Destination: Durban, South Africa.

As we cleared the sea buoy, we slowed and brought the ship around to the east to create a better lee and protect the pilot from the waves as he disembarked. Once the pilot was away, the captain ordered full ahead with revolutions for 19 knots, and we turned onto course 76 degrees.

"Mr. Connolly!" the captain called.

"Yes, Captain?"

"If you check the charts, you see that the Agulhas Current is strong here, about 2.5 knots, which will set us to the south until we reach our turning point outside the edge of the continental shelf. Calculate what our course should be to offset the effect of that southward set."

"Yes, Captain." I went to the chart, saw we had thirty miles to reach the intersect point, and calculated that we would set four miles in the one hour and thirty-six minutes hours steaming time required.

"Captain, it would be a four-mile set, so we should adjust course to 74 degrees to counter the southward set."

"Very well, Mr. Connolly, come to 074 degrees."

I echoed his order to the helmsman, who repeated it, followed by, "On course 074 degrees."

"Captain, I read in the caution notes on the chart that freak waves up to sixty-five feet preceded by a deep trough may be encountered in the area between the edge of the continental shelf and twenty miles to seaward. These can occur when a strong southwesterly is blowing, the sea is rough, and the barometric pressure is low."

"What does that tell you, Mr. Connolly?"

"Well, Captain, the wind is from the southwest and rising; the barometer is dropping, and seas are rising. Perhaps we should pay a little more attention to the sea and not post the lookout on the bow but on the flying bridge instead."

"Excellent suggestion. You're the officer of the watch. You do what you feel is prudent." He turned and left the bridge.

Since we only posted the bow lookout on the night watch or in foggy conditions, I didn't have to do anything but make a mental note to pass the info on to the second mate when we changed watch.

The helmsman, AB Sturm, said, "Mr. Mate, five years ago, I was sailing with Farrell Line, and we got pooped by a big wave hitting us aft, just a few miles south of Durban. It washed a couple of containers overboard."

"Thanks, Sturm. That's good to know."

We reached our turning point just as the second mate, Chuck, came up to relieve me.

"Hello, Chuck. We just turned onto course 049 degrees. We're at sea speed, no extra nozzles, but we're heading direct into a one-and-one-half- to two-knot current. Wind and seas are building, and the barometer has dropped but not much." I then related the warnings to him about the lookout.

"Okay, William, you're relieved," he said, and I went below to my cabin.

At 1700, I went to the salon for supper. Everyone was there except Mr. DeKuyper. With the following seas causing the ship to corkscrew, I thought he may have a bout of seasickness, and Fran, the chief steward, confirmed it when he told the captain he had just given Mr. DeKuyper Dramamine.

I watched surreptitiously as the captain and his wife ignored each other. Eunice kept up a continuous conversation with Grace O'Brien and Clara Simpson at the other table, while Meg sat, quiet and introspective. The second mate, Roy, sat on the opposite side of the table from Greg, the third engineer, and Bernie Simpson focused on his food, not speaking to anyone. Given the recent rancor, I was glad to see peace reigned in salon society for the time being.

As Meg was leaving, she leaned over and whispered, "Any word yet on whether you can stay with us in Durban?"

"Oh, yeah, I can. Tony said he'd cover for me."

"Wonderful. I'll tell Mum."

Grace O'Brien was giving me a history lesson on South Africa while she, Meg, and I sat at their usual table in the salon. An hour before, Meg had knocked on my cabin door and told me her mom wanted to talk to me.

"What about?" I asked, somewhat suspicious. I must have been obvious because Meg laughed and said, "Home." When I responded with a blank look, she followed up with, "Home...South Africa."

"Oh. What about home?"

"She'll tell you." She grabbed my hand and led me to the salon, knocking at her cabin door and collecting Grace on the way.

"Are you familiar with the history of Cape Town?" Grace asked.

"In general. I did a little research when I learned I would travel here."

"Then you know about the Dutch East India Company starting the first permanent colony here. What you may not know is the settlement grew slowly due to shortage of labor, so the Dutch authorities imported slaves from Indonesia and Madagascar. These were the ancestors of the cape's colored communities. They also imported many plants, so they changed the landscape and the population." Pausing, she got up, poured a cup of coffee, returned to the table, and continued. "There were wars. Britain captured Cape Town in 1795 and returned it to the Dutch in 1803. The Brits took Cape Town again in 1806, and in the Anglo-Dutch Treaty of 1814, the Dutch permanently ceded Cape Town to Britain, and it became the capital of Cape

Colony. Diamonds in 1867 and gold in 1886 brought an influx of immigrants. The interior Boer republics clashed with the coastal British from 1899 to 1902 in the Second Boer War. Britain won. In 1910, Britain established the Union of South Africa, unifying the Cape Colony, the two defeated Boer republics, and the British colony of Natal."

Another pause, another sip of coffee. "In 1948, the National Party was elected on a platform of racial segregation (apartheid), which led to the Group Areas Act, which classified all areas according to race. Due to certain areas being declared for 'whites only,' entire segments of coloreds were moved and their housing destroyed. Cape Town, Kaapstad in Afrikaans, is the legislative capital of South Africa, so politics are rife there."

Looking at me, she continued, "That's where we are in human-class relations now throughout South Africa. Apartheid is the law. Many people, more of British descent than Dutch, don't like it and want it changed, but that isn't likely in the near future, given the governing party in politics right now."

During this time, Meg hadn't said a word. Grace continued to stare at me but said nothing, so I asked, "Why are you telling me all this? It's interesting, I admit, and I see parallels between the race problems arising in the States and your problems here but—"

Grace interrupted. "I like you, and it's obvious that Meg is smitten with you." She held her hand up as Meg demurred. "I don't know where your relationship will end up, but I do know that neither I nor Meg will leave South Africa. This is our country, for better or worse. You need to know that." She rose, patted Meg on the shoulder, and left.

Afterward, Meg and I sat, holding hands. "Your mother makes it sound like an ultimatum. Is it?"

Hesitant, Meg looked at me and nodded. "For her, yes, it is. I told Mum I'm in love with you, and while we haven't talked about it, I would marry you if you asked. That's the reason for the talk."

Stunned by Meg's revelation about marriage, I didn't know what to say. Keeping it in perspective, we had a three-week, whirlwind romance going, I was in love with Meg. I liked her mother, though that may change if she becomes a mother-in-law, and now, I am told I have to live in a country whose apartheid system has already made it impossible to do things with my friend Greg.

"You said that for her, it's an ultimatum. What about you?"

There was silence, and then Meg said, "I don't know."

"Meg, I don't know what to say. I do love you, but I haven't thought about marriage because, well, I just haven't thought about it. As for having to live in South Africa, I haven't seen much of it, but I know I don't like your apartheid system." Reflecting on how far I had come from the lily-white environs of South Boston, where any stranger was "alien" but blacks were even more so, I found I was appalled at the stringent hypocrisy of the apartheid system.

Holding my cheeks in her hands, she said, "You can start to see the country and the people when we get to Durban." She had tears forming when she kissed me. "Let's just see about everything else."

"Okay."

When I relieved Tony, he relayed that the captain had slowed the ship down because he didn't want to go to anchor. The captain wanted me to notify him when we were an hour from the pilot station off Cape Natal. We were on course at 031 degrees, now doing revolutions for 13 knots, and our ETA at the pilot station was 0300 hours. The wind and seas had abated somewhat. The ship still cork-screwed, but in slow motion, making it easier to move about. At 0200 hours, I called the captain and notified him of our position. A few minutes later, he came on the bridge.

"Any traffic?"

"No, sir. We passed a southbound tanker an hour ago but nothing since then."

"Let me know when you pick up the Cooper Lighthouse near The Bluff at Cape Natal," he said, and he left the bridge. Forty minutes later, using the pelorus on the bridge wing, I had a bearing of 14 degrees on the Cooper light. It emitted a flashing red light every ten seconds. The estimated distance was fourteen miles, which put us eleven miles offshore, with eighteen miles to go to the pilot station. I called the captain and informed him. Five minutes later, he appeared on the bridge.

"Any traffic?"

"Nothing visible. Might be a small boat, twelve miles straight ahead. It keeps ghosting on the radar screen but seems to be on the same course as us, doing 8 knots. We'll be at the pilot station before we catch it."

"When the Cooper light is abeam, drop down to slow ahead," he said, and he walked into the chart room.

"Aye, aye, Captain." I called the engine room and let them know we would slow down in about forty minutes and be maneuvering a half hour after that. The engineers don't like surprises, and it's always prudent to give them a heads-up.

When the Cooper light came abeam, I rang the engines down to slow ahead. I could now see a few lights on ships at anchor. There are two segments of the coastal waters where anchoring isn't permitted. One is the direct approach to the harbor from the northeast, and the other is a one-thousand-yard-wide strip extending out three thousand yards at right angles from The Bluff at the tip of Cape Natal. Any other area is a safe anchorage, with most ships anchoring to the north and east in water ten to 20 fathoms deep. The captain came out on the bridge again.

"I count five ships at anchor, Captain. Two are close to the harbor approach channel, and three are farther east."

He walked out on the starboard bridge wing and looked aft and then forward and came back in. "Keep her steady as is until you're abeam of the breakwater; then, drop to dead slow, and take her between the two on the left and three on the right." Turning, he smiled and said, "Your first chance at ship handling. Don't screw it up sonny." He left the bridge.

While it wasn't really ship handling since there was no maneuvering involved, it still was a big deal for the captain to leave me alone on the bridge in congested waters. I was nervous and thrilled at the same time. By the time the second mate relieved me at 0400, we were easing past the last ship on the left. I told him what the captain's orders were and said, "I'm surprised he left me here alone."

Laughing, Chuck replied, "He was standing in the salon, looking out at the port, when I came in for coffee. Don't get too excited about him leaving you alone, but he told me he thought the 'kid' was doing fine."

My enthusiasm bubble burst, I was still happy with the captain's praise and went below with a smile and bolstered ego.

Up in time for breakfast, I opted to avoid meeting Meg or Grace, still reeling from the mention of marriage. When the ordinary seaman on watch knocked on my door and told me to report to mooring stations, I went aft and found that Sturm, Jaeger, and Goode had already brought the mooring lines out from the locker and faked them down on deck. Normally, on such a short run, we'd leave them out, but the weather leaving East London mandated that we secure them.

The pilot was aboard, and we were already in the approach channel, heading 215 degrees. The wind, still from the southwest, had moderated to 10 mph. Coming down the approach channel, the Island View Channel is straight in front, with the Island View wharf on the ocean side and the Salisbury Island tanker terminal on the island side. After clearing the inside breakwater, we turned hard right into the center of the harbor and eased our way between the T-jetty on the north and pier no. 1 on the south to our destination, the west side of pier no. 1.

Half an hour of maneuvering later, assisted by a single tug, we docked portside to the pier at the outer end of the pier. It was the port side because we had the two bulldozers to unload here, and they were stowed on the port side at the no. 2 hatch. Releasing the crew members from mooring stations, I headed for the salon to get a cup of coffee. Waiting at the top of the ladder was Meg.

Tentatively, she asked, "Are you still coming home with me?"

"Of course," I said, hoping the trepidation didn't show in my voice or face. "When are you leaving?"

"Ten o'clock. Mark, Mum's fiancé, is picking us up."

"Okay, let me check with the chief mate and throw a few things in my duffel. I'll meet you at the gangway at 1000 hours." This drew a smile from Meg and won me a kiss.

Chapter 16

THE FARM

At 1000, I was at the top of the gangway, duffel at my feet, heart on my sleeve, and lump in my throat. Then, the reality struck me. Meg and Grace were disembarking, not just visiting ashore. I might never see Meg again once the ship sailed from Durban. Though I was heading for a rendezvous, it could end up as a final farewell.

Two of the stewards were carrying their luggage to the bottom of the gangway, where a small, dusty, gray pickup truck, its paint weather-beaten by a hard sun, squatted. In front was a very old two-door convertible in what seemed to be immaculate condition. The luggage went into the back of the pickup, and the driver of the convertible got out and spoke to the steward. The driver of the pickup and the pickup drove off toward the pier gate. The convertible driver, a short, rotund man wearing a dark suit and bright-green bow tie, leaned against the rear fender and looked up to the top of the gangway.

Meg talked to Grace as they walked through the companionway door.

"Good morning William," Grace started. "Are you ready to visit and see how we Afrikaners live?"

Not sure if she had just issued a challenge or a welcome, I replied, "Of course."

Meg came up and kissed me, something she had not done before in the presence of her mother. I wondered if it was her counterpoint to Grace's challenge.

"The bags just left in the back of a pickup. There's a guy on the pier waiting beside a car. Your driver?"

Grace looked down to the dock, smiled, and waved. "That's my fiancé, Mark, and yes, he's our driver."

Noticing my discomfort, she said, "Don't worry; I won't tell him you thought he was the chauffeur. Unlike in the United States, being a chauffeur here and in Europe is a worthy profession. Mark was a chauffeur before he went into banking."

I was embarrassed by the inference that I was denigrating Mark; it simply demonstrated my surprise at his physical appearance. After hearing Meg, and, to a lesser extent, Grace, describe him during the voyage, I expected a tall, suave, debonair, Hollywood type of guy, not Mr. Ordinary.

Grace led the way down with Meg next and me in the rear. At the bottom, Grace rushed to Mark and gave him a long kiss, to the point at which Meg cleared her throat to get her attention.

Looking at Meg, Grace said, "Meg, I haven't seen the man I love in months. I deserve a kiss and hug."

"Yes, Mum," said Meg. Then, she added, "Hello, Mark. It's good to see you."

"Hullo, Meg." He stepped forward and gave her a hug. "Is this your newfound friend?" he asked, looking at me.

"Yes, it is. This is William."

Reaching out his hand, he asked, "Do you have a last name, or is Meg's memory slipping?" He was jovial and friendly.

"Hello, Mr. Vanderwahl. William Connolly, very nice to meet you."

"Likewise, William, likewise. Let's all get in, and we'll start home. William, put your bag in the stam...the boot...the trunk. Americans have a different word for lots of things."

"Yes, sir," I said, and I deposited my duffel in the stam. I had learned a new word, and I had only been ashore for one minute.

"Mr. Vanderwahl, what kind of car is this?"

"This, my boy," he said, patting the spare tire mounted on the running board, just behind the right front wheel, "is a 1938 Mercedes 320 Cabriolet. She's a beauty, isn't she?"

"Yes, sir, she is." With cream-colored side panels and doors, dark-blue fenders, and a dark-blue top, it was a picture of elegance.

"Hop in now, and we'll be off."

Grace got in the front with Mark while Meg and I got in the rear. I had never ridden in a Mercedes before; not many kids from Southie ever had. The interior was luxurious, in beige leather. The two orange fog lamps on the front looked out of place compared to the understated elegance of the rest of the car. I sat in the right rear, behind Mark, and before we started, Meg scooted over and snuggled with me. Wondering if either Mark or Grace would say something, I realized that Grace had done the same to Mark in the front seat. I felt I was on a high-school joyride.

Meg kept up a constant chatter as we rode, pointing out the sights, interspersed with comments by Mark, regaling me with the history of the city. As we left the highway and got onto the back roads, the condition of the roadway deteriorated. I asked Mark why he drove an old car on such bad roads.

"These cars were built to handle anything. In 1938, Germany did a lot of bad things, preparing for war, but the one thing they did right was build this auto. It originally belonged to an official in the Nazi party who shipped it to his nephew living in Cape Town, hoping to follow it. He never made it. The nephew sold it to my father, who stored it in a garage. I didn't know it existed until my father died in 1959. I restored it. The original color was green, but I changed it to its current cream and have been driving it since."

The modern city of Durban dates from 1824. British Lieutenant F. G. Farewell, coming from the Cape Colony, led a party of twenty-five men and established a settlement on the north shore of the Bay of Natal. One of the men accompanying Farewell, Henry Francis Fynn, befriended the Zulu king Shaka by helping him recover from a wound he received in battle. Shaka rewarded Fynn by granting him a thirty-mile swath of land along the coast, one hundred miles deep. They built a city, and Fynn named it d'Urban after the then-governor of the Cape Colony, Sir Benjamin d'Urban.

Voortrekkers established the Republic of Natalia in 1838 and had a series of battles with the Zulu tribe under King Dingane until prevailing over Dingane at the battle of Blood River. Thereafter, the continued tension between the Zulus and Voortrekkers prompted the British to build a fortification and attack the Voortrekker camp at Vongella, but they were defeated. Eventually, in 1844, the Afrikaners succumbed to military pressure and accepted British annexation.

As farming grew, owners couldn't attract Zulu laborers to work the farms, so they turned to India, bringing in indentured servants on twenty-five-ear contracts. As a result, Durban has the largest Indian population outside of India. The city seal reads *"Debile principium melior fortuna sequitur"*: "Better fortune follows a humble beginning." I thought, that is a motto I hoped to live up to.

Driving through the harbor and business district, I saw that the land was flat, but as we got farther away from the pier, the hills began. Mark was a good driver and handled the traffic, the descriptive monologue, and the occasional kiss from Grace all in stride. An hour and fifteen minutes later, on a one-lane road overgrown with trees, we pulled up to a gate and stopped. Meg said, "I'll get it," and hopped out of the car, calling for me to follow her. I got out my side and helped her open the gate. Meg ran back to the car, told Mark and Grace that we would walk the rest of the way, closed both car doors, and stood aside as the car pulled away.

Standing there, with Meg beaming, watching the car recede, my old nemesis, déjà vu, returned. I felt light-headed and dizzy. I lurched back against the gate and almost fell. Leaning on the gate, I bent over and vomited onto the grass as nausea swept over me. Stricken, Meg stood and stared.

"I'll be okay," I muttered. "It won't last." Standing up straight, I took deep breaths and waited. After a few minutes, the dizziness and nausea subsided, and I could let go of the fence. Closing the gate, I said, "Let's go; I'm okay now," and I reached for her hand.

"What was that?"

"Nothing fatal, just embarrassing. I'll explain everything later, but I need to get a drink of water." I was still a little weak in the knees, but we started down the road.

About a quarter mile in, Meg said, "There's a well behind that barn; you can get a drink there."

After I rinsed my mouth and drank, we sat on a bench inside the barn, and I told her of my history with bouts of déjà vu and the accompanying nausea and dizziness. "The physical part is bad, but the mental part is scary." I related my history of predicting that my grandfather would die of lip cancer and a few lesser events that made my mother wonder about me and told her how I had less frequent events as I grew older. "If you want to rethink marrying me, now's your chance," I said.

"You scared me…but no, I haven't changed my mind. Have you?"

"If you recall, when you first brought up the topic, I didn't know what I wanted. I'm hoping this visit will clarify things. Okay?"

Holding both hands and staring at me, after a few seconds, she whispered, "Okay."

"C'mon," I said, standing up, "show me the rest of your world."

Walking down the hard-packed, stained-orange-dirt road, I could have been in the backwoods of Georgia or Florida, except for the peculiar smell. "What is that smell?"

"What smell?"

"I can't describe it."

Looking around her and sniffing, she said, "Oh, I think you smell the num-num."

"Num-num? Sounds like a baby made up the name."

"It's got a much longer name, but everyone calls it num-num. It's a plum bush. We've got them surrounding the house, and this is the time of year, they bloom and bear fruit. You'll see when we get there. They have white flowers shaped like stars, and they smell even better at night."

"Why is that?"

"It just is, like the midnight jasmine that blooms only at night," she rambled on, delighted to be in her element and introducing it to me.

"I don't know, but tonight, we can leave the windows open, and you'll see for yourself." This statement triggered senses other than smell.

"Is that the main house?" I asked as we rounded a small bend in the road.

"Yes." She took off running, and I brought up the rear, not wanting to catch her but enjoying the view. At the bottom step of the veranda, she waited, and when I reached her, she grabbed me and kissed me, hard. It was wonderful.

"Let me show you," she said, grabbing my hand and pulling me up the three steps. As we reached the top, Grace and Mark came out, also holding hands.

"We thought you may have run into some lions," Mark said.

"You know there're no lions here. Too many people," Meg retorted.

"Yes, but there are ferocious felines of the Grace and Meg species," he said, and everyone laughed.

"We're going to have lunch if you're interested. By the way, William, I left your bag just inside the doorway."

"Thank you, sir."

"Please, call me Mark."

"Yes, sir…Mark."

Still clinging to my hand, Meg said, "I'm not hungry. Let me show William around, and we'll join you later. Get your bag, William, and follow me." She started off to the right of the house.

Shrugging at Mark and Grace, I went inside, grabbed my duffel, and dutifully trotted after Meg.

Meg's apartment was a two-room bungalow with an elongated stoep in front. A muted, mustard color fading to brown, with shuttered windows, it was unassuming and plain, except for the front door, which was painted a gleaming ebony. Num-nums lined the ground in front of the stoep.

Following Meg through the front door, I dropped my duffel in the room and turned as the door shut. Meg attacked me. Mind you, I didn't resist, but caught off guard at the initial onslaught, I took a full three seconds to adjust. We wrestled our way into the bedroom, dropping clothes as we went. When she bent down as she removed her panties, I was so hard it hurt. I wrestled with the condom until she pushed my hand out of the way and rolled it on, gasping, "Condoms are a bother." The first time didn't last long, the pent-up pressure for both of us exploded fast and left us both gasping. The second time was slower; we were more patient, exploring each other's bodies, sensuous and loving. I took in the feel of her hair and the smell of her body. Leaning back, I gazed at her body, perfectly curved and flawless, and the street-corner joke flew into my mind: "It would violate the Pure Food and Drug Act to screw someone as beautiful as her."

Culminating in the missionary position, her legs wrapped around my back, I rolled to the side, but we stayed intertwined, kissing and nuzzling in an ecstasy of emotion. She unwrapped her legs, massaging my hips with her thighs in the process, rolled onto her back, and stretched, a tigress in her lair. "We should take a shower before going back," she said and sidled her way to the bathroom. I followed her in, and she was on the toilet. Thinking she may be uncomfortable, I offered to wait outside, but she said, "Just remember to put the seat down," and I laughed. We ended up taking a shower together and almost ended up back in bed, but practicality reigned, and we went back to the main house. Welcome to Durban, William.

We walked in holding hands, and the room was empty. Leading me into the kitchen, a large room for the size of the house, with a six-burner gas range, a refrigerator, and an upright freezer (not a common sight, as most freezers were the low, horizontal models), she turned to me with a smirk and said, "I'll bet Mum and Mark had the same idea as we did." She giggled. I didn't point out that it was her idea, and I was simply a willing, nay, eager, participant.

She had opened the refrigerator and started poking around when Grace walked in, wearing a bathrobe. She and Meg exchanged glances and smiled, and then she said, "Mark is taking a shower. He has to go back to town for a meeting and won't return until late tonight, so it will be just the three of us for dinner. Do you have a preference?"

"No, ma'am, anything you cook is fine."

Meg chimed in, "Do we have any lamb? I'd love a lamb chop."

"Let me get dressed, and you rummage through the fridge and see what's there. Mark said he stocked up in anticipation of our return."

Mark left for downtown around 4:00 p.m. Grace waved to him from the stoep and then returned to the kitchen. Meg didn't find lamb chops but found pork chops, so that was our entrée. Grace created a glace for the chops from a dozen different ingredients, most of which were sticky and sweet. Meg tossed a salad, making too much, despite my warning her that I didn't eat leafy things. They completed the meal with broccoli and brussels sprouts and a bottle of GS Cabernet that Grace said was a local product and that there was controversy surrounding it.

"The companies GS and SFW are merging, and this wine, " she held up the bottle. "they won't let it out on the market because it is too young. Mark's bank is involved in the financing, so he inveigled a case from them as a present for me. Tonight, we will find out if the company was right or wrong." She proceeded to uncork and decant the wine.

Raising her glass, Grace toasted, "Here's to being home with friends and family," and we clinked and sipped. My wine knowledge was limited, almost nonexistent, so I said nothing when I tasted the wine and found it bitter, with a cloying effect.

"Damn," Grace said, raising a look from Meg. "They were right. It is young. Maybe in a few years, it will mellow." She took the glasses from me and Meg and poured them out into the sink. "I have a good Argentine Malbec you'll like," she said, and she returned in a few minutes with another bottle. She opened and decanted that one, saying, "Let it breathe awhile."

After dinner, where I refused salad five times and played with the brussels sprouts enough so that Meg stopped encouraging me to try them, Grace poured the Malbec and said, "Try this. You'll find that the mixture of blackberry, plum, and black cherry is distinctive."

I tried it and recognized that there were fruit flavors, none of which I could discern. I said, "It's great," completing my diplomacy act for the evening.

"Yes," Grace admitted after finishing one and a half bottles of the Malbec, "I am a little snooty about my wine, but everyone is entitled to one bad indulgence. Wine is mine."

Thinking to get in her good graces (no pun intended), I offered, "Ma'am, I can tell if it's red or white, but only after it's in the glass. It either tastes good or bad—no nuance, no flavors, and hopefully, cheap."

Grace burst out laughing. "An honest man. God, how rare that is." Patting Meg's hand, she said, "I think you may have made a good choice, dear." Standing, she teetered a bit and said, "I believe I've had enough for one evening." She went upstairs to bed.

Meg and I cleaned up and then went out and sat on the stoep. "Do you mind if we wait until Mark comes home? Mum hasn't been this tipsy in a long time, and I don't want to leave her alone."

"Sure," I said, and we settled into the love seat and snuggled, happy in each other's presence, friends as much as lovers. When Mark arrived near midnight, we said good night to him and, holding hands, walked back to Meg's cottage.

I awoke the next morning alone in bed to the ever-present aroma of num-nums. Just as I slipped off the sheets and stood up, Meg walked in from the bathroom, naked and beautiful, with tousled hair and sleepy eyes, and she noted my immediate reaction. Walking close, she leaned into my erection and rubbed against it. "Still energetic, I see. Two times last night wasn't enough? Good." And we went for our third wild ride.

After a breakfast of coffee and scones, Grace, no worse the wear for her imbibing, said that she and Mark were going to visit some of their neighbors. We were free to do what we wanted, but if we wanted to leave the property, we would have to wait until the Land Rover was returned from the garage. Mark had sent it for a check-up since it had sat idle for a month.

After they left, Meg flashed her faux-innocent smile and said, "Do you want to do it here in the kitchen?" to which I replied, "I prefer softer surfaces, and I wouldn't want to put any creases in that beautiful ass of yours."

"How thoughtful," she said, as she unbuckled my belt. We settled for the floor. I began to worry that I would run out of condoms.

As we rearranged our clothing, nothing removed, just pushed aside in our haste, I said, "Let's go for a walk; you can show me the rest of the property." I had brought along my sneakers and changed into them. Meg donned hers and grabbed a vintage WWI canteen, filled it with water, and handed it to me.

"Where did you get this?"

Wistfully, she said, "It belonged to Gramps, my dad's dad. Now, it's mine."

I gave her a gentle kiss and said, "Let's go." And off we went.

For three hours, we meandered on the edges of the property, thick with trees and brush where the land was not cleared for farming. We climbed a small hill and gazed at the valley, a series of rifts in a larger valley; we waded along a spring-fed gorge and skinny-dipped in a placid pond at the end of the gorge. She confessed that when she was nine years old, she, two girlfriends, and their two brothers (a year or two younger than they), used to skinny-dip here.

"You started young, I see."

Poking me, she said, "No, you ninny. It wasn't that way. We were just kids cooling off. We were still innocent then. It lasted a whole summer. A year later, we were too old."

On the way back, I remarked that I hadn't heard any monkeys, only a few bird calls.

"Some nights, you can hear them. Each year, the encroachment of civilization drives them deeper into the jungle."

"What kind of monkeys?"

"Only Vervets here. Up closer to Kruger Reserve, there are Samango monkeys."

We passed by the garden areas, and there were four young black people, two girls and two boys, tending them. When Meg saw them, she yelled in delight, "Bhule! Inyoni!" She ran toward them. I followed behind. When I reached them, Meg was holding hands with both the girls. Turning, she said, "William, these are my friends Bhule and Inyoni. They are sisters, and these are their brothers, Siyanda and Nomvula." The girls bobbed their heads in greeting, and the boys timidly shook my hand when I offered it, barely touching fingers.

"We grew up together here. Whenever their parents came to tend the garden, they came with them. I haven't seen them since I left for college."

They spent half an hour talking while I listened, the girls giggly and the boys quiet but smiling a lot.

"We have to go," Bhule said, "or we will miss our ride home." With hugs and handshakes, they left.

Walking back to the house, Meg explained their names to me. "Bhule means 'beauty' or 'goodness'; Inyoni means 'bird'; Siyanda, the older brother, means 'We are increasing'; and Nomvula means 'after the storm.' Their mother, Thulisile, meaning 'she who makes things quiet,' named Nomvula because he was born two days after a terrible storm, where the entire village flooded."

"Do you know their father?"

"Oh, yes. His name is Bhekizizwe, meaning 'Look after the nation.' Bhekizizwe and my father were friends, though they couldn't always show it because of apartheid. My father ensured that Bhekizizwe got travel passes so the family could travel safely between his home and here. He employed both him and Thulisile as caretakers here on the farm. The day after my father's funeral, Bhekizizwe gathered his family at the barn where you were sick, and he held a funeral of his own for him. Mum and I cried harder at that funeral than the prior one."

"Your father sounds like a very good man."

"Yes." Tears ran down her cheeks. "Yes, he was. The good thing is that Mark feels the same way about this stupid apartheid, and he has found a job for Bhekizizwe doing gardening and tending to properties the bank owns." Wiping her eyes, she smiled and said, "Remember my story of skinny-dipping?"

"Yes."

"You just met my swim mates," she said and laughed.

Supper that night started at 7:00 p.m., and Mark regaled us with stories of his days as a chauffeur in Cape Town and Durban, driving rich clients around. "A chauffeur was and still is a respected position. The chauffeur was entrusted with the lives of the master of the estate and his family. That's when I learned the difference between 'old money' and 'nouveau riche.' The old-money gentry were polite, never condescending, and appreciated your service. They never looked down their snoot at you. The nouveau riche mostly were full of themselves, hot air in an overstuffed balloon, acting as if they were better than you. They looked through you, as if you were paint on a wall."

I interjected, "You know, now that you describe it, I experienced that as well when I was crewing on sailboats as a teenager. The guys and ladies who had money for generations were always nicer than the ones who had recently acquired money. I think the old-timers were just more secure in themselves. They didn't look at me as a threat."

"Spot on, William, and it's an excellent lesson in keeping things in the proper perspective throughout life."

It was a wonderful four hours, a family gathering accepting the newcomer: me. Afterward, Meg and I sat on the stoep of her apartment and talked until 2:00 a.m. I finally broached the subject of marriage. "Meg, I love you. As much as the lovemaking has affected me, sitting at the table tonight and listening to you, your mother, and Mark talk, I realized what a wonderful person you are and how lucky I am to have someone like you love me. So, the answer to your question is, yes, I want to marry you, but we have a long way to go yet.

"I like your mother and Mark, and I like your home, but my life is the merchant marine. I've just started my career, and it will take me away from you for long periods of time, starting tomorrow morning. We both have to think long and hard about being away from each other. I've been living this life since I started college because I didn't get home often, and we would go on training cruises every year for six to eight weeks." Pausing to collect my thoughts, I said, "You've been away at college, but you didn't have a boyfriend back home, and you enjoyed the freedom and association of new friends while there. Now, you are back home where you want to stay, and it's clear I'll have to be the one to relocate. Even if I come ashore, I don't know what the job market is here in Durban or whether I can even get a job, being an American. So, let's play it slow, and see how it goes."

She took my hands in hers. Meg's tears had been falling throughout my soliloquy, and now she looked at me, kissed me softly and tenderly, and said,

"All right, I'll try. It will be hard without you here, but I'll try. Let's go to bed." There was no sleep that night, only alternate bouts of lovemaking and tears.

Mark took me back to the ship the next morning. I insisted that Meg stay home for selfish reasons. I didn't want anyone on the ship to see me crying. Mark gave me his business card when he dropped me off and told me to call him if I had any problems or needed someone to talk to. It was as close to a father-son conversation I'd had since Dad died.

As we sailed from Durban, the high-rise buildings disappearing into the mist on the North Shore reminded me of the view of Miami Beach, and for some reason, it made me homesick. I wondered if my future with Meg would disappear into the mist as distance and time came between us.

Chapter 17

LOURENÇO MARQUES

Sailed from Durban at 1300 hours on Friday 11/11/66. Light mist. Low clouds. Temperature 81 degrees. Wind calm, and flat seas, with a gentle rolling swell from the southwest. Destination: Lourenço Marques, Mozambique.

We cleared the pilot boat, and once we had Umhlanga Rocks abeam to port, the captain set a course of 070 degrees and set revolutions for 15 knots.

"Captain, there's plenty of water inshore and no charted shoals. Why do we go out so far before turning north?"

"Good question, Mr. Connolly," he said, putting me at ease, "but one you should have figured out yourself." This instilled tension again. "Did you check the caution notes on the chart?"

"Not yet, sir."

"I suggest you do so."

I went into the chart room and looked at the caution notes, an inset on most charts warning of general dangers or odd circumstances. After I returned to the bridge, the captain said, "Well?"

"Thank you, sir," I said, kissing his ass and ensuring I didn't incur his wrath for not checking prior to asking my question. "It says that strong currents, whose influence may extend to twenty miles seaward, have been experienced along this coast, setting directly onto shore for no apparent cause. Great caution should be exercised navigating in this vicinity."

"Now, you know why we go deep. By the way, Mr. Connolly, consistency keeps ships afloat. I recall you checked the caution notes on the prior chart because you noted the chance of a rogue sea. Do it every time, not just when you think you can impress the captain."

Chastened, I said, "Yes, sir, I will."

The plan was to stay on this course for thirty-seven miles until due east of Tongeat Bluff with its noticeable red cliffs and then change course to 042 degrees for another seventy-four miles until abeam of Cape Lucia. From there, we would sail on 012 degrees for eighty-three miles until abeam of Ponta do Oure, fifteen miles offshore, and then sail due north for fifty-one miles until abeam of the flashing red light at the north tip of Ilha da Incaha outside of the port of Lourenço Marques.

We were just coming up on our turning point at Tongeat Bluff when Chuck, the second mate, relieved me.

"You don't look happy, William. Missing your girlfriend already?"

Grinning, I said, "I didn't think it was that obvious."

Patting me on the shoulder, he replied, "Hey, she's a good-looking gal. There'd be something wrong with you if you didn't miss her. Leaving is a big part of a seaman's life. You better get used to it."

Nodding, I went below and turned in but couldn't sleep. I lay there, listening to a radio station from Johannesburg, until light poked through the porthole. Giving up on sleeping, I went to the salon for a cup of coffee. At 0630, Dennis, the chief mate, and Bill, the chief engineer, walked in together, talking. When they saw me, they stopped talking, said good morning, got their coffee, and went to their respective seats at different tables but never resumed their conversation.

"How'd your visit go?" Dennis asked.

"Fantastic!"

"Wow, that good?"

"Yes, it was." I told him about the farm; Grace's fiancé, Mark; and the people I met on the farm, also commenting on the 1938 Mercedes Cabriolet.

"Sounds like an interesting couple of days. Do you have any plans for when we call at Durban on the return trip?"

"No. I told Meg I'd send her a telex a day before we get there. Maybe Tony will cover for me again."

"I'm sure he will, and if not, I will."

Taken aback by his offer to cover my watches, I ventured to breach another, stickier subject. "Dennis, remember just before signing off in New York, you said we'd have a private talk about the 'events' of last trip. Are we going to have that talk?"

Leaning back, he said, "Yeah. Yeah, we should. Tonight, after dinner." He looked around as a few others came into the salon. "In my room, where no one can eavesdrop."

The midwatch passed, uneventful, and Chuck relieved me when we were fifteen miles south of our next change of course, abeam of Ponta Do Oure. As I walked off the bridge, the captain came up and ordered Chuck to slow down to 12 knots. We were in a stretch of the coast where a countercurrent, an offshoot of the Mozambique current heading northward at one knot, was prevalent, and this now helped us. By slowing down, we saved on fuel oil. At the border of Mozambique and South Africa, the name of the current changed from Agulhas to Mozambique.

Still stinging from the captain's rebuke earlier that afternoon, I went out on the bridge wing and asked him if I could get him anything before I turned in.

Smiling craftily, he said, "Thank you, but no, Mr. Connolly." In a lower tone that only I could hear, he continued, "I believe you learned a valuable lesson this afternoon. It isn't necessary to kiss my ass more than once after a mistake. More than once makes me think another mistake may be looming. Good night." He walked into the bridge.

Embarrassed and relieved, I tucked my tail and slunk below.

We were not due to start loading until Monday morning, so rather than pay dockage fees for an idle ship, the company ordered the captain to go to anchor. The local anchorage had thirty-six to forty feet of water and a good seabed for holding the anchor fast. Captain Coltrain didn't like going to anchor for any reason, but two days of dockage fees was a cost savings the company couldn't ignore, and he was a company man. The message about not berthing didn't come in until midnight, and Sparky, the radio operator, didn't give the captain the message until 0800, or the captain would have slowed the ship and crawled up the coast in order to save fuel. Sparky took some heat from the captain over that. He needed to yell at somebody.

I had finished running the ladders. Without Meg keeping me company, it was a drudge again instead of pleasure. Standing on the flying bridge, I enjoyed the sunshine on my face, smoking a cigarette; I was smoking more now that Meg wasn't here to chastise me. She smoked when we first met, but after only a week, she decided to quit and thereafter chided me to quit. I had compromised by only smoking on watch. Without her support, I was well on my way back to three packs a day.

As I was ruminating on the positive effects Meg had on me, Eunice's voice cut through my reverie and startled me. "Well, it's been a whole two days without Meg. You must be horny. Anything I can do to help?"

She was standing five feet away, wearing a bikini with a sheer something-or-other over it. Before I could respond, she put one hand on her hip and opened the sheer thing with the other. She continued, "I'm very good at helping."

"No, thank you," I said and walked toward the ladder.

Heading to my room, I thought, "Is she still screwing Tony? Is she that horny she needs two people banging her?" I would have to be careful because of two factors. First, she was the captain's wife, and that was playing with fire; second, she was right. I was horny and didn't know if I could resist such blatant come-ons. I was afraid to test my determination; it wasn't willpower, it was "won't" power.

That night after dinner, I knocked on the chief mate's door and walked in. Waving his hand, he said, "Close it," so I did. "I'm not going to explain all the details of what occurred last trip. You saw enough to know a few of us had a side venture going, carrying things that weren't on the ship's manifest. That US customs raid in New York could have been a bad ending for all of us, so we decided to cease and desist. There were a few leftover things we dumped on the way up to Boston, and that's that—done, end of story."

"Did you know Sparky was murdered?" I asked.

There was a slight pause, and he said, "I heard but never got the full story."

"He was. The night we were paid off, I found him in the alley past the bar, going toward Third Avenue. I saw the two guys running away who killed him, and they saw me. At first, I thought they'd come after me, but they took off, and when I went into the alley, Sparky had his tongue skewered to his chest by his own switchblade."

"Jesus," was all Dennis said.

"Yeah, my thoughts exactly."

We sat in silence for a minute, and then I continued, "I told you I heard Sparky telling someone to hurry, that it was going down right now. Thinking back, I'm sure it was a customs guy he was talking to. Who did you tell?"

More silence, and then he said, "Jesus, I told the captain."

"I doubt he killed Sparky. He doesn't seem the type to get his hands dirty. Who could he have told?"

There was even more silence, finally broken by Dennis. "Frankie, the Mafia boss. The captain knew him and his father from his days as pier superintendent. Frankie could take care of things like this. Jesus, I can't believe the captain would set up Sparky, but I can't believe he wouldn't set him up, either."

Figuring now was the time to get it all out in the open, I told him about Eunice coming on to me and Tony at the start of the trip, as well as her latest hit on me. I also told him about overhearing the argument between Eunice and the captain from the flying bridge. "The captain has a temper."

"Oh, I know. I've seen it firsthand, but I've never seen him get violent. I hope Eunice doesn't push him too hard. Every man has his breaking point." After another long pause, Dennis said, "That's enough for one night. I think it's best if you forget about everything that happened last trip."

"I already have, Dennis."

Lourenço Marques is the capital and largest city of Mozambique, and its largest exports are chromite, sugar, sisal, copra, cotton, and hardwood. It's also the seaport of choice for South Africa for its gold exports. It was originally surrounded by marshland; the Portuguese government saw the potential viability of the port in the late 1900s and changed the capital from the island of Mozambique to Lourenço Marques. It grew steadily thereafter.

It was a tempestuous time in Portuguese East Africa. In 1962, the Mozambique Resistance, the Front for Liberation of Mozambique (FRELIMO), was formed, and after two years of internal struggles, they fired the first shot when they attacked the military post in Cabo Delgado province. As the ship now approached the port of Lourenço Marques, FRELIMO had liberated most provinces in northern Mozambique, and things remained tense between FRELIMO and the Portuguese government.

The pilot boarded at 0500 on Monday, November 14, 1966, and we proceeded into port, a somewhat tortuous approach through shallow water. The river channel was only twenty-six to thirty feet deep. After an hour and a half of feeling our way along, we tied up at berth no. 3, one of five berths in a string along the north bank of the Matola River.

The chief mate informed us when we went to mooring stations that he anticipated at least two days in port. At breakfast he informed Tony, Chuck, and me that we would work three gangs of longshoremen, starting at 0800. One gang would load chromite ore in bulk into the no. 5 hatch's lower hold, the second would load bagged copra into the no. 4 lower hold, and the third gang would load baled sisal into the no. 1 lower-tween deck in the after end.

At 0730, Tony started to open the hatches. With nothing else to do, I told him I would give him a hand and went to open the no. 1 hatch while he opened the no. 4 and no. 5 hatches. I then returned to the officers' salon and had a few more cups of coffee and smoked cigarettes.

At 0900, the chief mate came in for a drink of water. He was sweating profusely, and while it was 83 degrees and humid, he didn't look right. When he sat down, I asked him, "You okay, Dennis? You look kind of gray."

"No, I'm feeling kind of weird. I haven't sweated this much ever, and I'm a little nauseous."

"You should go see the chief steward, check it out."

"Yeah, I will," he said and rose to leave.

"Want me to cover Tony for a coffee break?"

"Yeah." He was distracted as he went out the door.

I found Tony at the no. 5 hatch, peering over the coaming.

"Hey, Tony, take a coffee break. I'll cover for you." I told him about the chief mate.

"That's not good," he said. "Dennis tripped about a half hour ago at the forward end of the no. 4 hatch, and he went down hard. He banged his head on the hatch-coaming stiffener. There wasn't any blood, but still, he hit it hard."

"Go ahead and get your coffee. No rush. If Dennis isn't back when I go in, I'll check on him."

"Okay, thanks," he said, and off he went.

The chromite ore they were loading in the no. 5 hatch was a dirty-silver color in clumps of about four or five pounds each. The longshoremen were using the ship's gear to load, even though there were three electric gantry cranes on the pier. On shore, a small jitney pulled a string of four trams filled with the chromite. On the pier, they laid out a ten-foot square net, draped with thick canvas, and each tram pulled alongside the net and tilted its load into the net, one tram load per net. They then hoisted the net into the ship, and the men in the hold pushed it into position and lowered it. They then unhooked two of the four corners and dumped the load, returning the net to the pier to start the cycle anew.

At the no. 4 hatch, they loaded bags of copra, also using nets, but this time, they carried the nets out from inside the shed, already filled with bags of copra. To carry the loaded net, they used what we always referred to on the Boston waterfront as a "mankiller," a three-wheeled forklift with a boom extending from the front that could raise and lower the net. They called it a mankiller because if you turned a corner too fast with a load on the end, it tended to tip over, killing the operator. I watched them on the pier; the drivers seemed to be good and operated smoothly.

Watching the men in the hold was fascinating. The longshoreman running the winches would dump the contents of the net in the center of the hatch in the same manner as the chromite. Then, two men would lift a bag of the copra shoulder-high, and one man would run under it, trot to a corner of the hold, and toss it onto the ever-growing stack of bags, laying it out in perfect rows. They moved fast, and from above, it looked like a bunch of ants carrying things into the nest. Hot, hard work. I don't think I would have lasted an hour at it, but they seemed tireless.

Leaving there, I made my way up to the no. 1 hatch. They were loading bales of sisal into the forward end of the lower hold. The bales came in on large pallets. The men in the hold, two at a time, lifted a bale and walked it to the pile and stowed it. More hot, hard work.

Walking to the inshore side, I scanned the pier, noting the deep layer of dust so that every footstep created an eddy, and every time the forklift placed the pallet on the pier, a miniature dust storm appeared. As the winch operator lifted the load, a swirl of air trailed it, like the tail on a kite. Everybody, including me, exuded sweat, so the dust caked on exposed skin and clogged the nostrils, adding to the cloying mix of exotic aromas.

Tony came up while I was standing there and told me he hadn't seen Dennis. I told him everything was going well, and I'd see him at lunch time. I left.

Knocking on Dennis's open door, I got no response, so I walked through his office and knocked on his bedroom door beyond. There was still no response, so I opened the door and looked inside, and he wasn't there. I went to the salon and found him slumped over the table with his head on his arms. Tapping him on the shoulder, I said, "Dennis? Dennis, you okay?" He didn't respond. I checked to see if he was breathing; he was, and I ran to get the chief steward. When we got back, Joey, the pantryman, was there, trying to wake up Dennis.

"Leave him be," Frank, the chief steward, said. "Help me sit him up," he said, looking at me. We got him erect in the chair. He then told Joey to get a Stokes litter and two other men, so we could carry the chief mate to his room. He opened Dennis's eyes and looked at them. "One pupil is larger than the other."

I interjected. "Did he come and see you?"

"No. Why?"

"I told him to see you about an hour ago. He was sweating and said he felt nauseous. Tony told me he fell and hit his head on the coaming stiffener."

"Damn. Sounds like a concussion."

Just then, Dennis stirred, looked at Frank, and then vomited on himself and the table. Frank and I supported him until he stopped.

"Sorry," he muttered, as Frank and I supported him. Joey and both of my ABs came in then, carrying the Stokes litter. We carried Dennis to his cabin and put him in his bunk.

"Sit him up, and prop the pillows behind him," Frank ordered.

The others left, and Frank told me to notify the captain. Frank was unbuttoning Dennis's shirt as I left, and that's when the odor of vomit hit me. For whatever reason, it didn't bother me until then, but I was glad to leave and get a breath of fresh air.

When the captain and I returned, Dennis was mobile and had, with Frank's help, gotten his shirt and pants off. Frank was wiping his face and chest, cleaning the remains of his partly digested breakfast off him. Looking to Frank, the captain said, "What do you think? Do we need an ambulance?"

"No, I don't think so, but it wouldn't hurt to have a doctor check him over."

"I'll have the ship's agent get one down here," he said, and he left.

Dennis seemed more relaxed and was not sweating so much. "That was embarrassing. I'm usually a lot drunker when I throw up on myself."

Frank and I grinned, and Frank chimed in, "At least this was a medical condition from the whack to your head and not self-inflicted through overimbibing." He chuckled.

"Hey, Frank. You're not going to tell everyone you undressed me with no witnesses, are you?" It was an obvious reference to his being queer.

"What, and ruin my reputation? If I'm going to undress someone, I'd rather it be someone like him," he said, pointing at me, "than an old tubby like you." They both laughed while I stared at them. Addressing me, Frank continued, "Don't worry; both you and old tubby here are safe. I never have affairs with shipmates."

I gave him a sickly grin and said, "If you guys are okay, I have to get ready for watch." I backed out the door.

The rest of the day went fine, with no snags in the cargo operation. The doctor came aboard at 1400 and told Dennis to stay in bed for the rest of the day. If there were no more nausea or dizziness, he could resume normal duties the next morning.

The longshoremen had knocked off for the day at 1600 hours. I waited until after dinner and then went to Dennis's room and gave him a recap of the day's events. He looked and moved much better. As I was leaving, Frank came in to check on Dennis. I must have looked apprehensive because he laughed and asked, "Am I the first queer man you've ever met?"

"No, there were a couple of queer guys that tried to hit on me when I was a kid."

Looking serious, he said, "No wonder you're nervous. They weren't queer, they were pedophiles, preying on kids. They give us a bad reputation, not that many people say nice things about queers. Don't worry, young Meg doesn't have any worries about competition." He laughed. Dennis was laughing behind him.

"Frank, I didn't mean to offend you."

"You didn't, William. We are what we are. Just be yourself." And he patted my cheek like my ma would have, solicitously.

We continued loading through noon on Wednesday and sailed at 1500 hours for Beira.

Chapter 18

BEIRA

Sailed from Lourenço Marques at 1500 hours on Wednesday, 11/16/66. Light clouds. Temperature 80 degrees. Humidity 76 percent. Wind from the south at 6 knots and increasing. Waves two feet in height. Destination: Beira, Mozambique.

The captain walked off the bridge after we cleared the local ship traffic. Once he left, I was free to muse and daydream. I stared at the bright-green sea, tinged by the white of an occasional breaking wave. Feeling the head wind on my face was tantamount to meditation. Vigilant when entering or leaving port, I didn't think of Meg until we were an hour on our way. Thinking of her brought both exhilaration and melancholy, conflicting emotions I was learning to deal with. Chuck, the second mate, interrupted my daydreams when he relieved me at 1600 hours.

With revolutions for 15 knots and a two-knot head current, our ETA was Friday at 0500. The captain reminded Sparky that he wanted to see any messages from the company as soon as they came in, not wanting to waste more fuel if we didn't have an available berth on Friday.

We steamed for 149 miles before altering course to 027 degrees. We had a short run of fifty-two miles and then turned due north for another 107 miles to Ponta da Barra Falsa. Continuing due north, our next target was the Banco de Sofala, 151 miles away. Once there, we turned in to the final leg on a course of 303 degrees for thirty-four miles to the buoy marking the entrance channel of the port of Beira, Mozambique.

Located on the Pungwe River, Beira is a narrow, shallow-water port stretched out along the east side of the river. It sits north of the mouth of the convergence of two rivers, the Buzi and the Pungwe, the Pungwe being the longer of the two rivers. Although a well-equipped port, Beira is the stepchild port in Mozambique, overshadowed by Lourenço Marques.

We learned from the pilot the talk of the town was the new railroad station they were just putting the finishing touches on. While the station, located south of the port area, was for passengers only, the expanded railcar-holding area east of the station had high hopes for attracting more commercial business from the interior of Africa.

We had boarded the pilot at 0500 and were creeping up the river. Not being able to sleep since getting off watch at 0400, I now sat on the fantail, knowing I'd be called out for mooring stations within the hour. I was smoking, drinking coffee, and absorbing the strange fetid odor akin to something rotting in the underbrush; the cigarette helped mask the odor. As the day brightened, it seemed the river oozed rather than flowed, a filthy brown sludge, the result of heavy silting from both rivers.

The river channel hugged the eastern shore, close to the city, tucked into the land like two lovers spooning after sex—hot and steamy, but relaxed. At 0615, the chief mate called the crew out to mooring stations. With the assistance of one tug, we finished mooring and were ready to go to work loading by 0730.

After breakfast, I hit the bunk for a few hours of sleep. After a light lunch, at which the chief mate filled me in on the loading plans, I relieved Tony and went on deck.

We had two gangs of longshoremen working. One gang at the no. 2 hatch loaded thirty-foot-long mahogany logs into the aft end of the lower hold. One at a time, they lifted them, slinging the logs with wire-rope chokers, one at each end. Even though the hatch opening was large enough to allow them to fit in the hold, the longshoremen had "dipped" them so they could slide them closer to the end. Dipping is the method in which one sling is longer than the other so that one end of the log is "dipped." They lower the dipped end in first. This allows the log to be pulled closer to the end of the hatch before being released. This saves time and effort for the longshoremen, who wrestle the logs into their final resting places. Once in a while as they struggled with a log, one man would break into a chant of five or six words and would then shout "m'bele," and they would push in unison, sweat glistening on their backs and shoulders.

When the log landed in the hatch, men in the hold used log peaveys to work the logs into the sides of the hold and snug them up against the aft end. Once a log was in place, one man would jam a wood wedge at the end to keep it in place until they positioned the next log.

The second gang loaded cases of cashew nuts at the no. 3 hatch into the upper-tween-deck lockers, working both the port and starboard lockers, alternating pallet loads. The winch operator placed the pallet at the door of the locker, and the men would lift and walk the cases into the locker and stow them. In between loads, they stacked up the empty pallets, and at every tenth load, they would take out the empties. It was a smooth but slow operation. Things went well the entire watch. When Chuck relieved me at 1600, I told him they planned to knock off work for the day at 1700 and that the mate wanted the hatches closed, anticipating overnight rain.

At dinner that evening, not having Meg there to focus on, I listened to Clara Simpson and Eunice talk about their day in town. At breakfast, Clara bugged Bernie to go into town, and in between snuffles of food, he refused. Eunice volunteered to go with Clara. Eunice had always been polite but not overly friendly to Clara during the trip, so I was surprised by her offer.

I eavesdropped; it was easy to do since they both were loud. It seemed the better part of their day had consisted of imbibing cocktails at a local restaurant. They didn't slur their words, but the lips wrapping the words up in their respective cocoons were definitely loose.

By 1830, everyone had fled the salon except the ladies and me. Both kept looking at me, and given one's mothering predilection and the other's rapacious character, I knew I should leave before I got involved.

The ordinary seaman woke me at 2330. I splashed water on my face, shrugged into my shirt and shorts, went to the head and peed, and then headed to the salon for coffee and whatever the cook had left for the midwatch meal.

In the salon, I passed on the mystery meat, no doubt the remains of today's meatloaf, recognizable only by the name on the menu. Slathering peanut butter on a heel of bread, I took it and my coffee and relieved Tony up on the bridge. As usual in port, the AB and the ordinary seaman took turns at the gangway watch and didn't come up to the bridge unless called.

"Hey, Tony, anything happening?"

"It's raining." It was unnecessary, since it was teeming, and I couldn't miss it.

"Okay, I got it. You're relieved."

He said nothing, just leaned against the forward bulkhead and stared into space.

"What's the matter, Tony?"

He looked at his shoes, scratched his head, and said, "I don't want to go below. She's gonna be there, waiting for me."

"She? You mean Eunice?"

Nodding his head, he said, "Yeah. She backed off for a while and hasn't bugged me since Cape Town, but now she's back at it."

"Hell, you've already screwed her. What's the problem?"

Glaring at me, he said, "The captain is the problem. I know he knows, but I keep expecting him to walk in on us, and it scares the shit out of me. The other night, she knocked on my door, and when I ignored it, she went away but came right back and slipped a note under the door."

"What did it say?"

"'Open the door, or I'll start yelling.'"

"I take it you opened the door?"

He nodded.

"How long did she stay?"

"About an hour. Enough to fuck twice. She gave me a lecture because I heard a noise in the companionway and lost my hard-on."

"A lecture?" There was incredulity in my voice.

"Yeah. She grabbed my cock and said I needed to 'stiffen my resolve' because she didn't want to have to suck my dick every time to get it hard."

"Jesus."

"Yeah, she's weird, and scary, and incredibly sexy."

"So are you going to hide up here the rest of the night?"

"No," he said, sighing. "Maybe she's tired and won't be there." He went below.

At 0400, Chuck, the second mate, relieved me. By then, the rain had stopped, but everything was steaming, and the humidity hovered near 100 percent. I hadn't stepped outside, but my clothes were soaked from sweat and moisture in the air. On the way to my room, I put an ear to Tony's door but didn't hear anything. I felt sorry for him and was jealous, wishing I could have time with Meg the way he was having time with Eunice.

Later that morning at 0745, I stood on the inshore-bridge wing, drinking coffee and smoking as I watched the longshoremen climb the gangway. They dressed the same as yesterday, wearing baggy boiler suits, coveralls that were gray and dingy, having seen much use. As they climbed down the manhole into the no. 3 hatch and emerged in the open, they all shrugged out of their coveralls and tied them off at the waists before starting work. Given the temperature and high humidity, this seemed sensible. I was sweating just standing still, watching. Tony was on watch, and it looked like it would be a boring day.

I went down to the salon to refill my coffee and ran into Clara Simpson. After the session we'd had on the pool deck, she would always smile when she saw me. I felt sorry for her. Although she sat with her husband at mealtimes, they almost never spoke. Also, she had been dieting and exercising. Having seen Meg and I run the ladders a few times, she walked the ladders, slowly and steadily, and she had made enough progress that the weight loss was noticeable.

"Good morning, William."

"Good morning, Mrs. Simpson. How are you today?" I filled my cup as I talked.

"I'm fine, thanks. What's happening here today?"

"What do you mean, here?"

"Here, on the ship."

"Other than the loading operation, nothing that I know of."

"Tell me about the loading." She was apparently desperate for some company.

"Better yet, why don't you come up to the flying bridge with me? We can watch what's going on, and I'll explain it as they work."

"Let's go," she said, and I led the way back up.

Leaning over the forward rail, I explained to her what was happening and went into detail about why they were doing things the way they were. I don't know if she was that interested, but it was clear that having someone to talk to was enough for her.

After half an hour, she changed topics. "Did you have a good time visiting with Meg while we were in Durban?"

"Yes, I had a great time."

"I'll bet you miss her."

"I do, a lot."

Hesitant, she started, "You know…"

"What?"

"You were kind to me when I made an ass of myself a while ago and blubbered like a baby, and I appreciate that."

Embarrassed now, I looked at my shoes and didn't reply.

She continued, "I'm not nosing into your private life, just offering friendly advice. It's clear you and Meg are in love. I enjoyed watching you two moon over one another. It brought back a few good memories."

There was more foot staring.

"I talked to Grace and Meg a lot before they left, and they are both strong women. There's no doubt Meg is her mother's daughter. I admire strong women, more so because I know my own shortcomings. Anyway, being with a strong woman is a challenge, and it takes a strong man to accept a woman as equal in a relationship."

"Mrs. Simpson," I said, picking up my head and looking at her, "I don't think it's a question of me being strong enough to deal with Meg, or her mother. I'm young and maybe naïve, but I love Meg. I have never felt this way about another girl. Not even close. The thing I'm wrestling with is South Africa."

"South Africa?"

"Yes, a foreign country with foreign ways, one of which, apartheid, I already despise. I don't know if I can live there."

"Why would you? Take Meg back home. She's lived in the United States for four years, and she told me she loved it there."

I related Grace's speech and Meg's confirmation of staying in South Africa.

She was silent for a minute and then said, "I'd hug you, but that would probably make you uncomfortable." She patted my arm and went below.

I chain-smoked until lunch, staring onto the deck but aware of nothing but my inner struggle. When I saw the longshoremen head off the ship for their lunch break, I went below to the salon and relieved Tony.

Mr. DeKuyper sat at my spot, talking with the chief mate. When I walked in, he stood, but I said, "That's okay sir, stay there," and he resumed his seat and conversation. Bernie Simpson was stuffing his face with today's entrée, brisket. It was mediocre unless the chief cook ladled up his Texas barbeque sauce, and then, it was delicious. Today, it had sauce; Mr. Simpson both relished and wore his brisket well, his usual tucked-in napkin highlighted with reddish-brown spots from his chin drippings and heavier stains at the edges from mouth wiping.

Seated with Eunice at the captain's table, Clara Simpson played with a salad and drank ice water. Eunice talked, and Clara's occasional nod seemed only polite and not focused.

I sat opposite Tony, next to the chief mate, and I told Joey, the pantryman, to bring me the brisket, eavesdropping on Mr. DeKuyper's conversation. In low tones, he and Dennis were finalizing the plans for a weekend motor safari when the ship reached Mombasa. Throughout the trip, DeKuyper had little social contact with the other passengers but had befriended Dennis, and they spent many hours together talking when the ship was at sea.

DeKuyper, through his friends, two German expatriate sisters who ran a lodge at the foot of Mt. Kilimanjaro, had arranged for up to eight people to go there and stay for the weekend. He wouldn't be going. He had business to attend to in Mombasa, but he made sure we would be well looked after.

I asked, "Who's going, Dennis?"

"It's me; Fran, the chief steward; Bill; Greg; and Pat, from the engineers. And I have room for three more. You interested?"

"Yeah, I'd love to. How much is it?"

"Two hundred bucks a person, including transportation to and from."

"That's cheap."

Tony, sitting there listening, said, "I wouldn't mind going."

"Okay, you're in, too. Chuck already said he'd keep an eye on things over the weekend."

Tony said, "Think the Simpsons would want to go?"

Giving Tony a funny look, Dennis replied, "We don't want any passengers along. It's for the crew only, so if you want in, okay, but keep your mouth shut."

Tony looked at DeKuyper, thinking, "He's a passenger." But he said, "I understand. I won't say a word."

"Good." He turned to DeKuyper, "By the way, Pieter, how did you meet these German ladies?"

"I married one, but she caught me in bed with the other. I don't know why, but they still both like me." He chuckled.

On the flying bridge that evening, waiting to be called out for undocking, I heard soft steps and turned around, expecting Clara to offer another of her "Mom knows best" stories. They were well-meaning but not helpful. Instead, it was Eunice.

I don't know if I actually groaned, but she reacted as if I did.

"It's all right. I'm not going to bite you. After lunch today, after you left, Clara told me of your dilemma: the girl or the country. I have to admit, it's an unusual situation."

"Mrs. Coltrain, with all due respect, Clara shouldn't have told you that. She was trying to be helpful, and I'm not ungrateful, but you both should just drop the subject."

"A little testy, are we? Well that's understandable after a weekend of salacious sex. And now, as they say, help is only at the end of your own hand."

As I turned to leave, she put her hand on my chest and said, "Wait a minute. I apologize. It's been so long, I've forgotten what real love feels like." Shifting to stand in my path, she continued, "I will offer you one bit of advice."

Now, my sigh was visible, and her advice not wanted. Nonetheless, she continued.

"You're young, and like most young men, you let your little head lead your big head. Sex, while wonderful, is fleeting. Finding someone you can spend the rest of your life with is difficult, made even more so if you expect them to adapt to your ways. Every woman marries a man for what they like about him, hoping to change what they don't. A complete success at this makes for a miserable man, and a complete failure makes for a miserable woman. Two miserable people make a miserable marriage." She paused. "When two women gang up on a man, the women will win. Meg and her mother are two women. Think about it." And she left.

I'd had all the mothering I could take for one day, but the more I thought about it, Eunice's advice made me focus the most about what the future boded for me.

At 2000, the mate called us out for undocking, and by 2100, we were clear and stowed for sea.

Chapter 19

DAR ES SALAAM

*S*ailed *from Beira at 2000 hours on Saturday, 11/19/66. Cloudy skies. Temperature 78 degrees. Humidity 72 percent. Wind from the southwest at 4 mph. Calm seas. Destination: Dar es Salaam, Tanzania.*

We cleared the entrance buoy after dropping the pilot and changed course to 053 degrees. The captain set revolutions for 18 knots, with no need for extra nozzles. We stayed on 053 degrees for 369 miles and then altered course to 350 degrees and ran 306 miles until we were clear of Ilha Rongut. There, we altered course to 250 degrees and ran for 200 miles, keeping east of Mafia Island. At the northern tip of Mafia Island, we changed course to 345 degrees for twenty-two miles and then to 317 degrees for another twenty-two miles. Then, we went due west another nine miles to the pilot station. We entered the port of Dar es Salaam, Tanzania.

In the nineteenth century, Mzizima (Kiswahili for "healthy town") was a coastal fishing village on the periphery of Indian Ocean trade routes. In 1865, Sultan Majid bin Said of Zanzibar built another city abutting Mzizima and named it Dar es Salaam—literally, "the residence of peace." It is the largest city in Tanzania.

The city of Dar es Salaam came into its own when the German East Africa Company established a station there in 1887. The British captured German East Africa during World War I and renamed it Tanganyika.

Political developments, not the least of which was the growth of the Tanganyika African National Union, led to Tanganyika gaining independence in December of 1961.

Tanzania itself is a brand-new country, formed on April 26, 1964, when Tanganyika and Zanzibar signed an accord unifying the two nations under the name of Republic of Tanzania. Change was coming fast to Africa.

It was Tuesday, November 22, 1966, at 0600. It was hot, 88 degrees and steamy. Now, it felt like Africa, or at least what I envisioned Africa to be. We were into the short rainy season. April and May are the "long rains," and November and December are the "short rains." It is hot and humid all year round.

The pilot boarded, and we came into the harbor at slow ahead, doing 3 knots. The wind was from the west, and the combination of ship speed and opposing-wind speed created a wind effect of 10 mph. It was not enough to eliminate the sweat but enough to feel good on your face.

All I could smell were cloves. The entire harbor smelled of cloves. The water was clearer than in Lourenço Marques, because there was no river runoff. Anchorages were to our right and directly ahead. We passed a sharp point of land, Kigamboni, with three anchorage areas. Areas A, B, and C were ahead and to our starboard side, and anchorage area D was ahead and to port. The customs and immigration buildings were on the shoreline behind anchorage area C.

Clearing the headland of Kigamboni, we turned to port and headed for berth no. 3. The other three berths were occupied. Two tugs assisted us, and with only a light wind, they had no problem pivoting the ship and pushing us in portside to the berth, leaving only 50 feet at the bow and stern from the other ships. When we secured from mooring stations, I went in for breakfast.

The captain was in his office, meeting with the ship's agent and customs. Fran, the chief steward, occupied a corner table with immigration officials, checking off each crew member against the crew list. I got in line, checked in, and then sat and ordered bacon and eggs from Joey, the pantryman. The cook had gone overboard again on the fried onions, to the point that even Bernie Simpson, who never disparaged food, commented on the odor.

Tony had already eaten and was with the chief mate, getting instructions for the day's work. Bernie and Clara Simpson were pestering Fran, the chief steward, about getting a tour of the city, and Eunice sat by herself, drinking coffee and smoking, a Dunhill, same as the captain. Due to the heat and humidity, we kept the doors and ports in the crew quarters shut and the air-conditioning going full blast. I didn't mind the air-conditioning, but I disliked going back and forth from the heat outside to the cold inside. Because of the shut doors and the overbearing onions, the smell of cloves didn't penetrate. When my eggs and bacon arrived, I leaned close and inhaled, hoping to offset the odorous onions. The coffee acted as an olfactory overtone.

Halfway through my meal, Fran told the Simpsons that the agent had arranged for their tour. They would leave at 0900. This was the first time I had seen Bernie excited about something other than food. He showed it by thanking Fran profusely and spraying the food he was chewing over half the table. The man was a pig. When it happened, Clara lifted her hands back out of the way and gave him a look. Eunice, at the next table, just shook her head and dragged on the cigarette, blowing smoke imperiously into the air.

Soon after 0800, the chief mate came in, grabbed a cup of coffee, called to Joey the pantryman, ordered a bacon-and-egg sandwich, and then sat with me.

"Morning, William."

"Good morning, Dennis. How long do you expect us to stay in port?"

"Couple of days. The stevedore supervisor said they were busy, and we may lose a gang at noon to go to another ship. If we have to finish with one gang, then we could be here until Friday."

The labor situation in Dar es Salaam was far different from South Africa. There was a violent strike on the waterfront in 1948, but the labor movement didn't start until 1955. After Tanganyika and Zanzibar merged in 1964, the government disbanded all trade unions and created the National Union of Tanganyika Workers (NUTA) as the sole trade union in the country. This was a sham, since the union was controlled entirely by the government. As in South Africa, all the dockworkers were natives, but unlike South Africa, the supervisors were black.

Two gangs of longshoremen started work at 0800. One gang loaded cases of tea into the no. 4 upper-tween deck in the after end. The second gang loaded bags of cloves into no. 1 upper-tween deck in the forward end. When I came on watch at noon, Tony confirmed that we would only have one gang working in the afternoon. The chief mate decided to work no. 4 with the cases of tea. Standing on deck, I noticed that the aroma of cloves smothered all other odors. When I went into the hatch to check how the cases were stowed against the bulkhead, I could smell the tea. Leaning over a case, I inhaled deeply and promptly sneezed, evoking friendly laughter from the longshoremen. The tea had a strong, pleasant aroma.

Just as in Beira, the longshoremen wore drab, dusty coveralls, which were soon drenched in sweat. Unlike Beira, they didn't strip the coveralls to their waists but left them loose, open at the chest.

Using a six-foot-long tray, the dockworkers used a forklift to load a pallet of cased tea onto the tray and then hoisted it into the hatch. The cases were about eighteen inches square and had tin corner strengtheners. The winch operator would land the pallet in the middle of the hatch, and each man would grab a case and walk to the aft end and deposit it, building a wall across the after bulkhead.

When the wall reached head height, they started the next tier and repeated the process, progressing toward the center of the hatch. After erecting two tiers to head height, the third and fourth tiers were built to chest height. The next two tiers were one case lower. The seventh and eight tiers were knee-high, effectively creating steps. They then lay dunnage on the tiers to prevent damaging the cases when they stepped on them and walked up the steps with the cases, finishing the back tiers to the overhead and working their way out. With each two tiers finished to the overhead, they laid another two tiers knee-high. This brought them out to the edge of the hatch's square opening. By the time they knocked off at 1700 hours, they had filled in half of the space and still had a stairway the full width of the hatch from forward to aft. When they returned in the morning, they would climb the stairs again and fill in the spaces to end up with a solid stow.

Chuck relieved me at 1600 hours, and I beelined to the shower. When standing on deck and peering into the hatch; it had the same effect as standing in a sauna. My clothes were soaked within ten minutes.

At dinner, everyone who came into the salon smelled of or commented on the odor of cloves. The overpowering smell of the onions from this morning was now relegated to second place. As Dennis walked in, Eunice was sitting by herself; the captain's whereabouts were unknown. She asked him, "Will it smell this way for the rest of the trip?"

"Yes, ma'am, at least while in port. At sea, with the hatches closed, it won't be so bad."

Eunice wrinkled her nose, shook her head, and took a deep drag on the cigarette but didn't reply.

Missing were the Simpsons. Even when they had gone ashore before, they always came back in time for dinner. Sitting at their table was Mr. DeKuyper, eating meticulously, European-style—holding his fork in his left hand and his knife in his right and not switching after cutting his food. Eunice was staring at him, a slight smirk on her face.

Dennis sat and ordered. There was pot roast tonight—not bad—and the vegetables were fresh. "Any damages to the tea today, William?"

"No. They handled it pretty well. They built their stairway and stacked them well."

"Make sure they use dunnage as stepping boards before they climb the stairs. The exterior frames of the cases are strong but won't take the weight of someone stepping on them."

"They already did that. They were careful. I didn't see any broken cases. I'll tell Tony when I see him to keep an eye on them in the morning. He'll be on watch tomorrow when they start work."

In a lower tone, he said, "No, he won't. You will. I gave Tony the day off tomorrow." Glancing at Eunice, he said, "More 'escort' work for Her Highness."

I nodded. "Am I covering him tonight, too?"

"Nah, I'll take it."

"I don't mind. I'm not going anywhere."

Shrugging, he said, "Okay, I'll pop into town then and look around."

At 1900, standing on the bridge wing and leaning on the rail, struggling to light a soggy cigarette, I watched Tony leave, walking down the pier toward the gate. Half an hour later, a taxi pulled up to the foot of the gangway, and Eunice went down and got in, working her ass the full length of the gangway. Fifteen minutes later, Dennis and Mr. DeKuyper walked out to the gate, heading into town. I still hadn't seen the captain, so I went to the gangway watchman and asked him if the captain had gone ashore. He hadn't, or if he had, no one saw him go.

I headed below and found Chuck, the second mate, and told him I would relieve him early if he wanted to go ashore.

"Thanks, William. I'll take you up on that." He walked to his room to change. I felt like everyone was abandoning ship. Even though I was miserable missing Meg's company, it felt good to let the others get away and have fun.

After telling the gangway watchman that I would be on duty all night and would have a walkie-talkie with me if he needed me for anything, I went up to the chart room and worked on *Notice to Mariners* corrections, another favor to Chuck.

Two hours later, I was putting the charts back when the watchman called me and asked me to come to the gangway. I went down and saw Bernie and Clara Simpson arguing at the foot of the gangway. They were both drunk, he more than she. Indicating to the watchman to follow me, I walked down the gangway and inserted myself between them.

"Bernie," I said. "We're going to help you up the gangway and to your cabin."

He started to protest, and I interrupted, "I'll be sure and let the chief mate know if you cooperate with me." It implied bad news for Bernie if he didn't cooperate.

He nodded. "Yeah."

I told Clara to wait until I came back. Then, with me in front and the AB behind, we managed to get him into his room, leaving him flopped on his bunk.

Clara sat on the bottom platform, and I helped her up. She wasn't nearly as drunk as it first seemed, and she ascended the gangway under her own power, with me following behind.

At the top I asked, "Do you want to go to your room? I can get the key to Meg and Grace's cabin instead."

"Thanks, that would be good."

I got the key from Fran, the chief steward, explaining what I was doing, and he said he'd check on her later.

Unlocking the door, I let her in and handed her the key. She stood there, looking lost. "I would keep it locked. Fran said he'd check on you later."

"Thank you. This is the second time you've rescued me." She grabbed and squeezed both my hands.

"You're worth rescuing." I turned and left, pulling the door shut.

At midnight, I sat in the salon, drinking coffee and smoking, when Fran came in.

"You check on her?"

"Yes, she's fine. She thinks you're a saint." We both smiled.

"I checked on him, too. He's passed out but otherwise okay."

"Fran, you've been going to sea a long time. Is there a lot of this type of thing?"

"Among passengers, no. Among crew members, yes. I'm not a violent person, but there were times I really wanted to punch people in the nose, they behaved so badly." Standing, he said, "By the way, just for the record, you're no saint. But you are a pretty decent young man."

"Thank you, Fran. I take that as high praise, coming from you."

Smiling, he said, "Don't let it go to your head."

Dennis, Chuck, and DeKuyper came aboard around 0300. Dennis and Dekuyper were high, but Chuck was sober. Chuck changed clothes and relieved me, and I turned in.

At 0700, I was fortified by scrambled eggs, ham, and grits and working on my second cup of coffee, when Dennis came in to the salon, sat down with a thump, and ordered coffee from Joey and a glass of water. When he got the water, he took two aspirin, grimaced, burped, farted, looked at me, and said, "I'll be fine."

I told him about the Simpsons last night. Neither one had shown yet for breakfast, and he nodded.

"How many gangs today?" I asked.

"Don't know. We'll see when they show up. If it's only one gang, keep them at it in the no. 4 hatch, loading tea."

One gang showed up, and I directed them to work. I climbed down in the hatch with them to check on the dunnage laid across the tops of the cases they would step on. They followed the same pattern as yesterday, and everything proceeded well. When they broke for lunch, they had about two hours' work left to finish the hatch.

At lunch, Bernie Simpson resumed his trough status and was cramming ham-and-cheese sandwiches in his mouth, head lowered over the dish as if he was afraid he would lose a crumb. Clara was missing, and DeKuyper sat at the captain's table, eating toast and drinking tea.

Neither Tony nor Eunice had returned, and the captain still hadn't shown up. When Dennis sat down, I asked him if he had seen the captain since I hadn't seen him all night.

Shaking his head, he said, "No. I'll knock on his door after lunch."

Greg, the third engineer came in, waved, and said, "Understand you're working double duty." He raised his eyebrows and laughed.

I smiled, nodded, and returned to my sandwich.

Moving over from his regular spot into Tony's seat, he said, "It amazes me. The whole ship knows what's going on between Tony and the captain's wife, but everyone pretends it's nothing."

"Do you want to ask the captain what he thinks about it?"

Waving both hands, he said, "Uh-uh, not me. I'm just jealous of Tony. She is one sexy woman."

Addressing Dennis, he said, "Don't you think so, Dennis?"

Glaring at Greg, he replied, "Thinking can get you in trouble on subjects like this. Talking gets you in more trouble."

Waving his hands again, Greg replied, "Okay, I'll shut up."

"Good." Dennis returned to his coffee.

The one gang of longshoremen returned at 1300 hours and finished the hatch at 1515 hours. After shifting them into the no. 1 hatch to load bags of cloves, I went to the chief mate's office and asked him if they were going to secure the cargo of cased tea. The longshoremen had erected a wall that was ten feet high, and in any type of seaway, some were sure to fall over.

"We'll bring a gang of carpenters tomorrow to shore it up."

"Okay." I hesitated. "Did you check on the captain? I still haven't seen him."

Signaling me to close his door, I did, and he said, "He's in his cabin. He's been drinking and was out cold. The room reeked of gin. I've seen him drink before, but nothing like this. When he comes to, I'll see if I can find out what's going on, but I suspect Eunice pushed him too far, and this is how he's coping with it."

At 1600 hours, Chuck came up to the no. 1 hatch and relieved me. As I headed back for the house, I saw Eunice coming up the gangway. We reached the door to the house at the same time, and I opened it for her. She nodded and went in. I continued to the chief mate's room. Knocking on the door, I asked, "Dennis, you in there?"

"Yeah, come in."

I closed the door. "Eunice just came back. I haven't seen Tony yet."

"He's in his room. Got back an hour ago. Looks like he hasn't slept since he left here." He snorted in derision. "What a fuckin' mess."

"How's the captain?"

"Awake. He'll be fine. He was grumpy enough to seem normal, providing that bitch doesn't set him off again."

"Okay, I'm hitting the sack."

"Go ahead. You did good, kid."

Nodding my head, I left his cabin, went to my own, and crashed.

Nothing happened during the night watch, and I awoke at 0800 and went in for breakfast. Greg, Dennis, and I were the only ones there. Bernie Simpson passed me as I came in. Given the tone and topic of the last conversation we all had, no one spoke other than to say good morning.

When I came on watch at noon, I relieved Tony, who went and hid in his cabin. Eunice and the captain were at his table, neither one looking at or speaking to the other. Bernie and Clara sat together. She seemed chattier now, almost normal.

At 1245, I went and stood by the gangway, waiting for the longshoremen to return from lunch. Following the longshoremen up the gangway were six carpenters, carrying their tools. Once I saw that the longshoremen had settled in, finishing the bags of cloves, I went and watched the carpenters in the no. 4 hatch. They had already erected a wooden fence consisting of 4" x 4" uprights with one-inch-thick dunnage boards nailed horizontally to contain the cased tea. Now, they were stringing wire cable across the rear of the uprights to hold them in place. They attached the cables to turnbuckles which in turn clamped onto steel frames of the ship and stretched from one side to the other so that when they tightened the turnbuckles, the wires pulled the fence tight against the cases.

By the end of my watch, the carpenters had complete securing, the longshore gang had finished stowing the bags of cloves, and the chief mate decided they were tight enough in stow to not need securing. Chuck and I closed the hatches, and the bosun and crew dogged them down.

The sailing board had been set for 1900 hours so as to not mess up the meal hour. We sailed on time.

Chapter 20

⚬⟨∞∞∞⟩⚬

TANGA

Sailed from Dar es Salaam at 1900 hours on Thursday, 11/24/66. Overcast. 84 degrees with high humidity and a soft westerly breeze. Seas less than a foot high. We're bound for Tanga, Tanzania.

We had a choice of taking the inland channel, which had some shallow spots, or going out around Zanzibar and Pemba Island. Either way, it was a short run, so the captain chose the safer, offshore passage and set revolutions to make 15 knots.

Clearing the sea buoy, we set a course of 48 degrees for 27 miles, bringing us abeam of the flashing red light of Ras Makunduchi on the southeast corner of Zanzibar. Then, we altered course to 13 degrees for 87 miles, keeping 5 miles off the Pemba Island coast. Once we cleared Pemba Island, we altered course to 342 degrees and ran 56 miles to the ship channel entrance to Tanga Bay, with Yambe Island on the port side.

It was midnight. I had relieved Tony fifteen minutes earlier, checked the radar, and turned to go into the chart room when I saw the red light. It was the smoke detector, and it showed a warning in the no. 3 deep tank, starboard side. Immediately, I called the captain. He was on the bridge within three minutes.

"Mr. Connolly, reset the smoke alarm indicator, and see if it's a false alarm."

I reset it. Within five seconds, the red light came on again.

The captain said, "Mr. Connolly, roust out the bosun, and both of you go down the hold and check it out." Pausing, he said, "Take a walkie-talkie with you."

"Aye, aye, Captain."

Going below, I stopped at my cabin to get my flashlight and then woke up the bosun.

"Shit!" was his only comment after I explained the problem. He pulled on his pants and boots, grabbed his flashlight, and led the way to the manhole cover accessing the lower holds.

We climbed through the manholes and down the access ladders through the upper- and lower-tween decks and reached the manhole cover to the deep tank. The cover was an oval-shaped steel plate, thirty inches at its widest point, with two hinge bars at the back connected to the steel deck. At each side of the front on the cover was a U-shaped extension known as a retainer. A steel-threaded bar attached to the deck with a threaded ring on the top that acted as a turnbuckle (known as a "dog"), slid into the U-holes, and allowed the cover to be secured. I reached to undog the cover, but the bosun grabbed my arm.

"Don't." Kneeling down he placed his hand on the metal top of the cover. "Always check to see if it's hot. Don't want it to flame up in your face. Another thing: Loosen the dogs, but don't slip them off the retainers until after you've cracked the hatch. If there's pressure, the retainers will prevent the cover from flying up and hitting you."

Knowing I should have thought of that, I muttered, "Thanks, Boats."

His warning triggered memories of my fire training at the Boston Fire Department in my upper-class year at MMA. The instructor's comments on the last day of training were, "I don't care if you're 5 miles, 50 miles, or 500 miles at sea. If a fire breaks out, you can't call the fire department. If you do, you'll be talking to yourself. On board the ship, you are the first and only line of defense against fire, so you damn well better learn these lessons." The words were ringing in my ears.

We had to do two things on that last day. One: Escape from a cinder-block building, thick with smoke from tires burning inside it. Two: Stand in a circle of burning gasoline with another person and only a small CO_2 cylinder in your hand, and get both of you out of the circle. For problem number one, we had to remove our gas masks while inside the building. For problem number two, the "other person" wouldn't cooperate, and we had to carry them out while the observer kept pouring gasoline on the fire. They were valuable lessons in learning how to act in stressful situations.

Nodding, the bosun indicated with his hand that I should loosen the dogs. I backed them off four turns each, but the cover still sat on the rubber gasket. Looking at the bosun for guidance, he nodded, and I lifted the edge of the retainers. As soon as the cover cleared the rubber seal, thick, acrid smoke poured out, and I slammed the cover back down, coughing, tears running down my cheeks.

"Dog it," the bosun said, and I did.

Standing, I called the captain on the walkie-talkie but didn't get a response. There was too much steel between me and the bridge for the signal to get through. The bosun reached down to check how tight the dogs were and then said, "Let's go." He climbed up the ladder, me right on his tail, still coughing and blinking away tears. When I cleared the manhole at the lower-tween deck, he closed it and dogged it tight. We then continued to the main deck, and he dogged that manhole cover as well.

Pulling the walkie-talkie from its holster, I called the captain and told him what happened.

"You and Boats come to the bridge."

"Aye, aye, Captain." We went aft to the house and up to the bridge.

Addressing the bosun, the captain asked, "What do you think, Boats?"

Shaking his leonine head slowly, he said, "Not good, captain. There's something more than paper burning down there. That smoke was bad."

Nodding his head, the captain walked to the telephone and dialed the chief engineer. "Bill, we have a fire in the starboard side, deep tank in the no. 3 hatch. I'm going to release the CO_2 into the tank to see if we can suppress it." He listened to Bill's response, said "Okay," and hung up. Moving to the control panel, he threw the switch, which released CO_2 into the deep tank. He stared at the panel for a few seconds and then turned.

"Boats, open the hatch cover at the no. 3 hatch. The sea is calm, and we're only hours away from port, so it should be okay. Let's air out the hatch. That smoke could affect the cashews stored in the upper-tween deck."

Boats nodded and walked toward the door. "Make sure you hang the safety locks on the hatches when they're open. I don't want them slipping," the captain called after him. Boats grunted in return and kept walking.

I went to the head behind the chart room and rinsed my face, keeping my eyes open to clear the stinging. Back on the bridge, I checked the radar, saw no ship traffic, went out to the starboard wing, and visually checked all directions. Going back into the bridge, I asked the captain, who was standing inside the door at the starboard side and peering down at the deck, if he wanted me to turn on any deck lights for the bosun to work by.

"No, that will hurt our night vision."

I went back to the bridge wing and watched the bosun as he and the day-maintenance man undogged the securing lugs on the hatch. The clouds had cleared somewhat, and the moon, in a waxing-gibbous stage, splashed occasional shafts of moonshine across the deck.

The residual smoke in the hatch had drifted away. I still smelled it because it had clung to my hair and clothes, but the clove odor from the no. 1 hatch dominated once again.

When Chuck, the second mate, relieved me at 0400, I told him what occurred.

"Damn, it's a good thing it's in the deep tank. At least that's sealed and not in the open like the rest of the hatch. That could be a real shit storm!"

Leaving Chuck, I asked the captain, now out on the port bridge wing, smoking, if he wanted me to do anything before turning in.

"No, thank you, Mr. Connolly. We'll see what tomorrow brings."

"Good night, Captain."

"Good night."

Leaving my clothes outside my door in the net laundry bag, I took a shower and then turned in, thinking, "The bosun was nervous. I was shitting my pants, but the captain was cool as ice tonight. What a pro." I was fading off when it struck me. "We can't run away from a fire on board like you can on land. If you do, it means you're sitting in a lifeboat in the middle of the ocean." I fidgeted until dawn.

Tanga is the most northerly seaport city of Tanzania, close to the border of Kenya. It was originally a Portuguese trading post. The Sultan of Oman defeated the Portuguese around 1750 and controlled Pemba Island and Mombasa, Kenya. The town was a major hub of the slave trade until the Europeans abolished the slave trade in 1873. In 1891, the Germans bought the coastal strip of Tanzania from the Sultanate. The Germans developed a tram line within the city and built the Usambara railway. The production of sisal was the main economic driver in the early 1900s, which was interesting because sisal, a hemp-like fiber, was imported into Africa by the Dutch and British and Portuguese and grown commercially. Sisal was one of the first imports by Spain from Yucatan.

Tanga is a small, shallow-water port. The channel and anchorage range from 40 feet to 65 feet in depth, but there is only 12 feet of water at the cargo pier. We planned on loading bags of coffee at the anchorage, and the coffee would arrive in barges.

The captain anchored at 0730. When I entered the salon at 0800 for breakfast, Bernie and Clara Simpson were still there, nursing coffee, along with Eunice, who was smoking, and Mr. DeKuyper, who was drinking tea and reading a book. Bacon, eggs, and coffee had again relegated the aroma of cloves to second place, at least inside.

I expected a gang of longshoremen to be working, but nothing was happening. Chuck, the second mate, came in and told me the captain wouldn't allow any work in the no. 3 hatch until we knew the fire was under control. He planned on opening the manhole to the deep tank again at 1000 and checking on it. When he said the word "fire," Dekuyper picked up his head, and Bernie squealed "Fire? What fire?"

"Nothing to worry about," I said. "It's contained within the starboard-side deep tank, and we've flooded it with CO_2. It can't spread."

Just then, Fran, the chief steward, entered, and Bernie started to whine about going ashore.

"Mr. Simpson, we can get a small boat service to take you ashore, but if the wind picks up, you will have a problem similar to Ascension Island, when you fell overboard. Do you want to take that chance?"

Before Bernie could remonstrate, Dekuyper interjected, "I assure you, there is nothing in Tanga worth seeing. Certainly nothing worth taking a swim for."

Clara responded, "Thank you, Mr. DeKuyper. I think we'll stay aboard." Bernie glared at her but said nothing.

At 1000, I went to the no. 3 hatch coaming and looked into the hold. The bosun and day-maintenance man were loosening the securing dogs on the manhole cover. This time, they both wore oxygen-breathing apparatuses (OBA) to ensure they wouldn't be overcome by the smoke. The captain and chief mate stepped up beside me and peered down. When they cracked the cover, smoke poured out. The captain called down, "Any flames?"

The bosun shook his head no.

"Leave it open a few minutes, and see if it clears out."

The bosun waved at him, and he and the day man stepped into the hatch square. After an initial diminishing, the smoke grew heavy again.

"Shut it!" the captain yelled.

The day man jumped in and stepped on the cover to seal it, and he tightened the dogs.

"Set up fans, and blow the smoke out of the hatch," the chief mate ordered. Turning to the captain, he asked, "What now, Captain?"

"The milk powder is AID cargo, not worth salvaging. I'll have the chief engineer flood the deep tank. We'll have to deal with it in Mombasa."

"What about loading coffee here?"

"Order a gang for tomorrow morning. If anything is hot, it will cool off by then, and smoke won't be an issue."

Nodding, the chief mate walked off, followed by the captain.

After lunch, on watch, I checked the bearings to ensure that the anchor was holding and now had nothing to do for four hours. Dragging a stool out to the bridge wing, I put my feet up on the aft railing and lit a cigarette. This was the worst time.

The image of Meg, partly wrapped in sheets and giving me that come-hither look, hung like a billboard in front of me. I missed her so much, and not just the sex. I loved listening to her, the lilt of her voice, and the utter sincerity with which she addressed things. She was intense but not harsh. The way she held my hand with both of hers when deep in conversation. So unique, so Meg, and now, so distant.

Around 1430 hours, Clara Simpson came up to the pool deck and set up a lounge chair. I had waved at her earlier when she walked the ladders, a habit she adhered to every day. Since the incident when Bernie had hit her, a considerable burden and one which she planned on relieving herself of when they returned home, she had relaxed and seemed to be enjoying the trip.

Walking to the pool-deck door, I asked her if she wanted me to close the door, so she could have privacy.

"Thanks, but no. I need to get used to having young men look at me again." Her left hip was jutting, her hand on it.

She had lost at least twenty pounds, and with her belly and hips trimmer, her ample breasts were accentuated. "I don't think you need to practice. You'll have to beat them away with a stick. Besides, what makes you think young men ever stopped looking?" It was trite, but I knew she wanted to hear it. We had developed a reverse mother-son supportive relationship, the young man boosting the ego of the older woman. I had come to really like her. It seemed awkward at first, but we were buddies.

Doing a slow pirouette, arms akimbo, ending with an arching of her back, with her breasts prominent, she said, "Practice never hurts." Then, she burst out laughing, and I joined in.

"I better close the door," I said. "The eye strain is too much." I closed the door, hearing a soft, parting "Thank you."

The night watch passed uneventfully, and I slept in, passing up on breakfast. In the salon at 1100 hours, I was having coffee. The chief mate came in, grabbed a cup of coffee, and plopped down opposite me.

"What's the situation with the fire?" I asked.

"It's out. We opened the manhole cover at 0600 hours this morning. Other than some residual smoke, it was fine, so I opened the deep-tank cover, and we now have another swimming pool, this one filled with dirty milk."

"How you going to discharge it in Mombasa?"

"We'll pump it out and hope for the best. The plastic liner in the bags is what caused the acrid smoke. Most of the bags are still intact. If not, they'll be shoveling it into bins and dumping it ashore."

"How're the longshoremen doing loading the coffee?"

"Okay. I covered the deep tank to minimize the odor, and we'll keep the fans going in the hatch to dispel it. We're filling the entire lower-tween deck with coffee, and we need to keep it four feet away from the deep-tank openings."

"Got it. Anything else?"

"Nah. I'm just pissed off because it had to be someone's cigarette that smoldered and started the fire. The top tier of bags in the forward end were scorched. There wouldn't be enough oxygen to burn if it had been lower down. If the CO_2 had worked, we would have lost only about fifty bags. Now, it's all gone."

I relieved Tony when he came in for lunch.

"When is the last time you checked the anchor bearings?"

He gave me a stricken look.

In a lower tone, I asked, "You checked them, didn't you?"

He shook his head.

Getting up, I said, "I'll do it now."

The wind was minimal from the northeast, with no changes in the bearings. As I finished, Tony came on the bridge, followed by the captain, who went into the chart room.

Holding my finger to my lips, I whispered, "Nothing changed." Then, louder, I said, "I know you took them, but you forgot to enter the anchor bearings in the log, Tony."

"Thanks, William, that's why I came up." He went into the chart room and closed out the entry in the log.

I heard the captain say something but couldn't make it out. That it wasn't his usual stentorous tone told me he wasn't too upset with Tony.

The captain came out and went below, and I went in and logged in.

"Well? What did he say?"

"He said I need to keep my mind on important matters, regardless of distractions. I don't know if he was referring to the logbook or his wife, Eunice. It wasn't the words but the look he gave me. Weird."

The loading went fine. Working from a barge requires extra care since the barge can move as well as the ship. The mooring lines to the barge also need to be tended. The barges carried fenders to protect their hulls and those of the ship, but as the barge gets unloaded, it rises in the water, the lines slacken, and the barge drifts forward, aft or away, making it a moving target for the winch operator.

They used nets, and the longshoremen in the barge tossed bags into the net. The winch operator then brought the load aboard and dumped the net in the middle of the hatch. Two longshoremen then lifted a bag, and another man ran under it, trotting into a corner of the tween deck and dumping it on the growing pile. It was the exact same manner in which they loaded copra in Lourenço Marques. The plan was to load the entire perimeter of the lower-tween deck but to leave the square of the hatch open, so we'd have access to the lower hold in Mombasa.

When Chuck, the second mate, relieved me at 1600 hours, I told him the gang would knock off work at 1700 hours. No gang was ordered for the next

day, Sunday, but one gang would start again at 0800 on Monday. We anticipated finishing cargo operations Monday evening.

Sunday passed quietly, with my usual fantasies of me and Meg dominating
my mental musings. It wasn't made any easier when, in the middle of the
afternoon, Eunice sunbathed on the pool deck. She wore a bright-blue bikini
and had loosened the top as she lay facedown on the lounge chair, her breasts
bulging to the side, leaving little to the imagination. I paced a lot, and she
had her head turned toward the bridge. Of course, I looked at her every time
I came to the door separating the bridge and pool.

On one of the turns, she said, "William. Would you be so kind as to get
me some water?"

I figured, why not? She hasn't hassled me lately, so I may as well be polite.
"Sure. Be right back."

As I handed her the water, instead of reaching out, she rolled over, and the
bikini top slipped off. Imagination was no longer required. The puppies were
out of their pen, free to frolic.

"Oops," she said but made no effort to replace it, sipping the water instead. Standing two feet away, I couldn't take my eyes off her breasts. They
were magnificent. Finally, I raised my eyes to hers, and she said, "Thank you.
Your stare was a compliment. You can compliment me any time you want."
She lay back down.

I backed away, feeling the rising bulge in my pants. Closing the door to
the pool behind me, I leaned against the bulkhead, closed my eyes, and still
saw her nipples, jutting like ten-penny nails. It took all my willpower to not
go back through that door and bite them.

On Monday morning, it was raining, so we didn't open the hatches and start
work until 1030. Except for a deckhand slipping and falling overboard from
the small tugboat used to ferry the barges, tedium reigned. They finished
loading coffee at 1815. By the time the barge got away, it was 1900. The coffee
required no securing, so we weighed anchor at 1930 and sailed for Mombasa.

Chapter 21

MOMBASA

Sailed from Tanga at 1930 hours on Monday, 11/28/66. Light clouds. Temperature 83 degrees. Wind from the north at 10 mph and increasing. Dropped the pilot as we approached Yambe Island. Bound for Mombasa, Kenya.

Just clear of the northern point of Yambe Island, we set a course of 102 degrees for 7 miles to get us far enough offshore to ensure we were never closer than 5 miles to the coast. All coastlines have potential uncharted shoals, wrecks, or rocks, and this section of Africa has its share. Better safe than sorry. Altering course to 028 degrees, we ran for 37 miles. The captain set revolutions for 8 knots. With only 53 miles to cover, we were in no hurry. We then turned toward the coast and set a course of 342 degrees for the remaining 9 miles to the harbor entrance.

Mombasa is an island separated from the mainland by Tudor Creek on the north and Kilindini Harbor on the south. Kilindini means "deep" in Swahili, and the harbor is 35 to 45 meters deep. No one knows the exact founding date, but it was already a prosperous trading town by the twelfth century. It was a center for trade in gold, ivory, and spices in the premodern era and a key link in the Indian Ocean trading networks.

Vasco da Gama was the first known European to visit Mombasa in 1498. He was not well received. The Portuguese sacked the city two years later. Perhaps the inhabitants of Mombasa were prescient when Vasco da Gama first arrived. Between 1528, when the Portuguese attacked again, and 1826, there was ebb and flow of rule between various Sultans and the Portuguese. In 1887, administration of the city was ceded to the British East Africa Association, and in 1898, the Sultan of Zanzibar formally presented the town to the British.

The population of Mombasa, about two hundred thousand people, is diverse, with a smattering of Dutch, Portuguese, British, and other European nationalities, but native Africans, Swahili and Mijikenda, are predominant. The Brits run the country and are the upper class. English is the language of convenience used by all businesspeople.

The pilot boarded at 0600 hours, and we made our way into Kilindini Harbor. There was no predominant smell here; there was a mix of pleasant and unpleasant aromas, depending on the wind and location in the port. With the wind being from the east, there was a mélange of salt air, jungle, cloves from the no. 1 hatch, jungle rot, and diesel fuel. The water was clearer than in Beira, Mozambique. The creek created less silt than two rivers but was dirtier than Lourenço Marques in Mozambique, which also had two creeks but less water flow, as it was closer to the open ocean and salt water. We tied up by 0730 at berth no. 4, starboard side to the pier. The chief mate insisted we dock starboard side so that the dripping and slop from the flooded powdered milk wouldn't drop onto the powdered milk in the port-side deep tanks when they discharged it.

At breakfast, the chief mate explained that we would start discharging at 1300 hours. The local agent had screwed up and had not ordered the gangs for an 0800 start. One gang would start unloading the powdered milk from the no. 3 port-side deep tank. The second gang would load bagged cement into the no. 2 lower hold, forward end. When they finished the cement, they would shift to the no. 2 lower-tween deck aft and load bales of sisal. The third gang would load cases of tea into the no. 4 lower-tween deck in the center of the hatch, between the previously loaded tea from Tanga and Dar es Salaam.

"What's happening with the flooded deep-tank milk?" I asked.

"Nothing yet. A cargo surveyor should be here sometime today or tomorrow. Until the surveyor looks over the cargo, nothing can move."

Tony leaned in and asked, "Are we still going on the safari?"

Dennis glanced over his shoulder at the Simpsons and nodded. "Tell you later."

Mr. DeKuyper came in, nodded at the Simpsons, walked up to Dennis, and clapped him on the shoulder. "Well, old boy, I'll be leaving you here. I've got a van coming for me at 1100. I've enjoyed the trip. Could have done without the seasickness, but you and the crew have been quite pleasant."

Standing, Dennis shook DeKuyper's outstretched hand and said, "The pleasure was all ours. We've enjoyed your company."

Before he could stop himself, Tony blurted out, "You're leaving? What about the safari?" The look Dennis gave Tony shriveled his shorts.

There was a moment of silence, and then Bernie Simpson barked, "Safari? What safari?" When no one responded, he repeated, "What safari?"

Dennis replied, "It's a crew-only trip."

"Why?" He was indignant now. "Why crew only? I want to go. Is he going?" he asked, pointing at DeKuyper.

"No, Mr. DeKuyper is not going. He helped arrange the trip."

"Well, I want to go. I'm a passenger. That's the same as a crew member."

"You'll have to take that up with the chief steward," Dennis responded.

"Well, I certainly will." Bernie rose and stormed out of the salon.

Later that morning, when Mr. DeKuyper was ready to leave, I had nothing else to do, so I offered to help carry his bags and guns down to the foot of the gangway.

Standing there, he asked me, "Are you serious about Meg O'Brien?"

"Yes, I am, but what makes you ask?"

"Meg's had four years in the United States, perhaps long enough to consider living there. Her mum, Grace, on the other hand, is as South African as you can get. If Meg leaves, there'll be an awful rift between mother and daughter, and as a Yankee friend of mine once said, you don't want to be the ham in that sandwich."

"Yeah, I know. It's been on my mind a lot. No offense, but I don't know if I could live in Durban."

"No offense taken. There are things I don't like about my country, but I'm part of it; you're not. The bloody apartheid is tearing us apart, and I don't see that ending well." He paused and then said, "Never you mind. I'm sure things will work out for you."

The van arrived, covered in reddish-gray dust and belching diesel fumes. We loaded his bags into it. Shaking my hand, he said, "Tell Dennis I'll return Friday to see everyone off on the motor safari."

"I will." He climbed in, and they left. As I walked up the gangway, I thought, "That's two people now who have warned me about getting between Meg and Grace O'Brien."

At 1300, the longshoremen trooped aboard. The gang at the no. 2 lower hold loaded bags of cement from the British Portland Cement Company Bamburi production plant. The Bamburi plant had been operating since the early 1950s. Shipments of bagged cement had been limited since the onset of bulk shipments from the redeveloped pier at English Point, opposite Mombasa's Old Harbor.

The gang in the No. 4 upper-tween deck laid rolls of paper over the pepper stored in the forward end of the deck to segregate the cased tea and minimize any tainting of one by the other. Tea loaded in the aft end would fill the remaining space in the hatch.

The gang in the no. 3 port-side deep tank stacked the bags of powdered milk onto two pallets placed on a large tray. When the winch operator lifted the tray to the pier, the dock crew took the pallets off the tray with forklifts, and the cycle would repeat.

The afternoon passed with no incidents, and Chuck relieved me at 1600 hours. I took a shower and wrote a few lines in the log I had started. It had started as a letter to Meg but evolved into a diary/log. I intended to give it to her when we called back at Durban and start another one. It was easier for me to write about daily events in a logbook fashion, even with the intimate details of my feelings, than to do so in letter form.

Entering the salon for dinner, the odor of fried onions, the chef's favorite concoction, smacked me in the nose. This time, he had used them to smother a meatloaf—cruel and unusual punishment for innocent pieces of beef and pork.

I ordered the meatloaf from Joey, the pantry steward, and pleaded with him to minimize the onions. He was semi-successful. The mixed carrots and green beans, canned, since both are difficult to get in Africa, weren't bad with butter, salt, and pepper. Scraping the residual onions to the side, I dug in. Two bites later, Fran, the chief steward, came in, pursued by Bernie Simpson.

"Why can't I go on the safari? I'm a guest on this ship, and I should be able to do whatever you do."

Fran, until this point poised and unperturbed by Bernie's histrionics, stopped, faced Bernie, and said, "Can you create a menu? A work roster? Stitch a cut? Order stores and supplies? Hmmm? Then, it's clear you can't do whatever I can do."

My head snapped up, and so did that of Clara Simpson, who was already at her table.

Fran continued, "You and Mrs. Simpson may not go with the crew. Besides, there is only one opening. I am having the local agent see if he can book another safari for the both of you."

"If there's one opening, I'll go. She," he said, pointing his thumb at Clara, "can stay here."

Fran took a deep breath. "Mr. Simpson. You may not go as part of the crew's safari. Do you or do you not want to still go if I can book you a separate tour?"

Clara interjected. "I don't want to go." Glaring at Bernie, she said, "I've seen enough wild animals."

"Well, I want to go, so get me booked," snapped Bernie, and he walked out of the salon.

Fran walked over to Clara, bent over, and softly said, "I apologize for my rude behavior."

Touching his forearm, Clara smiled. "Don't worry, Fran. Bernie has a way of attracting rudeness."

Fran nodded and left, rolling his eyes as he went past.

Since Chuck was covering for both Tony and me over the weekend, we gave him Wednesday off, and he went shopping downtown. Returning late that afternoon, he showed us the statuettes he had bought at the local native market: two iron-wood figures of Masai warriors, armed with spears, two feet tall; an ironwood mask; and three smaller figurines he said were ebony but looked to be ironwood.

"It's interesting," Chuck said. "The market is across the street from real ritzy stores and is set up like an open-air flea market at home. Villagers bring their wares to the city in the morning and set up, but with them, there is no tomorrow."

"What do you mean?" Tony asked.

"When I got there around 1000 hours, these warriors," he said, pointing to the Masai statuettes, "were ten dollars each. I didn't want to lug them around all day, so I decided I'd buy them later. When I went back at 1530, they were closing up shop."

"How much were the warriors?"

"One dollar each. I wasn't going to argue, but I didn't want to cheat them, either. I must have looked perplexed because a tall black man in a suit and tie with a British accent and a bass drum voice was also shopping, and he explained it."

"Explained what?" Tony persisted.

"They believe they are here today, with no assurance of tomorrow. A dollar in hand today is better than nothing. At the end of every day is a fire sale. I told the Brit that I felt as if I was cheating them.

"He replied, 'Did you ask them to lower the price to one dollar?'

"No. I said."

'You cannot cheat someone if you agree to the price they are asking. Here, it is one dollar, is it not?'

"Yeah, you're right. I said, and thanked him.

"He said, 'You're welcome' then bestowed a great smile on me.

"Hell, of a deal, eh?"

Also on Wednesday, the cargo surveyor arrived midmorning and inspected the soggy mess in the starboard deep tank. He took less than five minutes to determine that the cargo was a total loss. During the discussion with Dennis, the chief mate, he pointed out that the date of manufacture on the bags was two years old. Powdered milk can go bad after a year, turning hard and yellow.

"It smells sour down there in the tank. Even if the dry milk hadn't turned bad, adding the water made it milk, and that won't last more than five days, even when refrigerated. The sooner you get rid of it, the better."

Dennis grunted. He had Tony track down the stevedore supervisor, and they discussed the best way to discharge the mess. The supervisor went on deck and called down to the men in the port deep tank. Two men from the gang climbed into the starboard side. They lowered a pallet into the opening, and the men tried to lift and stack bags onto the pallet. Every other one broke or shredded, so they gave up and returned to discharging the port deep tank.

Back in the salon, drinking coffee with the chief mate, the stevedore supervisor suggested they use tilting buckets—three-cubic-yard bins hinged on pivots so they could be unlocked and dumped after being filled. They could lift and throw the bags, broken or otherwise, until they had dug a hole in the cargo deep enough to lower the bin into and then push the bags into it, working their way back and forth along the edges. On the pier, they would bring in dump trucks and dump the bins into them.

"I can't think of anything better," Dennis said. "Can we start in the morning?"

"It depends on whether we can get dump trucks. They're not standard stevedore equipment," he said, laughing.

Friday was the earliest they could get the dump trucks, and they could only work from 0700 to 1200 each day. That ensured we would not have to rush back from our weekend safari. By Thursday night, the port deep tank was empty of powdered milk, the cement bags and the cased tea finished. That left the sisal to load in the aft end of the no. 2 lower-tween deck and the damaged milk to discharge.

Friday morning after breakfast, I stood at the forward rail of the flying bridge and peered down at the longshoremen struggling with the soggy bags of powdered milk. As soon as they starting to dig out a hole to place the tilting bin into, the odor of sour milk rose, bilious, stronger than the smell of cloves in no. 1 hatch.

The longshoremen had stripped off their coveralls and wore tattered shorts and knee-high rubber boots. Within minutes, they were streaked with milk stains. It took a half hour to dig out a hole big enough for the tilt bin to fit into; then, they slid the bags, whole or in pieces, into the bin. They worked their way around the perimeter of the tank opening. By noon, they had managed to remove one-eighth of the cargo. At this rate, we would be in port until at least the next Thursday.

In the salon during a coffee break, Dennis said, "I asked the stevedore if they could get a shore crane that could handle a clam bucket. That will be a lot faster."

"When will you know?"

"Not until Monday morning. If they can get one, they'll show up with it. They also said they won't work Sunday because they can't get enough dump trucks, so I sure hope they get that crane."

Chapter 22

THE LODGE

At noon on Friday, Dennis, the chief mate; Fran, the chief steward; Tony, the other third mate; Greg, the third engineer; Bill, the chief engineer; and I trudged down the gangway, carrying light overnight packs. Pieter DeKuyper greeted us at the door of the small fifteen-passenger bus that would take us to the safari lodge.

Bernie Simpson left earlier to join up with a group of tourists going to the same safari lodge. Clara stayed behind on the ship.

As we settled into our seats, before the bus pulled away, Pieter asked, "Does everyone have their passport? We'll cross into Tanzania, and every once in a while, the border guards ask to see them." There were affirmative nods and grunts from everyone, and Pieter signaled to the bus driver to go.

Dennis asked Pieter, who was standing in the aisle, "Are you coming with us? I thought you had business to attend to?"

"I am, and I do. It turns out the hunt organizer I was to meet here is up at the lodge, evaluating it as a base camp for hunts. I'll meet him there."

"That's great."

"I had the boys stock in a few treats for the ride. You'll find beer and water in the cooler in the back and sarmies and crisps in a box."

"What's a sarmie?" Tony called from the back.

"You Yanks call them sandwiches."

"Oh. What are crisps?"

"Potato chips," Dennis chimed in.

Pieter continued, "It's 278 kilometers to where we're going. Stateside, that would be a three-hour trip. On African roads, it'll take us about seven hours. We'll be going through the towns of Samburu, Mwatate, and Taveta in Kenya and then cross the border to the town of Moshi in Tanzania. That's when we go from tarmac to dirt roads. We should reach Moshi by 1600 hours. Questions? No? Good. Enjoy the trip." And he sat down.

The bus was air-conditioned—a rarity, according to Pieter—and a blessing on the Tanzanian leg of the trip because without it, the ride was on dusty roads with the windows open.

The highways in Kenya were in decent condition, and we averaged 45 mph. Crossing the border, all the border guards did was accept a gratuity from the driver and wave at us as we rolled by. The road condition deteriorated, and we slowed to 35 mph. At Moshi, we stopped for gas and for the guests to relieve themselves. There was a restroom at the gas station that was clean. When Greg commented on it to Pieter, he gave him a stern look.

"They're natives, not savages. They make a living from tourists and have learned what the tourists want."

We turned north, and within two miles of leaving town, we drove on dirt roads. There was no one ahead of us, which was good, because the cloud of dust the bus kicked up blocked our rear view completely. In five miles, we struggled on rutted-dirt tracks, with an occasional dilapidated bridge offering a risky crossing. At the third bridge, the driver steered off to the side, away from the bridge, and went down the shallow bank, heading for the river.

Dennis tapped Pieter on the shoulder. "Why isn't he using the bridge?"

Pieter seemed unperturbed, but he rose and went to the driver. When he returned, he told Dennis, "The bus is too big for the bridge. It won't hold our weight. The river is shallow here, so we'll ford it."

As we inched our way across the river, I looked at the underpinnings of the bridge. The metal beams were rusted and corroded, and at least every other one of the wooden trestles was missing or warped. The driver made a good choice to ford the river. As we crossed, the water never rose above the axles. I glanced around for signs of crocodiles or hippos but saw only boulders and mud banks.

Dennis, Greg, and Pieter struck up a three-way conversation. The rest of us were silent, listening. Greg had apologized to Pieter for his remark about the restrooms, and Pieter had launched into a lecture about foreign visitors, whether hunters or tourists, always presuming that every native was a cannibal or headhunter and never giving enough credit to them for their roles in African society.

"Greg, you're a black fellow. I was a bit surprised you asked the question rather than one of the others."

Dennis interjected. "I felt the same way, Pieter. I expected primitive conditions and was surprised at how modern and clean the restrooms were."

Wagging his long index finger in the air, he said, "I was raised under apartheid but lived out in the bush. In the bush, nature is your enemy, not the natives. My father, a stern, religious man, made me understand early on to accept people as God's creations. Look for the similarities, not the differences. When you're tracking lions or water buffalo in deep grass, the man beside you with better eyesight and hearing is your best friend, color be damned."

Greg asked, "Did your father ever get in trouble with the authorities because of his views on apartheid?"

"A few times, but since we lived away from the cities and most of the local white folks sympathized with my father's views on the problems of apartheid, it was only when we had visitors from Cape Town that the issue arose."

"Was he ever arrested?"

"Arrested, no. Detained, yes—twice. Once by a visiting constable who held him in jail over a weekend. After a night of drinking with our local chief constable, the visitor decided to forget everything. The second time, he was locked up overnight in the storage shed of that same chief constable, a good friend. The chief constable knew there was an inspection party due from Cape Town consisting of constables and political administrators. He knew my father well enough to know he might start a 'debate' with the visitors that could land him in serious trouble, so he locked him away for the night."

"Was your father mad at the chief constable?" Greg asked.

"Angry enough to call him a traitorous bastard." He laughed as he remembered. "My father never cursed, so hearing those words leap from his tongue shocked me. It took him a month before he forgave the chief."

The conversation died off as first Fran and then the rest of us rummaged through the cooler and boxes for sarmies and chips. Getting to and from the cooler was a feat, due to the bouncing of the bus on the rugged surface. Sitting in the seat, a water bottle between my thighs, the first bite I took of my sarmie ended up in my left eye as the bus jounced. I had to rinse the oil out of my eye before I could eat the sarmie. After two more hours and three bridges, all groaning in protest at the weight of the bus, we reached the lodge.

Only two stories high, the lodge occupied a low escarpment, overlooking a pond off to the right as one looked outward from the veranda. The side of the pond facing the lodge had little vegetation, but there were heavy undergrowth and stubby trees on the far side. Fed by springs and runoff from Mount Kilimanjaro, it was a watering hole for wildlife.

We arrived at dusk. Instead of going directly to the front entrance, the driver turned right and crept along a rutted track leading to the side of the building. When he stopped the bus, he stood, put a finger to his lips, and said, "You must be quiet, please. The animals are at the waterhole, and voices will frighten them. Follow the lady into the lodge, and she will explain everything once inside."

The last one off the bus, I paused and gawked. Even though it was dusk, the colors were muted but discernible. The veranda ran the full width of the building, which was faced with reddish stone, the line broken by the steps leading to the driveway turnaround in front. The structure faced south, with the pond to the right, and I could see the red-and-gold remnants of the sun painting the clouds. The stunning view of Mount Kilimanjaro, its snow cap perched daintily atop its rocky shoulders, rose behind and to the west of the lodge. I stood there, absorbing nature at its best. Sounds filtered in, the chirrup of birds, the chatter of monkeys, the faint yipping bark of a zebra, and as

I started up the steps, the trumpet of an elephant, already watered and leaving before the predators arrived, split the air.

Inside, a large reception room with a small desk and chair in the corner greeted me. The walls were panels of dark mahogany. Remnants of their luster still clung to them. Three miniature chandeliers with electrified faux candles dangled from the ten-foot-high plaster ceiling. The floor was stone, similar to blue stone and rough, not made for high heels. The guys from the ship, Pieter, and two ladies (obviously sisters because they looked so alike, one in a green dress and the other in yellow) gathered around the desk. The trim sisters had an athletic build, aquiline noses, and curly hair. The only difference was in the color of their hair. The woman in the green dress was a blonde, and the hair of the woman in the yellow dress had run to gray.

"Welcome, everyone," the woman in the green dress said. "I'm Gerta. This is my sister, Frieda. We're the proprietors of the lodge, and we're glad you're visiting us." She had not a trace of an accent, German or otherwise. "Please sign the guest book, take your key, and take one of the cards on the table. The card lists the rules of your stay here." Holding up her hands, she said, "Before you complain about having rules, please understand the rules apply to the outside areas where you may come in contact with wildlife. Here, inside the lodge, you may be as wild as you want." This evoked a few chuckles. "But outside, the animals rule the kingdom, and you are guests in their world. While not an official wildlife preserve we observe all the same rules set by the Park Service of Tanzania." She looked at us; no one asked a question, so she pointed at the desk, and we lined up.

I was last in line. Gerta, off to the side, engaged in earnest conversation with Pieter. Leaning into Greg, in front of me, I said, "I wonder if that one was his wife."

Before Greg could reply, a voice floated over my shoulder. "No, that was my mistake. Gerta is the smart one in the family."

Turning, I faced Frieda. "I'm so sorry," I said. "That was rude of me to talk about your personal matters."

She laughed, a beautiful lilt similar to Meg's. "You're turning red," she said, touching my cheek. "Don't be embarrassed; it's ancient history. We get along with each other quite well, considering Pieter was so randy and rash in his youth." Patting my cheek again, she said, "I liked the randy part." She arched her eyebrows. "It was the rashness that did him in."

Reaching out her hand, she said, "I'm Frieda, and you are?"

Shaking hands, I replied, "I'm, William, William Connolly."

By this time, Greg had signed in. As he turned away from the desk, Frieda stepped up and introduced herself to him and steered him away toward the door. I signed in, picked up my card, and followed them into a twenty-by-twenty-foot room with a bar at the far end.

A buzz of conversation guarded the door, confronting each entry but allowing everyone in. Besides our group, there were twelve other folks, including Bernie Simpson. As I moved toward the bar, Bernie interrupted DeKuyper and Gerta by pointing to Gerta and saying, "You're in charge here, aren't you?"

"Yes, sir; along with my sister, I am."

"I'm hungry. When do we eat?"

DeKuyper took a step toward Bernie, but Gerta raised her hand and said, "We've prepared a light meal for those of you who arrived late. We have the buffet set up right around the corner in the next room."

Without a thank-you, Bernie turned and walked into the next room. Dennis, along with everyone else in the room, had overheard the conversation. "Miss Gerta, I apologize in advance for that," He continued, struggling with the word. "Man."

Chuckling, she said, "My dear man, he is not the first rude guest we have encountered, and I am sure he won't be the last, but thank you for your sympathies." Turning to the center of the room, she announced, "Ladies and gentlemen, *mesdames et messieurs!*" Pausing for quiet, she continued, "We have a buffet set up in the room beyond." She pointed. "There is no rush. Please relax, and have a drink or two. I remind you, though, there is a 4:30 wake-up call for the morning if you wish to see the animals at the watering hole. For those who are on motor safari tomorrow, the wake-up call is at 3:30 in order to be on site at dawn."

Turning to a member of the other group, she asked, *"Est-ce que je dois le repeter en francais?"*

"Non, madame, merci beaucoup mais tous comprennent l'anglais."

"Good. My French needs help."

In a decidedly French accent, he replied, "You did well, Madame Gerta."

As people drifted into the next room, I stood next to the Frenchman at the bar. "Hello," I said, offering my hand. "I'm William."

"I am Jean Paul," he said, shaking my hand gently.

"Are you a tour guide?"

"I am. I work from Mombasa and Dar es Salaam, depending on where the tourists arrive."

"Did Mr. Simpson come with you today?"

"Ah, Simpson, *oui*, yes. He was added to the group late. The others are all from France, on a tour of Africa. From here, I return them to Dar es Salaam, and another guide will take them onward."

"I hope Mr. Simpson behaves himself."

He gave a Gallic shrug and a noncommittal sideways movement of his head.

"He's a passenger on our ship, but we wouldn't let him come with us."

This drew a smirk. "I think I know why."

"Sorry. Can I buy you a drink?"

"Merci, but no. I am awake early. *Bon soir."* And he left.

The light buffet held roast beef, ham, Muenster cheese, weiner schnitzel, three varieties of potatoes, salad, four types of bread (the best of which was a rich, dark pumpernickel), cheesecake, and German chocolate cake. I made a slab sandwich of the pumpernickel and roast beef and took a huge slice of chocolate cake.

People sat, scattered at six different tables. I noticed Greg with Frieda and Fran, our chief steward. Frieda felt an immediate kinship to him when she found out his occupation. Bill and Tony were with three folks from the French tour. Bernie sat by himself at the furthest table. I opted to join two guys and two girls from the French tour group.

"Hello. May I join you?"

The guys hesitated, but both girls said, "Oui, *certainment.*" One of them moved to make room for me at the table.

"Merci," I said, and I sat down between the girls.

"*Parlez-vous francais?*" one guy asked.

"I just did. I'm afraid that's about it; sorry."

One guy and both girls laughed. The look from the guy who asked dripped acid.

Their names were Luc, Andre, Elain, and Yvonne. We chatted for half an hour, with Yvonne finding a number of reasons to place her hand on my thigh. It may have only been a spontaneous reaction by her, but my state of abstinence brought an immediate overreaction. When they got up to leave, I told them I was going to just relax a bit. In reality, I had to wait for my overreacted member to fade before I stood up. When I got up, the only ones left in the room were Greg and Frieda. She waved at Greg, telling him to stay while she instructed one of the staff cleaning up. I said good night and then realized I didn't know where my room was. "Frieda, excuse me, but where is my room?"

"Through that door and up the stairs. All the rooms are on the second floor."

"Thanks. Good night."

Through the door and up the stairs, the hallway was plain; I had expected something more exotic. I found my room at the far end of the hall. The old-fashioned skeleton key turned with ease, and I entered a culture warp. In front of me, a mural of the jungle, replete with exotic birds and a boa hanging from a tree limb, a la the Garden of Eden, covered the wall. The left wall held a pride of lions in the distance, resting with a bright sun shining on them. A mosquito net hung from the ceiling and draped itself around a four-poster bed. The posts were hand-carved teak, and on the footboard, a carving of five hyenas was frightening to behold. The detail was extraordinary.

Continuing around the bed, I saw another mural on the far-right wall depicting a cave entrance, with the door to the bathroom in the center of the entrance. The bathroom held only a toilet and basin sink. Nothing exotic there—just the necessities.

Only after I crawled into bed did I notice that the headboard had two naked women in a shallow carving. The women were embracing each other. Instead of being salacious, there was something maternal and loving about the scene. I thought, "I'm young and horny; I have two naked women with me in bed, and I think it's maternal and loving." The artist must have been a genius to make me think that. I drifted off, not sure if I would be awakened at 3:30 or 4:30.

Chapter 23

SAFARI

At 0330 hours, there was a gentle tapping at the door. Today was safari day. I stretched, took another lingering look at the two women carved into the headboard, thought about Meg, and sighed. The windows were open, and the distant night sounds of the jungle percolated in—the chirping of birds, the sloughing of something in the brush, the gabble of monkeys in the trees—all wrapped in a fragrance of mountain gladiolus and impatiens kilimajari. These two were the dominant flowers in what is known as the forest zone, extending from 800 meters up to 2,800 meters in elevation.

I took a deep breath, rose, and went to the bathroom. After dousing my face and shaving with hot water, I followed the aroma of roasting coffee down to the buffet room, where I found our group, except for Greg, drinking coffee and eating Danish pastries.

"Where's Greg?" I asked Dennis.

Looking around, he shrugged. "I don't know. I hit the bunk before he did."

As I poured my coffee, Frieda, now wearing a loose-fitting shirt, khaki pants, and trail boots, walked in, followed by Greg. She addressed us while Greg got coffee. "Good morning, everyone. I hope you all slept well. In fifteen minutes, you will board the bus for the trip into the bush. Please be as quiet as possible when leaving and after you arrive on site. The animals are used to the bus and its engine noise, but they don't react well to the sound of human voices."

She paused to see if there were questions. "There's bottled water and box lunches on the bus. I suggest you use the toilet now. There are no facilities in the bush, and squatting down in lion country is not recommended." The last was said with a wry smile.

Dennis and Fran headed for the bathroom. Inching up beside Greg, I said, "Hey, the last thing I saw last night and the first thing I see this morning is you with Frieda. Get lucky?"

Flustered, so different from his usual, calm demeanor, he stared at his coffee cup and said nothing.

"Wow, I was half kidding. Now, I'm jealous." That evoked a grin from him.

"She's a very interesting lady," he said. "Don't embarrass her with any stupid comments, please."

"I won't. I promise. Not another word from me."

Dennis and Fran returned, and Frieda herded us toward the side-door exit, the same way we had entered last night. She stopped us at the door and said, "Joseph is your guide, your driver, and your host. He is in charge. Please pay attention to him."

Treading softly, we boarded the open-top Volkswagen minibus with seating for twelve. It was fitted with handrails along the edge of the open roof line so that anyone standing up could maintain balance. Standing in the aisle, I found that my head and shoulders stuck above the roof line.

Frieda, who had boarded the bus last and stood beside the driver, introduced us to Joseph, a tall black man dressed in safari shorts and shirt, wearing sandals. She wished us a fun trip and then went back into the lodge.

Joseph closed the bus door and rolled out of the driveway. We all peered out the windows, expectant, curious, and in my case, excited. Once away from the lodge, Joseph told us what we should expect, but there was no guarantee that we would see any animals. He explained that once we got to what he called the "sanctuary area," we would roam the dirt tracks and try to get close to the animals, but he could not leave the tracks and chase the animals into the bush.

At 0445, with the sky lightening, we parked on a dusty trail, engine running, with patches of prairie and elephant grass to our left. A savanna-type jungle with tight trees, but not wet, as a rain forest would be, was ten yards to our right.

"Look," he whispered, pointing left and front. "Lions." It took a minute, but we spotted a small pride of eight lions, all female with two cubs, just starting to stretch and rise from their sleeping spots, their rictus grins evolving into yawns. The cubs were big enough to be weaned from their mother and seemed intent on pestering two of their aunts, who put up with their antics for a few minutes before wandering off.

Standing at the back of the roof opening, I had my eight-millimeter movie camera out and running, hoping there was enough light to catch the scene. So intent were we on the lions that Joseph surprised us by slamming the bus into gear and starting down the road. I made a grab for the handrail and avoided falling. Greg and Bill, both standing in front of me, weren't so lucky. Greg landed flat on his back at my feet, and Bill crashed into me, butting me in the groin with his head before flopping face first onto the floor.

Despite the pain of Bill's head butt, at the trumpet of the elephant, I turned and looked toward the jungle. A bull elephant with huge tusks, gray but stained with red dust, was thundering toward the bus. He came out of the jungle eighty yards behind us and chased us down the road, screaming in rage, warning us to stay away from his turf. He had closed to thirty yards before Joseph got the bus up to speed.

Camera fixed on the elephant, I yelled, "How fast are we going?"

Dennis, recovered and hunkered down right behind Joseph, answered, "About twenty-five."

"Slow down; let him get closer." And to my delight, Joseph slowed down to where the elephant was only ten yards behind us. It didn't last long. Giving another threatening trumpet, the elephant stopped and glared at us. Joseph also stopped but kept a fifty-yard space, just in case. When the elephant rushed a few steps forward, Joseph moved the bus forward again, and then it was over. The elephant stopped, took two steps, trumpeted, and turned back into the jungle. Joseph put the bus in neutral but left the engine running.

Everybody talked at once until Joseph reminded us to be quiet. We had traveled a quarter mile down the track, and now the lions, who had ignored all our activity, were behind us to the left.

"Look," Joseph said, pointing to the left and a little ahead of the bus. "Eland."

An eland is a large, tan antelope with spiral horns, the male darker than the female. The males weigh up to 2,100 pounds and the females up to 1,300 pounds. They are slowest of the antelopes, with a top speed of 25 mph, but they can't maintain that speed for long. They can jump over nine-foot-high fences.

Putting the bus in gear, Joseph started forward. "How many lions do you see?" he asked.

Looking back, I said, "Just one and the two cubs."

"We will get closer to the eland. I believe the lions will hunt them."

An eighth of a mile down the road, the jungle on the right thinned out. Another eighth of a mile past that, the jungle stopped, and a track crossed our track. Joseph turned left toward the eland, went about two hundred yards, and stopped. "Watch," he said, and we did, staring at the herd of about sixty eland. For twenty minutes, there was nothing, and then a lioness erupted out of the grass, startling the herd into flight, right at the bus. As we watched in awe, the eland fled past us, fewer than fifty yards away. Another lioness hiding in wait shot out of a clump of elephant grass, silent and deadly, slamming into a male eland and knocking him to the ground. There was a brief struggle while the lion secured its grip on the throat of the eland, and then the other lionesses, panting and growling, arrived to finish him off. I had forgotten to use my camera, so fascinated by the kill.

As Joseph backed the bus away, I filmed the lions feeding. Even the two cubs with their babysitter had arrived, and just before we got out of sight, a male lion, obvious by his magnificent, dark-brown mane, showed up and claimed a seat at the feast but not without growling and snarling from the lionesses. Back at the intersection of the original track, Joseph stopped the bus.

He whispered, "You had a good day. An angry bull warned you to go away, and lions made a kill. That does not often happen." He smiled. "Very good day, indeed."

At 0730 hours, it was full daylight, and it seemed that we had been in the bush for days. Joseph told us to help ourselves to the cooler, and we did. I went forward and asked him if he wanted anything.

"A water, thank you, but I will get it. Before, with the jungle so close, I could not leave the seat. Anything could happen, as you saw when the bull attacked. In open ground, nothing big can come close without my seeing it."

"Let me," I said and brought him a bottle of water and a packet of crackers.

"How long have you been doing this, Joseph?"

"Oh, many years."

"You don't look that old."

"I started with my father, who worked for Mr. DeKuyper when he was young. My father was Mr. DeKuyper's gun bearer." The pride was obvious in his voice.

"Mr. DeKuyper told us about your father. His name was Joseph, too, wasn't it?"

"Yes." A great smile split his face. "Mr. DeKuyper has been a good friend, helping me to get my education in the missionary school."

"Then you are Swahili. They are a noble tribe."

Growing solemn, he said, "Thank you. It is not right to boast, but I am proud of my ancestors. How do you know of the Swahili?"

"I read about them. When I knew I was traveling to Africa, I researched about the areas I would be visiting. The Swahili and the Zulu tribes are prominent in the history of Africa."

"Ah." He nodded his head in agreement.

Dennis interrupted us. "Joseph, I have to piss. Is it safe to go outside?"

Holding his hand up as a signal to wait, Joseph went to the roof opening and looked in all directions. "You may go, but only just outside the door."

Joseph returned to his seat and opened the door, and Dennis stepped off, took one step, and relieved himself, hurrying back inside.

"We will return to the lodge now. Most animals rest during the day." Making a U-turn on the track, he crept along at 10 mph, the dust from the road swirling up and drifting down through the roof opening. "Look!" Joseph called out. "A baby eland." Sure enough, just at the point where the jungle encroached again, a baby eland was walking on the jungle side of the road. Joseph closed the distance for us to get a better look. The baby trotted toward the road, and Joseph sped up and cut him off. The baby stopped and then started again and made a barking sound. Joseph kept even with him. I was filming this from the roof top when Dennis yelled, "Look out!"

I spun around and saw an adult female eland running straight at the bus. Camera still running, I gaped as she leaped over the open roof, her hoofs clearing my camera by inches as I leaned back and fell into the seat. By the time I stood up, mamma and the baby were turning back behind us.

"Holy shit. That was close."

Everyone talked at once, and Joseph just smiled. No need to be quiet now.

Joseph took his time driving back, stopping to point out animals resting in the grass, none of which we spotted on our own, except for the giraffes. They were obvious. Every time we stopped, the dust would catch up and surround us, unwilling to let us escape. We even overlooked elephants that were standing still against a backdrop of trees fewer than one hundred meters away until Joseph chided, "Do you not see them?"

Dennis said, "Now I do, but I smelled them. Christ, I feel like a kid again. I loved going to the zoo, but this is so much better."

"It sure is," chimed in Bill. "That elephant scared the shit out of me."

"How do you think I felt?" I said. "First you head butt me in the balls, and then I'm face-to-face with a pissed-off elephant."

"Yeah, well, I hope you enjoyed it 'cause it's the last head you're getting from me." And everyone broke out laughing, getting the double-entendre "head" joke.

But Fran had the best line when he added, "Bill, I didn't think you swung both ways."

Everyone but Joseph laughed hard. No one explained it to him.

We arrived back at the lodge at the stroke of noon. On the way, Dennis had asked everyone to chip in for a tip for Joseph, and each of us donated twenty dollars. As we exited the bus, Dennis handed the money to Joseph, and his eyes went wide.

Putting his hands behind his back, Joseph said, "No, sir. That is too much money."

Reaching out and pulling Joseph's hand, Dennis crammed the cash into his palm and said, "It's not too much. You are a great guide and fun to be with, and we all appreciate you."

Lowering his head, Joseph mumbled, "Thank you, sir. Thank all of you." Then, he shook Dennis's hand.

Inside the lodge, everyone hurried to use the bathroom and clean the dust from faces and hands. We gathered back in the dining room; both Greta and Frieda were there, along with the French tour group and, of course, Bernie Simpson.

Greta started, "I hope you had a good trip?"

"You bet we did," Dennis interrupted and related our experiences from that morning.

"I must admit," Greta continued, "those are far beyond the normal sightings. We were waiting for you to return before starting lunch. Everyone, please sit, and enjoy the meal."

Everyone scattered to different tables. The overhead fans rotated slowly but succeeded in moving the air. It was warm but not hot; the humidity was lower than I expected, and I commented on it to Greta.

"Remember, we are at 1,100 meters elevation. Climbing Mount Kilimanjaro is like traveling through all four seasons. We are at the early fall season here."

The French men, Luc and Andre, sat with Greg and Frieda and were engaged in a lively conversation. I found myself with the same two French girls, Elain and Yvonne, which was fine until Bernie Simpson came and plunked himself down, not offering a word of introduction. The girls did not look happy.

Addressing Yvonne, I asked, "What did you do this morning?"

Bernie barked, "You're wasting your time talking to these 'frogs.' They don't speak any English."

"Oh?" I said. "How do you know?"

"Because they didn't answer anything I said to them."

I looked at Yvonne; her tightlipped smile made it clear that neither she nor Elain wanted anything to do with Bernie.

Playing along, I asked Bernie, "Well, other than insulting them by calling them frogs, what did you ask them?'

He was oblivious to the idea that he was insulting them. "I asked them how come they don't speak English. I didn't like the snacks they had on the bus, either. It looked like goose shit on a cracker." This last elicited a gasp from Elain.

Putting both hands on the table, I leaned in and stated, "Bernie, you're a passenger on my ship, and I've let a lot pass because of that, but I have to tell you, you are the biggest asshole I have met in years. You're rude, ignorant, and insulting, and I suggest that you keep your opinions to yourself. Have you ever heard the term 'ugly American'? Well, that's what you are, and as a fellow American, you embarrass me."

Bernie turned red and stood up. Just as he opened his mouth, Dennis, who heard everything I had said, stepped up to Bernie, grabbed him by the right arm, and said, "Excuse me, Mr. Simpson, but there's something I need to discuss with you. It's urgent." And he pulled Bernie behind him and into the deserted bar. There was a muttering of voices and then a smacking sound and a thud. Dennis walked back in to the room and announced, "I apologize for Mr. Simpson's behavior. He's decided to spend the rest of the day in his room."

Elain and Yvonne stood and cheered, yelling "Bravo, Monsieur Dennis!" Similar remarks came from others in the room. Dennis sat down and resumed his lunch amid a buzz of gleeful chatter.

An hour later, in the bar, I sat with Dennis, Greta, Frieda, Greg, Fran, and Mr. DeKuyper, having a drink. "Dennis?" DeKuyper asked. "What did you do to get Bernie to hide himself in his room?"

"I'd rather not say. If there's a problem later, I don't want any of these guys to get in trouble." He indicated the crew members.

"Dennis," Fran said. "There are only friends here. Whatever you say, we've already forgotten it."

Looking around at us, he decided. "I asked him to stay away from everyone for the rest of trip because he was causing an international incident."

There was a pause, and then Fran said, "And he agreed?"

"No. He said, 'I don't have to listen to you,' and I punched him and knocked him on his ass."

DeKuyper's jaw dropped, Greta and Frieda laughed, and Fran said, "Good."

I asked, "What did he say then?"

"Nothing. I told him to go to his room and not to show his face again until he could behave in a civil manner. Then, I came back and finished my lunch."

Greta said, "I'll check in on him later and make sure he's okay."

Fran sniped, "Just bring him room service; that'll keep him quiet." And we all laughed.

I took a nap, the room cool in midafternoon, and woke up at 1700 hours. Still gritty from the safari, I showered and went down to the bar. It was empty except for the bartender.

"Hello. I thought most folks would be here this time of day."

"No, sir, the veranda is where you can see the animals gather at the watering hole. You may order a drink there, or I can make one for you right now, and you can take it with you."

I ordered a Cuba libre and brought it out to the veranda. There were Quiet-Please signs at all doors leading to the veranda. I arrived last, and Yvonne waved me over to her table for two in the far corner. The entire guest contingent except Bernie was there, conversing in whispers, leaning in and appearing intimate.

"What are you drinking?" Yvonne asked.

"Cuba libre," I said, and she wrinkled her nose.

"Have wine. They have an excellent Riesling."

"I've never tasted Riesling."

"Try mine," she said, offering her glass.

I sipped it, and, having a sudden urge to keep Yvonne happy, I agreed, and she waved at the waiter and ordered a glass for me. Me being me, I chugged the cuba libre before the wine arrived.

The table squeezed into a corner of the veranda faced the landscape in front, and both chairs were set behind it so both persons would have a view of the watering hole. There were faint shadows everywhere since Mount Kilimanjaro blocked direct sunlight, and a gentle breeze wafted in the aroma of the impatiens, fighting everywhere among the tree roots for space to grow.

The closeness of the seating gave Yvonne the opportunity to pat my knee and thigh. I didn't object.

"I haven't seen any animals yet," she said.

"It's too early. Most of them come at dusk or later. Did you go on your motor safari this morning?

"No. We'll go tomorrow morning with Joseph."

For the next hour, we sat and sipped our wine, breathed in the jungle fragrance, and watched the waterhole. The breeze had died, exaggerating the heat and humidity, but there were no mosquitoes. To compensate for the heat, Yvonne rolled up her sleeves, unbuttoned the top two buttons on her blouse, and fanned herself by flapping the fabric of the blouse, an impromptu peep show. Just then, Greta, who had walked out a few minutes earlier and was making the rounds of the tables, said, "They're coming," and we all stared at the waterhole. Barely discernible in the fading light, a group of monkeys had gathered at the far edge, drinking while two of them stood guard. After five minutes of drinking and jerking about to false alarms, they drifted back to the trees.

Greta, standing beside me and leaning against the wall, whispered, "Look to the left. Hyenas."

Try as I might, I couldn't see any movement. It was too dark.

Greta whispered again, "Dinner is ready." And she worked her way back to the door, passing the message along. Yvonne and I stood and headed in.

We sat with Greta, Dennis, and Pieter and enjoyed the buffet, similar to last night's spread.

"Greta," I asked, "we're a long way from a grocery store. How do you get the fresh meat, bread, and dairy items?"

"The bread we bake ourselves. Depending on how many guests we have, we fly in fresh produce and meats from Dar es Salaam."

"Where is the airport? How come we didn't fly here instead of taking the bus?"

She laughed. "'Airport' is a rather grand name for it. There is a grass strip, two kilometers south of here, and the maximum weight the pilot allows is 150 kilos. The pilot flies here every week on his own business, and we have prevailed upon him to assist us when needed. It works well for us and him. He flies things in, and we maintain his vehicle and provide lodging whenever he requires it."

Yvonne headed for bed around 2200 hours, and the rest of us soon followed.

There was a tapping at my door again, this time at 0430 hours. I debated for a while whether I should get up and watch the animals at the watering hole or just roll over and go back to sleep. The animals won. After scrubbing my face, brushing my teeth, and using the head, I went down, collected a cup of coffee in the dining room, and then meandered out to the veranda.

The French party had left for their safari, and the only ones on the veranda were Fran, Tony, and me. We sat in silence until Tony spotted a small group of antelopes approaching the waterhole. They were skittish, and only a few had drunk when they stampeded. We never saw what spooked them.

Next were the monkeys again. They seemed more nervous than last night and jumped around a lot but stayed long enough to drink. Just as I stood to go get another cup of coffee, four giraffes appeared, stately and almost elegant in their approach. One of them, obviously a male because of his size, stood guard while the others bent to drink. That was a vulnerable time for them, as they splayed their front legs wide and bent over to drink. When they finished, they stood guard for the fourth giraffe as he performed his ritual of bowing to the water gods.

We sat there for another thirty minutes, but other than a few small antelopes (I think they were dik-diks), nothing else showed up. Passing up breakfast, I went back to bed.

I woke up at noon, showered, shaved, and went down to lunch. All the guys from the ship were there. As I sat down, the French group, including Bernie, arrived back from their tour with Joseph, and the noise level increased. Everyone talked at once, in French and English, asking about their trip.

Yvonne came over, sat, and shuffled her chair close.

"Hello, Yvonne. I have two questions. Did you enjoy the motor safari, and did Bernie behave himself?"

"Yes, I did, and yes, he behaved himself. He sat in the back and never said a word to anyone, not even Joseph." Patting my knee, she said, "It was exciting. Joseph is such an interesting person. We saw lions and elephants and antelopes, but we did not get chased and did not see the lions hunt. You had much more excitement than we did." She capped that off with a slide of her hand up my thigh and a squeeze just short of the main target.

Trying a last-ditch effort of conscience, I stammered, "Yvonne. I love what you are doing, but…" I was not sure how to continue without seeming like an idiot. "I'm engaged, and I don't think she…Meg…my fiancée…would appreciate my getting…intimate with you."

Smiling, she looked at me and said, "How wonderful. A man with a conscience. But I am not looking to marry you, just have sex with you." And with that, she reached the main target, gave him a gentle squeeze, arched her eyebrows, and said, "But it is your choice."

Lunch comprised another "light" buffet of bratwurst, three different cheeses (including one that smelled like an old shoe), weiner schnitzel, potato salad, green salad, the same four types of bread, and for dessert, apple strudel. I grabbed a slice of the schnitzel, stuffed a huge bratwurst between two slices of pumpernickel, daubed it with mustard, and washed it down with a stein of beer. During lunch, Yvonne kept her hands to herself, keeping them busy with food. She was a prodigious eater.

Burping on the way to the desert table, Yvonne came up behind me.

"I can tell you enjoyed the bratwurst." She laughed and then said quietly, "I'm going up to shower. My door is open if you want dessert other than strudel." She pointed at the table and walked away. I stared at the strudel for a few seconds, and then picked up a piece and returned to my table, thinking, "This strudel had better be damn good."

We boarded the bus at 1500 hours to return to the ship. Both Gerta and Frieda were there with hugs for everyone. Pieter DeKuyper shook hands with everyone and thanked Dennis for teaching Bernie Simpson manners. The French contingent, with Bernie in tow, were due to depart at 1600 hours, but none of them were around when we pulled out of the driveway. Seven hours later, the bus stopped at the foot of the gangway, and our safari adventure came to an end.

Chapter 24

AFTERMATH

A t 0700 on Monday, I was eating breakfast in the salon, the familiar odor of fried onions clinging to everything. Clara Simpson sat, pushing food around on her plate and staring at the bulkhead. Bernie was absent from his usual place. For him to miss a meal was a rarity, so I leaned over and asked Dennis if anything happened to him.

"Nah. He didn't get back until 0200 and left a note on Fran's door that he wanted his breakfast served in his cabin."

When we sailed from Beira, Clara had asked Fran, the chief steward, if she could move to the cabin Megan and Grace had occupied. Fran accommodated her, and the arrangement with her and Bernie occupying separate cabins had remained that way since.

"Has he said anything to the captain about your punching him?"

A pained look on his face, Dennis said, "I told the captain last night when we got back."

"What did he say?"

"'I hope there weren't any witnesses.'"

I laughed, shook my head, and said, "Nope, never happened."

The only cargo operation left was the discharge of the water-damaged powdered-milk bags. The stevedore had gotten a truck crane with a clam bucket, and they were unloading it into dump trucks on the pier. Dennis had insisted they lay tarps across the deck where the loads swung overhead, minimizing the mess on deck, but milk stains splattered all over the pier, and the dump trucks oozed a trail of milk when they pulled away.

I relieved Tony at noon and watched, bored, as the continuous sloshing and splashing of sour milk went on. Every hour, the longshoremen would stop for ten minutes while the crew cleaned up the residue in the tarp on deck. They piled the torn bags into another, separate tarp, which would empty into a dump truck at the end of the operation.

The stevedore had convinced the dump-truck operators to stay for the entire day, so our estimated time for completion was noon tomorrow.

Dennis had given Chuck the day off since he had covered for everyone on the weekend, so I stayed on watch. The longshoremen knocked off for the day at 1700 hours. After checking all the mooring lines, I completed the log of the cargo activities, took a shower, and went to eat.

Bernie was there, adorned with a magnificent black eye. He sat alone, silent except for the occasional slurping sound, which had become his trademark. Clara sat with the captain's wife, Eunice, at the captain's table, both stealing conspiratorial glances at Bernie.

As everyone was finishing, Chuck came in from his day ashore. He had a few more trinkets from the local market, but he also carried a four-foot-long box, twelve inches wide and eighteen inches high.

"What's in the box?" Dennis asked.

"The deal of a lifetime. Look."

I pushed a few dishes aside, and he set the box down gingerly on the table and opened it. Inside was a carved elephant tusk, a little over three feet long. The top of it depicted a Japanese garden and Shinto temple, but the amazing part was the intricate carving on the inside. Looking through the windows and doors of the temple, the exposed interior had ornate frescoes carved on the walls. The detail was incredible. The entire tusk sat on an ebony board, polished to perfection with a silver handle at each end.

"Where did you get it?" I asked.

"At an upscale shop across the street from the native market."

"How much did it cost? You didn't get this for a dollar."

"Three hundred and twenty-five bucks. They started at four hundred, but I haggled them down."

"That's still a lot of money."

"Yes, it is, but in five years, this will be worth a fortune. There's a movement on to stop hunting elephants for their ivory, and that will make the value of this go up. Besides, it's beautiful."

Everyone except Bernie had crowded around to get a good look. Eunice commented, "I have a friend in New York, a patron of the arts who collects ivory artifacts, and she agrees a ban on the taking of ivory is coming. This will be worth a lot of money in a few years. Other than the value of the ivory, the artwork is amazing, so delicate, like lace. You better wrap it up well to protect it."

Greg, peering at it, asked, "How much does it weigh?"

"Don't know, but I'm guessing forty pounds or more. I held it on my lap all the way back to the ship in the taxi ride. It's fastened tight to the ebony, and the handles are screwed deep into the wood, so I'll tie it down to the desk in my room by the handles."

When Chuck took the tusk to his room, everyone but Clara and I drifted away. I was on my second cup of coffee when she came and sat by me. Reaching out and tapping my hand, she said, "So how did Bernie get the shiner?"

Mustering an innocent face, I asked, "What shiner?"

"Oh, come on. Someone had to slug him. He didn't get that by walking into a door. He must have irritated someone more than usual."

Smiling, I said, "He is good at that, isn't he?" I looked into her eyes. "Let's just say he deserved it—retribution of a sort for what he did to you."

"Who?" she asked. "I want to thank him. Was it you?"

"No, although I wanted to. It was someone higher and bigger than me, and that's all you're getting out of me."

She thought about it for a few seconds, smiled, and said, "Ah, I think I know. Thank you." She got up and left, leaving me wondering if I hadn't gotten myself and Dennis into trouble again with my big mouth.

Later that night, Clara knocked on Dennis's open office door. He came out
of his bedroom.

"Hi. What can I do for you?"

"Could you come by my cabin in about twenty minutes? There's something I want to give you."

Puzzled, he said, "Yeah, sure. See you in twenty minutes." When Dennis
tapped on Clara's door, she opened it and gestured for him to come in, closing
the door after him. She wore a bathrobe, open at the top far enough to display
ample cleavage. Despite himself, Dennis stared at her cleavage before looking
up at her.

"Thank you for giving Bernie that shiner."

Taken aback, he asked, "Who told you that?"

"A friend, and don't worry, I'm grateful. Bernie deserved it. In fact, I'm so
grateful I've decided to do something I've been thinking about for a while."
She stepped up and kissed him on the lips, soft at first and then with ardor.
Dennis, shocked, still responded as she hoped. He kissed her back.

Pulling apart, Dennis held her at arm's length. "You sure this is a good
idea?

"I think it's a wonderful idea," she said, as she opened her robe.

An hour later, they were still intertwined, smiling, and purring like kit-
tens. Dennis said, "You have a remarkable way of saying thank you."

"Do I? Well, I can be very grateful to someone who helps me in difficult
situations. If you're not busy tomorrow night, come back, and I'll thank you
again. I'm so grateful, I may have to thank you every night." She grabbed his
dick and gave it a playful shake.

I slept in the next morning, getting to the empty salon at 0900 and settling
for toast and coffee. With nothing else to do, I went on deck with Tony and
watched the longshoremen finish discharging the milk slop from the deep
tank. It was a mess, and the putrid odor of sour milk enveloped the ship.
At 1030, they finished, and the crew hosed down the deep-tank bulkheads.
Arrangements for a tank truck to be alongside had been made by the ship's
agent, and the engineer on watch coupled a hose from the deep tank cargo

outlet to the tank truck and pumped the residue into the truck. The sour odor persisted, so Dennis left the deep-tank cover open and dropped in a few fans to circulate the air.

At 1600 hours, we buttoned up the hatch and sailed for Tamatave.

Chapter 25

TAMATAVE

Sailed from Mombasa at 1600 hours on Tuesday, 12/6/66. Sparse clouds. Temperature 82 degrees. Wind from the southeast at 5 mph. Dropped the pilot as we cleared the harbor entrance. Bound for Tamatave, Madagascar.

Clear of the harbor entrance, we sailed on a course of 163 degrees for fifty-eight miles to clear Pemba Island and reach a position of 5 degrees south latitude and 40 degrees east longitude. From there, we set a course to pass south of Aldabra and its smaller brother island, Assomption, taking into account that we now had a two-knot southerly set from the Mozambique current.

Once clear of Assomption, we continued to the Glorioso Islands, ninety-seven miles northwest of Madagascar. We needed to keep Grand Gloreuse, the largest of the islands, to our north. Passing the northern tip of Madagascar, we swung onto course 165 degrees and ran the coast until abeam of the mouth of the Onive River, a tributary of the Mangoro River, then changed course to 204 degrees and ran 127 miles until offshore of our destination.

Tamatave, the chief port of Madagascar, is on the Indian Ocean side of the island. It is connected by the Malagasy Railway to the capital, Antananarivo. The main exports are coffee, sugar, cloves, and rice, although our only cargo to be loaded here was black pepper. This was a "showing of the flag" visit, done every third or fourth trip, more for commercial politics than for profits.

Founded in the eighteenth century, Tamatave centered around a European trading post. King Ramada I captured the town in 1817 and made it the chief port of his kingdom as part of his efforts to unite the entire island. King Radama I was the first Malagasy sovereign to be recognized by a European state. Raided and occupied a number of times by the French, in 1894, Tamatave became the base for their conquest of the interior of Madagascar. During the colonial period, owing to the swampy character of the soil and crowded native population, epidemics often hit the town. The French drained the neighboring marshes and, in 1895, relocated the native population from the town and resettled them in a village to the northwest. The bubonic plague broke out in 1898, brought by ships from India, and again in 1900, but it was less severe due to the relocation of the native population.

Tropical cyclones are regular visitors and devastators of Madagascar. In 1927, Tamatave was severely damaged by a cyclone and was subsequently re-built. That destructive cycle continues today. October to April is the main cyclone season, with occasional damaging visits in May and June. The climate is of tropical rain forest, but there is no real dry season since there is rainfall in every month. February through April is wettest, and September through November is driest.

The city center is on a sandy peninsula, projecting at right angles to the main coastline. The city and the harbor are protected from the east by a large natural reef, and although open to the north, there is another large reef due north of the northernmost tip of the port, which aids in deflecting heavy seas during storms.

Two days and sixteen hours after sailing from Mombasa, we picked up the pilot one mile out from the north jetty. Once clear of the jetty, we inched our way southwest, bypassing the planned-expansion area of the port and docking portside to the pier at the main cargo pier, sticking out like a chopped notch in a log. Past that, the harbor narrowed and split into two channels, where only smaller boats and ships moored.

The cargo operations started at 1200 hours and completed that night at 2100 hours. I never got ashore but looking out from the bridge, I found that the buildings were ordinary, no grand cathedrals or mosques and no imposing government structures. I don't think I missed anything of interest. There were two incidents during our stay that caught everyone's attention. The first was the chief cook getting into a fight on the dock with the ship's supply-company driver. The chief cook, who had been on the dock, watching the driver in the process of stacking cases of canned goods and some fresh vegetables onto a pallet, said something to the driver that apparently offended him. The driver said something to the chief cook, who punched the driver, knocking him to the ground; then, he jumped on him and began slamming his head against the pavement, all the time screaming at him.

I was coming out of the house at the top of the gangway when I heard the commotion and looked over the side. I yelled to the gangway watchmen, "Call the chief mate!" I ran down the gangway to pull the chief cook off the driver. Straddling his back, I grabbed his shoulders and pulled. He came up, turning and swinging. I ducked and backed up. Holding my hands in front, I inquired loudly, "What the fuck are you doing?"

He stared at me blankly, eyes twitching and shifting; he slumped his shoulders and collapsed into a sitting position on the ground. I walked around him to the driver, attempting to sit up. His nose was broken, and there was blood on the ground where his head had hit it. I squatted beside him to assess the damage and steady him.

"Jesus," I heard from the chief mate as he reached the bottom of the gangway.

"Better get Fran here, or call an ambulance," I told him. "This guy is pretty banged up."

He called up to the watchman and instructed him to get Fran and have him bring his kit. Turning to the chief cook, still sitting on the pavement, he asked, "What the hell happened?"

No response.

"Can you hear me, Jim Bob?" He was louder now. "I want to know what happened!"

The cook ignored him and stared at his feet.

When Fran arrived a few minutes later, he saw the blood on the back of the driver's head, gently blotted it, and then looked at the driver's eyes. "Not good, at least a concussion. Dennis, call an ambulance."

Looking at me, "Keep him sitting up. Don't try to stand, and don't lay him back down."

Talking to the driver, Fran asked, "Can you understand me? *Comprenez-vous?*"

The driver nodded, winced, and said, "I understand. I speak English."

"Good." nodding in agreement with himself. "I believe you have a concussion. I'm going to put a loose bandage on the back of your head to try to stop the bleeding. It seems your nose is broken, but that's not serious. You need to sit still, and if you feel like you're going to faint, tell him," he said, pointing at me, "and he will support you. Okay?"

There was a feeble "Yes."

"Good." He proceeded to bandage his head.

In the meantime, Dennis talked to the stevedore supervisor, who had watched the entire bout. He said he didn't hear what the cook and driver had said, but he saw the cook punch the driver and pound his head on the ground. The cook still hadn't moved.

It took fifteen minutes for the ambulance to arrive. It was a boxy white Peugeot, with a rear-hinged door for moving a stretcher in and out and a side-hinged door on the right side for walk-in access to the back. The driver and passenger doors slid backward on rails. Fran explained to the attendants, both of whom wore white lab coats, what had happened and what he had done for the driver. They sat him on the tail, checked his eyes, helped him to lie down on the stretcher, and left, one in the back with the injured man and the other driving.

"Fran," Dennis called. "Let's get the cook up to my office, and we'll try and sort this out. In the meantime, have someone finish loading our supplies onto the pallet, and get it aboard. When they're done, have them lock the truck up, and bring me the key."

"Will do, Dennis."

With Dennis looming behind him, Fran crouched in front of the chief cook. "Jim Bob, you need to get up and go to the chief mate's office. You understand?"

Jim Bob lifted his head, nodded, and stood up. Dennis followed him up the gangway.

In Dennis's office, Jim Bob sat at the table, leaning over his clasped hands. Scrawny, 5'6" tall and weighing 150 pounds, Jim Bob was a bag of bones from New Orleans, Louisiana—a white Cajun from the bayous.

When Fran arrived, Dennis started. "Okay, Jim Bob. Tell me what happened."

Without lifting his head, he said, "I dunno. One minute, I was counting the cases the guy was loading, and the next, Mr. Connolly was asking me what I was doing. I dunno what happened."

Dennis then related what the stevedore supervisor told him.

Jim Bob looked up, eyes twitching frantically. He asked, "Why would I hit him?"

"Wait here a minute." Motioning to Fran, he stepped into his bedroom.

"Fran, he looks like he's high on something."

"That's what I thought."

"Go search his room. See if you can find any drugs. It's not booze. We'd smell it if it was."

Ten minutes later, Fran returned and called Dennis outside. "It's PCP. I think they call it angel dust. He's got about a hundred capsules. I also found a couple of pounds of marijuana."

"What did you do with it?"

"It's locked in my medicine cabinet."

"Okay. We gotta do something. I asked the agent to check on the injured driver. If he calls the cops, Jim Bob is in a world of shit. In the meantime, I don't want him near the galley. God knows what he's been doing to the food, and there're too many knives there." Stepping back inside, Dennis confronted Jim Bob.

"Look at me, boy." Jim Bob lifted his head and looked up at Dennis.

"You're in a pile of trouble. We just cleaned out your angel dust and marijuana. You are confined to your room. If you so much as stick your head outside the door, I'll lock you in handcuffs and leg irons. If that guy you beat up brings the police in on this, you'll be arrested, and then the only thing we can do for you is notify the US consulate. You got that, boy?" There was no response, so Dennis yelled, "I said, you got that, boy?"

"I gotta pee," was the reply.

"Jesus!" Dennis shook his head. "What a fuckin' mess. Fran, let him go to the head, and then put him in his room."

At 1630, the agent who spoke English with a strong French accent came aboard and informed the captain and chief mate that the delivery driver had a concussion and a broken nose but nothing more serious. As per the captain's orders, he had also called the main office in New York, explained the situation, and they had authorized the payment of any medical expenses for the driver.

The captain asked, "Have you told the injured man the company will cover his medical expenses?"

"Yes, Captain, I did."

"What was his response?"

"He was happy. He wished to know why the cook attacked him?"

"And?"

"I told him the man is mentally ill and that the company would send him to a hospital. He was satisfied, so both the cook and the company are, how you say, 'off the hook.'" And he smiled.

"Thank you. I will be sure and tell the folks at home what a good job you've done."

Smiling and nodding his head, he asked, "Is there anything else to do?"

The captain said no, but Dennis held up his hand. "Wait a minute. Here's the key to the man's truck. It's locked up at the foot of the gangway. Please arrange to have it returned to the supply company."

"Of course." He took the key and left.

The other thing that caught the attention of the officers at dinner was the captain's wife, Eunice. She walked into the salon, the aroma of gin following her and enveloping everyone in its path. She stepped up to Bernie Simpson and said, "In case no one has told you lately, you are an insufferable bastard, a poor excuse for a man, and if you had any balls, I would cut them off." She then flounced, tossed back her head, and stared at Bernie, daring him to comment.

After a few seconds, the captain said, "Perhaps you'd like to sit down and have dinner, Eunice."

Pivoting slowly, she took a step to the captain's table, leaned over, and said in a not-so-quiet voice, "Remember our conversation in East London? Nothing has changed, so don't try to kiss my ass. It's no longer yours to kiss." Standing erect, teetering slightly, she looked around the salon, and total silence greeted her. With that, she steered for the door and left.

Bernie, not having the nerve to say anything to Eunice, now turned to the captain and said, "She's your wife. You shouldn't have let her talk to me that way."

The captain lit a cigarette, took a long drag, blew it out, and said, "Mr. Simpson, there is very little that Eunice and I agree upon nowadays, but her opinion of you is one of them." Rising, he picked up his coffee cup and left, leaving Bernie puzzled as to whether he had been insulted again.

Cargo operations had finished at 2130 hours, and the ship was buttoned up. When I relieved Tony on the bridge at midnight, I noticed that Eunice was sitting in a deck chair back at the pool. Whispering to Tony, I asked, "Is she waiting for you?"

"Yeah, she's been there since 2200."

"Well," I said, smirking, "you better get going before she cuts your balls off."

"She won't. She's already told me she's going to make me wear them out fucking her."

"You're relieved. Have fun." As he walked back to the pool deck, I heard her say, "Do me justice, Tony, or I'm coming back for William afterward."

The captain called us out for undocking at 0600 hours. Tony must have done well by Eunice because she never knocked on my door.

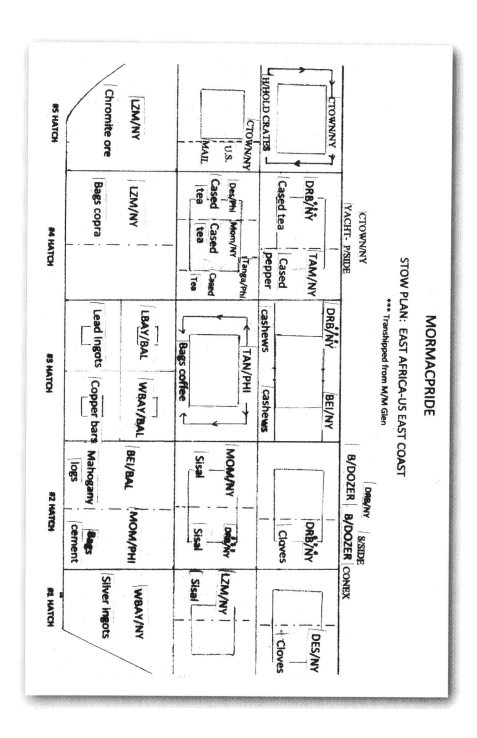

MORMACPRIDE

STOW PLAN: EAST AFRICA-US EAST COAST

*** Transhipped from M/M Glen

Chapter 26

DURBAN— HOMEBOUND CALL

Sailed from Tamatave at 0700 hours on Saturday, 12/10/66. Light rain. Two miles visibility. Temperature 81 degrees. Wind from the east at 12 mph. Bound for Durban, South Africa.

Coming out of Tamatave, we ran at 100 degrees for seventeen miles to get far enough offshore to avoid any shoals and then headed 196 degrees until abeam of Faradofay. We then changed course to 241 degrees until we cleared Cape Sainte Marie at the southern tip of Madagascar. There, we set a course of 253 degrees, straight across the Indian Ocean to Durban.

When the sun came out on the second day, both Eunice and Clara spent that afternoon and the next on the pool deck. Eunice was in a clinging, bright-yellow two-piece, and Clara's cheeks and boobs hung out of a magenta one-piece suit. They looked and sounded like high-school girls, laughing and whispering, probably comparing notes on the sexual performances of Dennis and Tony.

The trip took three days and three hours, every waking minute of which I thought about Meg. I lived in a permanent state of horniness, envisioning her naked body, recalling the smell of her hair and muskiness after sex, the softness of her breasts. Glimpsing the appendages on display by Clara and Eunice didn't help the situation. The night watches were easier because there was only my imagination to fuel my erotic thoughts—no live specimens. Tonight, the last night at sea before docking in Durban, a three-quarter moon sprayed twinkles across the sea. Lunar decorations.

Earlier, at dinner, Dennis agreed, after a sufficient amount of pleading, to give me the first two days off so I could see Meg. He also told me they had received a wire from the office in New York instructing him that, besides our scheduled loading, we would transfer cargo, ship to ship, from the *MorMacGlen*. The *Glen* had struck a submerged object leaving East London and sliced through steel-hull plating on the port side of its no. 3 hatch. It was not enough to sink the ship but enough to keep the bilge pumps running. Since the ship wasn't in danger of sinking, the port authority wouldn't give them a berth to discharge cargo directly to the pier. The schedule was too tight with other ships in line, so we would transfer as much of its cargo as we could. They hoped that would lighten the ship enough to get the damage above water so that they could weld it. The *MorMacGlen* was at anchor inside Durban Harbor, with a self-induced list to starboard and a temporary patch to minimize leaking.

We approached the pilot station from due east and boarded the pilot at 1015 hours. It was a bright, sunny day with a southeast breeze; we moved into the approach channel heading 215 degrees. The wind had moderated to 10 mph. Our destination was the west side of pier no. 1. This time, we docked starboard side to the pier at the outer end. The *MorMacGlen*, at anchor and waiting for us to berth, now approached from the rear. It also came alongside the starboard side to us, thus matching up hatches.

After lowering the gangway, I released the crew members from mooring stations, headed to my room to clean up, and then went to the salon to get a cup of coffee. Sitting at the table were Meg and Grace. Stunned, I didn't react until Meg jumped me, wrapping her legs around my waist and almost knocking me over. I couldn't talk because her lips smothered mine. I didn't want to talk. It took all my control to keep from running my hands up and squeezing her ass, something I knew her mother wouldn't appreciate with a dozen people looking on. We came up for air, and she let go of her leg lock on my hips, sliding to the deck.

"I didn't want to wait." Breathless, face aglow, and blue-green eyes gleaming, Meg turned and grasped my right arm with both of hers.

"Hello, William," said Grace.

"Hello, Mrs. O'Brien. This is a nice surprise."

She laughed. "You know whose idea this was."

"How did you know when we would dock?"

With a look of incredulity, she said, "You are joking! Meg has been following your itinerary via the local agent since the day you left. No doubt they'll be happy they won't get any telephone calls for a few days."

"I have two days off. I have to be back on Thursday by noon." Looking around, I saw that Dennis was missing, so I said, "Let me check with the chief mate. You can either stay here, or you can come with me while I pack a few things."

Just then, Clara Simpson came in, and Grace greeted her with a hug.

Meg said, "I'll wait in your room. Mum can stay here and talk to Clara."

Dennis was in his office, talking with the stevedore superintendent and the chief mate from the *MorMacGlen*, Gabriel Santorini. He was short, five feet five inches, with trim build, shaved head, and a gigantic red handlebar mustache. Dennis introduced me to him.

Grasping my hand and shaking vigorously, he said, "Hi, Bill. Call me Gabe." I don't know if it was the presumption of calling me "Bill" or just instinct, but I took an instant dislike to him.

"Hello, sir." Turning to Dennis, I said, "Meg and her mother are aboard. Do you need anything before I head out?"

"No. You're good. You'll be back at noon Thursday, right?" It was more a statement than a question.

"That's right. See you then." Nodding to Gabe and the stevedore superintendent, I walked out.

As I opened my room door, Meg grabbed me, pulled me in, slammed the door, grabbed my head, and pulled me down to kiss her. It was a great kiss. It took me all of five seconds to get a raging erection, and she knew it, pressing in hard against me. Leaning her head back but maintaining the groin pressure, she waggled her hips, eliciting a groan.

"Stop," I said. "I have to walk upright when I leave here."

Flashing a guilty grin, she said, "Okay," and pulled away.

I threw a few things in my backpack: shorts, T-shirts, one pair of long pants, one semi–dress shirt and the extra condoms I had gotten from the ship's store last night. Fran, the chief steward, couldn't resist commenting, "Only a dozen? You'll be there for two days. Sure that's enough?"

Grabbing my back pack, I said, "C'mon, let's get this show on the road." I locked my door and followed Meg to the salon. Grace and Clara were still gabbing. I guessed what the topic of conversation was when Grace looked at her watch and said, "My, what restraint. I thought you'd be longer getting packed." Meg smiled, and I turned bright red.

Giving Clara a hug, Grace said, "Let's go." We followed her out and down the gangway to a waiting Land Rover, new but dusty, not like Mark's 1938 Mercedes 320B Cabriolet, which was pristine.

"I thought you had an older Land Rover. It was out for repairs when I was here."

"It was, and that now belongs to Meg. This is mine," Grace replied. "I had just ordered it when you were here. It's a 1966 model 11A 88."

It was a two-door, pale green car, with the classic recessed grill and headlights with big, boxy front fenders. It was a hardtop; many had canvas tops. On the edge of each front fender was a rearview mirror. Missing was the oversized bumper that extended up to the hood level and outward, which took the brunt of foliage hits in off-road driving. She must not be planning to go into bush country with it.

Meg said, "You get in front with Mum. I'll ride in back." She jumped in ahead of me. I tossed my backpack in with Meg and climbed in. The seats had padding, but not like American cars. A few miles on the rough roads outside of Durban convinced me that any off-road driving would guarantee a sore ass.

Grace rattled on as we drove through Durban, playing tour guide, and Meg leaned over the back seat, rubbing my neck and playing with my hair, something I found irritating but put up with when Meg did it.

Grace didn't drive as fast as Mark had, so it took an hour and a half before we pulled up to the gate and stopped. This time, I got out and opened it, closing it again after Grace pulled through. The last time, I had a déjà-vu experience and embarrassed myself by vomiting in front of Meg. I felt queasy, recalling it. Meg must have noticed because as I climbed back in the car, she asked, "Are you all right?"

"Yeah, just embarrassed. Remembering last time."

Grace gave me a quizzical look, so I explained about my déjà-vu incidents, including the one where I had impressed Meg by throwing up in front of her.

"Do you get them often?" Grace asked, in her mother mode now.

"Less and less each year. They're more embarrassing now than frightening. It doesn't last long when it appears. Some folks think that déjà vu is just a delay in sensory input—you see it, but it only registers in the subconscious. After a delay, it registers in your conscious, making it seem like a memory. Either way, it's weird."

After a quarter of a mile on the same stained-orange-dirt road, we pulled up to the main house. As I opened the car door, the aroma of the num-num flowers wafted over me, a permanent reminder of Meg's and my first night of lovemaking with the windows open.

Grace said, "You and Meg are on your own until dinnertime, when Mark returns."

I grabbed my backpack, and Meg grabbed my hand and tugged me toward her bungalow behind and to the right of the main house. As we approached, I remarked how the glossy ebony door stood out from the mustard-brown color of the walls.

"Why did you paint the door in glossy paint when everything else is flat paint?"

Pulling me forward, Meg stopped, stared at the door, shrugged, and said, "I don't know."

I carried my backpack all the way into the bedroom before dropping it on the floor, grabbing Meg and kissing her—long, deep, passionate kisses. Unlike the first time in this room, we undressed rather than stripped each other and took our time making love. As I reached for a condom on the dresser stand next to the bed, she shook her head. "You don't need that. I'm using an IUD."

"What's a UID?"

"Not UID. IUD—intrauterine device. It's a method of birth control."

"I never heard of it. Are you sure it's safe?" Images of a pregnant Meg flitted through my mind—not an unpleasant thought, but a nervous one.

"Yes, it's safe. I got one from my gynecologist after you left here." Smirking now, she said, "I felt if we were going to spend so much time in bed together, wrestling with a condom is cumbersome, and I like the naturalness." She rubbed her pelvis against me. "Don't you?"

"No, hate it," I said, slipping inside her.

As we were lying on the bed, naked, hands meandering over the peaks and valleys of each other's bodies, gently, not urgently, Meg asked, "Did you miss me?"

Getting up on one elbow, I looked down at her, brushed her lips with mine, and replied, "Every minute of every day."

"That's all?" She feigned displeasure.

"That's all. If there was more time, I would have missed you more."

"All right, that will have to do." She pushed me back and straddled me.

At 1700 hours, after taking a shower together and making love in the shower stall, we took another shower. It was less precarious, since we stuck to washing. Walking hand in hand to the main house, wrapped in the smell of num-nums and serenaded by the rustle of the wind in the trees, I realized what an idyllic scene this was, and some of my concern about living in South Africa eased. Just before reaching the corner of the main house, I stopped, held Meg's chin, and ever so gently kissed her. "You make it easy to love you, Meg."

Nestling her face in my neck, she murmured, "I hope so."

Turning the corner, we saw that Grace sat in a cane chair on the stoep, one of two on each side of a small, knotted vine-table that was two feet square. There was a glass of red wine in her hand as she waited for Mark to return home.

"Well, Meg." She addressed her but looked at me with a faint smile. "You look…refreshed."

Meg didn't react, but I felt the scarlet rising from my neck to my cheeks and ears.

"Come and sit with me. I have an excellent Cabernet you should try."

I strained to remember the wine she had served when I was here last; it popped into my head. "I thought you liked Argentine Malbec."

"You remembered, and yes, I do, but I also like several Cabernets and a few Pinot Noirs."

Sitting in the chair opposite the table from Grace, Meg pulled the chair next to me forward and turned it to face me and Grace. There were three empty wine stems on the table; Grace held her half-full stem in her left hand, swirling it.

Meg rose and poured wine into two glasses, one-third full. "Plenty of room to swirl without spilling," she said.

"Exactly how long do you swirl it? I asked.

Meg shrugged, looking to Grace for the answer.

"No exact time, William," Grace offered. Demonstrating by lifting her hand and swishing the wine about, she said, "The idea is to infuse air into the wine and let it breathe, but like other things in life, if it feels good, just keep doing it!"

This got a "Mum!" reaction from Meg and another scarlet wave from me.

At 1830, the wind died down, and the sounds of monkeys and birds, no longer masked by the rustling of tree limbs, escaped from the jungle canopy and visited us on the stoep. We had sat, not talking, absorbing the jungle essence for about ten minutes when I heard a car approaching.

"That should be Mark," Grace said, rising and walking to the top of the steps. A few seconds later, Mark's classic Mercedes 320B Cabriolet appeared, trailing a stream of dust. He pulled to the side, away from Meg's cottage, and parked beside Grace's Land Rover.

Getting out, he reached back in the car and emerged with his briefcase in one hand and a magnum bottle in the other. Holding the bottle up as he walked toward the stoep, he said, "A surprise, Grace—something to celebrate William's visit."

Grace first kissed Mark and then relieved him of the magnum and examined it. Mark shook hands with me and kissed Meg on the cheek. "Welcome back, William. You can tell us all about your adventures at dinner." He walked into the house.

"My goodness!" Grace exclaimed. "This is a very fine wine."

Meg and I stared at her. Continuing, she said, "Mouton Rothschild, Pauillac, a fine red blend and quite dear in price. I shall have to reward Mark for this wonderful gift." Holding the bottle in the air like a trophy, she paraded into the house. Meg and I smiled at each other. Holding her glass imperiously, she said, "Bring the wine William, and I will reward you." She pointed at the table.

"Of course, madam," I said. Bowing and picking up the bottle and my glass, I followed her into the dining room.

It was a family dinner, with Mark and Grace treating me like a son-in-law, an established member of the team rather than a boyfriend trying out for the varsity. It felt good to be accepted. In between the all-green salad (which I ignored), roast lamb, fried potatoes, German chocolate cake, and three bottles of wine, I regaled them with tales of Mombasa and the safari. They roared when I told them that an anonymous person had punched Bernie after doing his ugly-American routine.

Grace interjected, "Clara told me a lot in the short time I talked with her this morning. While she wouldn't tell me, I suspect I know who the 'anonymous person' is, and I heartily approve of his actions."

At 2300, Mark looked at his watch and announced, "Some of us have to work tomorrow, so if you will excuse me, I am going to bed."

"Good night, Mark," I said. "Thank you for your hospitality."

"Not mine, William," he said, sweeping his hand to include the ladies, "*our* hospitality, and you're welcome."

I offered to clean up, and Grace accepted, following Mark to their bedroom. As I picked up the dishes, Meg dropped a glass, shattering it but luckily missing her foot. That's when I realized she wasn't tipsy—she was drunk. "Sit down, Meg," I said, leading her away from the glass on the floor and ensconcing her in a soft chair in the living room. "I'll clean up."

She gave me a lopsided smile and said, "Okay."

It took fifteen minutes to clean up everything, including the broken glass. I turned out the kitchen light as I walked to Meg, leaving only the dim glow from the nightlight by the door. Meg was asleep, but a kiss woke her. She wrapped her arms around my neck and said, "Take me to bed." It was a worthy thought, but it was all I could do to get her upright. We stumbled back to the cottage, with ample moonlight to light the way, and with some fumbling help from Meg, I undressed her and got her into bed. I undressed, peed, and brushed my teeth. When I got back, Meg was snoring. "This must be a prelude to married life," I thought, and laughed aloud. Crawling into bed beside her, I rolled her onto her side to stop the snoring, whispered, "I love you," and went to sleep.

The grind of Mark's car-starter motor woke me. It was 0630. Filtered sunlight peeked through the gauze curtain, splashing dabs of light on the bureau and wall. The now familiar aroma of num-nums pervaded everything. Looking at Meg, I saw that she hadn't twitched all night, so I sidled out of bed, did the three S's in the bathroom, and came back to the bed. I leaned over Meg; the first less-than-perfect effect displayed itself as morning breath. Sour wine isn't romantic, so I kissed her on the forehead, dressed, and walked to the main house. Going in, I brewed a pot of coffee and then took a cup out to the front stoep and sat, enjoying the serenity and coffee until I was interrupted by Grace a half hour later.

"Good morning, William." Looking around, she asked, "Where is Meg?"

"She's a little under the weather this morning. She's sleeping in."

"Is she ill?" concern on her face.

"No. Hungover."

Putting her hand to her mouth, Grace giggled. "Oh, my. Now, I'll have something to chide her about." She giggled again. She went in and soon returned with a cup of coffee and joined me on the stoep.

"William," she said, in a serious tone, "are you in love with Meg or just in lust with her?"

Caught by surprise, I hesitated a few seconds, looked at Grace, and then answered, "Both."

Grace blinked but didn't reply, so I continued.

"I love to talk to her, listen to her expound on life here in South Africa, her growing up, her aspirations. I love to sit and snuggle and not say a word. I could do that for hours with her, something I've never wanted to do with any other girl. Just seeing her smile makes me want to smile. Meg is incredibly sexy, so I would have to be dead to not want to sleep with her, but it's so much more than sex. Meg is…incredible."

"That's a lovely answer, William." There was moistness on her cheeks. "Meg is my life, and I want to see her happy."

"So do I, Grace. Let me ask you a question." I was treading on dangerous ground. "What if Meg wants to move to the States, with me?"

An iciness came over her. "If she would be happy there, I would have to agree with it…but I don't think she would ever be really, happy anywhere except here, at home."

After a minute, she rose. "I have to get dressed." She left. The battle lines were drawn, and I now knew that if I tried to take Meg away from South Africa, I would have a war on my hands—one I don't think I could win.

Chapter 27

NEW YORK ECHOES

Dennis was not happy that Gabe Santorini, the chief mate from the *MorMacGlen*, had heard "stories" about the guns and explosives smuggled aboard the *Pride* on the prior trip. Right after William had left his office on the way to Meg and Grace's home, Gabe raised the subject.

"That's bullshit, Gabe. Who told you that?"

"Just a story going around the pier in Brooklyn. They say Sparky got involved, and that's why he ended up dead."

"That kind of story can get people in trouble, and I don't appreciate you spreading it around."

"I'm not spreading anything around. I'm just telling you what I'm hearing out there. Besides, I don't care what a guy does on his own time. No skin off my ass. Who knows? I might take advantage of an occasional opportunity if it fell in my lap."

Dennis let out a *harumph*, a sure sign of his irritation. Switching the subject, he asked, "What are we getting from you to load?"

"We're matching hatch for hatch, so we're transferring cased tea for New York from the no. 4 hatch; cashews for New York from the no. 3 hatch; and sisal and cloves for New York from the no. 2 hatch. That will get us high enough, and we can move oil and water between tanks to give us enough of a starboard list, so the welders have a clear area to work."

"Any cargo damaged from the water?"

"Yeah, the bottom three tiers of coffee bags got wet, and there may be seepage into one tier above. Once we get the repairs done, we'll transfer the good coffee into the upper-tween deck and dump the damaged stuff ashore."

"No damage to the deep tanks?"

"Nah, we were lucky. We had them sealed up tight, so the water sloshing in the hold didn't penetrate."

"Damn lucky," Dennis commented. "The agent said they canceled all our bookings to make room for your cargo. The only thing we'll be loading from the dock is the two bulldozers we brought here a couple of weeks ago."

"Why?"

"The stevedore dropped one when discharging, and the buyer refuses to take just the one left. So, they're sending them both back to New York."

Shaking his head, Gabe commented, "They're all fucking nuts. Both dozers will end up at auction, and Frankie's boys will get them for a song."

"Frankie? As in Frankie who runs the docks and other things in Brooklyn?"

"The same. His guy always seems to be the high bidder at the auctions, mainly because no one else is bidding when he bids on something."

"Gabe, how do you know Frankie?"

"I'm a Brooklyn boy, and my name is Santorini. How could I not know about Frankie?"

Dennis *harumph*ed again. "Is that where you heard the stories?"

Gabe shrugged, rolled his hands, and said, "Who knows? Maybe." He stood up. "I gotta go. The old man," he said, referring to the captain of the *MorMacGlen*, "wants to know what's happening with the cargo operations." Offering his hand to Dennis, he said, "Maybe we can work a few things out."

Dennis shook his hand but remained silent. After Gabe had left, Dennis wondered if Captain Coltrain's relationship with Frankie had anything to do with Gabe's parting remark.

The longshoremen started at 1300 hours, and Tony was busy opening the hatches. In the no. 3 and no. 4 hatches, they used the *Glen* gear for the cargo operation, but in the no. 2 hatch, they used the *Pride* gear because one of the booms on the *Glen* sustained damage. Tony double-checked that the bosun's gang had topped up all the booms in the nos. 3 and 4 hatches as high as possible to get them out of the way.

Normally, the winch operator only needed to get the load swung out over the pier and then lower it, but "the pier" was now comprised of the hatches of the *Pride* at no. 3 and no. 4 and the hatch of the *Glen* at no. 2, and the space was tighter. As a result, the winch operator focused on the signalman at each hatch; they weren't standing directly over, and the movement was a lot slower.

Work progressed without incident, and at 1700 hours, the gangs knocked off for the night. Tony washed up and went to the salon, where Eunice, the captain's wife, greeted him.

She sat at the captain's table with Clara Simpson, waving her hand at the clouds of cigarette smoke she had created, and beckoned him over. Tony bent over next to Eunice. Low enough so that no one except Clara and Tony could hear, she said, "I'm horny. Be at my room at 7:00."

As Tony stood up, Clara averted her eyes. She appeared sympathetic enough to not embarrass him.

Tony sat and ordered dinner from Joey, the pantryman. As the food was being served, Dennis arrived and slammed into his seat, upset about something.

"What's the matter, Dennis?

Glaring at Tony, Dennis eased his look, and he asked, "Anything strange happen today on deck?"

"Strange? No nothing strange. Is something wrong?"

Dennis shook his head and avoided continuing the conversation by ordering dinner.

The captain never came in for dinner, so after dessert, Dennis went to the captain's office and knocked on the open door.

"Come in," the captain called from his bedroom.

Closing the office door behind him, he walked to the bedroom door. "Captain, is there something going on with Gabe Santorini that I should know about?"

The captain stared at him for a few seconds and then said, "There may be. I don't know yet."

"What the hell does that mean?"

"Just what I said, Dennis," he said, emphasizing every word. "I'm waiting to find out what's going on. I'm expecting a telephone call tonight that will enlighten matters."

"That call, it wouldn't happen to come from a certain guy in Brooklyn, would it?"

Pausing, the captain lit a cigarette. "Dennis, I had hoped that our business relationship with the 'gentleman' from Brooklyn had ended, but it is clear now that it will end only when he decides it will end."

"That's what I was afraid of. Who else besides you, me, and Gabe know anything?"

"I have no idea who knows what on the *Glen*, but aboard here, it is only you and me. I hope no one else needs to get involved."

Dennis let out a *harumph* and walked out.

Chapter 28

CRISIS

Meg appeared an hour later, wearing light-green gym shorts and a loose T-shirt that showed she wasn't wearing a bra. She was bleary-eyed but still vivacious. I decided not to tell her of my conversation with Grace, to avoid a possible argument between them. I didn't want to irritate Meg and cut off the flow of affection coming my way. Cowardly? Manipulative? Maybe, but I wasn't taking any chances on ruining the last full day we would be together, at least for the foreseeable future.

"Coffee?" I asked, holding up my cup.

She leaned over and kissed me, the mint of her toothpaste having dispelled the early morning breath. "Love some," she said, and she plopped into the adjacent seat.

Going to the kitchen, I poured her a cup and topped off mine, bringing both back to the veranda. Setting the cups on the table, I leaned into Meg and nuzzled her neck, evincing a cooing sigh. "Something you need to know. Grace knows you have a hangover. She'll try to blackmail you. At least, that's what she said."

"No problem." She tilted her head back, arching her back and pulling my lips to hers. "She'll have to get used to a lot of things now that you're in our life." Trading her hold on me for the cup, she took a long swig of coffee.

"Want some breakfast?"

She eyed me skeptically. "The man can cook, too? I am a lucky woman."
Nodding, I said, "Yes, you are, but I'm a luckier man."

"That's right, and I think you should get lucky right now." Dropping the coffee cup on the table she stood, grabbed my hand, and pulled me to my feet, moving off the veranda. We ran all the way back to the bungalow, leaped up the front steps, and slammed the heavy ebony door in our rush to get naked. Meg pulled the T-shirt over her head, and my lips caressed her nipple before she finished the movement. Letting out a soft moan, she pulled my head in tight as I pulled down her shorts. I walked her back to the sofa, my tongue worked from one nipple to the other and my hands roaming her back and cheeks, rubbing and squeezing. With a firm grip on both cheeks, I moved south, tongue flicking over her belly button and darting around the edges of her vulva, probing vaginal lips and finding the clitoris. She collapsed onto the sofa and wrapped her legs around my neck.

"Oh, God! Stop, I'm coming." She halfheartedly tried to pull my head up, but I persisted until she shuddered, slamming herself against my lips. Standing, I dropped my shorts and slid into her, coming to an orgasm within seconds.

We lay there for a few minutes, half on and half off the sofa, her legs knotted around my waist, our breath returning to normal.

She cradled my cheeks; her kiss was gentle, tender. "We'll save that for special occasions."

"Special occasions?"

"Yes. Like morning, or afternoon, or evening. Special."

Unwrapping her legs, she said, "Let me up; I have to pee." And we both giggled.

"Me, too." I stood up and offered a hand as she stood and walked to the bathroom.

We finished our business, ladies first, went into the bedroom, and lay down, curling into one another, arms and legs entwined. We drifted off to sleep.

Waking to a wet sensation, I found Meg's lips surrounding my penis. When I groaned, Meg lifted her head, smiled, and said, "I thought I'd get even."

Letting her have her way, I twitched and moaned until she raised up and impaled herself on me, grinding her hips and pressing hard.

"Wait," I said, grabbed a pillow, and stuck it under my ass, giving me better penetration and Meg a bigger smile. This was a slow-motion fuck. She rode me like a horse. Incredible! Five or six times, I stopped her to keep from coming until she got to the brink and climaxed, with me coming seconds later. She collapsed and lay there, spent, until I slipped out of her and drifted off to sleep.

Meg woke me with a kiss, wrapped in a towel and smelling fresh from the shower. "Shower's empty. Your turn."

Grunting, I nodded, rose, and walked into the bathroom, stopping to pee again before stepping into the shower. When I came out, towel wrapped around my waist, Meg was sitting on the sofa, dressed in a lime-green sunsuit, a bright contrast to her red hair. Raising my hands, pretending to shield my eyes, I said, "That suit will blind people in direct sunlight."

She pouted, stood, and walked toward the bedroom. "If you don't like it, I'll change."

"Whoa, I'm teasing. You look great in anything." I was surprised she took my comment seriously. A lesson learned in my "dealing with Meg" class.

"Okay," she said, smiling again. "Get dressed. I'm hungry." She pulled off my towel and slapped me on the ass to hurry me along.

We walked hand in hand to the house from the bungalow, gazing at each other and smiling. The walk was hot, humid, and dusty, but we didn't notice anything except each other. As we climbed the steps of the veranda, it was just past noon. Grace wasn't there to greet us, so Meg called upstairs for her. When she got no response, she gave me a curious look and went upstairs. She screamed, "*Mum!*" I bolted up the stairs after her.

Spread eagled on the floor, wearing only panties, Grace looked as if she were posing for *Playboy*—except she was unconscious. "Is she breathing?" I asked as I dropped to my knees beside her. Meg, on the other side, leaning over her, didn't answer, so I pushed her back and put my ear to Grace's lips and then her chest. No breath and no heartbeat. First-aid training kicked in, and I tilted Grace's head back to open her air passage, pinched her nose, and breathed into her mouth, and then I started pumping on her chest. I had been in the first class at Massachusetts Maritime Academy to get this resuscitation training, and this was the first time I'd used it for real. In between breaths, I told Meg to call a doctor, and she stumbled to the phone.

I lost track of time, just trying to maintain rhythm, but it couldn't have been more than a few minutes. I was beginning to feel the strain. As I leaned in to breathe again, Grace moaned. I listened to her chest and detected a heartbeat. I rocked back on my heels. It struck me that Grace still appeared naked, or nearly so. She had a red space between her breasts from my pushing, and I felt embarrassed to be hovering over her.

"Meg!" I called, not realizing she stood behind me. "Get a pillow and a sheet to cover her up. Is the doctor on the way?"

She handed me a pillow and pulled the sheet off the bed and draped it over Grace. Just then, I heard an odd whooping sound, a siren. Meg turned and ran downstairs.

The doctor charged into the room. He said, "Move away! I'm Dr. Graul." I rolled back off stiff knees, clambering to my feet. Meg hovered at the door, so I went and hugged her. We both watched as the doctor listened to Grace's heart with a stethoscope. Turning, he instructed Meg to have the ambulance attendants bring the stretcher. When Meg left, he said, "Who are you?"

"I'm William Connolly, sir, Meg's boyfriend."

"Ah!" was his response, and he turned back to Grace, adjusting the pillow to ensure that her head still tilted back, keeping her air passage open.

The attendants arrived; in retrospect, they were a comical-looking pair, their physical looks and actions reminding me of Stan Laurel and Oliver Hardy. I felt almost afraid that they would drop the stretcher once they loaded Grace on it, but they got her down the stairs and into the ambulance without any mishaps.

The doctor climbed in the back of the ambulance and hooked Grace up with an oxygen mask. He told one of the attendants to follow the ambulance in his car. Apparently, they had followed him to the farm. As they closed the door of the ambulance, Meg called, "Where are you taking her?"

"Saint Aiden's" was the muted response, and off they went.

"Wait while I get Mum's keys, and we'll follow them," Meg said. Less than a minute later, she reappeared, and we climbed into the Land Rover and followed the dust trail of the ambulance.

We never caught up to them, but Meg knew where to go, and considering her state of mind, she focused amazingly well on driving, pulling into the parking area as they unloaded Grace.

It would be a while before we could visit Grace in her room. In that time, to distract Meg, I asked her about the hospital, and she related its history. The original Saint Aiden's was inspired by Rev. Dr. Lancelot Parker Booth, an English doctor who set up a missionary school in 1886 for Indian laborers and a dispensary behind the school. After he left in 1906, another doctor from India, Reverend C. M. C. Bone, along with a nurse only remembered as Miss Cole, set up a sixteen-bed hospital in a house across the street from the mission school. This was the original Saint Aiden's hospital. Getting by the political problems of the Group Areas Act in 1960, when the hospital was declared a special zone, the hospital board sought and managed to get permission to expand their premises. A month ago, the new Saint Aiden's church, adjacent to the hospital, had been dedicated. Meg added that both her father and Grace's fiancé, Mark, had done a lot to help the hospital during the difficult times.

When she mentioned Mark, I interrupted. "Mark...you need to call him and let him know."

Putting both hands to her cheeks, she said, "Oh, God." She ran to the greeter's desk and asked where the telephones were. She disappeared around the corner.

Sitting there, I thought back to my last encounter with Grace, wondering if the stress induced by my implying that Meg would move with me to the States triggered the heart attack. Pending guilt loomed over me, but I brushed it away, secure in the belief that I hadn't caused the problem.

Meg returned. "He's coming directly. The bank is only ten minutes from here. Thank you for reminding me." She started to cry. I gathered her in my arms, and we stood in a corner of the lobby until Mark strode in the door and spotted us.

It was an hour before they let Meg, Mark, and me into the room where Grace lay, hooked up to an IV, oxygen mask, and other wires monitoring her heartbeat, displayed on a screen beside the bed. Grace's eyes were open, but she didn't seem responsive. Doctor Graul was in the room, consulting with two other doctors who left when we came in. Dr. Graul greeted Mark, telling him that Grace apparently had a heart attack. She was lucky that Meg had found her and called him. Any longer, and she may have gone into cardiac arrest.

It was then that Meg interjected. "But Mum was dead when we found her!"

Mark snapped around, and Dr. Graul said, "No, she wasn't!" Motioning for us all to leave the room, we followed him outside. "Why would you say that, especially in front of your mother? She's been frightened enough by this."

"But it's true," Meg insisted. "Before you got there, she wasn't breathing, and her heart had stopped. William saved her."

Everyone stared at me, and then Dr. Graul said, "I wondered what caused the redness on her chest. Did you use the resuscitation process?"

"Yes, sir. In my last year of school, it was part of our first-aid training. I'm glad I paid attention in class." I emitted a sickly snicker.

Dr. Graul put his hand on my shoulder and said, "My boy. We're all glad you were a diligent student. When she is stable, I will let Grace know but not now. The less stress, the better." Stepping back, he said, "You may all visit with Grace but only for five minutes. I've sedated her, and she may already be asleep, but a little handholding never hurts." Turning to William, he smiled. "After all, she just came back from the dead."

Meg and Mark preceded me, and I held back at the door. "Doctor."

"Yes?"

"There's no need to tell Grace at all. When we found her on the floor, she was almost nude, and it may embarrass her to know I saw her in that state."

He paused. "William, I won't tell her if you don't want me to. We won't know for a while how badly her heart has been damaged, but knowing that you brought her back from the brink, I think that a little embarrassment is the least of her problems."

Chapter 29

COERCION

Tony stood at the railing by the gangway, watching the longshoremen climb aboard the ship. Half of them crossed from the *Pride* onto the *Glen* via the brow gangway erected between the two ships at the aft end of the no. 3 hatch. Tony, still bothered by the chief mate's "Anything strange happen today on deck?" remark, knew that Dennis was perturbed about something.

It was the same load plan as the previous day. The no. 2 lower-tween deck loaded packs of sisal using the gear on the *Pride*. Using *Glen* gear, they loaded cases of cashews into the no. 3 upper-tween deck aft and cases of tea into the no. 4 upper-tween deck aft. It was easy for Tony since they were only loading at half the normal rate, due to the poor line of sight for the winch operators. He had plenty of time to muse about last night's tryst with Eunice.

They had incredible sex. Doing it on board with the possibility of the captain walking in on them didn't seem to affect Eunice but heightened the nervousness of Tony and, in a weird way, made it more exciting. He and Eunice had enough practice now that his fear of the captain had waned to simple apprehension. He no longer lost his hard-on at every strange noise. What resurrected his fear as they lay naked on her bed was Eunice's question: "Would you like to spend some time with me in New York?"

"Why would I do that?" he responded.

Fixing him with a "Just how stupid are you?" look, she passed her hands across her body, saying, "For more of this, what else?"

He didn't reply.

"I do enjoy your company," she continued. When he still didn't reply, she said, "I'm not looking to adopt you, for Chrissake." Her petulance and sarcasm were rising. "A few weeks, maybe a month. I'm divorcing Marcus, and I could use some company for a while."

"Marcus?" he thought. He didn't know the captain's first name. "Look, Eunice, I'm sorry, but your request surprised me. I never expected to see you again after this trip. One thing is for sure: I won't be welcome on this ship if Captain Coltrain is here, so I have to find another ship. That will probably take a few weeks, so sure, I'll stay with you."

"Good," she said, reaching out and stroking his penis. "Now, put that marvelous tongue of yours to work."

At 1000 hours, Tony went in to the salon for coffee, expecting to grab a cup and take it on deck. Dennis, the chief mate, waved him over to the table.

"Everything going okay, Tony?"

"Yeah, it's slow but steady."

"The *Glen*'s mate watching his side of it?"

"Yeah. The junior third's name is Jack. Nice guy out of Maine Maritime. Graduated two years ago. He was on watch yesterday afternoon, so I guess he's covering for the other third mate like I'm covering for William. Real talkative. He doesn't like their chief mate."

"Santorini?

"If that's the chief's name, yeah."

"That's him. Did Jack say why he didn't like him?"

"He's just a mean prick, always ragging on Jack and the other third mate, trying to embarrass them. When they were in Walvis Bay, Jack and the other third mate were at a bar when Santorini came in, drunk and carrying a briefcase, and he insisted on buying them a drink, buddy-buddy-like, way out of character. When they left, they took a taxi to the pier. He told me they don't let private cars or taxis onto the pier and that the guards are strict there.

"Anyway, as they got out of the taxi, Santorini said, 'Damn, I forgot something at the bar. Take my briefcase to my room while I go back to the bar.'

"They thought nothing of it and did as he asked. At the gate, the guards questioned about the briefcase. It was obviously heavy. They said, 'No idea. It's the chief mate's, and he asked us to take it aboard. He's the boss, so we're taking it aboard. It's heavy. May be bottles of booze.'

"The guards laughed and waved them through. Jack left the briefcase in the chief's room. When Santorini returned, he banged on Jack's door, demanding the briefcase, right back to his usual prick self. Jack walked to his room and showed it to him, sitting on the floor beside his desk. Santorini threw him out of his room, no thanks, nothing."

"Tony," he said, a look of incredulity on his face. "That is one hell of a story."

"Well, I told you, Jack is talkative."

"Okay. Let me know if Santorini interferes in anything. If he does, I'll handle it, okay?"

"Sure, Dennis." Tony went back on deck.

Just before noon, as the longshoremen broke for lunch, Tony saw the *Glen's* chief mate, Santorini, crossing the brow gangway. He was carrying a large briefcase in his right hand. Santorini leaned to his left to offset the weight. Tony trailed behind him as he entered the house and climbed the stairs, passing the salon deck and continuing up to the officer's quarters.

Tony went in to the salon, nostrils assailed by the ever-present odor of fried onions, eyes and ears greeted by the smile of Joey, the pantryman, and a "Howdy, Tony." He sat down as Dennis entered and joined him at the table.

"I just saw Santorini go up. I thought he was heading to see you."

"Didn't see him."

"He was carrying a briefcase like the one Jack described. It looked hefty."

Dennis shook his head, gave a *harumph*, and ordered lunch from Joey.

As they waited for the food to arrive, Dennis said, "I see Bernie's here. Where's Clara?"

"Eunice said she and Clara were going ashore this morning. They've become real pals since they have something in common. They both hate their husbands."

Dennis smirked, remembering how Clara had "thanked" him after returning from the safari weekend. "That's true, but considering the delicacy of the situation, I hope you're smart enough to not be too obvious in consoling the distraught wife."

Tony hung his head. "Sorry, Dennis, but you know none of this was my idea."

Joey brought their lunch; Dennis had a ham-and-cheese sandwich and Tony, a ham-and-egg sandwich. They busied themselves eating. Finishing first, Dennis rose, nodded at Tony, and went to his office. Sitting at his desk, he pondered Santorini's visit. He could only have gone to the captain. Stewing on it a few minutes, he called the captain on the phone, reluctant to walk into his office and chance bumping into Santorini.

"Yes!" He received the usual stentorian greeting.

"Captain, if you're alone, I'd like a minute with you."

"I'm alone, Dennis. Come on up."

Dennis knocked at the open door and entered, as the captain walked out of his bedroom. Because of their illegal complicity on the previous voyage, he knew the captain wouldn't get offended at his brusqueness, so he asked, "What was in the briefcase, Captain?"

The captain lit up a cigarette, smiled, and said, "Word gets around fast."

"It was obvious, and it was heavy enough that he struggled with it."

Nodding, the captain took a long drag on the smoke, blew it out, and said, "I don't know what's in the briefcase. It's locked and sealed. But it is full, and it is heavy. I had to lift it to put it in the safe."

"So now we're messenger boys, making deliveries? Is it for Frankie back in Brooklyn?"

"Yes, Dennis, it is. Frankie made it a special request when I talked to him on the phone. Said he would very much appreciate it if I were to personally deliver it to him when we reach New York. I didn't ask what it was, and he didn't offer to tell me. I think it's better that way."

"Is this it, or are we getting any other surprises from Santorini?"

"This is the only thing that concerns Frankie. I want nothing to do with Santorini beyond this package."

"Good. I don't like the son of a bitch, and I sure don't trust him."

"I agree with you."

Chapter 30

BEGINNING GOOD-BYE

I leaned against the wall while Meg and Mark, on opposite sides of the bed, hovered over Grace, each holding a hand, trying hard to appear cheerful. It was more for each other's sake since Grace had drifted off to sleep, or, at least, was comatose from the drugs. We were there for ten minutes when the nurse came in and ordered us out of the room.

Mark suggested the cafeteria. Meg and I followed without comment. Mark pointed to a table, and Meg sat down. "Would you like a tea? I'm having one."

Meg shook her head, I said no, and Mark went toward the food counter.

Sitting beside Meg, I draped an arm over her shoulder; together, we were an isle of loneliness in a Sargasso Sea of angst among other groups of people in twos and threes, awaiting news of loved ones. I said, Grace will be fine. This was scary today, but she's here, alive, and in good hands."

Sighing, leaning into me, Meg said, "But she wouldn't be if you weren't here." Turning, she kissed me softly and sweetly. "Thank you."

Smiling, I said, "You're welcome. No charge for the medical consultation." It extracted a weak grin.

Mark returned and sat opposite us. "William. Thank you for saving Grace." It was blunt and direct.

"Meg, we have to focus on what's best for your mum. The medical expenses are covered through my health-insurance plan at the bank. This hospital is part of the National Health Care System, but my plan will supplement that. Dr. Graul will ensure that only the best doctors attend Grace." Pausing, he said, "You do know that, don't you?" He reached across and held her hand.

Blinking back tears, Meg nodded.

"Good," he continued. "William, what's your schedule?"

"Don't know when we're sailing, but I have to return to the ship tomorrow by noon."

"Where do you go from here?"

"Cape Town, a two-day run."

He sat, silent for a minute. "It's best if you both return to the farm tonight." Meg started to protest.

Shushing her, he said. "I'll stay here with Grace. The hospital has a few guest beds for instances like this. No doubt, I can use one for the night. Come back in the morning. If Grace needs anything, I will call you before 7:00 a.m. No arguing. We both have enough stress."

Meg nodded.

"Good. Off with you now. Get something to eat and a good night's rest. I'm sure there will be better news on Grace in the morning."

Offering to drive, I felt relieved when Meg smiled and declined the offer.

"My stress level would overload, watching you trying to navigate and drive on the left side of the road. I'm okay."

Rush hour, what there was of it, was on the wane, and we reached the farm in an hour.

As we walked into the kitchen, I asked, "Want something to eat? Remember, the man can cook." This drew another wan smile from Meg.

"Let me see what's in the refrigerator," I said, opening the door and rummaging. "There's lamb and potatoes left over." I talked into the fridge, my voice muffled by the door.

"That's fine. You want me to heat it up?"

"No, I'll do it." I lifted the dishes and placed them on the counter. "How about a glass of wine?"

Cocking her neck as if listening (Grace had the same mannerism), Meg nodded. "Make it white." She went into the bathroom while I busied myself with the food and poured two glasses of wine. Red was preferable, but the white was already open.

Thirty minutes later, we ate, standing at the counter, side by side, occasionally touching hands. When finished, I cleaned up while Meg went to her mum's room. After cleaning, I sat at the end of the table and waited. Fifteen minutes passed. As I was wondering if I should go look for her, she appeared, carrying a small overnight bag.

"Some of Mum's things. Underwear, makeup kit, pajamas."

"That reminds me. I have to take my things when we go to the hospital tomorrow morning."

A stricken look appeared, and she cried, "You're leaving me!"

There was no rational response to that statement, so I got up and hugged her, letting her cry. I don't know how long we stood there, but she pushed away, took a paper napkin from the counter, wiped her eyes, blew her nose, took a deep breath, and yelled "Fuck!" Then, she giggled.

"Feel better now?"

"A little. Let's walk to the bungalow. I need to move around."

"Sure. Want to bring the wine?"

"No. Right now, I want you, holding me, being here." She reached for my hand and led me out the door.

We lay in bed naked, her idea. No sex. I had an involuntary erection when she snuggled against me; it went away. The heightened intimacy was chaste.

At 0530, I awoke, undraped her arm from across my chest, and went to the bathroom. On return, standing over her, admiring her magnificence, a deep sense of loss washed over me, knowing that after today, I might never see Meg again. I felt estranged, as if looking from a cliff top, making her somehow unattainable. I had never felt so vulnerable nor so reliant on anyone else. I was hopelessly in love with this woman.

As I was standing there, gazing down, she stirred, rolled over, and smiled. "What are you doing?" she asked.

"Realizing how my life has changed now that you're part of it."

"That's a good thing, right?"

"No, that's a great thing."

Stretching, she asked, "What time is it?"

"A little before six."

Reaching for my hand, she pulled me beside her. "That was nice, lying there with you all night, but now I need you to make love to me. I can't forget about Mum and the fact that you're leaving, so I need a distraction, and you are good at distracting me."

We made love—slow, gentle, urgent only at the end. Then, we rose, showered, dressed, and left for the hospital at 0730.

We found Mark walking back to Grace's room from the cafeteria, tea and scone in hand.

"How is Mum?" Grace asked.

"Much better, Meg, much better. They chased me out of the room twenty minutes ago to do some tests. Have you had breakfast?"

We both shook our heads. "I'm not hungry," Meg said.

"Have something. Grace will chastise me thoroughly if I don't watch out for you while she's indisposed." This elicited a smile from Meg, but she still declined food.

Dr. Graul emerged when we reached the room. "Good morning, Meg, William. Give the nurse a minute to reassemble Grace before you go in. She vomited this morning when she drank too much water, and they are changing the bedding."

Noting the stricken look on Meg's face, he hurriedly continued, "Everything is fine. Grace is doing amazingly well. Her EKG looks normal. She has no outward signs of distress."

The nurse walked out of the room, and Dr. Graul motioned for us to go in. Meg led the way. Grace sat up in bed, propped up by pillows. Her face erupted in a smile as Meg ran to the bedside and hugged her; then, they both cried. Mark and I waited near the door until Grace took note of us, and then he stepped forward and, in a pretentiously stern tone, said, "Well, Grace, now that you've given us all a bloody good fright, what do you have to say for yourself?"

She paused. "I love you. I'll try not to do it again."

"Bloody right, you won't." A huge grin belied the severity of his tone, and then the three of them started talking.

Dr. Graul tapped my shoulder, leaned in, and whispered, "I told Grace you saved her life. She asked me what happened. I didn't tell her the state of undress she was in." I smiled and nodded. He then turned and left the room.

A few minutes passed; there were smiles etched on their faces as they gabbed. Grace looked at me and said, "I believe I owe you a rather large thank-you."

"You don't owe me a thing. I'm grateful my training paid off and we're having this conversation."

"You are the most diplomatic young man I have ever met," she said, and I blushed.

Meg rose from the bed and wrapped her arms around me. Her face was buried in my chest, and a muffled "Every day, I find more reasons to love him" escaped.

Staring right into my eyes, Grace said, "Yes, I see that." Remembering our last conversation on her veranda, I knew she had signaled a truce. Grace smiled. I smiled and nodded, content in the moment.

"I've gotta go. I'm due back at the ship by noon."

Mark said, "I'll drive you. I have to check in at the office."

Surprised, I was glad Meg didn't insist on driving me. I didn't want a scene at the gangway. "Thanks, Mark. I have to get my bag from the car." Holding out my hand to Meg for the keys, she took my hand and said, "I'll walk you to the car."

The hospital seemed deserted at that hour; there were only two people in the waiting room and no one at the reception desk as we passed through, silence clinging to us. Meg unlocked the Range Rover, and I retrieved my bag. Setting it on the ground, I pulled Meg close, inhaling the scent of her hair, hoping it would last. "I'll call you from Cape Town," I said.

"No! Call me tonight."

"Will you be home? I don't have a number for the hospital."

"I'll be home. Mum is doing fine. Mark will keep her company."

Mark appeared at the entrance to the hospital. "My ride is here."

Meg clutched the sides of my face and kissed me fiercely. "I love you," she said and ran toward the entrance before I could respond.

At 1145, I was climbing the gangway of the *Pride*, wondering what the hell was happening in my life.

Chapter 31

STRANGE CARGO

I dropped my bag in my cabin and went looking for the chief mate., finding him in his office.

"Good morning, Dennis. I'm back."

Looking up from the cargo loading plan, he glanced at his watch. "Good. Find Tony, and relieve him. Let him bring you up to speed on what's happening."

As I turned to leave, he asked, "Everything okay with the girlfriend?"

Rather than go into a long-winded explanation, I said, "Yeah, everything's fine." and left to find Tony.

I bumped into him, literally, leaving the mate's office.

"Hey, welcome back, William."

"Hi, Tony. Dennis told me to relieve you. What's going on with the loading?"

"Wait a minute. I have to tell Dennis something." I followed him back into Dennis's office.

"Dennis. You said you wanted to know if anything strange was happening."

Dennis lowered his pencil and looked up. "Yeah?"

"When we started to load the cloves into the no. 2 upper-tween deck, the chief mate on the *Glen* relieved Jack, the junior third mate."

Dennis shook his head. "What's strange about that?"

"Well, he climbed down the hold and then when he came up, he crossed onto the *Pride*, came to me, and told me I could take a coffee break, that he'd watch things for a while."

"What did you do?" Dennis challenged.

"Told him I couldn't leave unless you said it was okay. He tried to convince me it was okay, and when I ignored him, he stood at the rail for a while, watching a few drafts of cloves get loaded. Then, he left and went back aboard the *Glen*."

"Okay, Tony. Thanks. Santorini is a strange bird. Anything else?"

"Nope."

"Bring William up to speed." With that, we left.

"The gang's knocked off for lunch, William. Let's eat, and I'll catch you up on things."

After two days ashore, the familiar smells of fried onions, coffee, and baked bread seemed new. A peanut-butter-and-jelly sandwich and a glass of milk did it for me. Fresh supplies had arrived, and milk was a treat. Tony had a cheeseburger. In between mouthfuls, he apprised me of the cargo plans and related most of the story from Jack, the *Glen*'s third mate, about Santorini, the chief mate.

"Sounds like an odd duck," I said.

"Yeah. Not the friendly type at all. He was pissed when I wouldn't leave the hatch, like he tried to hide something. Fidgety, bouncing from foot to foot. If he was, I couldn't tell. Nothing but cloves came over the side."

"I'll keep an eye out. Maybe he'll try the same thing with me."

Tony shrugged and switched topics.

"How's Meg?"

I related the whole thing with Grace, including her being seminaked on the floor.

Tony behaved like a guy. "Nice tits?" he asked.

"C'mon, Tony, she was dying!"

He just raised his eyebrows, so I added, "Yeah, they were nice, but I bruised them pushing on her chest."

"Well, I'm glad she's okay. She seemed nice enough."

"Compared to whom? Eunice? How's that going? Still getting your night-time exercise?"

"Not so loud," he said.

I looked around at the salon, empty except for the two of us. Waving my right arm, I said, "Who's here to hear?"

Leaning in, he told me about Eunice's offer to stay with her for a while in New York.

"Hey, a real gigolo."

"Why not? I can't stay here on the *Pride*."

"That's true. Without Eunice to intercede, the captain would make your life miserable."

"Eunice told me she and the captain are getting divorced. It's all her idea. She made it clear she has all the money, and she is leaving him high and dry. They've had a couple of knock-down-and-drag-out fights, and she avoids him as much as possible now. She's a vindictive bitch, and she used to taunt the captain, but now she seems a little afraid of him."

"I don't know, Tony. When Bernie Simpson hit Clara, it was the captain that sicced Dennis onto Bernie. I don't see him as being violent toward a woman."

"Maybe not, but Eunice knows how to push his buttons, and everybody has their limits."

"Maybe. Anyway, I gotta change into my uniform. See you later."

I changed into my hot-weather uniform: short-sleeve khaki shirt and short pants. I arrived on deck at the gangway by 1250. I watched the longshoremen climb the gangway, dressed in the standard dingy, dusty, coveralls, but they were all smiling and bobbing their heads in greeting as they crossed the top of the gangway and went to their respective places.

Curious, I went to where they were loading cloves in the no. 2 hatch and looked down into the hold. Everything looked normal. They were laying the bags of cloves in even tiers across the forward end of the upper-tween deck. A stevedore tray—an oversize pallet of eight feet by six feet—was being used to transfer the bags from ship to ship. In the semidarkness of the far corner, on the port side nearest to the *Glen*, I saw what appeared to be blue netting on part of the bags that seemed to be separate from the main stow.

I climbed down through the manhole into the upper-tween deck and looked at the bags with netting. They were not lying loose; they were on pallets. Finding the induna, the gang boss, I asked him, "Why are these bags separate, on pallets, and covered with netting?"

He spoke English with a singsong lilt. "The boss mate from the other ship tell us to leave them that way."

"Were they stowed that way on the other ship?"

Bobbing his head, he said, "Yes, Mr. Mate, same way."

"When did they come aboard?"

He seemed puzzled at the question, so I pointed at my watch. "What time did you load them?"

Understanding, he said, "Last load before mealtime."

Thanking him, I told him not to cover them with other bags until I returned. I went back on deck to find Dennis. Something wasn't right.

Knocking on his door, I walked into Dennis's office.

"Dennis, I think I know why the chief mate from the Glen wanted Tony off the deck this morning."

"Why?" he said, looking apprehensive.

"At the last minute, before they broke for lunch, they transferred two pallets of bags covered with blue netting. Left them on the pallets and stuck them in a corner. The chief mate told them to do it."

"Shit! That bastard's up to something." Getting up, he said, "Don't let them bury the pallets."

"I already told them. They won't cover them unless I tell them to."

"Good. Go back, and watch them. I gotta talk to the captain." We both left.

"Captain, that motherfucker is up to no good. It has to be drugs: marijuana or heroin. The smell of the cloves hides the odor of the drugs. Do you think Frankie is involved in this?"

"No, Dennis. If this was Frankie's thing, I believe he would have let me know, like he did the briefcase. I think Santorini is flying solo on this, whatever it is. Why don't you invite Mr. Santorini aboard to have a chat with us? I don't like mysteries, especially the kind that puts me at risk."

Dennis let out a *harumph* and stormed out.

Santorini was standing by the no. 2 hatch, arguing with me, when Dennis came out of the house. Dennis came up behind him and grabbed his shoulder, whipping him around. He hissed, "What the fuck are you trying to pull?"

Santorini threw his hands up in the air. "Whoa, big guy! Take it easy."

Sticking his face right into Santorini's, he said, "This is my ship. You don't say jack shit to my mates on my ship. Got that?"

Backpedaling and squeezed between Dennis, the hatch and me, Santorini had no retreat. Not knowing if a fight would break out, my city-kid instincts kicked in, and I angled myself to hit Santorini from the side if he threw a punch at Dennis.

"Captain Coltrain wants to talk to you, right now. Do we need to ask your captain to sit in?"

"No. No, Dennis," he said, looking around nervously. "Whatever the problem is, I can straighten it out."

"Good. Let's go."

Santorini walked toward the house. Dennis asked me, "What was he arguing about?"

"He told me the two pallets were special samples, and he wanted them covered up to prevent someone from stealing them. That's when you showed up."

"Okay, don't let them cover them." He grinned. "I could see you were ready to sucker-punch him. I was tempted to let you." He walked off, leaving me to watch the cargo operation.

In the captain's room with the door closed, Santorini and Dennis stood while the captain sat in the chair behind the desk.

"You have a decision to make." The captain addressed Santorini. "Tell me what's going on and who is involved. You already know we have mutual acquaintances in Brooklyn. That's why the briefcase is in my safe. I don't believe for a minute that our 'mutual acquaintance' is part of your other shit. That being the case, you are standing alone, and your balls are swinging in the breeze, an easy target. So what do you have to say?"

Sweat on his forehead, shifting from foot to foot, Santorini looked back and forth between Dennis and the captain.

"I will not ask you again, Santorini, and I'm not a patient man."

Blowing out a deep breath, Santorini nodded. "Okay, I'm doing a guy a favor."

"If the guy's name is not Frankie, I don't give a shit," the captain barked.

Shaking his head, he said, "No. This guy is in the Bronx."

The captain raised his eyebrows. "Dangerous game you're playing. Competitor of Frankie?"

"No. I swear. Frankie has his turf; this guy has his. No competition."

There was silence for a few seconds. "I'm waiting," said the captain.

Blowing out another big breath, he said, "It's heroin."

"How much?"

"A lot. A hundred and fifty kilos."

The captain considered this a moment. "This isn't the usual trade route for heroin. Most of it is through the French Connection. Where did it come from?"

"Nigeria."

"That's a long way from here."

"They had an uprising there a few months ago. Everything is topsy-turvy. This shipment ended up in Southwest Africa and was put aboard the *Glen* in Lüderitz Bay."

"Put aboard?"

"I didn't know it was there until after we reached Cape Town. Sailing from Lüderitz Bay, the pilot handed me an envelope as he disembarked. It contained instructions to call someone in Durban when we got to Cape Town. They told me what it was, where it was, and what to do with it when we get to New York. They also reminded me that if there was a problem with the authorities, I would get blamed for everything. I'm the chief mate in charge of cargo. The shit was already on the ship, so I was the perfect fall guy."

"Nice story, but I don't buy it. What's missing? You said you were doing a guy a favor."

There was a pause, and then Santorini continued. "They sweetened the pot. I owe a bookie a lot of dough. They'll scrub the books if I deliver the heroin."

"And you believe they'll do it?" Skepticism dripped off every word.

"I didn't think I had a choice. What now?"

"Well, you aren't sailing with us, so how is the delivery supposed to be made?"

"The stevedores will just unload it in Brooklyn along with the regular cargo and then deliver it. They must have to grease someone at the pier."

"Like I said. You're playing a dangerous game. Brooklyn belongs to Frankie. I can't imagine he'd be happy knowing this stuff moved through his pier and he didn't get an 'honorarium.'"

Cornered, desperate, he said, "So what now, Captain?"

The captain stared at Santorini for a good thirty seconds. "Nothing now, Mr. Santorini. I don't know anything. Dennis knows nothing. All I heard today is a ridiculous story about drugs being smuggled. Not on my ship. Only a rumor. You agree?"

Santorini nodded.

"By the way, you will not set foot on my ship again, understand? You have any business to conduct, send a junior mate."

Nodding his head again, Santorini rasped, "Yeah, I got it."

"Good-bye, Mr. Santorini."

Dennis escorted him to the brow gangway and then returned to the captain.

"Hell of a spot this bastard placed us in, Dennis. I don't like these two pallets sitting there. Might as well wave a flag saying, 'Look at this.'"

"We could dump it overboard on the way back."

Musing, the captain stroked his chin and then lit up a Dunhill Switch from the black box. "Dennis, what I see here is an opportunity. I have no idea who the gentleman from the Bronx is, but I do know Frankie. I don't want to be part of anything that smells of a rat concerning Frankie."

"So what do we do?"

"I'll contact Frankie. For now, keep the pallets separate but accessible. Put them near the manhole access so we can get to them when at sea without having to open the hatch."

"Okay, Captain." Dennis rose and went looking for William.

He found me at the no. 4 hatch, deciding to only tell me enough to ensure my silence.

"William."

"Hey, Dennis."

"Listen, there's something fishy with those two pallets, but we don't know what. I think it may be drugs."

I held up both hands in front of him. "Wait a minute, Dennis. We had this conversation before, at the end of the last voyage. I didn't want to know then, and I don't want to know now. I see two pallets of cloves, and that's all I see."

"Okay, kid. You won't get dragged into anything."

Lowering my hands, I said, "Thanks, Dennis."

As he left, Dennis told me, "Have the gang move those two pallets of cloves underneath the manhole access, and leave them there."

"Will do," I said. Thinking, Dennis must plan on dumping the stuff overboard when we're at sea. Please don't do it on my watch. But I knew that from Dennis's perspective, there was less risk than on Tony's or the second mate's watch.

Cargo operations had ended for the day. Dennis had informed us that we planned on sailing tomorrow at 1500 hours. Everyone arrived at the salon for dinner at the same time, a rarity since Eunice tried to avoid the captain and Clara avoided Bernie. I was the center of conversation. Everyone wanted to hear about Grace, and I related the story, omitting any lurid details.

Much to my embarrassment, Clara blurted out, "My God, William, you saved Grace's life." Then, with a snide look at Bernie, she added, "Yours, too." She was remembering when Bernie fell out of the boat at Ascension Island.

Eunice clapped her hands, slow and melodramatic. "A regular hero," she said, but she smiled as she said it.

Even the captain chimed in. "Well done, Mr. Connolly. I will note that in my voyage report."

Standing, I said, "If you'll excuse me, I told Meg I'd call and check on how Grace is doing. Would it be all right if I use the agent's phone at the gangway, Captain?"

"Certainly."

Retrieving the number from my room, I called, not sure if Meg was home yet or still at the hospital. There was no answer. After ten rings, I hung up, disappointed. Two steps away from the phone, it rang. The watchman had stepped away to give me privacy, so I answered the phone. It was Meg.

"I just called you at home. How did you get this number?"

She laughed. "The local agent gladly gave me this number in exchange for an agreement to never call him again. I have been a pain in the derriere, keeping track of you."

"How is Grace?" I asked.

"Mum is doing great. Dr. Graul is amazed at how well she's recovering. There's no evidence of damage to her heart. None! Dr. Graul keeps shaking his head, mumbling, 'I don't understand.'"

"That's good news. I told Clara and Eunice what happened. They both send best wishes to you and Grace."

"I'll tell Mum. Good news! I'm coming to the ship tonight instead of going home."

My pulse quickened. "When will you get here?"

"I'm going home to change and get some things for Mum, but I should be there soon after eight o'clock."

"I can't wait."

"Me, either. See you soon."

I told Dennis about Meg staying overnight.

"Lucky you. Keep the noise down. No screaming," he said, smiling.

"I'll try," I said, a wide grin decorating my face.

"I was talking about Meg." We both laughed.

Meg arrived at 2015 hours. They wouldn't let the car onto the pier at that hour, so the roving guard drove her to the ship. Clara and Eunice insisted on talking with Meg, so we squirmed for an hour before we got to my cabin. We were naked in no time. My bunk wasn't anywhere near as large as Meg's bed, but we didn't fall out of it despite our gymnastics. It was a wonderful night that ended too soon when my alarm rang at 0700 hours.

We walked through the salon, where Meg said good-bye to everyone. I walked her to the gate as we held hands. At her car, we kissed.

"I'll call you from Cape Town."

"You said that before." A desperate smile caught her tears. "This will be so hard. I miss you so much already."

"We'll get through it. Go on. I don't want you to see me cry." Leaning down, I kissed her, her arms clinging to my neck. "I love you," I said as I stood, turned, and walked to the gate, not looking back, for fear I'd get in the car with her and drive off.

We went on sea watches at midnight, but Tony had covered for me again because Meg was there, so I took his eight-to-twelve watch, going on duty after I dropped Meg at the gate. The induna at the no. 2 hatch had moved the two blue-netted pallets of cloves to the starboard side, right under the manhole access, and had left a small pocket of space around them as they finished building the stow of bags. When they finished transferring the cloves from the *Glen*, they swung the ship's gear out of the way, and a truck crane loaded two bulldozers on deck on the starboard side of the no. 2 hatch. They also loaded a conex box, a metal cargo van (8' x 8' x 8') with a lockable door at one end. Conexes were the precursor to full-size containers that were twenty and forty feet long and were just getting popular in the seagoing trade. These were the spare parts for the dozers. Shipped earlier to Durban on a different ship, they were now getting returned together because of the damage to one bulldozer.

Dennis had them stow the conex next to the manhole access cover. The door was locked but not sealed.

By 1400 hours, all cargo was loaded and secured. At 1500 hours, we were underway.

Chapter 32

HIDING THE HORSE

Sailed from Durban at 1500 hours on Friday, 12/16/66, at 1500 hours. Slightly overcast. Temperature 73 degrees. Southerly wind at 13 mph and increasing. Seas at 8 feet; rollers, not cresting but threatening to. The captain set revolutions for 17 knots since we were riding the 2.5 knot Benguela current down the coast.

Dennis sat in the captain's room, listening to him explain the latest complications with the heroin in the bags of cloves.

"I talked to Frankie before we sailed. I wish I hadn't."

"Oh shit," Dennis commented. "What now?"

"Frankie is unaware of Santorini's dealings, and he's not happy someone in the Bronx will be the recipient. Santorini was correct when he said they each have their turf. What he left out, but I suspected, is that they don't tread on each other's turf without permission."

"Where does that leave us?"

"In shoal waters, Dennis, no place a deep-draft ship wants to be. Frankie wants the heroin 'horse,' as he called it, I hadn't heard that nickname before, to still be delivered in Brooklyn."

"And how do we accomplish that?"

"We have to remove it from the cloves and store it separately. That means we need to find out what bags contain the heroin, cut them open, remove the heroin, and then resew the bags of cloves. The cloves will get discharged and delivered. Frankie is setting it up, so he's in the clear, no matter what. Hopefully, no one finds out until the stuff is off the pier in Brooklyn."

"How are we supposed to deliver the heroin?"

"Frankie left that up to us—quote, 'You guys are the experts at moving shit.'"

Silence persisted for a minute, and then Dennis said, "How about if we stick the stuff in the conex with the bulldozer parts? Frankie is supposed to end up with the dozers anyway."

The captain nodded. "Not a bad idea, Dennis. Let's think about this." He drummed his fingers on the desktop. "The cloves hide the odor of the heroin, but we don't want the conex smelling like cloves. Too obvious a connection."

Dennis leaned back in the chair, eliciting a squeak. "How about we break open a case of tea and a case of pepper? The tea will offset the smell of heroin, and a little pepper inside the conex will set any sniffer dogs sneezing."

The captain thought about it and nodded. "Let's do that."

"The bosun will have to help with this, Captain. He can do the heavy work and resew the bags."

"Okay. Boats will keep his mouth shut."

"What can I offer him? We gotta give him something."

"Tell him five hundred bucks."

"Is there anything in this for us, or we just being patsies for Frankie?"

"There's five thousand dollars for you when the briefcase gets delivered. Frankie said he would have 'something extra' for us if he gets the heroin."

"Jesus. That's a lot of money. What the hell is in the briefcase?"

"Told you. Don't know, don't want to know."

"One other thing. Santorini will squeal pretty damn loud when he gets the blame for this. He'll finger us."

"Yes, I discussed that with Frankie. Santorini is his problem. That can mean a lot of things, but I wouldn't want to be in Santorini's shoes when he gets back to Brooklyn. Get Boats going on this."

"Will do."

Dennis knocked on Boats' door. Boats came out, shirtless, his rodeo belt buckle peeking out from under his beer gut. He was tall, six feet, three inches, and his ruddy face had seen a few too many fists, but it went well with his massive, bare biceps and hands like small boulders.

"Boats, I've got a job for you. Let's take a walk so we can talk."

"Okay, mate," he said, grabbed a tee shirt and pulled it on. He exited the port door onto the main deck and headed toward the fo'c'sle locker, the mate in tow. Stepping into the locker, Boats waved his arm in a welcoming gesture and said, "The office is open for business."

Dennis sat on a five-gallon bucket of paint, backdropped by a wall full of shackles of various sizes. Boats leaned against the bulkhead. The smell of hemp and fish oil permeated the locker, masking the odor of cloves from the hatches. In five minutes, Dennis had explained to him what needed to be done, including the five hundred dollars.

"No rush on this, right, mate? We're done loading in the no. 2 hatch and won't have to open up until New York, so we can wait until we clear Walvis Bay, right?"

"That's right, Boats."

"Okay. Let me think on it. Does the conex have a seal on it?"

"No."

"Good. They check the seals to see if they're in one piece when we discharge."

Dennis paused. "Gave me an idea, Boats. I can let the agent at Durban know that the container had a seal when it came aboard and that he needs to add the seal number to the manifest. It'll look like the lazy stevedore checker didn't record it when loading. We'll be doing them a favor, covering their screw-up. There are extra seals aboard. I'll give them a number off one. When you're all done, you put the seal on the conex door, and we've got our alibi."

"Whatever you say, mate."

On the way back aft, Boats stopped at the conex on deck, opened the door, and inspected the interior. There were four crates of varying sizes inside. Crawling in, he saw there was a space, three feet square and two feet deep, behind the front cases, not visible from a casual inspection. It was the perfect hiding hole for the heroin. To minimize odor, he would wrap the heroin in plastic, tape it shut, and hose off the plastic with seawater before placing it inside.

The next morning at 0730, I returned to running the ladders again. Clara, who normally only worked out in the afternoons, did her best to keep up on the opposite side. I told her that it worked better if she used the port ladder and I used the starboard one because she slowed me down. In truth, watching her jiggling ass in front of me had the same effect as when Meg ran, and I didn't need the stress.

I finished and went to the flying bridge to cool off. Clara had already gone up when she stopped running. She was up against the forward rail, arms stretched overhead, enjoying the salt breeze.

"You're doing better, Clara. You ran a few more reps today. Got a goal in mind?"

Turning, she lowered her hands. "Yes, I hope to get to the point where these," she said, running her hands over her hips and ass, "ripple instead of jiggle." She started singing Frank Sinatra's version of "High Hopes." We both laughed.

"It's good to have high hopes," I told her. "If you aim high and fall short, you're still higher up than when you started."

"Wow." She cradled her chin with her hands in a Kewpie-doll imitation. "He's cute and philosophical."

I blushed.

"I love it when you blush," she said. "It makes me think you're innocent, even though I know better."

She leaned back, elbows on the top rail, tensioning her breasts. I don't think she did it to impress me—it was just a natural reaction—but once again, I was impressed. "So, William, are you going to marry Meg?"

"I think I'd like to." I stared in her eyes to avoid staring at her breasts, guilt inherent in the thought. "But I don't know how the whole Grace thing will play out."

"You think Grace will oppose you marrying Meg?"

"No...I think she likes the idea, but I don't think she'll let her leave South Africa. There's no way I can live in South Africa."

Clara pondered that. "I think you're right. In my talks with Grace on the trip over, her protectiveness was evident. It surprised me she let Meg go to the States for college. Grace means well, but if she's the cause of you and Meg breaking up, there are fireworks in the future. Two strong-headed women on a collision course." She shook her head. "Now, I, on the other hand," she said, smirking and waggling her breasts, "would never let you go, no matter what my mother told me."

Trying to keep it in a light vein, knowing that I was on thin ice, I said, "Clara, don't take this the wrong way, but you could be my mother."

"Yes, I could. More's the pity. But if I were Meg's mother I would tell her to marry you yesterday."

Chapter 33

CAPE TOWN—
HOMEBOUND

*N**ight watch, 0200 on Monday. We were ten miles to the northeast of the pilot station off Green Point Light. Forty-five minutes earlier, I had warned
the engine room we would soon reduce to maneuvering speeds. When I notified
the captain, he reduced speed to dead slow ahead and told me to "crawl down the
coast, Mr. Williams. Get me to the pilot at 0530."*

When the second mate relieved me at 0400, I relayed the captain's message
and went to my cabin to catch a few winks before being called out for docking.

The ordinary on watch woke me up at 0630, and, eyes grainy, I went aft
and oversaw the crew tying up. We had clear weather, and like the first call at
Cape Town, the early sun tinged the top of Table Mountain with an orange
glow.

A good-size sea was running, with ten-foot rollers. Cape Town has a history of large rollers as high as twenty feet, seas that never break until they hit
the shoreline. During World War II, a couple of Liberty-class ships, dodg-
ing the German U-boats, developed cracks in their hulls from the stresses
created when the wave period—the time it takes between crests at the same
spot—shortened to the point that the middle of the hull hung almost fully

suspended in air. Today, the arm of Green Point eclipsed the rollers, and we docked with no problem, starboard side to the same pier as our first call.

Tired but not sleepy, I ate breakfast. The captain and chief mate arrived late to the full salon, noisier than normal, due to meeting with port officials and the stevedore supervisor.

"Morning, Dennis," I greeted him as he sat. "What are we doing here?" I meant, what cargo were we loading? When sailing from Durban, the agent never told Dennis what the cargo would be. Tony was there, not needed on deck since cargo operations wouldn't start until 1300 hours.

"Not much. Looks like household crates, mail, and a yacht."

"Where's the stowage?" Tony asked.

"The household crates go in the no. 5 upper-tween deck. Spread them around the hatch, but make sure the square stays open. Put the mail in the no. 5 lower-tween deck, forward end. There's only about sixty bags. The thirty-six-foot yacht we'll load at the no. 4 portside on deck, using the jumbo boom. It will be a direct lift from the water, so make sure the slings get placed right when it clears the water. Also, make sure they tie the slings together, so they can't slide apart. Don't want a shit-coosh maker."

Tony and I looked at him, but Tony asked first. "What's a shit-coosh maker?"

Dennis laughed. "That's when you get something high in the air over water, and it slips. When it hits the water, all you hear is, *shit*! Followed by a big *coosh*."

We both laughed, more to make Dennis feel good since it wasn't that funny.

At 1300 hours, one gang of longshoremen came aboard and started loading sacks of mail. Dennis walked out and stood with me on deck beside the no. 5 hatch.

"MorMac must have scrambled for this cargo," he said. "Usually, Farrell Lines gets the mail. The fact we're carrying it makes the rumors realistic."

"What rumors?"

"MorMac and Farrell are supposed to be discussing some sort of joint service. Any time the lines get together and cooperate, it usually means they're cutting back...on ships and crew. Never good news. When they finish the mail sacks, go down and check for tears in the bags. They never break the seal, but they will, on occasion, slice open a bag and peek inside."

"Sure thing, Dennis."

He walked back into the house, and I leaned on the hatch coaming and stared into the hold.

At 1430, they completed the mail and moved into the upper-tween deck to load crates of household goods. Measuring 8' x 8' x 8', the crates are reusable, with one side acting as a door but screwed shut. Moving companies deliver them to the shipper, usually individuals, who fill them with everything found in a house: furniture, refrigerators, stoves, clothing, anything that isn't flammable or explosive. The moving company then secures them and transports them to the port for shipping.

As a mate, I keep a close eye on them because people can sometimes be stupid and stow gasoline containers or paint cans. The only way we know is if we see stains on the crates or smell gasoline. Dennis had told us some bizarre stories of things found in the crates, the worst of which, on a trip to Argentina, was thirty sticks of dynamite; five ten-gallon cans of gasoline; and five thousand rounds of ammunition. The gasoline had leaked.

When they questioned the shipper, who also happened to be a passenger on the ship, he said he had bought a farm in the northern plains of Argentina and needed the dynamite to clear stumps and rocks. When they refused to load the crate, the passenger went off in a huff and missed the sailing.

The second mate relieved me at 1600 hours. With time to kill before supper, I went up to the flying bridge to have a cigarette and relax. Stubbing out my third smoke, I looked over the rail to the pier and gaped. Walking up the pier toward the gangway with Clara was Meg. I ran down the ladders and met them at the top of the gangway.

Clara led the way. "Look what I discovered," she said, making way for Meg, who leaped into my arms.

After kissing, I sputtered, "What are you doing here?"

Clara interjected, "That's no way to greet your lover. You're supposed to say, 'Oh, I've missed you. Isn't it wonderful you're here?'"

Ignoring Clara, I hugged Meg and whispered, "You know I've missed you. I missed you before I left."

Clara, still trying to be the center of attention, said, "Meg decided to join us for dinner; she missed everyone so much. I don't think she mentioned you, William." She smiled.

Grabbing me by the arm and pulling me toward the door, Meg smirked at Clara and said, "No need to mention him. He's the center of my world, so there!" She stuck her tongue out at Clara, and they both giggled like teenagers.

Everyone was on best behavior at supper. The captain, who hadn't spoken a word to Eunice in public for weeks, shared a table with Eunice and Clara. Dennis sat with the captain, so Meg could sit next to me. Even Bernie, ruling his one-table empire, said hello to Meg. The chief steward, Fran, whom all the passengers loved because of his constant attention to them, came in to say hello, and the captain invited him to sit with him. I think he needed a buffer between him and Eunice, and it worked. Eunice was gracious and alternated comments between Clara, Fran, and Meg.

By 1900, all but Clara, Eunice, Fran, Meg, and I had left. As he exited, Tony leaned over and whispered, "I got you covered tonight on the midwatch."

As Fran rose to leave, he asked Meg, "Shall I make up a room for you for the night?"

"That won't be necessary, Fran, but thanks," she responded.

Fran smiled. "Never hurts to ask." He then kissed Meg on the cheek and walked out.

Clara stood and said, "Fran, you are a wonderful man. What a shame you're queer. Such a waste."

Realizing that I no longer thought about Fran as being queer, but only as a good shipmate, I was surprised and dismayed at her comment. I looked to Fran.

Bowing to Clara, Fran replied, "Thank you, Clara. I take that as the complement it was meant to be." He blew her a kiss and then left.

Clara looked at me and read my face. "I hope you don't think I'm insulting Fran. I love the man. Wish all men had his qualities."

"You know, Clara, the longer I know Fran, the more I have to agree with you."

The next morning, the salon was again crowded. As Meg and I neared the door, she grabbed my hand and pulled me back. "Can we get coffee and go back to your room?"

Handing her the key, I said, "Sure. I'll get the coffee. Go back, and wait for me."

When I walked in, all eyes swiveled and focused on me. Clara was the only one who spoke. With a smile in her voice, she said, "Good morning, William. Is Meg too tired to eat?"

I heard throats clearing and a few sniggers from the others in the room when I replied, "No, she's fine. I'm a little tired." Then, I grabbed two mugs of coffee and returned to my cabin.

I kicked the bottom of my door since both hands were full. Meg opened it and took one of the mugs. "The sailing board is posted. We leave at 1600 hours this afternoon," I said, taking a sip of coffee and sitting on the edge of the bunk. Meg occupied the chair at the desk.

She nodded but didn't reply.

"Am I going to get lucky again and find you walking up the gangway when we get to Lüderitz Bay and Walvis Bay?"

Meg shook her head. "No. This is it. Traveling into Southwest Africa is difficult." She lowered her mug and cried, softly at first and then sobbing.

Putting my mug on the desk, I gathered her in my arms, cradling her, letting her cry.

"I didn't believe it before when you left." Emotion stifled her words. "It would only be a few weeks when you left for Kenya, and I knew I could come to Cape Town and surprise you, but now you're really going, and it will be months before I see you again." She shuddered and sniffed. Stepping back from me, she grabbed a tissue from the box on my desk and blew her nose.

With her red-rimmed eyes swimming, she said, "You are coming back, aren't you?"

I stared at her, but before I could answer, she continued, "I thought about not using the IUD and getting pregnant, sort of insurance, but I couldn't do it."

"Meg. I am coming back. I love you and want to marry you. What I can't promise you is whether I'll stay in South Africa. There's nothing but trouble ahead with the apartheid system. We've got a lot of racial problems at home, too, but our government seems to be trying to fix them. Here, they're reinforcing the problem. I don't want to be part of that.

"I'm just starting in my career. Don't know how many years I'll sail, but I know I won't quit, not yet. I have three years' commitment for my navy-reserve commission. After that, I can't say, but I love sailing." I trailed off. "I've been dealing with loneliness a long time. I'm just wired that way. Can you deal with it?"

She reached out, held my hands in hers, and said, "I don't know. I hope so."

"Your mother made it clear she'd be unhappy if you left to go to the States with me. In the States, she's not my problem unless you make it a problem. She's your mother, not mine. Ultimately, you have to decide."

"I have to go the bathroom," she said, grabbing a tissue as she opened the door. I leaned against the edge of the bunk and waited, something both of us would have to get used to.

When she returned, she had washed her face. Picking up her overnight valise, she took a deep breath, let it out, and said, "We'll have to see how it goes. Walk me to the gate?"

Meg didn't want to see anyone, so we walked off the gangway and out to the gate. That's when I asked her, "How did you get here?"

"I drove." She pointed across the road to her mum's new Range Rover. "Couldn't trust the train schedule. I would have had to go to Johannesburg and then down to Cape Town and might have missed you."

Opening the door and putting her valise in the back seat, I kissed her. When she got in, I kissed her again, hoping the taste of her would linger. "Be careful. I love you." I once again turned my back on her and walked away. It was harder this time.

Returning to the ship, I got a cup of coffee and sat in the salon, feeling sorry for myself, until Clara walked in. She came right up, patted my head, and said, "Good-byes are terrible. Think ahead to when you can say hello again." She smiled and left.

I finished my coffee, went looking for Tony, and found him on deck, watching them load the yacht.

"Hey, Tony, thanks for covering for me last night. I'll take over if you want to go do something."

"Thanks, William, but I'm good."

Looking at the yacht still being hooked up in the water, I exclaimed, "Hey, that's an S & S."

"What are you talking about?" said Tony.

"Sparkman & Stephens, S & S, that's the builder. It's a thirty-six-foot Gulfstream, a beauty. I wonder how it got here?"

"I'll tell you," a booming voice behind us said. When I turned, Dennis stood behind a tall, skinny guy with wispy hair. The voice did not go with the body. "I sailed her here."

Reaching out an Ichabod Crane arm, he shook hands with me and Tony. "My girlfriend and I sailed her from Marblehead to Puerto Rico and then to Cape Town. Took three months. Had to stop at Ascension Island for repairs and supplies. Quite a trip. My plan was to sail up the African coast, through the Suez Canal, into the Mediterranean, and then back to Marblehead."

"What happened?" I asked.

"Two things. One, I ran out of time. Have to go back to work. Two, the girlfriend got fed up with me and flew home. Told me she would tell everyone at home what an asshole I was." Smiling, he said, "The jokes on her. Everyone already knows I'm an asshole. She's the only one that didn't."

Turning to Dennis, he said, "You'll take good care of her, won't you?" indicating the yacht. "She's the only female I know that I haven't disappointed." He guffawed.

I said, "She's awful small to be in the middle of the Atlantic Ocean."

Scratching his chin, he said, "I realized that when the waves got up to twenty feet high. Too late then. I was halfway here. Before we left, I had them add under-deck strengtheners to the securing points of all the stays. When we dropped the mast, I noticed they were stressed. Without the extra strengtheners, we might have lost the mast. As it is, we bounced around under nothing but a storm jib for three days."

Much later, after the yacht was aboard and secured, I climbed aboard for a good look. The Gulfstream 36' is a sloop, with only one mast with a full jib going to the top of the mast, which gives it more sail area. The mast had been lowered and wrapped with the boom in a specially built cradle on deck to protect it during the handling of the yacht, loading and unloading. A dark-green hull with a narrow white pinstripe running the full length, and the deck—which was painted dull gray, a color that small-boat sailors avoided since seagulls loved to shit on it—were both weather-beaten. The low-slung cabin with its natural wood, stained and varnished, needed refurbishing. The Atlantic crossing had taken its toll on the brightwork. Brightwork is any part of a yacht's woodwork that requires regular sanding and varnishing. It gives each yacht its distinct look but is a pain in the ass to maintain. As I climbed down, I looked at the stern and read the name: *Sea Bitch*. Aptly named by a guy who had little respect for women.

At dinner that night, Clara, Eunice, and I sat in the salon, talking. Clara and Eunice were well into their second bottle of wine. I drank coffee. Clara felt she needed to cheer me up and was doing her best, but it fast became a drag, so I changed the subject and told them about the yacht owner and his comments, ending with the name of the yacht.

"What is his name?" Eunice asked.

"I don't know. He never offered, and I didn't ask."

"Asshole will suffice," Eunice said. "I hope the *Sea Bitch* drowns the son of a bitch." And raised her glass in a toast.

Chapter 34

LÜDERITZ BAY

S̲ailed from Cape Town at 1630 hours on Tuesday,12/20/66. Weather clear. Temperature 71 degrees. Wind southeast at 15 mph. We dropped the pilot at Green Point, and the captain set revolutions for 10 knots.

The captain sailed due west for an hour to ensure that we were clear of the breakwater at the port of Saldanha, sixty miles northwest of Cape Town, before turning north onto course 315 degrees to parallel the coastline. Just prior to sailing, the agent had notified him that there was no berth available at Lüderitz Bay until Friday morning. With time to kill, we idled our way up the coast.

I dismissed the crew from their aft mooring stations once the tugboat dropped away from us. Feeling morose and more than a little sorry for myself, I climbed to the flying bridge and lit a cigarette. We had a beautiful view of Table Mountain over the stern as we sailed away, the setting sun reflecting off the face of the cliffs. Watching the mountain fade into the distance, I felt a wave of melancholy hit my heart, washing over it like a rock at high tide. Thinking back on our last conversation, I wondered if I had been too harsh telling Meg that she would have to choose between me and her mother. Her final comment, "We'll have to see how it goes," now had me wondering if she hasn't resigned herself to our breaking up. Wiping away the unbidden tears, the more I thought of it, the more I believed she would side with her mother.

Lüderitz Bay is just a dent in the desert coast of South West Africa, one of the most inhospitable coastlines in Africa; it was named Angra Pequena ("Small Bay") by Portuguese explorer Bartolomeu Dias in 1487. Dutch explorers sought minerals without success in the eighteenth century. Later expeditions in the early nineteenth century failed to find minerals but discovered the abundance of ocean wildlife. Whaling, fishing, seal hunting, and guano-harvesting enterprises sprang up, and Lüderitz Bay became a trading post.

Harvesting guano used as fertilizer, like the California Gold Rush, created a frenzy of activity by 1843 on Ichaboe Island, only fifteen acres in size, twenty-eight miles north of Lüderitz. The cold Benguela Current provided rich nutrients for the fish, and colonies of cormorants, gannets, and penguins feasted on the fish and deposited the guano. At its peak, six thousand seamen and 350 ships worked the island under miserable conditions. They dealt with cramped, makeshift accommodations; there was no medical facility and a lack of food and water. With initial depths of twenty-five feet of guano, in two years, they scraped the island clean of two hundred thousand tons, making the owners rich. Today, the seabirds have reclaimed the island.

In 1883, Heinrich Vogelsang, acting on behalf of Adolf Lüderitz from Bremen, Germany, purchased Angra Pequena from chief Josef Frederiks II of the local Nama tribe. In 1886, the town was renamed Lüderitzbucht in his honor.

There was a dark side to the town. From 1905 through 1907, during the Herero Wars, German authorities set up a concentration camp on Shark Island, a peninsula shaped like a shark, to house members of the Herero and Nama tribes, where between 1,000 and 3,000 tribesmen died under harsh conditions of forced labor.

After the discovery of diamonds in 1909, the town boomed. In 1915, after the German capitulation of World War I, South Africa took over the administration of German South West Africa.

Besides working in the diamond trade, lead and gold are also mined and exported in ingots, but fishing is the mainstay of the port. Because the harbor has a shallow, rocky bottom and great care is needed when docking, more ship traffic is being diverted to Walvis Bay, farther north.

The pilot wanted us to dock at the single commercial pier, but the captain refused. The depth alongside at mean low water is only eighteen feet, and we were drawing eighteen feet, six inches aft. The chief engineer couldn't get the ship flatter without also making it deeper. We could fill the forward ballast tanks but couldn't lighten anything aft. Half an hour of arguing with the agent over the pilot's walkie-talkie got an agreement for us to anchor, and they planned to use barges to bring the lead ingots to the ship. However, we would have to wait another day before loading.

Now, the captain was really pissed off. Someone should have checked the depth alongside the pier at Lüderitz before we sailed from Cape Town. We always take our draft at sailing, so someone could have called ahead and arranged for the barge ahead of time. At normal speed, we could have arrived early Thursday morning, worked two days, and sailed Friday night. Now, we were facing two days of overtime or additional layover time.

Customs and immigration agents had to come to the ship by boat, courtesy of the pilot, and they were upset, joining the captain, the agent, and the pilot in that irate state. When I came into the salon to identify myself to the immigration agents, the silence (except for an occasional grunt) lay like a pall on everyone, and the tension was palpable. I eyeballed Fran, the chief steward, helping the captain with the crew papers, and he raised his eyebrows and shrugged his shoulders in such a dramatic fashion that I laughed. Everyone stopped what they were doing and stared at me.

The captain, assured of a scapegoat, barked, "What's funny, Mr. Connolly? Please let me in on the joke."

Instinct told me to play it cool and make no wiseass remarks, but I couldn't help myself. "Captain, I haven't seen so many irritated people in one room in my entire life. Thought I'd cheer it up some." Then, I waited for the expected volley of verbal shit.

From across the salon came a high-pitched voice, the senior customs agent. "Bloody right." Turning to the captain, he continued, "Captain, everyone's been a bit cheeky, not our usual convivial selves. I apologize for my grumpiness and that of my fellow Lüderitz chaps. What say we follow this young mate's lead and cheer up, eh?"

Standing, knowing that customs and immigration can make or break your stay at a port, the captain said, "Gentlemen, I accept your apology and offer ours. Perhaps a libation would help ease the way." Turning to Fran, he said, "Fran, please take the gentlemen's drink orders. I'll cover this." He pointed at the paperwork on the table.

Just like that, I went from potential shark bait to hero. Everyone in the salon smiled, some shamefaced, and began jabbering to one another.

Afterward, sitting in Dennis's office, he said, "I watched the captain when you opened your mouth back there. If that customs agent hadn't piped up, I think the captain would have had you in irons, tied to the rail on the flying bridge, waiting to get into deep water to throw you overboard. What the hell possessed you to say that?"

I shrugged, made a face, and said, "I figured, what the fuck? Couldn't undo my laugh."

Dennis shook his head. "You continually surprise me, William."

Eunice and Clara asked to go ashore, just to play tourist, despite being told the only things to see in Lüderitz Bay were sand and disinterested people. Bernie Simpson asked to go, and to my surprise, Clara agreed, despite an eyebrow raising by Eunice. The agent agreed to have a boat at the gangway by 1000 hours for anyone who wanted to go ashore. At 0930, Tony asked me to cover for him. Eunice had asked him to accompany her ashore.

"No problem, Tony. You've covered for me plenty, but isn't your going with Eunice a little blatant? What happened to 'We'll be discreet'?"

"Nah, no screwing around this time. She wants me there to be a referee if Bernie acts up with Clara. It sucks, but..." He shrugged his shoulders.

I found Dennis in his office and told him I was covering for Tony and why.

"Fuckin' Eunice. She doesn't know when to back off." Lowering his head into his hands, he muttered, "I hope this doesn't blow up." With his head still lowered, he waved me out of the office.

The day passed without incident. Every hour, I checked the bearings to ensure that our anchor held fast. The second mate had also gone ashore. I told him

I would cover his watch for him since I had nothing else to do but feel sorry for myself. There were six charts in need of *Notice to Mariners* updates, and I did that while chain-smoking, spilling ashes on the charts. Skipping lunch, I settled for a lemonade to help flush the nicotine from my mouth.

Dennis had the day workers and three of the off-duty watch standers scraping rust and scale off the forepeak deck. All day, the whirring of electric chippers and screeching of scrapers on metal serenaded me. Deciding that the deck paint didn't hold up well enough, Dennis opted to coat the deck with fish oil. Since we pointed into the wind at anchor, a smudged aroma of cloves and fish oil overcame the deadening effect from cigarettes and assailed my nostrils.

The AB from the four-to-eight watch stayed on the bridge while I went below for supper: baked ham, potatoes, green beans, and, of course, pound cake. Arriving back on the bridge, I told the AB to go eat and standby in the crew mess; there was no need to stay on the bridge with nothing to do.

Lighting up a cigarette, I heard Greg Russell, the third engineer, knock on the window of the starboard bridge-wing door.

Opening the door, I stepped out. "Hey, Greg. What brings you up here?"

Stretching, pulling both hands behind his back and wiggling his shoulders, he said, "A little fresh air. Thought I'd get a sniff of the land, but all I can smell are those freaking cloves and fish oil."

"Haven't seen you much, not even at meals. What've you been doing?"

"Studying. Learning a few things. No sense going ashore. Nothing a black man can do there—at least, not this black man."

"Yeah, this apartheid shit sucks. I told Meg I couldn't live here because of it, and if we get married, she'd have to come to the States."

"What did Meg say?"

"She said, 'We'll have to see how it goes.'"

"That doesn't sound too encouraging. Does she like it that much here, or is she getting cold feet in your hot relationship?" He smiled to ease the harshness of the statement.

"It's her mother, Grace," was my rebuttal. I hoped that Greg wasn't right about Meg rejecting me. "I think Meg would come with me to the States, but she knows her mother wants her to stay, and with Grace being sick, that gives her an edge to dump a guilt trip on Meg."

"Does her mother advocate apartheid?" Greg asked.

"Shit, no! Meg's dad was a behind-the-scenes opponent of it, helping local natives get special travel and work passes. Her mother helped him. I don't know if her new, soon-to-be stepdad, Mark, is for apartheid, but I can't believe Grace would be attracted to someone with radically different views on it."

"I gotta tell you, William, ever since we first called at Cape Town and couldn't go ashore together, I've been studying the situation. Apartheid is a time bomb, ready to explode. I don't know enough to predict when, but what I have learned assures me it's inevitable."

"What have you learned? Tell me about it. I may have to argue the point someday with Meg and Grace."

Leaning back with his elbows on the rear railing, he said, "I've gotten a few books and read news journals about apartheid and the attempts of the South African government to spread apartheid to all of South West Africa like they did in South Africa. It turns my stomach, but it's fascinating reading. Lately, it's become South Africa versus the world. "You have to know the history. The United Nations, since its inception, has been squabbling with South Africa over the apartheid system. The arguments intensified in 1957, when South Africa refused to recognize the authority of the Trusteeship Committee, a branch of the UN, and refused to recognize the authority of the International Court of Justice in deciding who would ultimately control South West Africa.

"In 1959, rioting broke out in the town of Windhoek when the government extended urban apartheid to South West Africa. The government shoved it down their throats by forcing the removal and relocation of natives from Windhoek to a remote location similar to what they did in South Africa.

"Things heated up on the international front in 1960, when Ethiopia and Liberia, as members of a special seven-nation committee formed to investigate conditions in South West Africa, applied to the International Court of Justice to issue a binding judgment against South Africa. In 1962, the world court declared they had jurisdiction to decide the issue. South Africa protested. The case is still going on today."

"Man," I interjected. "I thought it was a local problem."

"No way, William. In 1962, a political party, the South West Africa National Union (SWANU) was formed, and a second political party evolved, South West Africa's People's Organization (SWAPO). Last month, SWAPO, under the umbrella of their new organization, People's Liberation Army of Namibia (PLAN), started a war in Ovamboland. That's an area along the northern border of South West Africa, abutting Angola."

I sat for a minute, thinking about it. "There's no way I'd live here. This is getting worse, not better."

"You bet your sweet ass it is. Things are getting hot fast, and the shit is already hitting the fan. It's just a question of how much and how fast." Stretching again, he said, "I gotta go. Hope I didn't scare you with my history lesson."

"I don't know if 'scare' is the right word, but you sure as hell woke me up."

As he walked away, he said, "True love is wonderful, William. You can always hope."

At 2100, the local launch brought our passengers back to the ship. I watched from the top of the gangway as they climbed aboard. The second mate assisted Bernie Simpson onto the gangway. He paid attention this time and didn't go for a swim. Tony helped the ladies as they stepped from the launch to the foot of the gangway and then followed them up.

Nodding to Bernie and Chuck as they passed me, I said, "Welcome back, ladies. Hope you had an enjoyable day."

Eunice, pointing ahead at Bernie walking in the doorway, sniped, "Except for that ass, it was fine." She turned to Tony. "Ten minutes." It was a demand, not a question. Then, she turned and went into the house.

Tony nodded, closed his eyes, took a deep breath, and sighed. "Cover for me?"

"No problem, Tony."

Clara had stepped aside, letting the others go ahead. "It wasn't that bad," she said. "Bernie was just being Bernie, rude and impatient. I'm used to it, Eunice isn't."

"Anything in particular happen? I asked.

"Only at dinner. We stopped at a nice German restaurant. Eunice insisted because it had a Christmas tree in the window and she said she wanted to get in the Christmas spirit. Bernie made a scene, whining because they didn't have any American beer. Eunice made him sit at a separate table." Giggling, she said, "I think the waiters drew straws to see who would wait on him. The manager sent us free dessert at the end of the meal. Bernie asked for a piece, and they told him they had served the last of it to us." She paused. "That made the best chocolate cake even better."

"I'm glad you had a good time, Clara."

"I did. Even Bernie couldn't ruin it."

Smiling, I asked, "Anything else exciting happen?"

"Not exciting, no, but the taxi driver warned us to be careful. It was a woman. She told us she was the only lady taxi driver in Lüderitz. We asked her to take us to a restaurant, someplace different, offering native food. She got protective. Told us we shouldn't go to the black neighborhood. There was an insurrection starting, and it's best for white people to stay away from the black areas, and vice versa."

"I wonder if a male driver would have warned you."

"I don't know. She sounded apprehensive. Whether for us or herself?" She shrugged. "I'm going to bed," she said. "Maybe I've had a little too much to drink."

I watched her waggle her way to the door, left hand trailing along the bulkhead for balance. I waited a minute and then followed her, making sure she made it to her cabin, and then I went to the bridge. Chuck relieved me at 0400 hours.

A loud *boom!* woke me. It was 0915. Too late for breakfast. I did my ablutions, grabbed a cup of coffee, and wandered out on deck to see what was going on. Tony was coming up out of the manhole at the forward end of the no. 3 hatch. He went to look over the starboard side coaming, yelling down into the hold. The longshoremen were working from a barge on the port side.

"Hey, Tony, what's up?"

Looking irritated, he replied, "The dumb fucks just dropped two lead ingots onto the tank top in the starboard deep tank."

"Shit," I said, looking over the edge at the men below. "Anyone hurt?"

"No, but it was close. They put a dent into the deck, but it's not too bad. Thank God, it was lead and not steel. It would have punched a hole through the tank top."

"How did it happen?" I asked.

"They slung the wire the wrong way on the bundles, and it slipped."

Lead ingots weigh a ton apiece and are shaped like upside-down Chunky candy bars, with wide tops and narrow bottoms. When the longshoremen lift them, they slide the wires under the wide parts. If they don't snug them up, the wires can slip. Everything seemed to be moving along okay now. Having someone drop a one-ton block of lead beside you will cause you to pay attention.

"So, Tony, did you get any sleep last night?"

His gloved hands on the hatch-cover track, he looked over his shoulder at me. "Enough." He paused. "When Eunice gets pissed off, she seems to energize. She works at it. Wore me out." Looking down into the hatch, he shook his head. "Man, my dick is sore."

"Lucky you. My dick is unemployed." We both laughed. I went back to the salon and got another cup of coffee.

At lunch, Dennis told me the gang would knock off at 1700 hours that day and planned on finishing loading by 1700 hours tomorrow. We loaded one thousand tons, five hundred tons in each of the port and starboard after deep tanks, and by 1800 hours, the barge was clear. The pilot was aboard, and we weighed anchor.

Chapter 35

WALVIS BAY

Sailed from Lüderitz Bay at 1800 hours on Sunday, 12/25/66, Christmas day. A light haze, visibility limited to one mile. Dead calm. We dropped the pilot as soon as we cleared Shark Island head and set course for 310 degrees, out past the sea buoy.

The captain remained on this course for ten miles, ensuring that we were in at least fifty fathoms of water, before he turned onto 355 degrees. On this leg of the trip, the coastline was all desert, with little area elevated over ten feet above sea level. That made for a poor radar image. The fathometer was more reliable, so we never turned it off until we docked at Walvis Bay, a distance of a little over 300 miles.

Fran cooked the turkey, traditional fare for Christmas dinner. He said the chief cook wanted to add onions to it and Fran had to guard the oven all day to protect the turkey. It was an excellent meal and everyone, including Eunice and the captain, were polite, if not convivial. Clara gave a Christmas present to everyone aboard. For the smokers, she gave a carton of cigarettes each and for the non-smokers, she gave a bottle of whiskey, their choice of type. Popular with the officers and steward's department before, she was now the Queen of the Ocean in the eyes of everyone. I wondered how Meg was celebrating Christmas.

At 1300 hours the next day, we turned east, heading in to pick up the pilot at Walvis Bay. The entire shoreline lay swathed in a golden haze, a reflection of the sun off the water and sand. It was not quite a mirage but shimmered enough to make the captain nervous until we boarded the pilot, one half mile north of Pelican Point, the headland creating the bay and protecting the town from ocean storms.

Walvis (Whale) Bay is a natural, deep-water harbor colonized by a succession of nations since the Portuguese navigator Bartolomeu Dias first anchored his flagship *Sao Cristovao* in Walvis Bay on December 8, 1487, while trying to find a sea route to the East via the Cape of Good Hope. He never staked an official claim on behalf of Portugal.

In the late nineteenth century, the United Kingdom occupied Walvis Bay and allowed the Cape Colony to annex it in 1884. Located just north of the Tropic of Capricorn, in the Kuiseb River delta, the town is built on sand. The area receives less than four inches of rain per year, making it one of the driest cities on earth. Despite the arid conditions, it stays relatively mild due to cold offshore currents. Like Lüderitz Bay, fishing is a mainstay industry.

The port area is flat, with four small warehouses and not much else. The town, set back from the port, has a perimeter of sand two hundred yards wide, between the warehouses and the entrance to the pier. Outside the gate is a small commercial area, with offices for solicitors (attorneys), a maritime-supply store, a curio shop, and a small administrative office for customs and immigration.

After docking, we went through the usual process of clearing customs and having our IDs checked by immigration. The customs officials were Afrikaners, descendants of the Dutch and very reserved—not hostile but not friendly, either. After the customs men left the ship, the friendly immigration officer, Michael Fitzpatrick, British by nationality but Irish by stock, as evidenced by his love of whiskey and his good nature, announced that he was now off duty for the day and settled in to the corner of the passengers' table. After being presented with a bottle of scotch, he regaled the passengers, myself, Greg, Tony, and Dennis with the difficulty of "living among these damn Dutchmen."

Whereas the customs men were stiff and cold, especially with Greg, Michael Fitzpatrick was the soul of conviviality, telling us the history of the town, where to go for a good meal, and, despite the Calvinists, where to go for a good woman, tipping his imaginary hat and apologizing to Eunice and Clara for his "blunt speech."

Eunice caught him by surprise when she retorted with, "What, no information where to find a good man?"

Supper was over, and the crew had drifted away by the time Michael Fitzpatrick stood and made his way to the gangway. For the last half hour, he and Greg had conducted a deep discussion about apartheid and what it was doing to the country. Shaking Greg's hand, Fitzpatrick said, "Mr. Russell, you will be well advised to stay aboard the ship while you are here. Since the start of the troubles up north in Ovamboland, the police are overreacting to any provocation. It is dangerous for a black man, and it's becoming dangerous for a white man. Tensions are even higher since the prime minister was assassinated in parliament."

"When did that happen?" Greg asked.

"A few months ago, September sixth. A crazy man, Dmitri Tsafendas, stabbed Verwoerd, the prime minister."

"That sounds like a Greek name."

"Partly. Officially a white man under apartheid rules, Tsafendas is of mixed race. He has a Greek father and a Mozambique mixed-race mother. Everyone who wants to blame all the troubles on the coloreds now have a reason to act stupid. These are bad times."

"Thank you for your advice, sir, and for the verbal guided tour of Walvis Bay. I enjoyed it. Everyone did."

The next morning at breakfast, Greg repeated Fitzpatrick's warning to all the officers, deck and engine. "I'm not going ashore here; that's for damn sure," he said.

Wanting to stretch my legs and look around, I said, "We won't get ashore again until New York, two weeks from now."

Bill, the chief engineer, said, "I'm going up town. I have to mail some letters."

"I'll go with you," I said. "When are you going?"

"As soon as I take a shower." He left.

"Tony, I'll be back by noon. Doesn't look like there's a lot to do here, other than the place to find a good woman Fitzpatrick told us about. I have a feeling they won't be open for business this time of day."

Coming off the top of the gangway, Bill and I could see the gate behind the cargo shed, with about two hundred yards of blowing sand between the shed and the gate, but the paved road went down to the far end of the shed and paralleled the fence line, adding another two hundred yards to walk.

Since the shed doors were closed and we had to go to the end of the shed, we stayed on the road all the way to the gate. At the gate, we told the two guards—one tall and blond, the other dark, short, and stocky—we needed a taxi to go to the post office and asked them to call one.

"Happy to oblige, gents," the blond one said, "but the post office is only six blocks that way." He pointed up the street leading away from the pier. "Then, take a left, and it's one block at the corner."

"Okay. Never mind the taxi," said Bill. "We'll walk."

As we passed the gate, one of them, the swarthy, bearded one, stepped out and called, "You'll need your seamen's cards to get back in the pier."

I waved at him, "Thanks. We've got our IDs."

He half saluted and went back inside the guard shack.

Bill and I walked, dust blowing around us. The road fronting the guard shack was Fifteenth Road and headed straight into town, and the intersecting road closest to the fence is First Street. Rail tracks were off to our right, with one siding leading at an oblique angle forward and to our left. We crossed the track at Third Street, passing the immigration building. At Seventh Street, we turned left, and one block down on the right, we found the post office.

While Bill went in and negotiated the proper postage, I leaned against the building and people watched. There wasn't much traffic, either pedestrian or vehicular. When Bill emerged, I commented to him about the lack of people.

He stopped, looked around, and nodded his head. "Yeah, it's strange. Tuesday midmorning, and it's a ghost town. I asked the postal clerk if there were any tourist places of interest, and she said no, they don't see a lot of tourists here."

Looking around, I said, "Let's walk a few blocks and look."

"Sure. Why not?"

We headed up Sixteenth Road, going away from the pier, nodding at the few people we saw. Some acknowledged us by nodding back. Most ignored us. We reached Union Street, and the houses were fewer and further apart.

"What do you think, Bill?" I asked.

"Let's go down here." He indicated a right turn on Union Street, which we took.

We walked about ten blocks and turned back toward the pier when we reached Fifth Road. Half a block down, there were five men standing on the sidewalk, talking, in front of an old church on the left. As we approached, the discussion seemed heated. They were arguing in Afrikaans about the church. Since they blocked the sidewalk and Bill and I were curious, we stopped and eavesdropped. They didn't notice us for a good two minutes. One of them, a fiery redhead, turned to us and said, in English, "Hullo. Are you chaps lost?" His tone wasn't friendly, but neither was it hostile.

"No, sir," I replied. "Bill and I are crew members on a ship and are stretching our legs and seeing what's to see here in Walvis Bay."

"Yanks, are you?" His tone was friendlier.

"We're Americans, yes."

Reaching out, he shook hands, introducing himself. "I'm Josef Stellenbosch." He also introduced his friends, but I didn't catch any of their names. Josef had a crushing grip. He was five or six inches shorter than me and built like a fire hydrant; his hands were disproportionately large for his body.

"Bill and I were curious about your arguing. We've walked about twenty blocks, and you're the first group of people we've seen. We thought maybe it was a holiday."

"No, no holiday. The heat, dust, and sand keep us indoors unless we have to come out."

Bill asked, pointing at the church, "What's going on here? You were pointing at the church while you argued."

"We're deciding what to do with the church." Just then, the others said they had to leave, shook hands with Josef, and waved at us as they walked off.

"Let's step across the road," Josef said, "and I'll tell you."

I looked and saw a two-story house of concrete block, slathered with peeled and fading stucco. Originally red, the paint had lost the war to blowing sand. It looked like most of the houses we had passed in our walk through town. We crossed the street and stepped onto a low porch; Meg would call it a stoep.

"Take a seat. I'll get us a beer." He went inside while Bill and I sat in dilapidated rocking chairs. He returned with two open pint-size bottles and a quart bottle of Hansa Pilsner, handing the small bottles to Bill and me. "Cheers," he said, clinking bottles, and then he collapsed into the third rocking chair, banging into the wall as he leaned back and drained a third of the beer.

"That," he said, pointing at the church across the street, "is the Rhenish Mission Church. We don't have a lot of history here, but that is a big part of our history. It's the oldest building in Walvis Bay, and it's unique." Taking another big swig of beer, he continued, "The church was prefabricated in Hamburg, Germany, and shipped here and erected in 1881 on Seventh Street, down by the harbor." He took another swig of beer. "In 1918, the businesses wanted more room to spread near the harbor, so they dismantled the church and moved it to this location.

"Under those rough plaster walls is a beautiful, hand-wrought wooden structure. They slapped the plaster on it when they rebuilt it to save the wood from rotting. Last January, the sixteenth, to be exact, we held our last service. Since then, vagrants have used it, and the exterior and interior are fast falling apart."

"What can you do about it?" I asked.

"That's the conversation we had when you boys walked up. Some of us old-timers would like to turn it into a museum or preserve it somehow, but that takes money." He rubbed his thumb and two fingers in the universal symbol of money. Then, he chugged the last of his beer. Looking at us, he asked, "You want another?"

"No sir," I said. "We have to get going."

"Thank you for the beer," Bill said, "and the history lesson."

Both of us stood and let Josef crush our hands one more time. Turning right off the porch, we walked down to the fence line at the western end of the pier and followed it back to the gatehouse. Bill said his back was getting tight. He wasn't used to walking.

The same two guards checked our IDs. I could see the doors to the cargo shed were open, so I said, "Let's cross the open lot, Bill. We can cut through the shed to the ship and save a few steps."

"Fine," he said, and we walked into an open lot, nothing but sand. Halfway through it, my shoelace came untied, and I knelt to tie it. As I did that, Bill bent over and stretched his back. I stood, and we continued. Fifteen yards from the shed door, an open-top Land Rover slid to a halt in front of us, throwing up a cloud of sand. The driver stayed where he was, but the passenger, a guard in uniform, ran around the Rover toward Bill and me. That's when I saw the gun he held, an Uzi. It was pointed straight at me.

I held up my hands and yelled, "Whoa, take it easy!" Bill, seeing the driver pull out a pistol and point in our general direction, put up his hands.

The Uzi guy stepped closer and demanded, "What did you pick up?"

Confused, I looked at Bill and then back at the Uzi guy and said, "What are you talking about? I didn't pick up anything." By that time, the driver had approached and stood on the far side of Bill, pistol in hand.

"We saw you on camera. You bent over and picked up something crossing the field."

"I didn't pick up anything." I was indignant but nervous. "My shoe came untied. I tied it."

"What about you?" He asked, looking at Bill. "You picked up something, too."

Bill, shaking his head, replied, "I was stretching. My back hurts. We walked a long way today."

The driver took three steps backward and said something into his walkie-talkie in Afrikaans. When the reply came back, he ordered us to strip.

Bill reacted first. "Strip? Here?"

"Here. Now." This was the reply.

We got our shirts off but both struggled with our pants, trying to keep from falling. The pistol guard took our clothes over to the hood of the Rover and searched them, turning the pockets inside out. He then turned back to us and said, "I said strip. Shoes and socks, too."

Embarrassed but too nervous to say anything as the Uzi guy stared at us, the muzzle never wavering, we stripped, birthday suits exposed to the sun and sand, mine partly tanned, Bill's lily-white except for his hands and face.

The pistol guard searched our skivvies, undershirts, shoes, and socks and talked into the walkie-talkie again. Acknowledging the reply, he motioned for us to approach the Rover and said, "Get dressed. You can go."

Leaning against the Rover for balance, I struggled into my clothes, opting to carry my socks. I hated the feeling of grit between my toes, and I would have had to sit on the ground to get my socks on. Working up a little pluck, now that the Uzi wasn't pointed at my navel, I said, "I don't understand. All I did was tie my shoes. What's the problem?"

The driver had holstered his pistol and his manner, while not friendly, was conciliatory. "This area is a diamond field, or at least it used to be, but diamonds are still here in the open ground. This entire area is under camera scrutiny. When you bent down, they alerted us to stop you."

Bill and I looked at each other. "Can we go now?" Bill asked.

"Go on," the Uzi man said, and he climbed back into the Rover. They kicked up another mini–dust storm, leaving, as Bill and I walked into the shed toward the ship.

As we topped the gangway, I told Bill I was going to take a shower. I had fifteen minutes until I relieved Tony on watch.

"Me too. Maybe I'll stop shaking by then." He went to his room.

I found Tony in the salon at exactly noon. He told me what was happening with the cargo operations, and I relieved him and then told him what happened. Everyone, including Eunice and the Simpsons, was stunned, saying they were glad they didn't go ashore. Eunice couldn't resist. When I got to the part about Bill and me standing buck naked in the field, she said, "What a sight. Too bad we missed it."

Chapter 36

MOVING THE HORSE

Sailed from Walvis Bay at 1900 hours on Wednesday,12/28/66. Weather clear. Dusty haze from westerly wind off the desert. Dropped the pilot short of Pelican Point and set course of 290 degrees for one hour to clear the shoals. Settling in on course 323 degrees. Seas less than three feet.

The first night out of Walvis Bay, Boats started the chore of digging out the heroin from the cloves. He had run two cargo lights down through the manhole cover at the no. 3 hatch and hung them from the sides of the ladder, pointing outward to illuminate the pitch-black area as much as possible. Draping a small tarp over the top of the manhole cover served to block the light from being seen on deck. A corner of the tarp was wedged into the hinge; the heavy cover didn't cut the electric light cords.

He laid plastic sheeting on the deck in the space he worked, roughly ten feet by ten feet. He was not worried about having loose cloves on the deck; there were always leakers, but he needed to ensure that the weight of the bags stayed consistent. He planned to cut open a loose bag of cloves from the general stow and use that to replace the weight of the heroin. An old, metal baling scoop he stored in the corner of the fo'c'sle locker worked to move the cloves from bag to bag and to scoop from the deck.

There were two pallets, thirty-six bags per pallet, six tiers of six bags each. Each bag was 3' x 4' x 1' and weighed 110 pounds. Boats sighed, knowing the hard work in front of him. He lifted the first bag off the pallet, placed it on end, cut the threads in the end seam, and started poking with a two-foot-long iron bar. He had wrapped a loose piece of burlap around the poking end and then secured it with twine. This would stop the bar from breaking open the heroin packs. As he finished, he resewed the seam and rubbed dirt and cloves over the new threads to disguise the "new" look.

In the third bag, he found heroin. There were ten kilos in the bag. Presuming they were consistent in their packing, he needed to find fourteen more bags, for a total of 150 kilos.

Setting the ten packs aside, he poured cloves from the general-stow bag back into the ransacked bag, guessing the weight, and he then resewed it and placed it on the "inspected" pile.

He started at 2015 hours, just after the watch changed. At 2345, when he expected the midwatch to come on duty, he stopped. The ordinary seaman on the watch maintained a lookout at the bow. The chief mate had instructed everyone to use the port side, walking back and forth to the bow to avoid having to climb over the lashing holding the bulldozers in place. It was a safe, prudent, and legitimate concern and worked out, keeping the crew away from what he was doing since the manhole cover was on the starboard side. Boats' only concern was possible noise, so he sat in silence for thirty minutes before resuming his work.

It was hot, heavy work, but Boats was diligent. By 0400 hours, 150 kilos of heroin lay on the plastic on the deck. "It feels like I moved a horse," Boats thought. "This shit is aptly named."

He had piled the bags from the first pallet on the deck and then used the empty pallet to stack the bags from the second one. All he had to do now was restack the bags from the deck to the second empty pallet and replace the blue-rope netting. Knowing it would get light at 0430 hours, he knocked off for the night. Using a rag to loosen the hot light bulbs, (there were no on/off switches), he felt his way up the ladder and pushed up the manhole cover, being careful to not let it clang back against the frame. When he got out, he unplugged the cargo lights and hung the plugs on the top rung of the ladder. Closing the cover, he folded up the tarp and stuffed it between the steel scantlings that supported the catwalk. It would be secure there unless they ran into rough weather.

Looking up at the bridge, he saw the second mate smoking on the port wing, leaning into the headwind. Boats worked his way aft to the house, went in, and took a piss, something he had held in for the last hour. He stripped, walked to the shower naked, and did his best to scrub off the smell of cloves. He walked back, naked, to his room, dried himself, and hit the rack. If Eunice had seen him naked, she would have been all over him.

Two hours later, the ordinary seaman on watch woke him, as he did every working day. Boats stretched, went to the crew mess, grabbed a cup of coffee, and looked for the chief mate.

"Morning, mate," Boats said, knocking on his door at the same time.

"Morning, Boats. Come in. Close the door, will you?"

Boats closed the office door and sat in the chair in front of the desk.

"Well?" asked the mate. "How did it go?"

"I got it all done. Had to handle every bag. The ones with heroin had ten packs each."

"That's a lot of work. Good job!"

"Yeah, but I think we got a problem."

"How so?"

"I gotta wrap the packs in plastic so they fit into the hole in the conex. I can't do that in the tween deck; it won't fit through the hatch-cover opening. Then, I gotta wash it down to get rid of as much odor as possible. I hafta do that on deck. That's wet and noisy, with the water hitting the plastic. I gotta wrestle the stuff into the hole in the conex. That's three hundred pounds." He stopped and stared at Dennis.

Dennis sat silent for a minute. "Looks like we need to change the plan. How much plastic sheeting you got?

"Plenty."

"Okay, let's line the hole in the conex with the plastic and leave enough overlap at the top to wrap it all up when the keys are inside. How are the keys wrapped?"

"Some kind of wax paper. They seem watertight."

"Good. Here's what we'll do." He laid out his plan.

The second day out of Walvis Bay, we were heading home. The weather had been grand: bright sunshine, powder-puff cumulus clouds, temperature in the low seventies. I had resumed my workout regimen of running the exterior ladders, and my newfound workout partner was Clara. I worked out twice a day, at 0800 and at 1700 hours. Clara usually joined me for the afternoon workout.

True to her word, she had maintained her regimen and diet, existing on salads, protein, and water. I estimated she had lost over thirty pounds. After the workout, I would sit up on the flying bridge and cool off for half an hour. Clara would go to her room and shower. We usually ran on opposite sides of the ship, but today, as I followed her up the last ladder, she stopped, and I rammed my head into her ass. Embarrassed, I apologized. She laughed and continued up to the flying bridge.

Going to the forward rail, she grasped the rail and slowly did bends and stretches, loosening her hamstrings, which give me, standing four feet behind her, an intimate view of her ass and crotch, barely hidden by her Lycra leggings. Lowering her torso, she let go of the railing and lowered her head toward her feet. Looking back, she caught me ogling her ass and smiled. She gave a little wiggle and then stood, turned, and said, "It's nice to know a young stud like you still looks at my ass, but William, you have a lot to learn about giving head to a woman."

I laughed, but it was uncomfortable, given our buddy-buddy relationship, and I was a little embarrassed at being caught looking. I must have blushed because she said, "Oh, he's turning red. How innocent."

I expected her to laugh. When she didn't, I noticed that she stared at my crotch, which came to life involuntarily.

Arching her eyebrows, she stepped close, reached, and cupped my cock and balls. She whispered, "I have a cure for this. It's in my cabin." Then, she let go and stepped back. "It will be there for you any time. Knock and enter." Blowing me a kiss, she went down the ladder toward her cabin.

Now, it was my turn to lean against the rail and stretch, hoping my erection went away. It had been over a week since leaving Meg in Cape Town, and Mary Palm and her five sisters had put me to sleep every night. Clara's offer was uppermost on my mind as I descended the aft ladder. As I was deciding to take a shower and knock on Clara's door, my conscience alive but pushed to the rear, Dennis, the chief mate, intercepted me as I came out of my cabin.

"I want to talk to you, William." He wagged his head in the direction of his office, so I followed him. In the office, he closed the door and stood in front of me, rather than sitting at his desk. He seemed nervous. Taking a deep breath and blowing it out, he blurted, "I got a problem, William, and I need your cooperation."

Puzzled, I shrugged and said, "Sure, Dennis, what is it?"

"Tonight, on your watch, there's going to be a little activity on deck by the bulldozers. I want you to instruct your ordinary and AB to stand their lookout watches in the crew mess. No need to go to the bow. Also, no autopilot. Keep the helmsman at the wheel so he doesn't wander around the bridge and look down at the deck."

I knew that something to do with the "cloves" would be happening, and it must have shown on my face.

"William, when we had our conversation, I told you I wouldn't get you in trouble, and I meant it. If you don't look, you won't see anything. By the end of your watch, it will be over. End of story. Okay?"

"Sure, mate, no problem."

Nodding, he said, "That's all. Thanks." I left. Any thoughts of jumping Clara's bones were now long-distance memories.

The weather had turned, and when I climbed to the bridge, a light mist was falling. Tony had turned the radar on; the captain didn't use it in clear weather, day or night. I used that as my excuse, telling his helmsman going off duty to tell my ordinary to stay in the crew mess. No sense getting wet. I would call him if I wanted him.

The helmsman grunted, nodded, and left, giving my helmsman, AB Sturm, the course before he left. I relieved Tony and then instructed Sturm to steer by hand.

"Aye, aye, mate." He took it off autopilot and steered by hand. He was German. He didn't question orders from officers.

Walking out to the port-bridge wing, I lit a cigarette and stayed in the lee of the bridge. The wind came from over the starboard bow. Stubbing out the cigarette, I snuck a peek before I went back inside, but I only saw dark shadows, nothing identifiable.

Dennis had waited until 0015 before meeting Boats on deck by the conex box. The rainy weather played into their hands. Everything was wet, so no one would think twice about seeing a wet area around the conex. Boats had placed the plastic sheeting in the space inside the conex that afternoon under the pretense that he was checking the securing. No one questioned him. No one ever questioned Boats. Now, down in the hatch, he passed the heroin, four packs at a time, up the ladder to Dennis, who placed them on a piece of plastic on the main deck. When they were all stacked, Boats unplugged the cargo lights and dropped the cords down into the hatch, closing the manhole cover and dogging it down. Then, he used the small hose he had placed there that afternoon and sprayed the block of keys, washing any residue toward the scuppers at the ships rail. He then rinsed his and the mate's boots, flushing that residue toward the scuppers.

Dennis stepped into the conex, banging his shin and muttering a barely audible "Fuck!" before whispering, "Hand them to me."

Boats handed the heroin to Dennis, two packs at a time, and Dennis stowed them on the plastic sheeting in the hole in the center of the conex. Hand fitting each pack, it took Dennis half an hour to complete the job. He climbed out, and Boats climbed in, folded over the excess sheeting, and taped it in place. Boats then spread loose tea leaves all over the pile, having previously spread tea leaves on the floor under the plastic sheets. He left the remains of the case of tea just inside the door. The last thing he did before closing, locking, and placing the seal on the conex was spread loose pepper on the floor, inside the door.

As he and the mate walked aft to the house, they threw their gloves overboard. Boats looked up and thought he saw a face at the window of the officers' salon, a woman's face, but then it was gone.

Chapter 37

WOMAN TROUBLE

The next morning, the rain persisted, so I skipped running the ladders and headed straight for breakfast. All the engine-room guys were there, oil soiled, with smelly coveralls and dumb jokes. Dennis just nodded. Tony, looking a little pale, said, "Morning" and left to relieve the second mate. The captain was absent, but Clara and Eunice huddled at the table, whispering in each other's ears. Bernie Simpson sat alone, as usual, communing with his altar of food, piled high.

"Morning, mate," Joey, the pantryman, said.

"Glad someone's talking," I said, and I ordered scrambled eggs, toast, bacon, sausage, and milk, the last of the fresh supply.

"Yeah, mate, seems like everyone's a little grumpy today."

"The captain been in?"

"Nah, he ordered breakfast in his cabin earlier."

"Coffee, too, please, Joey. Thanks."

"Coming right up."

On my second cup of coffee, I was still waiting for breakfast when the second mate came in. He grabbed a coffee and a piece of last night's pound cake and walked out. Bernie got up and left as the engineer watch standers and the chief engineer left, so we were down to Eunice, Clara, and me.

Joey brought the food and then returned to the pantry. As I cut the sausage, Clara sat down opposite, followed by Eunice. "We need to talk."

Motioning with my fork, I asked, "We?" I thought she must be pissed at me for not knocking on her door last night.

Clara shook her head. "All of us."

I looked at the plate. It was obvious what I wanted to do, because Eunice said, "Eat. We'll talk." So, I stabbed a piece of sausage and ate.

Eunice started. "There's something strange going on."

Still chewing, I didn't respond.

"Last night, I saw the chief mate and another man on deck doing something in the metal box on deck."

Not wanting to seem dumb, I offered, "You mean the conex box?"

"Whatever you call it." She was testy now. "Next to the bulldozers."

"Yes, they call it a conex box."

"What were they doing there so late at night?"

Knowing full well what they did, I said, "I have no idea. Why don't you ask him?"

"No. He'll run to Marcus, and that will set him off again."

It took a second to remember that "Marcus" was the captain, and then the significance of what she said hit me. "Set him off again." Recalling my conversation with Tony, I wondered now if the captain had threatened Eunice. She certainly was apprehensive.

Clara interjected. "Eunice, Dennis seems like a nice man. I'm sure he was just doing his job."

"In the middle of the night? Besides, the other thing, in the captain's safe..." She stopped.

"What other, thing, Eunice?" I asked.

"Never mind," she said, her head swiveling. "Never mind." She got up and left.

Clara stood. In a very quiet voice, she said, "Finish eating, William, and then please, come and see me. Eunice is worried. So am I."

Wolfing down a few more bites, I chugalugged the milk and drank the coffee, thanked Joey, who had probably overheard everything, and then left.

Going to the head and peeing, I returned to my cabin, brushed my teeth, and sat on the bunk, wondering what to do. After half an hour, I tapped on Clara's door.

She opened it, and I walked in, greeted by the smell of a clean body, fresh from the shower, and a hint of a flowery aroma. Clara wore a robe of baby-blue terrycloth, belted so that lots of cleavage showed.

"What's that smell, like flowers?"

She turned and picked up a small vial from the bureau, holding it out. "Lady Manhattan. You like it?"

I was not big on perfumes, but this was subtle, so I answered, "Yeah, it's nice."

Clara sat on the bed and flounced, or as nearly as a woman of her size could flounce, grabbing a pillow and settling against the bulkhead. The robe exposed more cleavage, and when she drew her legs up to sit cross-legged, for a second, I could see far enough up to know what she had for breakfast. To hide my immediate erection, I sat in the chair.

"So, Clara, what's going on?"

"You know Eunice is getting divorced?"

"Why don't you presume I know nothing, and tell me what's on your mind."

"Okay." She spent the next thirty minutes relating arguments Eunice and the captain had—how Eunice admitted spiting the captain and rubbing it in, until one day, he held up his hand (Clara demonstrated) and told Eunice, "Enough! Shut the fuck up, or I swear, I will throw you overboard."

"What did Eunice do?" I asked.

"She shut up and left. She said he had never talked that way to her before. It frightened her.

"The next day, Eunice insisted I accompany her to the captain's room. She asked for her jewelry back from his safe.

"'Okay,' he said. He went into his room, and she followed. I stayed in his office but heard her ask, 'What's that?'

"'None of your damn business,' he snapped. A minute later, she came out, clutching her jewelry box, and we left.

"'What were you arguing about?' I asked her.

"She replied, 'There's a briefcase jammed in his safe. It took up most of the room, and when I asked what it was, he barked at me. It looked out of place, and I was curious because the lock part was covered with a wax seal.'" Clara paused. Looking down, she realized how much of her was exposed and looked at me. Holding the edges of the robe like a man grasps a vest when orating, she said, "I didn't do this on purpose." But she didn't close the robe, either. Even with all the weight she had lost, she was still full-bodied, and I still had an erection.

Trying to stay on topic, I said, "Look, Eunice may be scared of the captain, especially since she's been fucking Tony for the whole trip and rubbing it in the captain's face. If she's been avoiding the captain since she got her jewelry, why would he hurt her? Seems like he wants nothing to do with her now."

Clara fidgeted for a minute and then blurted out, "She knows the combination to the safe, and she's thinking of taking the briefcase and hiding it, to ensure that he won't hurt her. She'll return it in New York."

"Steal it? She doesn't even know what's in the briefcase. What if it's nothing but paperwork?"

"She thinks it's valuable because of the way he reacted when she asked him about it."

"That's crazy. He reacted to her being a bitch and sticking verbal daggers into him every chance she got."

"Maybe, but she can't see that. I don't know what to do."

"Why do anything? It's Eunice's problem, not yours."

"We're friends. I don't want to see her get into trouble, and to tell you the truth, when I heard the captain's voice that day, it sent a shiver through me."

Standing, my erection dissipated by the distraction of the seriousness of the situation, I told her, "Tell Eunice to just stay away from the captain. If she does, she'll be safe. He isn't going to risk his livelihood and do something stupid unless she drives him to it. For God's sake, get her to back off."

"I'll try," she said.

Clara shuffled forward and sat on the edge of the bed, spreading her legs as she did so.

Startled, I focused on the absence of pubic hair, except a thin line directly above the vulva.

"Since you're here, let's not waste the opportunity." She opened her robe, exposing the largest nipples I have ever seen, erect and ready for action.

I should have left. It was now or never, but when she unbuckled my belt and unzipped my pants, I couldn't move. Maybe too much blood had left my brain for my dick. Maybe I didn't have the moral gumption to say no. When her lips touched the end of my dick, there was no debate, no argument. I groaned and came quickly.

Pulling back, Clara sat on the edge of the bunk and wiped her mouth with the sleeve of her robe. "William, that was supposed to be foreplay. What about me?" She leaned back and spread her legs.

I bent over, and she reached for my head, thinking I was going down on her, but I pulled up my pants. Thinking of Meg, guilt washed over me. Shaking my head, I headed for the door, Clara's voice trailing me. "It's my turn, dammit. William, it's my turn."

I still heard her through the closed door as I walked away.

Chapter 38

HEAVY WEATHER

The rain persisted, deepening my already glum outlook. I was missing Meg, semi-convinced that she'd break up with me because of her mother's insistence on living in South Africa, and I was horny. I dwelled on Clara's open-robe invitation more than I should have. It was New Year's Eve, and no one aboard was in a party mood.

Eunice's behavior bothered me, too. Her idea of stealing the briefcase from the captain and holding it hostage to ensure her safety seemed dumb, but I understood her reasoning, even if I didn't agree with it.

Did she tell Tony? I wondered. If not, why not? Why me? Perplexed, a little anxious, and more than a little curious, I mused about whether I should mention it to Tony. I still hadn't resolved my dilemma when I went to relieve him at 1145.

Skipping lunch, neither hungry nor in the mood for confrontation with Eunice or Clara, I went straight from my room to the bridge after returning once to get my sou'wester. The rain was heavy and the seas building when I stepped onto the bridge.

"Hey, Tony," I called out, and then I noticed the captain standing in the door of the chart room. Nodding in his direction, I said, "Captain." I looked around and didn't see Tony. I looked through the ports in both wing doors, closed due to the weather, and didn't see him outside, either.

The captain said, "Apparently, he's picked up some bug. He's in his room, puking and shitting, a regular whirling dervish. I relieved him an hour ago."

Sturm, my AB, arrived then to relieve the helmsman. The captain waited until they had exchanged information on the course and switched positions before continuing. "I asked Fran to check on him, make sure he drinks water. Dehydration is a problem when both ends are failing you." He showed a wry smile.

Given what Tony and his wife had been doing, I expected hostility from the captain, maybe even glee at Tony's discomfort. Perhaps the captain felt sorry for him, knowing Eunice much better than Tony did.

He gave me the course, 315 degrees, and the speed. He noted no traffic, and I relieved him.

The wind howled in the rigging; on the Beaufort scale, I estimated it to be a six or seven. Seas were twelve to fifteen feet and growing. Coming from slightly west of north, the wind drove the rising seas hard, slamming them into the starboard bow, causing the ship to shudder every fourth or fifth wave. At 1400 hours, AB Jaeger replaced Sturm at the helm, telling him the bosun wanted to see him when he went below. Twenty minutes later, leaning into the starboard bulkhead, peering through the rain, I saw the bosun, Sturm, and the day man, working their way forward, checking the lashings on the yacht and the bulldozers, clinging precariously whenever a wave broke over the top of the rail.

When Chuck, the second mate, relieved me at 1545 hours, the wind had increased, so foam streaked off the tops of the breakers, and an occasional green sea smashed onto the starboard deck at the no. 2 and no. 3 hatches. Just as I was leaving, the captain appeared and ordered Chuck to drop speed to 12 knots.

I knocked on Tony's door, checking on him. There was no answer, so I opened the door and looked in. No Tony. Going to the head, I heard him retching as I opened the door. Tony sat on the toilet, holding a pail in his hands.

Looking at me, he said, "This, sucks! Nothing left to come up. Nothing but the dry heaves now."

"Anything I can do?" I asked.

Waving me away, he said, "Stay away. Don't you catch it, whatever the hell it is."

Nodding, I backed out and closed the door.

The ship rolled enough so that I had to walk with my arms out, deflecting off the bulkheads. Not seasick, but wary of the possibility, I grabbed a few packs of saltines from the salon and washed a half dozen down with a few sips of water. I checked with Dennis and told him about Tony, asking him if he wanted me to cover his watch for him.

"You and Chuck split it. He'll stay on until 2200. You pick it up then, okay?"

"Sure." I paused. "Is Eunice or Clara sick? They were with Tony in Walvis Bay."

"I don't think so. Haven't seen either of them, but I figured they were hibernating due to the weather."

"The captain slowed down to 12 knots when Chuck came on watch."

"Yeah, I could feel it. Chuck is charting the latest weather report. The isobars are getting tight. Heavy winds coming."

At 0215 hours, with the speed down to 8 knots, winds of 60 mph and thirty-five-foot seas, a ten on the Beaufort scale, the ship pitching and tossing, I heard a snap, followed by a loud crash from starboard. I couldn't see anything through the porthole, so I went onto the bridge wing, slamming the door behind me. Clinging to the forward windscreen, I peered over the top, rain driving into my face like pellets from a shotgun. I still couldn't see much, so I went inside. As I picked up the phone to call the captain, he walked onto the bridge.

"Heard the noise, captain. Went onto the wing but can't see anything."

"Go get Dennis and Boats, and go see what happened. I'll turn on the deck lights."

When I got to Dennis's room, he was coming out. I relayed the captain's orders, and we got Boats, already waiting for us.

"Port side," Boats said. "Safer." And we followed him out the port-side-companionway door, the lee side of the ship.

On deck, the rain and spray were constant, shimmering in the glare of the deck lights. The wind, pulling and grabbing at our clothes, alternated between a screech and moan in our ears. Boats crabbed his way, hand over hand, to the forward end of the no. 3 hatch, me and Dennis following in his wake. At the forward end, he clambered over the piping and structural steel and worked his way to the starboard side, partially protected by the ship's gear housing and winch platform. He faced disaster.

The conex box, slammed all night by breaking waves, had succumbed to the bashing. One of the front wire-cable lashings, the inboard one, had snapped, and with every wave and bounce, the others were loosening and stretching, allowing more movement with every sway. Between the time he pointed at it and the time Dennis got close enough to see, the offshore lashing broke, letting the next wave slam the conex into the blade of the bulldozer directly behind, creasing the conex and straining the frame.

"I'm gonna get some ropes and hooks!" screamed the bosun, trying to be heard over the wind. "We'll hook the top-corner castings, take a strain, and try to tighten it like a Spanish windlass. Wait here."

Going to the port side, he headed to his locker in the bow.

I heard Dennis saying something but couldn't make out what it was, so I yelled, "What'd you say?"

"Motherfucker! That's what I said!" he roared back.

I started to inch out on to the deck, but Dennis grabbed my ankle. When I turned, he shook his head.

"Wait for Boats!" he shouted. "Too dangerous alone."

Waiting, the back-and-forth pounding continued, each wave slamming the conex into the dozer blade. The crease in the back of it grew, bowing the forward frame. Each pitch forward pulled it away. The lashing wires on the rear of the conex limited its port-to-starboard movement, but they strained with every lunge forward.

Boats arrived, carrying two coils of one-inch hemp line and two eye-hooks. He took one of the eye-hooks and threaded the line through it, doubling its size. Watching him, I did the same for the other hook.

He was still shouting, straining to be heard. "You," he said, pointing at me, "are gonna try to place the hook on the top of the corner casting. I'll hang onto you." He nodded at Dennis. "You lead the line back over the steel crosspiece on the bulkhead. Loop it twice, but leave slack until he places the hook, and then pull it tight. When we get the inboard one on, we'll try for the offshore one."

"Ready?" We nodded. Waiting for a break between waves, he yelled, "Go!"

I jumped out on the deck, skidding to a halt when my left hand and nose met the door of the conex. Disregarding the pain, I leaped up, grabbing the roof of the conex with my left hand and searching for the corner casting hole with my right. I hit it on the first try, dropping but hanging onto the rope to keep tension on the hook. Boats grabbed me, and with Dennis pulling on the rope and Boats pulling me, holding the rope and letting the pitching of the ship do the work, we snugged it up. After one more wave cycle, we had tightened it enough so that only the offshore side of the conex was hitting the dozer blade.

Soaked and blinded by salt spray, with a bloody nose and banged-up knuckles, I looked at Boats and said, "What's next?"

He laughed and slapped me on my back, knocking my knees into the steel cross member and yelled, "Let's do it again!"

We got into the same positions. Boats, timing the waves, shouted "Go!" I went, this time to the outboard side, farther away from shelter and closer to the rail and the raging ocean.

I got the hook placed on the second try, and like the first, I held onto the rope to keep the tension on the hook. That's what saved me: my death grip on that rope. As I turned away from the conex to go back, a solid wall of water hit me, slamming me into the door of the conex. Dazed and sputtering but still aware of the situation, I sensed a body washing by me on the deck, toward the scuppers. Instinctively, I reached out and grabbed at it. It was Boats. The same wave had driven him headfirst into the door, right beside me, and knocked him out.

With the ship rolling to starboard, I spread-eagled, the rope in my left hand and Boats in my right, tearing my shoulders apart. Dennis saved the day.

Abandoning the rope, he leaped across the deck and grabbed Boats. Between the two of us, we got him back in the lee of the hatch cover before the next wave broke over the gunnel. Sitting him on the deck, up against the bulkhead, I leaned in and yelled at Dennis, "I got him! Try to tighten the rope." Four waves and much subsequent forward pitching later, it was tight enough so that the conex no longer slammed into the dozer blade. It still moved but didn't crash into anything.

Dennis tied off the end, came over, and shouted, "Let's get the fuck out of here!"

Lifting Boats, conscious but woozy, between us was difficult. Threading our way back to the port side and into the house was like walking through a moving obstacle course, but we made it.

A half dozen crew members greeted us at the door. We were in tight quarters, but they took Boats from me and Dennis and sat him in the crew mess.

"Get Fran," Dennis ordered. "Tell him to bring his first-aid kit." Facing me, he said. "You better sit down, kid."

"I'm okay, Dennis."

Grabbing my arm, he ordered, "Sit." He led me to a chair. He picked up a roll of paper towels and stuck the entire roll up against my forehead. "Hold this, and don't move."

I sat there, puzzled, until I wiped my eyes, and my hand came away covered in blood. I can deal with blood if it's someone else's—not so much when it's mine. So, I sat and took deep breaths, open-mouthed gasps.

Fran arrived. Dennis told him, "Boats maybe has a concussion. William, his forehead's cut wide open."

Seeing me staring back at him, the paper towels at my head, Fran turned to Boats and asked him questions. Sometime later, I felt a hand on mine. It was Fran, removing the paper towels.

"Let go, William. I have it." He looked at it and then said, "Lie down on the table. It needs stitches. It'll be steadier that way." I lay down but had to roll over and spit out blood immediately. That's when I realized my nose had broken.

"Can't lay down," I gasped. "Have to breathe through my mouth. I'll sit still. Go ahead, stitch it."

Seventeen stitches later, he finished. "I can set your nose," he said, "but it will hurt like hell."

"Go ahead. Everything's going to hurt later, anyway."

He did, and it did, then and later.

The second mate came up early and finished my midwatch. Dennis told me to hit the sack, which I did, after stripping off my soaked clothes, but there was no sleeping tonight. With the ship rolling 15 to 20 degrees or more and pitching heavily, I pulled up the crash bar on the side of my bunk to stop me from rolling out, bunched two pillows together, and squeezed myself into a corner. I had popped four Tylenols before climbing into bed but couldn't tell if it helped or not. My forehead burned, and my nose ached. I don't know if I slept or drifted in and out of consciousness, but I wasn't awake for part of the next six hours.

At 1000 hours, I fought my way to the head. Hanging onto the bulkhead with one hand and little William in the other, I peed without dripping all over myself. Getting dressed and putting on my socks and shoes was a chore. Every time I bent over, it felt like the stitches in my forehead would snap. I thought the pressure on the bridge of my nose would make my head explode. Though my nose bled again, I stuffed a tissue up each nostril to stem it and then made my way to the salon.

Joey, the pantryman, had the salon in storm mode. All the doors on the cabinets were closed, slide bars on the sides of the tables were raised, and there were no loose cups or plates on the sideboards. Wet napkins served as place mats to keep dishes from sliding while eating.

I poured a cup of coffee only two-thirds full to keep it from spilling and looked out the forward ports. The rain had stopped, but the wind and seas were still high.

Joey came in. "Hey, Mr. Connolly, how are you doing?" Looking at my head, he made a face and said, "Damn, that must hurt."

"It does, Joey."

"Can I get you anything?"

"How about some toast?"

"Got it. Sit down and relax. You want butter or jelly?"

"Jelly. Thanks, Joey."

Nodding, he went into the pantry.

Dennis stuck his head in the door. "How are you feeling, William?"

"Sore, but I'll live. How's Boats doing?"

"He'll be okay. He's got a concussion and doesn't like being told to stay in bed. He ignored my advice, but Fran told him off, and damned if he didn't do as he was told. It's odd." Shaking his head, he said, "The toughest guy on the ship only pays attention to the meekest guy on board. Oh, Fran also told him you saved his life. Knowing Boats, he'll be pissed off because he has to say thank you." He laughed and turned, but I called him.

"Dennis, how did Fran know I grabbed Boats? He wasn't there."

"No, but he was there when I told the captain."

The captain refused to let anyone else go on deck, so the makeshift lashing that Boats, Dennis, and I had created had to suffice. Dennis knew it wouldn't hold up if the severe weather persisted.

Tony remained out of service. Fran forced him to keep drinking water by threatening to hook him up to an IV. Tony hated needles, something apparently only Fran knew, and the threat worked. His puke/shit cycle had slowed, so he was in the head only every forty-five minutes.

The pain from my forehead was constant but not severe, and as long as I didn't bend over, the nose didn't bother me. I found Dennis in his office and told him I could stand watch. He checked with Fran before agreeing to it.

I returned to the salon and asked Joey to make me a peanut-butter-and-jelly sandwich. When he brought it, I asked him if he had seen any of the passengers.

"Both ladies were in for breakfast. The weather don't seem to bother them none. Haven't seen Mr. Simpson." He chuckled. "Thought nothing would keep that man away from the table."

I smiled. Laughing hurt. It took a while to eat the sandwich. Chewing and breathing had become mutually exclusive actions. At 1150 hours, I relieved Chuck, the second mate.

"Wow, William," Chuck started. "You look like shit!"

Despite the pain, I laughed. "You should have seen the other guy."

"You sure you're okay to stand watch?"

"I'm good, Chuck. Even Fran said it was okay, and he has the last word on anything medical."

"That he does. Well, the good news is that the rain is over; everything else is terrible news. We're in a wind storm, rare for this time of year but not unheard of. I finished charting the last weather report, and we have a big high-pressure area to the north. Since we're in the southern hemisphere, the winds are rotating counterclockwise, and the pressure gradient is steep. I calculated that the wind speed for the next twenty-four hours should be in the forty-mile-per-hour range."

"That's not too bad, Chuck. The anemometer read 50 mph yesterday afternoon."

"I know. I said I calculated 40 mph. Ten minutes ago, the anemometer was reading sixty and gusting higher. Either I stink at transferring the data to a chart, or the weather service screwed up in their readings. I'm blaming it on the weather service."

"Any change in the wind direction?"

"No, and there won't be until we get further north, closer to the equator, or the high-pressure area drifts east. Or both."

"Okay, Chuck. What's our course and speed?"

"Still heading 323 degrees. We're making revolutions for 8 knots, but my star sights this morning show us making 5.5 knots."

"You been on watch since 0400 hours?"

"No, Dennis came up for a couple hours and gave me a break."

All this conversation happened as we stood facing each other at the binnacle, each of us holding onto one of the captain's balls. These are the iron balls used to adjust the magnetic compass for deviation. They're placed on slider bars on either side of the binnacle and adjusted periodically.

"Okay, Chuck. Anything else?"

"Yeah, hang on. It's gonna be a rough ride. I don't think your nose can take another hit."

As he turned to leave, I asked, "How are we splitting Tony's watch?"

"I'll stay on until 2200. You take it from there. If he's still sick tomorrow, I'll stay on watch until 1000, and then you come on, okay?"

"Okay, Chuck. See ya."

The weather continued to worsen. While the wind held between 55 and 60 mph, with occasional gusts to 70 mph, the seas continued to build. Heavy foam flew off the crests and speckled the troughs. Every wave broke at the crest, washing over the starboard-deck area.

Dennis relieved me for lunch at noon, but I grabbed a sleeve of saltines, peed, and came back to the bridge. At 1300 hours, the captain came up, looked out both sides, and went below without saying a word. The rotary windshield screen, which rotates by using centrifugal force to dispense the rain from the screen, couldn't keep up with the sea spray. I spent most of the time hanging on to the rail at the forward end, peering through the porthole, worrying about the conex. It moved. A lot. I hadn't heard any noise yet if it was slamming into the dozer again, but I couldn't hear much over the roar of the wind.

At 1400 hours, the captain came up again, peered through the forward porthole, and ordered me to bring the ship direct into the seas and take them head on. Just as I gave the order to the helmsman, Sturm, we took a huge wave over the starboard side. Green water came all the way to the house, amid a crash and grinding noises. The captain and I looked out the porthole together and saw the conex bounce off the dozer blade and roll over the starboard rail, into the sea. Gone!

By the next morning, the wind had dropped to 20 mph, but it took another full day for the seas to moderate to where the captain allowed Boats and Dennis to go on deck and assess the situation.

Inspecting the area, Boats picked up one of the original lashings that had broken, the bottom end still attached to the deck. Whistling, he held it up to the chief mate and muttered, "Damn. Looks like the wire slipped right out of the swage fitting. Never seen that before." There was no sign of the temporary rope lashings we had used.

Dennis walked outboard and looked at the sides of the dozers along the railing. "Boats, look at this. The conex broke the binder on the forward-chain lashing. Thank God, the other seven chains held. Get one of your guys, and replace it." He shivered. "Jesus. If the dozer had broken loose, it would have taken the whole rail with it."

The captain watched Dennis and Boats from his cabin's forward porthole. A few minutes later, Dennis knocked on his door. "Come in, Dennis. Close the door."

He sat in the chair opposite the captain; each had the same thought: "How the fuck do we tell Frankie his heroin blew overboard?"

Chapter 39

CONFRONTATION

Except for meals, Eunice hadn't ventured out of her cabin during the storm. After her mental slipup during her conversation with William about the briefcase in the captain's safe, she had cornered Clara and insisted she say nothing more to William or anyone else about the diamonds. Clara, intimidated by Eunice, didn't admit she had already told William about Eunice's plan to take the diamonds.

"I won't tell him, Eunice, but I don't think you should take the briefcase. If he catches you, you've given him an excuse to hurt you."

Eunice was adamant but realized she needed to keep Clara on her side. "Okay, Clara, I'll think about it."

On Sunday, the day after the conex had washed overboard, the seas were still rough but getting calmer. Eunice walked the passageway every half hour, leaning against the bulkhead to hold her balance, peeking into the captain's room when the door was open, trying to gauge an opportunity to steal the briefcase. Where to stow it after she took it puzzled her. No area would be sacrosanct from search. The captain was God aboard ship and could do whatever he liked. There were no rights of privacy she could invoke. The answer came two days later at 2:00 a.m. on Tuesday from a recovered and freshly screwed Tony.

Lying on her bed, naked, with hand on Tony's chest and moving lower, she asked, "Is there any part of the ship where no one goes when we're at sea?"

Distracted by her roving hand, Tony didn't think of the oddness of the question, only of giving Eunice what she wanted: an answer. "We can access anywhere if we have to, but no one ever goes into the chain locker forward, or the rope lockers aft."

"Why not?"

"No need to. Nothing in the chain locker except the anchor chain, and we stow the mooring lines in the aft rope lockers."

"Do you lock them?"

"Sometimes in port, if the mate thinks there may be chance of stowaways, but not at sea."

Eunice sensed he was about to ask her why, but she nipped that problem in the bud with a gentle squeeze of his most sensitive area, successfully distracting him.

The next morning, Wednesday, standing on the flying bridge facing forward, with her hair tossing in the wind, Eunice realized that the forward chain locker was too exposed. Anyone on the bridge, or the captain and chief mate, from their forward rooms, could see her if she walked to the chain locker in daylight. She knew from standing on the bridge at night with Tony that she could be seen at night if the weather was clear. Abandoning that choice, she walked down the series of exterior ladders and walked aft to the fantail. Lighting a cigarette as an excuse, should anyone accost her, she leaned her back against the taffrail and studied the doors to the rope lockers: typical, watertight doors with three dogging bars, one at the top, the bottom, and the side opposite the hinges.

Taking a drag on the cigarette, Eunice walked to the port side and looked up the deck. She saw no one and repeated this at the starboard side. Tossing her cigarette off the stern, she tried the securing dogs on the starboard locker, and although it was straining, she unlocked them and opened the door. A musty, old hemp smell washed past her. Looking inside, there were mooring lines faked down on the deck, spaces in the center of the coils and gaps where the lines didn't touch as they rounded the corners.

Closing and dogging the door, she peeked forward again to ensure that she was alone and then opened the port-locker door. Same conditions. Closing and dogging that door, she made a mental note to wear sneakers when she stowed the briefcase. She'd have to clamber over the mooring lines to access the far corner.

Lighting another cigarette, her hands shook. She was tough and able to handle most situations, but larceny was new to her. She stood there a few minutes, smoking, calming her nerves, and then went to her cabin.

Lunch in the salon was quiet. Crew members rotated in and out, nodding and grunting greetings. Greg, the third engineer, sat engrossed in a technical manual. Neither the captain nor chief mate made an appearance. Clara and Eunice sat together, not whispering but close to it. Bernie Simpson sat alone behind his tower of food. As I left, I walked past Bernie, just rising from his chair, and grabbed him as he slipped and nearly fell. Up close, he reeked of booze. He didn't thank me, just glared in my direction.

Two hours later, I was leaning on the starboard bulwark, staring into the salty breeze, enjoying the sunshine on my back and shoulders. Clara interrupted me, tapping on my shoulder.

"William." She was tentative, almost plaintive. "I'm afraid."

"Of what, Clara?"

"Bernie. He's been drinking a lot. He got in my face, saying he'll never let me divorce him."

"Yeah, at lunch, when I stopped him from falling, he reeked of booze. Did he hit you?"

"No, but he said he'd kill me before he lets me divorce him. I think it's finally sunk in with him that he's got nothing if I leave."

"I thought he had a business at home."

She paused. "It's my business. Bernie's an employee. I've kept the business separate from our personal lives. I don't know what will happen in a divorce. My lawyer will have to be better than Bernie's, I guess, but until I get home and change my will, Bernie gets most everything if I die." Another pause. "He's gotten rough, but he's never threatened to kill me before. I'm scared!"

"I don't know what to say, Clara."

"I do." It was Eunice. She walked through the pool deck door and shut it behind her. "Now, you've got two women who believe their husbands want to kill them. How are you going to protect us?"

Staring at them for a long five seconds, I said, "I can't protect you unless you try to protect yourselves. We've got a week to go before we reach New York. Go to meals together. If you come on deck, do it together. Hell, go the bathroom together. When you're in your rooms, keep the doors locked. Stay away from the crew spaces and open-deck areas." I took a deep breath and started again. "I don't think either Bernie or the captain will try to kill either of you, but it's clear you believe it, so stay away from them. Don't do anything to confront them. Got that?"

Clara nodded, and Eunice said, "Yes."

"Good."

No sooner had the word escaped my lips when the door to the pool deck swung open and slammed against the metal stop, a loud clang jarring the air. I turned, and Bernie stood there, swaying.

He glared at Clara. "You bitch," he snarled. "All the years I put up with your shit." He sputtered, and spit flecked his lips. "You think you're gonna just toss me away like a piece of garbage?" His voice rose as he staggered forward. "The fuck you are!" Shouting now, he reached for Clara.

Stepping between them, I caught a feeble punch on my shoulder. Shoving him back, I told him, "Back off, Bernie. You're drunk. Go sleep it off."

Weaving in front of me, he screamed, "Screw you! Screw all of you, the same way she's trying to screw me." Tottering, he put his hands on his hips, ample resting spots. He took a deep breath and started to cry.

Stunned, I stood there a few seconds and then turned to Clara and said, "You should go below, to your room."

Unfortunately, Eunice couldn't control herself and said, "Look at Mr. Tough Guy, crying like a baby."

Bernie screamed, "I'll kill both of you!" He lunged forward, aiming a hay-maker in Eunice's general direction, but I stood between Bernie and Eunice. Young reflexes won. I ducked and gut-punched him, my fist sinking deep into his flab. As he exhaled, his eyes bulged, and he sank to his knees. He couldn't hurt me as he gasped for air, but city-kid instincts and maybe a mean streak made me knee him in the face. Catching him on the right cheek, I heard the splat of his nose breaking, and he spilled over backward onto the deck, where his head made a dull thud.

The women had backed up a few steps but stood mute—a rarity, especially with Eunice.

"Damn it Eunice," I said, "you need to learn to keep your mouth shut. You're becoming a self-fulfilling prophecy." Rubbing at my face with both hands, I said, "Both of you, go to your rooms. I'll tend to Bernie."

When they left, I called into the bridge, keeping an eye on Bernie. I instructed AB Sturm to put the ship on autosteering and go find the chief mate and Fran, the chief steward, and to bring them to the bridge.

Bernie stirred, so I helped him get to his feet and sat him down on a deck chair at poolside. All the fight had gone out of him. Fran arrived first, followed by Dennis and Sturm. I ordered Sturm back to the helm, closed the bridge door for privacy, then explained to Dennis and Fran what had happened, stressing that Bernie said he'd kill both Clara and Eunice.

Fran said, "Let me take him below and clean him up. I think you broke his nose. He's got a cut on the back of his head, but it isn't bleeding much. He may have a concussion."

During the entire conversation, Bernie just sat there, staring ahead, not reacting at all.

Dennis said, "Go ahead, Fran. Fix him up, and then put him in his room. When you're done, come find me."

Fran nodded, helped Bernie get up from the lounge chair, and led him away.

After he left, I told Dennis what occurred with Clara and Eunice prior to Bernie showing up and then asked, "What do you think, Dennis?"

"I understand why Clara is afraid. Bernie is an asshole and bully. After what happened here, I think he might lose his temper and do something stupid." He paused. "I still can't see the captain losing it and hitting Eunice, though she's capable of pulling his trigger." Shaking his head, he said, "I just don't know."

"Should we put this incident in the ship's log?" I asked.

"Do you want it on the record that you slugged and kneed a passenger?" he threw back at me, shaking his head.

"No!"

"I didn't think so. Come see me after you get off watch."

Chapter 40

GUARD DUTY

I went straight to Dennis's office after being relieved by Chuck and knocked on the open door. There was no answer from the bedroom, so I went to the salon and found him drinking coffee and eating pound cake. When he saw me, he stood and motioned for me to follow him. We went to Fran's office, and Dennis told us to come to his room, so we paraded up the passageway to Dennis's office, closing the door behind us. Dennis went to his desk while Fran and I sat in the chairs before him.

"Fran," Dennis began, "I'm going to tell you something that must stay in this room. Don't tell anyone," he said, pausing, "not even the captain." Dennis waited for Fran to acknowledge his request and then related what I had told him. Fran didn't react until Dennis told him Eunice was afraid that the captain wanted to kill her.

"My God." He put his left hand to his lower lip. "She's serious?"

"Dead serious," Dennis said, not realizing how ominous it sounded.

Fran sat there for a while, head lowered. When he raised his head, he wore a look of resignation on his face. "They had some terrible arguments," he said.

"Who?" Dennis asked.

"The captain and Eunice. I've heard them."

"How terrible?" I asked.

His left hand again rubbed his lower lip. "Terrible. The last time, the captain threatened to kill her."

"Jesus!" Dennis and I said at the same time.

"We've got to keep them apart," Dennis said. "We got a week until New York. Clara will stay away from Bernie, but Eunice, I don't know. She's her own worst enemy."

While he was talking, I was thinking of the briefcase and how Eunice wanted it as her life-insurance policy. It could work…or it could backfire and become her death-assurance policy. Should I tell them or not? I opt not to tell them.

"William, I want you to check on Clara every hour you're awake, even when on day watch. I'll tell the captain what happened with Bernie and Clara. That way, he'll be fine with you leaving the bridge to check on her. I'm not saying anything about Eunice. The less we bring her to his attention, the better."

"What about night watch?" I asked.

"I'll check on her at night," Dennis replied. "Fran, as much as you can, try to check on Eunice the same way. Let her know she can come to you at any time."

"I think she prefers Tony," Fran said, a wry smile lightening the seriousness.

"And I think you're right, but Tony is just another hand grenade she's likely to pull the pin on and throw at the captain, so I'm hoping to minimize that explosion."

"Hugs," Fran said. "I'll give her hugs. I'm a better hugger than Tony." He laughed aloud, Dennis and I joining in.

"Okay, guys," Dennis said. "This is serious shit, so let's pay attention."

Fran knocked gently on Eunice's door. "Fran," he responded to her "Who is it?" query.

She opened the door but stood there, blocking access.

"May I come in?" he asked, and she moved aside, closing the door after he entered.

"Eunice, I'm aware of your concern about the captain possibly threatening you."

She interrupted. "There's no 'possibly.' It's already happened. More than once."

Holding up both hands, Fran continued. "Yes, I know. The chief mate, the third mate, William, and I met, and we are taking these threats seriously. That's why I'm here."

Eunice took a deep breath, nodded, and leaned back against the edge of her bunk. "Sorry, Fran. Once again, I barked at the wrong person, I know."

"That's okay. It goes with the job." He paused. "Dennis and William will check on Clara regularly. They've asked that I do the same for you. I'll need your cooperation."

"What do you want me to do?"

Taking a breath, tucking in his chin, and raising his eyebrows, he said, "Stay away from the captain, for starters. Try to stay in your room as much as possible. If you need to get out, stay in sight of other people at all times."

"That's it?" she asked.

"Well, it would help if you didn't antagonize the captain. That's best accomplished by staying away from other crew members. It shouldn't be too hard. We'll be in New York in about a week."

To his surprise, she laughed. "Fran, you are the soul of discretion and tact. You mean, keep Tony out of my room and my bed."

Nodding, he said, "That would be helpful."

"All right, Fran. I'll do my part. Thank you." She hugged him, and he left.

While Fran talked to Eunice, Dennis was in Clara's room, spelling out the rules for her.

"I don't feel safe here," she said. "The lock is flimsy, and I could break the chain lock just by leaning on the door. One kick, and Bernie could break it in."

"That's true," Dennis said. "I'll have the bosun weld a couple of braces on the side frames and hang a metal bar on the inside. Bernie won't be able to get past that."

Reaching out and holding both of his hands, she said, "Thank you Dennis. I thanked you in a special way before for protecting me. I'd like to thank you again." She placed his hands on her breasts.

"That was special, Clara," he said, feeling her nipples in his palms, "but I think it's best all around, if we stick to business."

"If you say so," she said, letting his hands drop.

As soon as Fran left, Eunice decided to take the briefcase as soon as possible. Having someone check on her regularly added to the difficulty of doing it undetected. Mealtimes were not good; everyone expected her to be there. They probably wondered where she was right now. She sat and stewed for fifteen minutes, interrupted by a knock on the door. It was Fran again.

"The chief mate will have the bosun weld a security bar on the inside of your door. Right after supper. He's going to put one on Clara's door as well. Both of you should wait in the salon until the job is done. It gets stinky and smoky when they weld."

"Thanks, Fran. I'll do that."

The salon was in full swing when Eunice entered and sat with Clara. The engineers seemed extra-loud as they traded barbs and good-natured insults, a standard mealtime practice. Even Greg raised his nose out of the book and contributed an occasional remark.

Dennis had already relieved Chuck, the second mate, so it was William, Tony, and Dennis when the captain came in and sat with them, leaving Clara and Eunice alone at his table. Bernie, as usual, was his solitary self, kept company only by his appetite and stained napkin.

"Captain," Dennis acknowledged.

The captain nodded. "Dennis, I was thinking, how about a movie tonight?"

We had a pull-down screen and a projector, put on board for the use of the passengers, and about twenty movies, but no one had ever asked to see them.

"Sure, Captain. Anything in particular you want to watch?"

"No, I'll let Fran pick the movie. Let the crew know they're all welcome to watch. Let's make it for 1930 hours. Remind them there will be ladies present."

Dennis stood, tapped on his cup to get everyone's attention, and announced the movie. We then all ordered dinner and settled in.

At 1930 hours, the salon was packed. The only ones missing were the bosun, finishing up the security bars on Clara's and Eunice's doors, and the watch standers. Tony had relieved Chuck early so that Chuck could watch the movie. The bosun came in twenty minutes into the movie, whispered in the chief mate's ear, and then leaned against the bulkhead and watched the movie.

The movie, *In Harm's Way*, starred John Wayne, Kirk Douglas, and Henry Fonda. Based on the 1962 novel *Harm's Way*, by James Bassett, it recounts the lives of several US Navy officers and wives based in Hawaii at the start of World War II. The title of the film comes from a quote by John Paul Jones: "I wish to have no connection with any ship that does not sail fast, for I intend to go in harm's way." One of the movie characters had an unfaithful wife engaging in drunken escapades with other officers.

As I watched, I couldn't help but think of the captain and Eunice and stole an occasional glance their way.

The movie had two reels, and our projectionist, Joey, the pantryman, changed reels while a few of us took a pee break. Coming out of the head at the end of the passageway in time to see the dog on the watertight door leading aft being shut, I peeked through the porthole and saw Eunice, clutching something to her chest, walk down the ladder and run, clumsily, down the starboard side, aft to the fantail.

Why was she running? Opening the door, I crossed to the port side, went aft, and peeked around the corner in time to see her shutting the rope-locker door. I ducked back and went forward to the end of the locker and watched as she reversed her path, climbed the ladder, looked back over her shoulder, and then went back inside the house. Whatever she had carried wasn't with her. She must have left it inside. Following her, I rejoined everyone in the salon. Eunice sat next to Clara. She eyed me as I came in. I ignored her.

At the reel break, seeing that the captain was not moving, Eunice had gone directly to the captain's room, opened the safe, taken the briefcase, closed the safe door, and reset the dial to the same number it was on, just in case the captain looked. She hoped he wouldn't need to get anything from the safe until they reached port, afraid to raise his suspicions. As she climbed the ladder and reentered the house, she felt as if someone were watching her. She looked over her shoulder, not seeing anyone. The only one to come into the salon after her was William, but he went to his seat and watched the rest of the movie without looking her way. A little out of breath, something Clara noticed, Eunice told her, "I ran up the steps to get back in time."

Chapter 41

CONFLICT

After the movie, Clara and Eunice lingered in the salon until all but Dennis and I had left.

"William," Dennis said, "walk the ladies to their rooms."

"Sure, Dennis." Facing the women, I said, "Ladies, follow me, please?" Nodding, they followed me out the door, leaving Dennis at the table drinking coffee.

In front of Clara's room, Eunice said, "There's something I have to tell you." She pointed to Clara's door. "Inside."

Clara unlocked the door, and we went in, closing and locking the door.

Clasping and unclasping her hands, a nervous sign, Eunice said, "I took it."

"Took what?" I said, just as Clara mouthed, "Oh no."

"The briefcase."

"Why?" I was pissed off now because the job of guarding her just got more difficult. "What good will it do you?"

Without questioning how I knew about the briefcase, she said, "He won't come after me. He needs it. I'll give it back in New York."

"Eunice." My patience was wearing thin, not believing a woman as smart as she could be so dumb. "Have you told the captain you took the briefcase?"

"No."

"Well," I said, sarcasm dripping from my voice, "if he doesn't know it's gone, why would it be leverage to keep him from killing you?"

There was a shocked silence, and then Eunice whispered, "Oh…oh, God."

"What's in the briefcase?"

"I…I don't know. I didn't look."

"Christ, Eunice, where are your brains? You've put yourself in a no-win situation. Say nothing, and the captain will do whatever he intended—if, in fact, he intended to do anything at all. Tell him, and you'll piss him off even more. He'll have yet another reason to hurt you, and if there's nothing valuable in the briefcase, there's no additional risk to him." I paused. "Don't you see that?"

"I do now," she said, defensive and frightened.

Leaning back against the door, I asked, "Where's the briefcase?"

"I hid it," Eunice replied.

"Where."

Silence. Eunice shook her head.

"You don't trust me, so you won't tell me, right?"

Defiant now, but shaking, she said, "I'm afraid."

Watching her, my anger faded. She was afraid and had infected Clara with her fear. "All right, Eunice. Don't tell me, but don't tell Clara, either. You have no right to drag her any deeper into this. Understand?"

Eunice nodded her head.

Looking at Clara, I asked, "Do you understand? You…know…nothing! That keeps you safe, at least from the captain."

Clara also nodded her head.

"Good. Eunice, since you don't know what's in the briefcase, and wherever you hid it, it's too dangerous to look now, say nothing. Dennis, Fran, and I will keep up our guard routines as best we can. C'mon, I'll walk you to your room. Go inside, and bar the door. Don't come out unless it's me or Fran at your door. Okay?"

Eunice took a deep breath and sighed, "Okay."

After hearing the bar drop on her door, I went to my room and got a flashlight, knife, and fid and went to the aft rope locker. I now knew what Eunice had been carrying when I followed her and had an hour before they'd call me for my watch.

Entering, I closed the door and turned on my flashlight. She had dropped the briefcase flat on the deck. It was invisible from the doorway, but, standing in the center of the coiled mooring line, I saw it.

Resting the flashlight on the line, I didn't bother to scrape the wax off since I didn't know the combination anyway. Instead, I jammed the point of the fid into the top of the lock and hit it with the heel of the knife. It took three good whacks before it sprung. I opened the other two latches, lifted the lid, and gasped. The reflection from my flashlight off the diamonds lit the entire locker.

The diamonds were in clear, cellophane bags, stapled shut. There weren't just diamonds. Other cellophane bags of emeralds and rubies created a kaleidoscope of color. There were also gold coins in plastic and cardboard sleeves. The Krugerrands I recognized, not the others. They looked uncirculated, not a mark on them.

Closing the briefcase, I secured the two unbroken latches, pushed back, and stared at it, myriad thoughts running wild in my head. First, the captain probably didn't know what was in the briefcase since it was sealed, but he must know it was valuable, so Eunice's instincts weren't too far off base. Second, if he found that it was gone, he would tear the ship apart looking for it. There would be no telling him now that Eunice took it. He'd strangle her on sight. Third, did Dennis, the chief mate, know about it? Was this another one of their illegal projects? Finally, what was I going to do? I had thirty minutes to decide and act before I had to go on watch.

It took two minutes to decide. Picking up the knife, fid, and flashlight, I went to my room, checking first to see if anyone was on deck. I grabbed my canvas backpack, dumped the few items in it on my bunk, and returned to the rope locker. Ten minutes later, I was back in my room, the contents of the briefcase in my backpack and the briefcase sinking in the wake of the ship. When the ordinary seaman knocked on the door, alerting me to my watch, the items on the bunk had been stowed, and the backpack hung in plain sight on a hook, innocuous and innocent, unlike me.

Chapter 42

ASSAULT

O ther than my pangs of conscience, the night watch passed without incident. Chuck relieved me at 0400. I tossed and turned in my bunk
until 0600, staring at the backpack on the wall, wrestling with the dilemma
I had created. I hadn't started the problem, but I was finishing it, for better
or worse.

I took the briefcase because I didn't trust Eunice to not try to retrieve
it, regardless of my warning to her. Now, the contents were mine. Instead of
focusing on how to return them when we get to New York, wayward thoughts
of keeping and fencing them kept intruding. Although I'd never done business with them, I knew two guys back in Boston who fenced stuff for the local
potheads. What I had may be too big for them to handle, but they might be
able to lay it off to someone bigger, like the small bookies do, assuming that
the diamonds and I got off the ship intact.

At breakfast, the crew zipped in and out. I had escorted Clara from her room,
and Fran had done the same for Eunice. When the captain came in, he sat
with the two women and said good morning. They returned the greeting. The
captain's cordiality made it clear he hadn't discovered the briefcase was missing. Bernie didn't show until 0730 hours. When he did, it was apparent why
he was late. Bernie was loaded. His clothes were wrinkled, he had a stubbly

beard and bloodshot eyes, and he could barely walk, slurring his words when ordering breakfast.

Given that the captain and Bernie sat with the women, each a potential and different threat to them, Dennis and I lingered over coffee, watching.

Bernie mumbled something unintelligible, spilling his coffee on his shirt, smoothing some wrinkles. Clara looked at me, and I nodded discreetly toward the door. As she stood, followed by Eunice, Bernie yelled, "Bitch!" and lunged at her across the table, falling sideways to the deck.

Clara took a step backward, leaving Eunice closer to Bernie. When he came up off the deck, he held a dinner knife in his hand.

I jumped up and started toward Bernie, but the captain was closer. Just as Bernie thrust the knife toward Eunice, the captain tossed his hot coffee in Bernie's face and grabbed for his knife arm, missing it. Unlike the shirt, the wrinkles on Bernie's face remained.

Bernie, screeching, instinctively clutched at his face with both hands, too drunk to realize that one of them held a knife, and stabbed himself in the right cheek. He dropped the knife as I reached him and pushed him back across the table, keeping him pinned by pressing my knee into his crotch. That stopped everything but his mouth from moving. Blood dripped onto the table and his shirt. I had blood on my hand where I leaned on his shoulder.

"Bitches," he blubbered. "Both of you. I'll kill you! I'll kill you!" Then, he ran out of gas.

Dennis said to me, "You got him?"

"Yeah."

Turning to the women, he said, "Go to your rooms, now." They fled.

The captain, after missing his grab at Bernie, stepped back and let me finish the job. Now, he called, "Joey!" The pantryman had been hiding. "Get Fran. Tell him to bring a first-aid kit."

"Yes, sir," Joey replied, and he ran out the door.

I still stood over Bernie, who was spread-eagled across the table. Dennis grabbed a napkin off the table and pressed it to his cheek, where the knife had penetrated. We stayed like that, Bernie whimpering and bleeding, until Fran arrived.

"What happened?" Fran asked.

"He's drunk. He tried to stab Eunice and Clara," the captain replied.

"Sit him up," Fran directed.

Dennis, standing over Bernie's head, asked, "You gonna behave yourself, Bernie?"

Bernie whimpered, "Yes." And Dennis lifted his head while I unclamped his shoulder and stepped back.

Removing the napkin, Fran said, "Damn, that's ragged. Open your mouth."

After looking, he said, "I'm going to have to stitch the inside of his cheek, too. He nicked the tongue, but it won't need stitches." He went to work cleaning the wound, numbing it with a shot of Novocain and then stitching it, inside and out. When finished, he bandaged the cheek.

"Bernie," Fran said. "Those stitches have to stay for five to seven days. We'll be in New York by then, so you can go to a doctor to get them removed. In the meantime, no solid food, just liquids."

Bernie nodded, eyes moist, nose running. He was a mess.

Fran continued, "I'll give you hydrogen peroxide. You should gargle for thirty seconds every two hours. If you don't, the wound will get infected."

Bernie nodded again.

"Those liquids will not include alcohol," the captain added. "I'm having your cabin searched, and I'm confiscating all alcohol. Except for using the bathroom, you're confined to your cabin. If I find you anywhere other than the bathroom or your cabin, I'll handcuff you to your bunk in your room until we reach port. You understand?"

"I understand." Bernie had to mumble due to the alcohol, stitches, and swelling.

"Good. Stay here while your room is searched. Dennis, keep an eye on him. William, go toss the cabin."

Nodding to the captain, I asked Bernie if the cabin was locked. He shook his head no, and I left.

The cabin was a pigsty. It reeked of booze and body odor. Candy wrappers, empty potato-chip and pretzel bags, and empty liquor bottles covered the floor, bed, and furniture. I found two full bottles of VO, a bottle of gin, a bottle of vodka, and a six-pack of club soda. I left the club soda and brought everything else to the salon and put it on the captain's table.

"That's it, Captain. I left him a six-pack of club soda. The room is a mess. It hasn't been cleaned in a while."

Fran, sitting with the captain, said, "Let me get it cleaned now, before he goes back," and he left. When he returned, he said, "The bedroom steward told me Bernie wouldn't let him in the room to clean it. He should have brought it to my attention."

For twenty minutes, we all sat there, silent. The bedroom steward stuck his head in the door and announced that the cabin was ready. Dennis and I stood, helped Bernie to his feet, and guided him, one on each arm, to his room, and then returned to the salon.

"Dennis," the captain said, "make sure all the officers know about Bernie's restriction. Fran, you let the stewards' department know. If they see him anywhere other than in the head or his room, they are to immediately report it to Dennis."

"Aye, aye, Captain," Dennis replied. Bernie nodded.

The attack shook Eunice; she was surprised the captain had jumped to her defense. Was it just a reaction, or did he still care enough for her to protect her? If so, would he really try to kill her, or was she overreacting? Yes, he'd said he'd kill her, but that was in a fit of anger. Bernie had done the same thing. Everyone said stupid things when they were angry. The conflicting thoughts had her stymied. What to do?

Chapter 43

DEADLY CONFESSION

Monday, January 9, 1967. Four days had passed since Bernie's breakfast attack. We were back in the northern hemisphere, with fair weather and calm conditions aboard. Dennis and I still checked on Clara but were more at ease with Bernie confined to his room. The captain had allowed Bernie to come out of his room for a half hour in the morning and a half hour at night, but he had to stay on the boat deck. Last night, Tony had to cut Bernie's visit short because Eunice and Clara came on deck, and Bernie had approached them. Tony reported it to Dennis and the captain.

Fran still escorted Eunice to and from meals. The captain sat with them and even engaged in conversations. Perhaps the deep freeze between Eunice and the captain had thawed.

Eunice had not attempted to retrieve the briefcase. Convinced that she would have told me it was missing if she had tried, I did my best to convince myself there was nothing in my backpack that didn't belong there.

That night, after dinner, Eunice decided to put the briefcase back in the safe. The captain had been cordial ever since the attack, and she now believed she had let her emotions rule and overreacted. She knew their marriage was over, but saw no reason to aggravate the captain any further by telling him she had taken it. True to her word, she had even stayed away from Tony after promising Fran she would.

Not knowing when she'd get an opportunity to put the briefcase back, she felt she needed to have it close, so when the opportunity arose, she could do it fast. At 2200, she put on her sneakers and dark-blue sweat suit, grabbed her pencil light on the keyring, and walked out the aft door, standing at the rail like she was catching a little fresh air while she checked for anyone on deck. Seeing no one, she walked to the fantail, opened the rope-locker door, and stepped inside, closing the door behind her.

Eunice turned on her light, stepped into the middle of the rope coil, and shone her light in the corner. Nothing but dust. She gasped and leaned over the rope to get a closer look. Mixed in the dust were fragments of wax, the same wax that had sealed the lock. The briefcase had disappeared. Panicked, eyes wide, breath rasping, she thought, What do I do? I better get out of here before I'm caught.

She shut off her light and opened the door. Seeing no one, she stepped out, closed and dogged the door, peeked around the starboard corner, and then ran forward, up the ladder and into her room, where she closed and barred the door, collapsing onto her bed, shaking, angry and afraid. She spent the next two hours wondering what had gone wrong.

When I relieved Tony at 2345 hours, we talked for a few minutes before he went below.

"Eunice hasn't bothered me ever since Bernie pulled that stunt in the salon. That may be a good thing, but I'm getting horny."

"We're only a few days out from New York. You can pull your pud for that long."

A sheepish grin appeared. "Yeah, I guess so. With everything that's happened, I wonder if she still wants me to stay with her when we dock?"

"Be prepared either way. She's been talking to the captain during meals. Not exactly lovey-dovey, but they're talking. Maybe she'll give him a reprieve."

"Yeah. Oh well, it was a hell of a ride. Good night." He went below.

An hour later, standing on the starboard-bridge wing, enjoying the salt tang and breeze in my face, I felt a tap on my shoulder and jumped around, startled. Eunice stood there. She motioned for me to follow her and walked aft to the pool deck. The clouds covered the moon and stars, but it was light enough to see her strained, nervous face. "William, I have a problem."

"Now what?" was my initial thought, but I kept silent.

"It's gone. The briefcase is gone."

How quickly your mind adjusts to your being a thief! I hadn't thought of the diamonds as hers or the captain's since I was busy mulling over the trustworthiness of the fences in Boston. It was easy for me to look shocked. "How do you know? You weren't going to check on it."

"I wasn't, but I decided to put it back in Marcus's safe without telling him. With everything that's happened, I hoped to avoid any further confrontations with him. When I went to get it, it had disappeared."

"Where did you hide it? It's safe to tell me now." I played the role to the hilt.

"In the rope locker on the stern."

"There are two rope lockers. Did you look in the right one?"

"Yes, it's gone. There were scraps of wax on the floor from the wax seal that was on the lock."

Scratching my head, I said, "I don't know. Anyone in the deck department could have gone in the locker and found it. Since you can't return it, I'd just keep quiet. Nothing you say will change anything. Only Clara and I know you took it. I'm sure as hell not going to say anything to the captain, and I doubt if Clara will, either. You better hope he doesn't need to get anything from his safe until we reach port. In any case, he has no reason to suspect you any more than anyone else aboard."

"But I feel guilty. I was going to return it, and now I can't."

"C'mon Eunice. Don't you think it's a little late to feel guilty? Look at the circumstances that caused you to take the briefcase. Who started all this shit in the first place? You did, so knock off the guilty crap. Just go back to your room, and keep your mouth shut."

She stepped up close, leaned in, and said, "You know, you're a real prick when you want to be." She turned and walked down the ladder.

Back in her room, pissed off that she had brought this on herself, she stewed about being told off by William. The more she thought about it, the more she looked for a scapegoat. She thought, What if William took the briefcase? He had said anyone in the deck department could have done it. He was in the deck department, and he was the only one who knew she had taken it. Dammit, it had to be William. Determined to get even, she decided to tell the captain and lay it all off on William.

The captain was awake, sitting in his bunk and reading, when the door to his office opened. "Who is it?" he called out, swinging his legs to the deck. As he stood, Eunice came in, closing the door behind her.

Leery, he asked, "What do you want?"

"We need to talk," she started, "or rather, I'll talk, and you need to listen."

"What's new?" he snorted.

"This is serious, Marcus." She was now standing right in front of him.

"All right, talk."

She told her tale of taking something without saying what she took or where she took it from, implying that William was part of the plot. As she spoke, the captain wondered, "She's pissed at William because, unlike Tony, he had resisted her wiles and didn't leap into her bed, so she's trying to get him in trouble." He didn't react to her saying she took something until she mentioned the briefcase.

"Stop," he said, turning to the safe. He opened it, turned, and glared at her. "Where is it, Eunice?" he asked, walking toward her.

"That's what I've been trying to tell you. I hid it, and William took it. I don't know where it is."

"Bullshit!" he yelled and slapped her, hard. Eunice didn't make a sound, but she caught her foot on the rug and fell backward, hitting the back of her head on the metal doorjamb. The captain heard a loud crack and then nothing.

He stared at her, waiting for her to get up, but she didn't move. Bending down, he saw that her head was at an odd angle, and she had stopped breathing. He stood up, picked up the phone to call Fran for help, and then slowly lowered the phone back onto the cradle. It was an accident, but everyone aboard knew they were squabbling and she had threatened to divorce him. This would be hard to explain. On the other hand, if she simply disappeared, he'd have a lot less explaining to do.

Checking his watch, he waited twenty minutes until 0220 hours. The midwatch would have changed helmsmen and lookouts, so no one should be on deck. A smear of blood covered part of Eunice's face from her nose, and there was a cut on the back of her head where it struck the jamb, but there was little blood since she died instantly when her neck broke.

He wrapped a towel around her head, hefted her onto his right shoulder, and opened the door, breathing heavily already. He looked out and then scuttled aft to the door leading to the boat deck. Knowing that the light from the passageway would shine out on the deck when he opened the door, he counted on the lifeboat hanging in its davit to block the view of the bridge watch.

Sweating now and gasping from the strain, he swung open the door and shut it quickly after him, wrapping the darkness around him. Waiting a minute to ensure that no one on the bridge had looked over the side at the glare of light, he stepped to the railing and heaved the body overboard. Her feet hit him in the head as they went by, almost pulling him over the rail with her.

Exhausted, he leaned on the rail, gasping, letting his breath and strength return, and then he returned to his cabin. Inside, he wiped down the doorjamb and checked for blood but found none. Sitting at his desk, he poured himself a shot of Pinch scotch, lit a Dunhill, sat back, and smiled an evil smile.

There's one more thing to do, he thought. He stood, retrieved Bernie's bottle of confiscated vodka and a bottle of VO, walked to the boat deck, and broke the bottle of VO against the foot of the davit, leaving the glass shards there. He then walked to Bernie's cabin, left the bottle of vodka on the deck outside the door, and knocked, then hurried back to his office.

Chapter 44

MISSING PERSON

Chuck had relieved me at 0400 hours, and I went to bed, tired, partly because of a lack of sleep and partly due to the tension brought on by Eunice. At 0730, I got up more tired than when I turned in, took a piss, washed up, and knocked on Clara's door to escort her to breakfast.

Clara greeted me with, "I'm still waiting for my turn." It was a not-so-subtle reminder of our encounter. I was so tired that even if I wanted it, and I didn't, I couldn't get it up.

The captain sat at the table and greeted Clara with a cheerful "Good morning." Bill, the chief engineer, and Greg, the third engineer, sat at a different table, looking over some diagrams and drinking coffee. Tony had come and gone, so I sat with Dennis and ordered breakfast. Chuck wandered in. Bernie and Eunice were missing.

Dennis asked, "Where's Eunice?"

Just then, Fran came in, went to Dennis, and said, "Eunice is missing."

"What do you mean, missing?" He stood and moved toward the door. Everyone stopped talking and looked at Fran.

"She's not in her room. I checked both bathrooms. She's not here."

Dennis said, "Everyone, go scour the ship. Check every cabin and working space. Bill, cover the engine room. Greg, help him. Fran, check the galley, serving spaces, and unlicensed crew rooms. William, come with me." I followed him out the door.

The captain called out, "I'll be in my room, Dennis."

We started with Dennis's room and office and worked our way through the deck and engineer officer's rooms. Then, we started with the forward passenger staterooms and worked aft. When we got to Bernie's room, we had to pound on it before he opened the door. The smell of booze hit us right away. Bernie was bleary-eyed and unsteady. The empty bottle of vodka lay on the deck beside his bunk. Shaking his head in disgust, Dennis looked in. "Where did you get this?"

Bernie stared at him, slack-jawed.

"Never mind. Just stay here." We continued our search.

We had no luck with the staterooms, so Dennis said to check the outer decks, starting at the flying bridge. I found the broken bottle of VO on the boat deck and reported it to Dennis. He sent me back to pick up the pieces, saying that it could be evidence.

Within an hour, we had searched every space aboard, including the cargo holds. Dennis even had Boats uncover the tarp and search the yacht on deck. Nothing.

The captain called Dennis, Fran, Bill, and me into his room. Looking stiff, old, and resigned, he began, "Gentlemen, it's clear that Eunice is not on board the ship. We'll have to notify the Coast Guard and the home office but before that, I'd like to get as many facts as possible. We should question the officers and passengers to find out the last time she was seen."

I knew that if I divulged I had talked to her last night on watch, I would become a suspect; if I didn't, and the helmsman reported seeing her, it would be worse, so I answered. "Captain, I'm probably the last one to see her. She came up to the bridge last night around 0100. Said she couldn't sleep. She stayed for about ten minutes, staring at the horizon, and then walked back aft through the pool deck and went below."

"Did you see or hear anyone else about at that time?"

"No, sir, but it was a cloudy night, pretty dark."

"Captain," Dennis said. "We found a broken bottle of VO by the davit on the boat deck. We could still smell the booze, so it was fresh." Pausing, he continued, "We also found Bernie, dead drunk in his room. He's still there."

The captain nodded, staring at the deck. After a minute, he lifted his head. "Mr. Connolly, was Eunice drinking?"

"Not that I could tell. I don't remember smelling any booze."

Nodding again, he said, "Dennis, bring Bernie here. All of you stay as witnesses."

Dennis looked at me, and we both left to get Bernie. Dennis didn't knock; he just opened the door and walked in. Bernie was asleep on the bed. Dennis shook him. "Get up. The captain wants to talk to you."

Bernie got up, rubbed his eyes, and said, "I have to pee."

"Drink and pee. That's all you're good for. Go on," Dennis said, pushing him toward the door. When Bernie went into the head, Dennis followed and held the door open with his heel. Just before they came out, Dennis said, "Wash your hands, dammit. You pissed all over yourself."

In the captain's office, Bernie stood, swaying, looking around, nervous and confused. His tongue kept poking his sutured cheek, pulsating it, like a frog breathing.

"Bernie," the captain said. "There's a few questions I need to have you answer. Do you understand?"

Bernie nodded.

"It's important you pay attention. This is a serious situation."

Bernie nodded and poked his cheek again.

"Where did you get the liquor?"

"Someone left it outside my door."

"When did they leave it?"

"Last night. I heard a knock. When I opened the door, no one was there. When I stepped into the passageway to look, I kicked the bottle over."

"Was it before you went for your nighttime walk?"

Bernie squinted; you could see the struggle going on in his brain. "I don't think so. Yeah, it was after." He nodded in agreement with himself.

"Just one bottle at your door?"

Another squint. "Yeah, vodka."

"When is the last time you saw Clara or Eunice?"

"Captain, I told you I was sorry about that. It was the booze." He stopped, sensing a trap.

"I'm not talking about when you stabbed yourself, Bernie. When is the last time you saw Clara or Eunice?"

"When I was walking on deck. I saw them both. A day ago?"

"Are you sure?"

"It might have been two days ago. I don't know."

"You came after them and started to argue. The third mate intervened and sent you back to your room. Isn't that correct?"

"Captain, I just wanted to talk to Clara."

"After being warned not to talk to either Clara or Eunice, you persisted. When you're sober, you yell; when you're drunk, you attack. You're a creature of habit. You've developed patterns and follow them." He sounded like a prosecutor presenting his case.

"I just wanted to talk to her, Captain. She's my wife."

Dennis interjected with a loud *harumph.* "Not for long, you piece of shit!"

Bernie visibly cringed, and the captain said, "Dennis, mind your mouth." He rubbed his chin and then said, "Take Bernie back to his room. Mr. Connolly, stand guard outside his door until further notice."

I marched Bernie back to his room, closed the door, and leaned against the bulkhead, my brain going 100 mph on a diamond-edged guilt trip.

"What do you think, Dennis?" the captain asked.

"I don't know, Captain." He was amazed at how calm the captain had been during the interview, considering he suspected Bernie of killing his wife. "He's an asshole and a drunk, but did he throw Eunice overboard? I don't know. He can barely stand up. If he did it, it would have been hours ago, before he got so drunk."

"Bill." He addressed the chief engineer. "What do you think?"

"It looks suspicious as hell, Captain. He's the prime suspect to me."

"And you, Fran?"

"Captain, the man has serious problems and is violent when he drinks. It's a real possibility that he may have killed Eunice." He shuddered.

The captain leaned back in his chair and closed his eyes. When he opened them, he sighed and said, "I'll send a wire to the home office. I'd like each of you to write a statement outlining the events as you know them to be. Dennis, ask Mr. Connolly to write a statement as well. That will be all."

"Do you want Connolly to guard the door all day?"

"No. No, Dennis. Tell Bernie he's restricted to his room. If he comes out without permission, I'll shoot him."

All three of them sat up when they heard "shoot him."

The captain waved them out the door, a grim look on his face, but he thought, that sounded convincing. It should erase any doubts they may have about me being aggrieved.

Chapter 45

FALLING-OUT

Wednesday, 1/11/67. Clear weather. Light, high cumulus clouds. Tempera-ture 40 degrees. Moderate wind from the Northwest. Seas at eight feet. One day out of New York.

Dennis was worried. He feared Frankie's reaction to the news that the heroin had gone overboard. Frankie, a made man and capo of the local Mafia family in Brooklyn, was not a forgiving guy. Dennis would have been more worried if he knew the briefcase was also missing, but the captain hadn't told him about that.

He had doubts about Bernie throwing Eunice overboard. As much as the captain steered him and the others in that direction, Dennis knew that the liquor bottles, both the vodka in Bernie's room and the VO found smashed on the boat deck, had been in the possession of the captain, on his dresser top. How did they get from there to Bernie?

The reply from the New York office to the captain's report of Eunice going missing came back within hours of them receiving it. A company attorney would greet the ship at Brooklyn, and, apart from customs and immigration issues, no one would be allowed ashore until the attorney cleared them. The captain had shared the response with Dennis, Bill, and Fran, telling them to inform the crew of the restriction. He added, "Most likely, the police will be there as well."

With Bernie restricted to his cabin, Clara moved around freely but Dennis, Fran, and I still checked on her. Standing on the port-bridge wing, leaning forward into the wind, eyes closed, with sun on my face, I heard, "William?" It was Clara.

"Hello, Clara. Everything okay?"

"No, it seems nothing is okay, but I don't know what to do about it."

"This hasn't exactly been the cruise of your dreams, has it?"

She snorted a laugh. "No, it hasn't." She paused. "I'm worried about Bernie." Seeing the incredulous look on my face, she hurried, "It's over with us. I'm divorcing him, and yes, he's an asshole, but I don't believe he killed Eunice. I don't understand why anyone would, but it wasn't Bernie."

"Clara, I don't think he did, either. Eunice visited me on the bridge at 0100 hours. The broken bottle on the boat deck implies that she was attacked there. Every time Bernie has been drunk, he's also been loud. I think I would have heard something if there had been a fight on the boat deck. Bernie isn't capable of stealth, especially when he's drunk."

"No, he isn't," she agreed. "He's a lot of things, but stealthy isn't one of them."

"The police will show up when we dock. The company attorney will be there. Tell them what you believe and hope for the best. Bernie may want to get an attorney himself. That would be the smart thing to do."

"I guess. Thanks." She patted me on the shoulder and went below, saying as she left, "If you had any sympathy for a frazzled woman, you'd see it's really time for my turn now."

At dinner, the captain was absent. Dennis announced we would dock around 0600 tomorrow at Twenty-Third street in Brooklyn. He reminded everyone of the restriction to stay aboard ship until cleared by the attorney. He told Clara they couldn't make her stay aboard once customs and immigration had cleared her, but it would be prudent to do so since there would probably be police investigators there as well.

"What about Bernie?" she asked.

"Bernie stays until the police let him go."

After dinner, Dennis sat in the salon, drinking coffee, stewing, and worrying about the consequences of telling Frankie news he didn't want to hear. When William came by at 1930, Dennis was still there, so he sat down.

"Clara came up to the bridge today to tell me she didn't think Bernie killed Eunice." When Dennis didn't respond, he added, "I don't think he did, either," and explained his "Bernie is loud" theory.

He nodded. "I've had my own doubts. The problem is, if it's not Bernie, there's only one other probable suspect."

"The captain, I know. What are you going to tell the cops?"

"Don't know yet. Bernie's side of the story is obvious, but only you, me, and Fran know about the captain. What are you gonna say?"

"I'm telling them both sides of the story. They can sort it out."

Nodding his head again, he said, "Yeah, I think I will, too. Let the cops wrestle with it." He got up and left.

When he left, Dennis took a piss and then went to the captain's office and knocked.

"Yeaaahs?" The familiar, nasal drawl echoed from within, and Dennis entered.

Closing the door behind him, he said, "We need to talk."

"Do we? What about?"

"First, what are we gonna tell Frankie about the heroin?"

"We don't have a choice there, Dennis. We tell him what happened. It went overboard in a storm. The odds are, he'll believe us. He'll be pissed, but it's the cost of doing business. He loses his load. We lose our commission. That's the least of my worries."

"You mean Eunice?"

"No." He paused. "Remember the briefcase I was delivering as a personal favor to Frankie?"

"Yes."

"That, too, has gone."

"Gone where?"

"Ah. That's the question." He paused, not sure if he should give Dennis any more info. "Eunice took it, hid it somewhere, and then had an apparent attack of conscience and decided to bring it back. When she went to retrieve it, it wasn't there." He sat, silent for a minute. "She claims Mr. Connolly took it."

Dennis's head was spinning. "How do you know this?"

"Eunice told me. When she did, I presumed she was mad at Connolly for resisting her charms and dismissed her claim. Now, I'm not so sure."

"When did she tell you this?" Dennis demanded.

"What difference does it make? The briefcase disappeared, Eunice is gone, and the only link we have is Connolly."

Dennis sat and stared at the captain. "You killed her, didn't you? The briefcase did it, and you're setting up Bernie for the fall."

"Don't be ridiculous, Dennis. Focus on the problem here. How do we get the briefcase back?"

"You mean, your problem," Dennis said, his voice rising, standing up. "Not my problem. You killed your wife for a fucking briefcase, and you don't even know what's in it. You are one cold-hearted son of a bitch!" Dennis turned and walked out.

The captain sat there, alone.

Dennis went looking for William and found him in his room. "William," he said. "The captain just told me a story. He said you stole a briefcase from someplace Eunice hid it when she took it from him. What do you say to that?"

Stunned, my face registered surprise. "Stole a briefcase? What are you talking about?" I tried hard to show indignation instead of guilt. "I didn't steal anything. What's going on, Dennis? Are you and the captain trying to get me involved in one of your schemes?"

Holding up both hands, Dennis said, "Easy, kid. I had to ask. The accusation was bizarre, but I had to ask. I believe you."

"The captain told you this? Why would he accuse me?"

"Tell you the truth, William, I think the captain's lost it. I'm convinced now he killed his wife, and he's getting desperate." Standing up, he said, "Forget we had this conversation. Just tell your story to the cops tomorrow. Let them handle it."

After Dennis left, William knew he would be focused on, at least for the next twenty-four hours. He had to hide the diamonds, but first, he needed something to put them in. Somebody might recognize his backpack. Walking out and up to Eunice's cabin, he tried the door, opened it, and slid in. Pulling the curtain over the porthole, he turned on the light and saw a large red-leather shoulder bag. Dumping the contents into a dresser drawer, he opened the door, looked, stepped out, and closed the door quietly behind him.

In his cabin, he transferred the diamonds, jewels, and gold coins to the red bag, carefully checking the bottom corners of the backpack to make sure nothing stuck behind. He knew where he would hide them but couldn't do it until after he relieved Tony on watch. Sitting on his bunk, he took two Tylenol to relieve the tension headache building.

At 2330, the ordinary seaman knocked and alerted him to the watch change. Instead of going to the salon to check out the midnight meal, his usual routine, he took the red bag and went aft and up to the pool deck. The door to the bridge was closed so he shuffled forward and stuck the bag under a lounge chair close to the door. Retracing his steps, he went to the head, took a piss, washed his face, went to the salon, and saw Greg, the third engineer there, getting something to eat before he went on watch. Stomach in knots, he couldn't eat but felt he needed to look normal, so he took a piece of pound cake, wrapped it in a paper napkin, waved at Greg, and walked out.

"How's it going, Tony?" I said, walking in through the chart room.

"Hey, William. We're on the last stretch. Got some traffic. First ship I've visually seen in ten days."

"Where are they?"

"One on the starboard bow. Showed up when I first came on watch. It's tracking our course, but we've been overtaking her. She's fourteen miles off. The other one crossed our bow an hour ago, heading south, down the coast. She's almost out of sight."

"Anything else?"

"The Loran-C is reading strong. The chart is on the table, and our 2300-hour position is marked on it. Call the captain at 0400 hours."

"Okay, Tony, I got it. You're relieved."

Just then, Sturm, my AB, came in and relieved the helmsman, and Tony and his AB went below.

I checked the radar bearings on the two ships and confirmed their courses and speeds. I could barely make out the one to our south with the binoculars. Scanning the horizon, I saw nothing else, went out to the port-bridge wing, lit a cigarette, and waited for the watch to settle in and my stomach to settle. Feeling the coolness of the wind on my face, I realized I was sweating. Innocent people don't sweat when it's 39 degrees and they're standing still.

After stubbing out the cigarette, I walked through the bridge to the starboard wing and aft to the pool deck. I grabbed the red bag and walked forward to the door leading into the smokestack house. The smokestack with its big red "M" is fake. The real smokestacks are two tall, thin pillars aft of the house. I undogged the door and stepped inside. While it had a light switch, I opted to use my flashlight after closing the door.

On the stack casing, a ladder led all the way to the top. The engineers used it to inspect the casing and to access the top of the stack housing itself. Scantlings, metal frames, and strengtheners circled the inside of the smokestack house. Slinging the bag over my shoulder, I climbed the ladder. At the top, I slid the bag off, reached across, and jammed it into the space between the skin and the scantlings, about a foot wide. It nestled down into the space.

Climbing down, I looked up and couldn't see anything from below. Perfect. I stuck my flashlight in my back pocket and returned to the bridge. When I went into the chart room, under the red night-light, I saw that I had dirt stains on my hands. I told Sturm I was going to take a piss, went to the head, and washed my hands. In normal light, I saw two smudges on my pants leg, but I ignored them. If I brushed them, it might smear and be more obvious. Back on the bridge, I settled in to wait for morning and whatever it brought. Nerves or no nerves, I had to see it through.

Chapter 46

NEW YORK

*T*hursday, Thursday, 1/12/67, 0530. Clear day, 31 degrees, Light West wind.
*Low, two-foot chop. Twilight, with night-lights of New York visible ahead
and New Jersey to port. We approached Ambrose light, homecoming beacon to
New York. Home at last.*

The Ambrose lightship, one of a few that served the purpose over the years,
lay directly ahead. There were rumors that they were going to replace the ship
with a beacon or tower. Things never stop changing.

The captain had ordered the engineers to reduce speed and come off the
extra nozzles. We were doing 15 knots and slowing, expecting to pick up the
Sandy Hook pilot at 0600. With the pilot aboard, we proceeded through
Ambrose Channel into Lower New York Bay and then Upper New York Bay,
taking a right toward Red Hook and docking at the Twenty-Third Street pier,
MorMac's home base in Brooklyn.

When we broke out the aft mooring lines from the rope lockers, prior
to docking, I made sure they scuffed the deck as they pulled out the lines.
Whatever bits of wax remaining would be undetectable.

By 0740, we were secure at the dock, starboard side to the pier and finished with engines. Sturm, the AB, broke out the gangway, and we lowered it.
Standing there, I watched the parade of officials come aboard and get logged
in: US customs, immigration, marine-operations supervisor, three attorneys,

two guys in plain clothes that looked like cops, and a steward from the MorMac passenger department. When they all passed, I followed them to the salon, sat down, and ordered a fried-egg sandwich and coffee. Even Joey, the pantryman, who was usually jovial, seemed nervous.

Fran and the immigration official sat at the captain's table and ran the crew check.

Working my way through the sandwich and coffee, I sat and watched. On my second cup, one of the company attorneys came in, went to Fran, asked him a question and then turned and beckoned me. Shaking my hand, he said, "Hello, I'm Joel Estevan, attorney for Moore McCormack. We're conducting interviews in the captain's office. Please come with me."

I followed him to the captain's office, where the other two attorneys and the two guys I thought were cops sat, squeezed around the table. There was a single seat in front of the table, and Joel pointed to it. "Have a seat, Mr. Connolly."

As I sat, the captain walked out from his bedroom and stood, leaning against the bulkhead.

Joel started without introducing anyone else. "We're going to record this interview," he said, and I cut him off by holding up my hand.

"Who do you represent?"

"The company."

Getting testy now, and more than a little nervous, I said, "You're an attorney, a wordsmith, you're supposed to be accurate. What company?"

Obviously irritated, he knew he had screwed up. "Moore McCormack Lines."

"And who are these other people?"

He introduced the two attorneys, both of whom represented MorMac. The cops introduced themselves. Both were tall, over six feet and fit, dressed in khaki pants and blue sport coats. One had black hair and the other brown, both cut short. "Detective Dave Zantorus," the black-haired one said. "This," he said, pointing to his partner, "is Detective Jason DeLaney. We're with the NYPD, and we're here to investigate the circumstances surrounding the disappearance of Eunice Coltrain."

Nodding, I said, "Am I a witness or a suspect in this investigation?"

Joel started to say something, but I cut him off. "I'm not talking to you; you don't represent me."

After a few seconds of silence, Detective Zantorus responded, "Everyone aboard is a suspect until evidence proves otherwise."

"That being the case, why didn't you inform me of my Miranda rights? Since the Supreme Court ruled on that last June, it's supposed to be standard procedure. I do read a lot," I added.

Detective Zantorus smiled, a hard. sardonic smile.

"By the way," I continued. "I'm willing to talk to you, without a lawyer, but only with you two. No one else present."

Addressing Joel, Zantorus asked, "Do you have another private room I can use?"

"We can talk in my room," I offered.

Standing, Zantorus told his partner, "Hang in here." Extending his arm, he said, "Lead the way."

Having agreed to let Detective Zantorus record the conversation, I explained the background, about my suspicions regarding the captain and why I suspected him. I told him about how Eunice was a tease and was flagrant about it in front of the captain, adding that the chief mate suspected the captain, and went into great detail on Bernie's actions during the trip but opined that I didn't think he killed Eunice. I left out any references to the heroin in the conex and the diamonds.

"That's quite a story, William." He had relaxed, calling me William halfway through the interview.

"Yes, it is. Now, you understand why I was nervous. On board ship, the captain is God. If God gets vengeful, those below him get screwed."

At 1130 hours, Zantorus finished. "We'll get this typed up and have you read it and sign it."

"How long will that take? I'd like to sign off and get away from this ship as soon as I can."

"By tomorrow. I have other interviews."

"Okay. What do I do in the meantime?"

Shrugging, he said, "Your job, I guess."

I found Dennis in his office and asked him what was going on.

"We start cargo operations at 1300 hours, three gangs working in the nos. 2, 3, and 4 hatches. Start with discharging the bulldozers. The restrictions aren't lifted yet, so everyone stays aboard. Keep an eye on things." He paused. "Did you tell them?"

"Yeah, I told the detective everything, how I suspect the captain and I think Bernie is innocent. How about you?"

"I'm due to talk with them after lunch. I'm gonna tell them the same thing."

The watch passed, and cargo operations went smoothly, with no incidents. The longshore foreman, Ritchie, whom I had befriended last trip, was connected to Frankie, the Mafia capo. He greeted me like an old friend, pumping my hand when he first saw me.

"Everything going okay, mate? Heard some funny stories about what happened on the ship. Too bad about the captain's wife. The captain is a friend of Frankie."

The last comment stunned me. I had forgotten Dennis' comments about the captain and Frankie when we had our "talk" at anchor off Laurenco Marques. Was I now going to have to contend with Frankie because I gave the statement against the captain? What else could go wrong?

"Everything's fine, Ritchie. It was a crazy trip. Bad weather. We lost a conex overboard. Hope I never have passengers aboard again. Just too much trouble."

"Okay, mate." He slapped my shoulder and walked off.

The crew members hid in their rooms when they weren't on duty. At meals, the conversation was muted, the investigation hanging over everything, dampening spirits. There were night mates from the union hall so, even restricted to the ship, everyone was off duty after 1700 hours. At dinner, I sat, drinking coffee. Everyone but Clara had left the salon. She came over and sat beside me.

"I'm disembarking tomorrow afternoon, but I'll be staying in town for a few days. I've given Bernie until Monday to clear everything out of the house."

"Hope everything works out for you, Clara. Where are you staying?"

"At the Warwick Hotel. I wasn't sure where to stay, but the travel agent told me the Beatles stayed there last August, so I figured, why not?" Patting my hand, she said, "It's still my turn, William."

Nodding my head, I said, "I'm sorry about that, Clara. You deserved better treatment. Maybe under different circumstances?"

"Maybe," she said, and she left.

At breakfast the next morning, the captain announced that the restriction on leaving the ship would be lifted at noon, adding that we would pay off at 1500 hours that afternoon. Payoff was always in cash, so a security guard always sat with Fran and the company paymaster. I waited until Dennis left and followed him to his room.

"Dennis, I'm signing off. MorMac is a great company. Maybe I can catch another ship with them, but I don't want anything to do with Captain Coltrain."

Leaning back in his chair, he wiped his forehead with his hand, pushing his wispy hair back. "Don't blame you, William. It looks like he got away with murder. Tony says he's getting off, too. That's no surprise."

"Are the cops going after Bernie?"

"Don't know. I gave them the same story you did about the captain, but they don't seem interested in pursuing him, so Bernie's still the prime suspect." Standing up, he offered his hand. "Good luck, William." We shook hands, and I left.

An hour later, Fran knocked on my door. "William, there's mail for you." He handed me four letters, three from my mother and one from Meg. Meg had written hers one day after we sailed from Cape Town. It wasn't a Dear-John letter. It wasn't even a letter, it was a note, but it was an ultimatum.

"William, my love. It's only been a day since you left, but there's no sense postponing this. I love you and want to marry you, but I can't leave home and live in the States. Mum is right. This is my home. Please find it in your heart to come and stay with me here." It was signed, "All my love, Meg."

Damn Grace! was my first thought. She's browbeaten Meg into writing this letter. After a few minutes, I realized that, no, this was Meg. This was her relationship with her mother. There was no way I could break that bond. To try would inevitably sour our relationship. I couldn't live in South Africa, and Meg wouldn't leave. It was one hell of a whirlwind romance, but it was over. Wiping away a few tears, I chastised myself for admitting that it was more than the sex. I loved everything about Meg but not enough to live in South Africa. She had her limits. I had mine. I rinsed my face at the sink to wash away the evidence of tears.

Customs had already cleared the crew, so there was little risk of being searched. Taking the towel, I went to the smokestack house and retrieved the red shoulder bag containing the diamonds. No one was on the bridge to bother me. Wrapping the bag in the towel (it would have stood out for me to carry a red shoulder bag), I returned to my room, a newly hatched plan stewing in my head. Did I have the balls to see it through?

I went down on deck and found Ritchie, the longshoreman boss, the messenger man for Frankie, the Brooklyn capo. I asked him to relay a message to Frankie. That done, I went back to my room and waited. Given the contents of the briefcase, knowing the relationship between Frankie and the captain, I deduced that Frankie was the intended recipient of the briefcase. Nothing else made sense. Ten minutes later, I opened the door to a knock. It was Ritchie.

"Okay, mate. Frankie will meet you at the head of the pier at noon. I'll walk out with you when we break for lunch. See you at the gangway."

"Thanks, Ritchie."

"No problem, mate. See you at noon."

At noon, I followed Ritchie to the head of the pier, carrying my backpack. This time, Frankie sat in a big Cadillac. The driver opened the door, and I climbed in. Frankie shook hands and said, "What's all the mystery, William?" He had remembered my name.

Taking a deep breath, I began. "Frankie. Is it okay to call you that?"

He laughed. "Yeah, William, it's my name. It's okay."

"A lot of weird stuff happened on this trip, with the captain's wife in the middle of most of it."

Frankie gave me an odd look but stayed silent, so I took another deep breath and began again.

"I'm not stupid. I'm a city kid. I know what you do for a living, but I don't care, because I learned early on to mind my own business. I also learned to cover my ass, so people can't blame me for something they screwed up. This is one of those times."

As Frankie focused, I continued. "Two things; first, I think the conex box that washed overboard had drugs in it. Your drugs. Probably heroin. The loudmouth chief mate from the *MorMacGlen* didn't do a very good job of hiding it. If he had, they wouldn't have had to transfer it to the conex."

Holding up a hand, Frankie asked, "Who's 'they'?"

"The chief mate and the bosun, but I'm sure it was the captain who made the decision."

"Go on."

"The other thing is that the captain had a briefcase in his safe, also probably for you. The captain's wife feared the captain would try to kill her. They'd been fighting the whole trip, and everyone knew she was divorcing him. She didn't keep it a secret. She took the briefcase and hid it to use as leverage against the captain."

Frankie eyes were boring holes in me, but I continued.

"The captain killed her. I know he did. He threw her overboard and tried to blame a passenger for it. The guy is an asshole, but he didn't kill Eunice. The chief mate agrees with me." I stopped talking.

There was silence, then he said, "Okay, William, let's say everything you told me is true. What does that have to do with me?"

Now, I was going onto thin ice. "I told you I know how to mind my own business. When I signed off the last trip, it was late at night. I saw two guys, guys I wouldn't be able to recognize if ever asked, come out of an alley on Twenty-Third Street. I checked the alley. Sparky was there, with his tongue stuck to his chest with his own switchblade. Sparky talked too much to the wrong people." Pausing, I continued, "I think the captain talks too much.

There's no way I would know what I know if it wasn't for him talking to his wife, who ended up talking to me."

"You trying to tell me something, William?"

"Yes. I'm trying to tell you the screwups occurred because the captain didn't do things right. The conex washed overboard with the heroin. The briefcase disappeared, and Eunice disappeared. There's only one thing that's turned out right, in this whole situation."

"What's that?"

"I found the briefcase."

Frankie's eyes widened. Knowing the next few seconds would determine my fate, I kept on.

"I didn't find the briefcase itself. I found the contents of the briefcase. Eunice must have opened it and thrown the case overboard. She stuffed everything into her shoulder bag. The reason I know this is because she told me she had taken it and told me where she hid it." I shaded the story here to make my part in it look better. "When she disappeared, I retrieved it."

"Where is it?" There was ice in his words.

"Right here," I said, patting my backpack. "I thought you may know who to return it to."

Frankie said nothing for a good ten seconds. "You're a smart kid, William. I won't take that bag, because I wouldn't want anyone to think I had received anything from you. When you get out of the car, hand it to the driver. He'll ask around and see if he can find the rightful owner."

Nodding, I said, "I'll do that. Thanks for listening. For what it's worth, I think the chief mate has played it straight with you. The captain's the problem."

Reaching over, he took my hand with both of his. "You saved my father's life, and now you've resolved a very big problem. I don't forget people who help me."

"Thank you, Frankie, but you don't owe me a thing. Except for the captain getting away with murder, everything ended up where it should."

He gave my hand a squeeze and nodded and then let go. I got out, took the shoulder bag out of my backpack, and gave the bag to the driver, then walked back to the ship.

We paid off, and I said my good-byes to the crew members. I wished Dennis luck and then stopped into Fran's office. "Fran, thank you for everything. You've been a great steward and a better friend."

"William, you held up well under difficult circumstances. I wish you were staying aboard, but I understand why you're leaving. The captain has created a toxic atmosphere here."

I reached out to shake hands, and he hugged me. I hugged him back.

The last one I saw was Greg.

"Best of luck to you, William. I've enjoyed our talks."

"Thanks for the education on race relations, Greg. It's opened my eyes to a lot of things. By the way, no one else knows, but Meg wrote me a letter saying she wouldn't leave South Africa."

"That's too bad, William. I liked Meg. I liked her mother, too."

"Yeah. It wasn't meant to be. Are you staying on here?"

"No, I'll look for something. Word is they need engineers and deckies for ships running to Vietnam. Maybe I'll grab one of those."

"Good luck to you Greg." We shook hands and I left.

I followed Clara down the gangway, carrying my duffel bag with my backpack slung over my shoulder. The company had allowed the taxi to come to the foot of the gangway, small accommodation for what she had been through on the trip. A few minutes earlier, I had seen the captain walk down the gangway, in civvies, wondering if he was going to meet Frankie.

As the steward piled her bags in the trunk, Clara said, "Thank you, William. You've been the only bright spot on this crazy trip. May I have a kiss good-bye?"

I hesitated, thinking of the letter from Meg. "I'm in no rush to go anywhere. Is it still your turn, Clara?"

She took a slow deep breath. "Yes, it is," she said, and we got into the taxi.

As we pulled out of the gate and headed up toward Third Avenue, I heard sirens. A police car and ambulance pulled up in front of us, blocking the way. A crowd had gathered on the sidewalk. The ambulance attendants knelt beside a body in the gutter. We couldn't get around the vehicles, so I got out and walked to the sidewalk, asking what had happened.

"Some old guy got hit by a car. A hit-and-run."

I sidled closer to the medics and saw they weren't doing anything except loading the body on the gurney. Edging closer, they turned him over. It was the captain. I shuddered, wondering how much of what I told Frankie had contributed to this, and then realized that I didn't care.

Getting back in the cab, I answered Clara's silent question. "Don't know. Some guy got hit by a car. Hit-and-run."

"That's awful." She said. Wrapping my arm in hers, she leaned in, smiled, and said, "Shows we need to make every minute count."

I returned the smile. "Yes, I guess we do."

MARITIME GLOSSARY

1MC	A loudspeaker communication system used on ships in the 1960s.
Abeam	Direction that is at right angles to the fore and aft line of a ship.
Able-Bodied Seaman (AB)	Member of the deck department. Stands watches as a helmsman. Performs maintenance.
Bight	A loop or slack curve in a rope or wire.
Bitt	Either of a pair of posts on a ship's deck used for fastening ropes or cables, usually mooring lines.
Boatswain/Bosun/Bos'n	The highest-ranking unlicensed person in the deck department of a ship. Equivalent to a Chief Petty Officer in the navy. Usually a day worker, not a watch stander.
Brow Gangway	A short, flat portable gangway used to span short distances.
Burthen/Athwartships	Interchangeable terms meaning side to side rather than fore and aft on a ship.
Captain	Person in charge of the entire ship. Highest-ranking member of the crew

Chief Engineer	Highest-ranking licensed officer in the engine department. Usually a day worker, not a watch stander.
Chief Mate	Highest-ranking licensed officer of the deck department. In charge of cargo operations and ship maintenance. Usually a day worker, not a watch stander.
Coaming	The raised edging or border around a hatch for keeping out water.
Deckie	Anyone working in the deck department of a ship, either merchant marine or navy. A term used derogatorily by members of the engine department.
Fid	A conical pin or spike used in splicing rope.
First Engineer	Second-highest-ranking licensed officer in the engine department. Usually a day worker, not a watch stander.
Hawsepipe	The opening in a ship's bow where the anchor cable passes through.
Hold	That part of a ship where cargo is stowed. The lowest level of the ship.
Junior Third Engineer	Fifth-highest-ranking licensed officer in the engine department. Stands the eight-to-twelve sea watch.

Junior Third Mate	Lowest-ranking licensed officer of the deck department. Stands the eight-to-twelve sea watch.
Oiler	Member of the engine department. Stands sea watches and performs maintenance.
Ordinary Seaman (Ordinary)	Member of the deck department. Stands watches as a lookout. Performs maintenance.
Pelorus	A device used in navigation for measuring the bearing of an object relative to the direction in which the ship is traveling.
Second Engineer	Third-highest-ranking licensed officer in the engine department. Stands the four-to-eight sea watch.
Second Mate	Second-highest-ranking licensed officer of the deck department. Responsible for the navigation of the ship. Stands the four-to-eight sea watch.
Snipe	Anyone working in the engine department of a ship. A term used derogatorily by members of the deck department.
Sounding Tubes	Tubes extending from the main deck down into the lowest parts of the holds and tanks for taking soundings (reading the levels of liquids).

Swage Fitting	A fitting compressed onto the end of a wire. It could be an eye or hook.
Third Engineer	Fourth-highest-ranking licensed officer in the engine department. Stands the twelve-to-four sea watch.
Third Mate	Third-lowest-ranking licensed officer of the deck department. Stands the twelve-to-four sea watch.
Tween Deck	That part of a ship where cargo is stowed. Lower- and upper-tween decks are above the holds and separated by hatch covers.
WT Door	A watertight door, especially designed for ships.
Wiper	Member of the engine department. Stands sea watches and performs maintenance.

Walter F. Curran is a retired maritime executive living in Ocean View, DE. He has sailed on merchant ships and worked on and around the docks in Boston, Philadelphia, Baltimore, Jacksonville and San Juan, Puerto Rico. A member of the Rehoboth Beach Writer's Guild and the Eastern Shore Writer's Association, in addition to "On to Africa" he has also published a book of poetry, "Slices of life-Cerebral spasms of the soul," "Young Mariner" the first of the Young Mariner series and is currently writing the third book of the "Young Mariner" series.

Readers may contact Walt via email WFCALLC@GMAIL.COM or his author page at Amazon, HTTP://WWW.AMAZON.COM/AUTHOR/ WALTERFCURRAN

Made in the USA
Middletown, DE
27 January 2018